BITS OF STRING
TOO SMALL TO SAVE

RUBY PERU

ILLUSTRATIONS BY PHILIP HARRIS

PANGLOSS PRESS
PORTLAND MAINE

2017 Pangloss Press Trade Paperback Edition
Copyright © 2017 by Ruby Peru Mehrer

First published in the United States of America in 2017 by Pangloss Press
Ebook first published in 2017 by Pangloss Press
This ebook published in 2017 by Pangloss Press

Pangloss Press
32 Bishop Ave. South Portland, ME 04106
www.RubyPeru.com
First Edition

ISBN: 978-0-692-51345-3

For information about permission to reproduce selections from this book,
write to Permissions, Pangloss Press,
Submissions@panglosspress.com

Illustrations and Cover Design by Philip Harris

for Dad

Dear Reader,

This book is probably not for you. If you're an adult, you'll struggle to accept children as viable main characters. If you're a child, you might find it too full of big words and long sentences. If you're a teen, you may be disgusted by all the unattractive characters with really disturbing philosophies. If you're a grown man, you won't be able to admit you liked it. If you're a grown woman, how are you going to find the time to read it? If you're a boy, there's too much romance and seduction. If you're a girl, the seduction isn't the nice kind, and the romance is mostly doomed, so watch out.

But if you do enjoy *Bits of String*, and you're the kind of person who likes to know more about the author, the illustrator, our process, and even get some hints as to ElizabethAnn's next adventures, perhaps you'd like to stay in touch. If so, head to **www.rubyperu.com/fan-club** to sign up for my fan club and receive a free bonus.

Your friend,
Ruby Peru

BITS OF STRING
TOO SMALL TO SAVE

Contents

PART ONE

FIVE SYLLABLES WORTH OF GIRL

FIVE SYLLABLES WORTH OF GIRL

1

WHERE ELIZABETHANN DECLARES HER WORTH IN TERMS OF SYLLABLES

One sunny Saturday morning, ElizabethAnn Von Earp tucked her Mary Janes beneath her slight form, curled up on a wide window ledge, and gazed off through the glass, hoping to catch a glimpse of Grandma's International Scout careening from lane to lane, leaving its wake of flying garbage cans and splintered mailboxes, but there just wasn't much to see. Not much at all. In fact, in ElizabethAnn's town, rain never fell, grass never grew, and dust flew around everywhere like ticker tape being thrown at a parade.

An indoorsy child, ElizabethAnn grew up, clear to the age of ten, astoundingly innocent of life's impending misfortunes. She became neither carefree nor fun-loving but exuded a persnickety, fastidious, and overcautious air. Like most little girls in these sorts of drab, unexceptional, late-twenty-first century police states (and indeed like most little girls throughout the long, sad, but always fashionable history of time) ElizabethAnn took great pleasure in wearing cute dresses. These were usually in shades of pink or violet, with nicely shined patent leather shoes, sets of fluttering hair bows, slatherings of sparkly nail polish, and other such indicators of a cultivated nature.

ElizabethAnn's mother, whom we shall simply call Mrs. Von Earp (because she is best imagined with a sense of prim formality) click-clacked across the kitchen's linoleum and wiped her hands on a starched apron, drawing her daughter's attention.

"Liz, dear," began Mrs. Von Earp.

"Please, Mama, it's ElizabethAnn."

"Ann, dear," continued Mrs. Von Earp.

"E-liz-a-beth-Ann, Mama! The whole name, please."

"Darling, you know how your father and I feel about that."

"It's arrogance, I know. But that's not what Grandma says."

"One syllable apiece. That's all a Von Earp really needs."

"Grandma says I'm five syllables worth of girl."

"I never should have let her name you. Moment of weakness."

"Anyway, Mama, it's my name. I can't help it."

"How about LizAnn? Isn't that a little less cumbersome?"

"Elizabeth*Ann,* please."

"Annabeth, perhaps?"

"I'd go for Annabethlizzy."

"How about Lizabeth?"

ElizabethAnn sighed and replied, "When Grandma gets here, you can hash it out with her," then turned back to the window and its view of row after row of mute-toned ticky-tacky.

When ElizabethAnn ventured outside, she navigated the sidewalks with extreme wariness of the green, spiky cactus that grew in the rights-of-way. And, of course, she never went near the wind-worn granite outcroppings for which her town was actually a little bit famous.

"That's what I want to talk to you about, dear," Mrs. Von Earp said and clamped her lips into a hard, red line. She paced and sighed heavily, as if with the burdens of eons.

Despite her generally circumspect nature, ElizabethAnn really liked to have fun. Fact was, when safely confined within the front and back yards of her family's well-fenced, postmodern split-level, she even skipped and hippity-hopped and bounced high-quality rubber balls. When feeling particularly adventuresome, she even frolicked in the neighborhood's supervised swimming pools and roller-skated around its butter-smooth cement roundabout, with other growing girls from approved families. But what she particularly liked was when, on Saturdays, Grandma drove over in her unlicensed, jacked-up, pimped-out, original-orange International Scout.

Though delicate herself, ElizabethAnn enjoyed Grandma's not-so-dainty visits. In fact, she couldn't have explained why, but she only felt truly safe when she was with Grandma. Whether she rode shotgun while Grandma engaged in vehicular derring-do or just sat and twiddled the Scout's radio knob while Grandma pontificated, ElizabethAnn lived for Saturdays.

"I think," began Mrs. Von Earp, "that is, we, your father and I, think Grandma has become a bit eccentric lately. I should say a bit *more* eccentric lately, and, well, we've decided it isn't safe to have her just going anywhere, you know, just anywhere she pleases, saying who knows what to whom."

Mrs. Von Earp gesticulated wildly to emphasize her point, in a way that hinted at inner conflict between an abiding fear of disgrace and a limited kind of love for (if not an understanding of) her mother, the woman ElizabethAnn called Grandma.

"In short," continued Mrs. Von Earp, "Grandma won't be visiting this weekend because, your father and I, we've decided to put her in a home."

"A home?" asked ElizabethAnn. "You mean *our* home?"

She popped up from the ledge, delighted, and her hands fluttered in the air like baby sparrows.

"No, dear. A 'home' is a place where she … she won't get herself into trouble."

ElizabethAnn silently returned to her perch on the window ledge and scanned the horizon.

On his way to do the weekend's lawn sweeping, Mr. Von Earp momentarily paused before this little domestic tableau.

"Oh, Lizzy," he said. "Why don't you go out and play?"

"Elizabeth*Ann*, please."

"You know how your mother and I feel about that name."

"If you say so, Papa."

"Why don't you scamper along, now. And give Papa a smoochie."

He proffered his cheek to ElizabethAnn, and she kissed it dutifully as the Von Earp parents exchanged a conspiratorial look.

"What do you and Grandma talk about in that big, awful car, anyway?" asked Mrs. Von Earp.

"Elizabeth tells Grandma about her playmates, of course!" volunteered Mr. Von Earp.

"Elizabeth*Ann*, please," the child interjected in a small voice completely disconnected from the thoughts in her now scheming, whirring mind.

"I suppose she tutors you on your schoolwork a bit," suggested Mrs. Von Earp.

"Actually, we talk about the fragility of the space/time continuum," replied ElizabethAnn, scarcely aware of what she said.

"Cute!" responded Mrs. Von Earp.

"And parallel worlds," added ElizabethAnn. "Stuff like that."

She craned her neck to see farther down the street.

"Isn't that a Polly-Magoo!" exclaimed Mr. Von Earp, with a face-quake just short of a chuckle.

He grabbed his broom and backed out the door while Mrs. Von Earp pursed her lips and rolled her eyes.

"Grandma can tell you about it when she gets here," said ElizabethAnn, consciously suppressing a desire to chew at least one fingernail to the quick, "but I don't know if she will."

"She isn't coming, dear. That's what I'm trying to tell you. I already instructed the men to pick her up, this morning," said Mrs. Von Earp.

ElizabethAnn giggled, as a lighthearted child would do. "Of course she's coming, Mama," she said, with a sweet-looking smile. "You can't stop Grandma. No one can."

She pressed her nose against the windowpane and her warm breath made a fleeting cloud while ElizabethAnn secretly planned direct and immediate action. Grandma had trained her for this moment.

"You don't understand, dear," Mrs. Von Earp explained. "When the men come, that's the end. They're going to take her … away."

ElizabethAnn could hear the *whisk! whisk! whisk!* of her father sweeping bits of wind-borne trash off the backyard's green, grass-like carpet and knew her days of roller-skating and swimming parties and rubber ball bouncing had come to a screeching halt. Such girlish entertainments wouldn't mean anything if not punctuated by Saturdays with Grandma.

"Mama, can I take Jackson for a walk?" asked ElizabethAnn, through her still-sweet smile.

Now, as the story progresses in our minds' eyes, we imagine ElizabethAnn popping up with the nonchalance of any ordinary child on any run-of-the-mill day and grabbing the dog's leash from its nail in the closet, but keep in mind Jackson was too big a dog to be walked by a little girl of ElizabethAnn's slight stature. A leggy little wisp of a beanpole, ElizabethAnn weighed less than the dog itself and exhibited much less control over her gangly limbs and various parts. No right-minded parent would attach these two live beings together expecting a positive outcome, but Mrs. Von Earp—what with all that inner conflict muddling her reasoning—gave permission.

And anyway, thought Mrs. Von Earp, while justifying her ill-advised choice (not in these exact words, but actually with a series of rapid mental images) *every sidewalk extends to the horizon entirely unblemished with potholes or cracks, and a friendly policeman occupies a post on nearly every corner.*

No one in this town worried about transgressors or outlaws, since there wasn't but one tree for them to hide behind, and it (a gargantuan cottonwood Grandma had more than once lobbied town hall to preserve) had been thoroughly fenced off for the safety of all. In fact, the recent sawing down of the town's second-to-last tree—a staunch, looming oak—had come as one big relief to the whole community of Forest Hills, whose board of directors voted unanimously to change the town's name to No Oaks.

Mrs. Von Earp, eager to change the subject, suggested ElizabethAnn could even walk Jackson to the corner store, pick up a stick of butter, and bring it home to bake some strawberry muffins. So, (as you, dear reader, have rightly been fearing) ElizabethAnn clicked the leash onto Jackson's collar, deep within his shaggy, mottled world of fur.

While Jackson led the way outside, ElizabethAnn skip-hopped behind him (the better to appear carefree) but noticed where, in the distance, a dust devil gathered momentum.

Out on the sidewalk, Jackson shook himself, sneezed once violently, and lifted his muzzle to nose the springtime air: the gooey asphalt melting in the sun, the candy-bar wrappers drifting on the wind, the acrid refuse bins, the tangy essence of incinerated waste, the gamey monkeys.

The gamey monkeys? thought Jackson.

No Oaks didn't present as the world's most likely location for a monkey colony or even a single solitary monkey visitor. After all, the town featured no bananas, circuses, zoos, jungles, or known monkey sympathizers (or trees, if you'll remember, but one). A thinking person would simply discount the pungent aroma and assume someone's dog had rolled in something dead. But Jackson was no thinking person.

The dog turned his volleyball-sized head over his fuzzy shoulder and gave ElizabethAnn the look that meant, *Hang on, sister, we're about to chase a monkey.* But ElizabethAnn thought the look meant, *Put on your jacket, little pumpkin, there's a cold breeze blowing,* so she buttoned her thin cardigan up to the neck and wondered how to get started looking for Grandma.

Noting the communication problem, Jackson next gave her the look that means, *Run fast! Soccer hooligans on the loose!* But ElizabethAnn thought it meant, *Stop for a second, I have to do my business,* so she politely averted her eyes. Meanwhile, that monkey smell became progressively more piquant, until Jackson couldn't stand it anymore.

Jackson sized up little ElizabethAnn — her big brown eyes, her blue-flowered dress, her prissy little cardigan, her spotless patent-leather shoes, and her ponytails poinging up and out with the aid of tightly wrapped sparkly pink hair ribbons. Ever so gently—for Jackson's loyalty to his tiny mistress occupied an even larger part of his brain than his olfactory sense—the dog snatched a mouthful of her dress, picked her up, and ran.

Jackson followed the scent down the street, around the roundabout, through an empty lot, up a hill, across a busy boulevard, along its center median, directly over a four-lane thoroughfare, down an eroding escarpment, through a giant drainage pipe, up a steep embankment, and right through a populated playground.

Meanwhile, her mouth full of fur, ElizabethAnn hollered, "Foot me fown! Foot me fown!"

When Jackson crossed another street, ElizabethAnn, from her undignified, upside-down position, glimpsed a smear of original orange, heard a familiar rumble, and switched to screaming, "If's Grandma! If's Grandma!" but Jackson wouldn't stop.

His nose fixed on its musky quarry, the dog entered a trash-strewn alley. The orange blur followed, taking a corner on two wheels, sending plastic shopping bags, crushed cartons, and soggy junk mail whirling into the air like startled titmice.

Grandma, leaning her head of tousled white hair out the vehicle's window, shouted, "ElizabethAnn, is that you? Is that Jackson?"

"If's me!" ElizabethAnn hollered, arms flailing randomly, head clanking against the metal tags embedded deep in Jackson's shaggy neck roll.

The International Scout raced after the girl and dog, turbo charging to the best of its rusty, antique ability. Grandma drove with one hand, searched for her distance glasses with the other, and all the while shouted out the window, "It's time, kiddo! It's time! The time/space continuum is broken!"

Jackson banked on an empty dumpster with a resounding *ka-thong* and carried ElizabethAnn down a narrow access strip between two brick buildings. The dog barreled forward, lengthening his stride until he barely touched ground.

Approaching the dumpster, Grandma slammed on the brakes, but the Scout skidded into it, pea-gravel shooting out from under its tires like bullets. The Scout's front bumper crumpled with the impact, and one headlight exploded.

"Frangipani!" Grandma exclaimed, as she stumbled out the driver's side door, pinwheeling her freckled arms and shouting, "The polymer's been breached, kiddo! The separation of realities is no more!"

"If thif about …" yelled ElizabethAnn, whose entire body flipped and bounced this way and that like a ball in some kind of unwinnable sport without players. "The … space … time … continu …"

ElizabethAnn's voice faded away, while she herself became a jiggly, erratic spot in the distance.

"Yes," whispered Grandma helplessly, pulling up short and resting her slender wrists on her head and her white hedgehog of hair, as she was wont to do in anxious moments. Then Grandma snapped-to, realizing she knew where that narrow passage led.

She raced back to the Scout and peeled it off the dumpster with a certain amount of grinding, crunching, and tinkling of broken plastic, backed it at top speed all the way down the alley to the road, then burned rubber, off and away.

Jackson kept his grip on ElizabethAnn's saliva-soggy cardigan, even as she hollered her bouncy, disjointed questions into the air. He zipped out the other end of the passage between the buildings, across several acres of green, plastic turf that constituted the No Oaks Golf and Country Club. Then, Jackson hurled himself, along with little ElizabethAnn, in one giant leap, headlong and pell-mell, over a fence. Girl and dog finally landed in the one, single, solitary place (ElizabethAnn suddenly recalled, after years of not even thinking about it) that she knew she was to never ever go.

The Treacherous Prohibited Stream.

Here grew the one tall cottonwood tree that still existed in all of No Oaks, which everyone pretended either wasn't there anymore or had never existed in the first place, depending upon who you asked, if you had the guts to ask at all.

As for ElizabethAnn, she had never seen this tree, or any live tree, in her whole life. Until now, didn't even believe in them. In that most disquieting and disturbingly shady place, Jackson put ElizabethAnn down, right on the muddy bank of the swiftly flowing stream, and sniffed the heavily monkified air.

Though none too pleased about lying in the mud, ElizabethAnn retained her typically curious yet safety-conscious demeanor, springing to her feet and surveying her surrounds. She took one look at that tree and dutifully thought, *Who knows when it could rot and come crashing down on someone's roof? Who knows what ne'er-do-wells could be hiding behind it?* And, of course, *Who knows what sorts of centipedes and insecty things could be scrabbling around on the bark?*

ElizabethAnn noticed the stream forming a little eddy in the mud slough where Jackson had so ingloriously dumped her. The water engulfed her ankles, and she pondered, *It's hard to even count the dangers of water.* In No Oaks, most people avoided it in large quantities, preferring to bathe with vigorous rubbings of antiseptic gel.

The water in question pressed gently on the sides of her ankles in its hurry to gurgle off into the distance, and it made a cold little ring of feeling there: an unusual, but not altogether unpleasant, sensation for ElizabethAnn. Despite this novelty, ElizabethAnn remained a single-minded young lady, and a prideful one, so she turned her attention to Jackson, from whom she planned to demand an explanation. But just then, the ground shook. She heard a screech, a crash, a tinkling of broken plastic, and a holler in a certain familiar voice. Grandma pounded on the fence.

"ElizabethAnn? Are you in there?"

"Yes, Grandma. I'm here. I'm in water!"

"I've got to get over this fence! You can't go without me!"

"Where are we going, Grandma? Where *can* we go?"

"I've … got … to …" said Grandma, and ElizabethAnn heard a grunt.

"Grandma, what are you doing?" ElizabethAnn yelled, then she heard a crash and a muttered, "Frangipani!"

"Just trying to climb … over … this …" ElizabethAnn heard, followed by a sliding sound and an "ooph."

"Grandma?" yelled ElizabethAnn into the air over the fence. "Did you know Mama wants to put you in a *home*?"

"I know it, dear, that's just one of the reasons I've got to move on. Just one," Grandma yelled over the fence. "It's finally time for me to return to Bumblegreen, and you ought to come along. Yes, I think you really ought!"

ElizabethAnn heard the crunching of gravel and the *huph, chik, huph, chik, huph, chik* of someone repeatedly jumping as high as possible, but just at that moment, she also spied a tire swing hanging over the Treacherous, Prohibited Stream. She completely forgot about Grandma and ran and climbed into the tire, then stood in it, in the most dangerous manner possible, shouting, "Whee!" and "Hooray!" and "Waaaah-hooo!" with wild, uncharacteristic abandon.

She yanked on the rope and kicked the tree, trying to get the tire to swing faster, farther, and more unpredictably, for it's a fact: Every child who is not the biologically predictable offspring of tightly controlled breeding loves a tire swing, no matter how dangerous the stream flowing under it, how deep the water, or how far the potential fall.

In the unfledged minds of children (even naturally cautious ones like ElizabethAnn), once spotted, a tire swing over a stream is like meat to a dog, treasure to a dragon, sunshine to a flower — pretty much the only thing that matters in life.

Meanwhile, Jackson still smelled a monkey. He waded across the stream, nosed around at a heap of roots, overturned some rocks, and finally lay down in a disappointed heap, watching ElizabethAnn go berserk. Then, as if from out of nowhere, a monkey scampered right down the muddy stream bank.

Jackson saw it.

ElizabethAnn saw it, too.

Currently (and for the first time, really) a victim of the crude passions that lurk beneath the surface in even the most ideally molded spawn, ElizabethAnn tumbled off her questionable plaything into the stream, slogged to her feet, and took off after that monkey. Close on her heels ran Jackson, barking his excitement. Due to the hubbub, the two of them could no longer hear Grandma's repeated exclamations and incessant pounding on the other side of the high, impenetrable fence.

In No Oaks, any monkey would have been an out-of-the-ordinary monkey, but even ElizabethAnn grokked the exceptional nature of this particular beast. First of all, it wore a tight-fitting polo shirt with a prestigious-looking golden insignia embroidered over the left breast pocket, referencing the nearby No Oaks Golf and Country Club. Secondly, she noticed (but only after chasing the animal helter-skelter for several out-of-breath minutes, always just one frustrating arm's-length away) that the monkey wore the most fantastic gold watch ElizabethAnn had ever seen. Then, as she looked on (ineffectually squeaking out little "Hey you theres!" through belabored lungs) the monkey spoke into the watch.

"Cupcake, I'm running a little late," said the monkey into the watch. "Can you hear me? It's crazy, this GPS. You won't believe where I am now!" The monkey sloshed across the stream, huffed up an embankment, and leaped from rock to rock across a series of mud puddles. "I can monitor my heart rate with the press of a button," continued the monkey. "I'm monitoring here! See, I'm burning fat, as we speak."

ElizabethAnn dashed after the monkey with considerably less grace than Jackson, splashing water clear overhead as she galloped through the stream and slipped and slid across the mud puddles and rocks.

"Listen, I'm taking a shortcut," said the monkey into the watch. "Don't worry! I'm connected to satellites and spaceports and all kinds of things. I can't get lost. I even get shortwave radio. You wouldn't believe the things I hear. Police radio! Everything!"

As the monkey rounded a boulder, tumbled through a pile of dead leaves, and balance-walked along a downed tree limb, a very muddy Jackson caught up to ElizabethAnn, who had stopped to catch her breath in a patch of weeds. The pair heard a roar, saw a bright glow between the slats of the fence, and didn't even have time to duck for cover before a section of fence exploded. The half-wrecked

International Scout came barreling through, splintering old, dry wood and sending fence posts a-flying.

Behind the wheel, Grandma kicked at her smashed-in car door, shouting, "Wait for me, kiddo! Wait for me!" The door wouldn't give, so she climbed through her open window, adding, "Don't get too close to that tree!"

The monkey looked up. It had stopped beside the tree, so taken with finding the right buttons for call and hang-up, blood pressure, glucose level, body fat index, stock reports, and all that, that it had momentarily forgotten its mission.

"Oh!" was all it said, then it spoke into the watch again, saying, "Lemon-pie, are you there? Time me. Seriously, I'm going to be home in three minutes. I'm going to twinkle through time and space. I'm pressing the button. I'll probably get there an hour ago. Seriously! Let's see if it works."

The monkey moved some leaves aside from the base of the One Remaining Tree and exposed where the roots made a little hollow place that looked like a burrow for a bunny, a fox, a groundhog, who knows? In an instant, the monkey disappeared down the hole.

Grandma ran straight for the tree, calling, "ElizabethAnn, I think you're ready! You've got to come home with me!"

"Home?" asked ElizabethAnn, who was already farther from home than she had ever, in her entire life, planned to venture.

Then, Grandma dove right into that hole, after the monkey.

Falling prey to instincts she didn't even know she had, ElizabethAnn leaped to the stream bank, tiptoe-ran along the log, flopped to her belly in the leaves, and slid, head-first, right into the hole after Grandma.

Jackson, instinct-bound to protect ElizabethAnn, followed suit.

No ordinary hole in the ground, this. As her toes cleared the hole's opening, ElizabethAnn heard a loud jangling sound like something electronic having a terrible and sudden malfunction. This was followed by a hollow, spooky, windy sound, like a discount-store Halloween ghost trying to ride out a hurricane. The two-toned noise sent shivers up her spine, and ElizabethAnn thought it sounded like: *kedank shooshreek.*

Once in the limbo-land of the hole in the ground, ElizabethAnn felt herself being pulled forward through dark space like an iron filing to a powerful magnet (her eyeballs feeling uncomfortably more magnetic than the rest). Meanwhile, her brain and body suffered the distinct sensation of being blown apart and inspected for termites by steely-eyed, white-gloved, obsessive-compulsives. Shortly afterward, ElizabethAnn felt the distinct sensation of someone expertly packing her brains back into her skull and riveting her body parts together again, like jeans pockets.

Finally, ElizabethAnn landed in a giant pile of leaves and twigs. Her center of gravity completely kaput, she rolled down an incline—sometimes head over heels, other times left over right, and during odd moments in a cartwheeling fashion. Not surprisingly then, after she came to a stop at the bottom of the incline, spent some time utterly blacked-out, and eventually regained consciousness, ElizabethAnn, the normally exceedingly prim and proper pride of the Von Earp family, found herself in a completely unique location.

2

WHERE INSECTS DEMONSTRATE THEIR OEUVRES

ElizabethAnn looked up from where she lay on a soft, spongy, wet, and, she thought, uncommonly dirty surface covered with twigs and things. Though she didn't know it as such, she lay, in fact, on a rain forest floor, with a rain forest's characteristic depth of topsoil, dearth of undergrowth, canopy of leaves, and aura of mystery. A gentle breeze ruffled her dress. The rich scent of green growing things prevailed—a very different sort of scent, she noticed, from No Oaks' insecticide-and-hot-tar aroma.

Rising to stand, ElizabethAnn heard a tiny voice, about the decibel level of an ordinary fingernail clipping being clipped, singing a folk melody.

Hey, ho, nobody home
Food nor drink nor money have I none
Nary have we rainy weather
Still will we be merry-hee

Then, a second voice spoke: "Did you hear that song? I don't approve. What is a *hee*? They should leave off singing if nobody knows the rhyme."

A third voice answered the second voice's complaint: "Well I don't suppose you know how the line goes, now do you?"

"I certainly do. I think it's something about 'free.'"

"So you agree it ends in *ee*?"

"I don't!"

Another faint song interrupted the pair of arguing voices.

Live long, not strong
Sun and breeze and honey have I none
Barefoot and without a feather
Once we did eat berry-ee

"That's an interesting version. Do you agree it's correct to add a supplementary *ee* on the end?" replied the second voice.

"I don't! It's a profound error," protested the third voice.

ElizabethAnn felt a tickle on her cheek and smacked her own face, instinctively. The shock of it brought her to her feet, where she noticed hundreds of minuscule life forms circling her head and the bloody splotch of a dead bug on her hand.

"Christopher! Christopher! He's dead! Oh, my only boy!" exclaimed the third tiny voice in abject despair.

"I'm so sorry!" cried ElizabethAnn to the voice—clearly an overwrought insect parent on the edge of irreparable anguish.

"I didn't mean it!" she added, not knowing which way to look or which of the hundreds, perhaps thousands, of insects she should address. ElizabethAnn, being a well-mannered girl, certainly did not plan to stop apologizing until she lost her breath and passed out cold.

"Oh, come off it, Francine," said the second voice. "'My only boy,' my foot! You have twelve-hundred children a season and wouldn't recognize one if he bit your cheek himself."

"Spoilsport," groused the third voice.

Hearing that, ElizabethAnn's inner clockworks turned on the old emotional carousel. As each horse passed the brass ring, she felt guilt, anger, vengeance, sadness, despair-touched-with-self-loathing, and then back to anger. She wallowed in all of these in the usual childish manner.

"No sense being angry at a mosquito," said the second voice. "It's a waste of energy at the very least. Oh, and that other voice you hear? That's Francine. She's just *Francine*. Likes to have herself a little joke, you know, nothing to be taken personally."

How did you know … thought ElizabethAnn, but the second voice laughed before she even finished the thought.

"Ha! I'm an insect," replied the second voice. "I can see inside. Why do you think they call us *in*sects? We're not *out*sects are we? Look, kiddo, a good needling is all we're after; then, we take a peek inside the old noggin to assess the damage. It's a simple pleasure, and what's the harm?"

"Take Francine here," the voice continued. "She's a real practical joker—a pro, see? Not a hack like me. But she's been teaching me. She's designed a course of study specially aimed at helping me increase my oeuvre. So far, my main trick has been a certain piercing whine. Would you like to hear it?"

Before ElizabethAnn could say No Thank You Very Much, she heard the most intensely earsplitting, crystal-shattering, dentist drill-recollecting, frontal lobe-scrambling whine she had ever heard in her short life so far. In less than a second, her eyes bugged out, lips quivered, fingers spasmed, and nostrils flared to unprecedented diameters.

"Why don't you leave me alone!" she shouted, swatting at the buzzing creatures circling her head and adding, "And let me out of this horrible place!" Though, in reality, despite the dirt, insects, and potential hiding places for criminals, ElizabethAnn actually found the strange place, with its dappled light and cool fruity breeze, quite beautiful.

Immediately, ElizabethAnn realized the insect would see inside her head and know she had lied about thinking this a horrible place, so she tried to run away, but after a good deal of manic jogging every which-a-way, tumbling and fumbling in search of a hiding place, she discovered such actions do nothing to rid one's head of insects buzzing around it. Finally, ElizabethAnn sat on a pile of dirt and twigs and cried.

"Looks like my work here is done," said the second insect voice. "Goodbye."

No! What about me? thought ElizabethAnn.

"Oh. You? I don't know. Hey, how'd you get here, anyway?" replied the insect.

We were going for a walk, and then Jackson picked me up. I screamed, but he wouldn't listen, and ...

"Long story short, babe," interrupted the insect. "I have a whole schedule of other people to annoy today."

You could say I followed a monkey. Down a hole! ElizabethAnn thought-shouted at her inquisitor.

"Down a hole?" asked the insect. "You must be kidding. You mean you came through a portal?"

A what? thought ElizabethAnn, without meaning to.

"By 'a what' are you actually trying to imply it was some kind of accident?" replied the tiny but sarcastic insect voice.

No, it was on purpose, actually, thought ElizabethAnn, adding, *I certainly dove after the monkey on purpose, but I felt strangely compelled. But everything that led up to that was by accident. It was an accident that led to a purpose,*

"'By accident, on purpose?' I've heard of that," chirped the insect.

Yes, by-accident-on-purpose. That's it, ElizabethAnn thought.

"Just kidding. I've never heard of that."

ElizabethAnn sighed and cradled her round little head in her hands. Finally, she asked out loud, "Please, did you see an old lady with white hair, all sticking-out-like?"

"Can't say I did."

"What about a dog?" she asked. "And a monkey? Did you see a monkey come through here?"

"What's a dog?" asked the insect.

"You know, a *dog* — furry, four legs, floppy ears."

"I'd sure know if I'd seen anything like that!"

"Jackson probably just trotted home," ElizabethAnn mused. "He's probably back with Mama ..."

"Listen," said the insect she recognized as Francine, "was there a monkey involved?"

"I already said there was!"

"Mm-hmm," replied Francine. "Well, up you go then. And no need to get petulant."

"Up I go?"

"Anything missing, such as your dog thingy, chances are a monkey stole it," said Francine, adding, "and frankly, you can't talk to a monkey around here without you go through the duchess. She lives at the top of that cliff, way up there. Look."

ElizabethAnn saw where, in among the trees in the dense forest, a jagged, rocky cliff rose up and up and up, quite vertically, emerging from the ground like the prow of an enormous moored ship. ElizabethAnn looked up into the trunks of the tall, pencilish trees and peered up to where broad leaves waved about like sailors leaving port for the first time.

"Higher," said Francine.

ElizabethAnn looked higher. Much higher, up into the tops of the tallest of the trees, all overgrown with flowering vines, whose dinner-plate-sized blooms looked as tiny as stars in the night sky. She saw how tree trunks flanked the jutting spit of land, then she saw where the spit of land flattened out on top and another forest grew on its surface.

"See the forest at the top of that cliff?"

"Yes, thanks."

"Go up there."

"Pardon me, but how?"

"Climb that tree right there, then shinny out on that branch. See it? Way up there? Then you can just blip right over to the top of the cliff," said Francine. "At least, that's how the monkeys do it. Myself, I just fly or ride a wind current, but I'm practically microscopic, so, you know, different technique."

Despite the fact that ElizabethAnn wore her cutest cardigan and her best blue-flowered dress and had her hair poinged up just so, with the most darling ribbons tied in bows, and despite the fact that she had been paying a great deal of attention to keeping, as much as possible, proper young-ladyish manners throughout the whole debacle thus far, ElizabethAnn understood she had to do what she had to do. So, she braced herself, made her eyes into dark slits of pure cussedness, clenched and unclenched her untried little fists, and grabbed a branch, intent upon climbing that tree, shinnying that branch, and blipping over to the top of that cliff. (Whatever that meant.)

3

IN WHICH A SLOTH HINTS AT
THE NATURE OF MAGIC

Once she got the hang of tree-climbing, and all the dreadful grasping and heaving and mental problem-solving it entailed, ElizabethAnn found a rhythm. Pretty soon, she could shinny from branch to branch like a true adept.

She inched up tree trunks, straddled branches, and jimmied herself past knotholes and between awkward knobby things making very tight little spaces. But after about the tenth knuckle-smack, eleventh gob of sap in the eye, and twelfth painful raspberry from sliding past rough bark, ElizabethAnn realized the decision to climb this tree couldn't be taken back (not without falling several stories), and it might not have been a good one.

If she could have given up, said to someone, "Okay, I surrender! You win!" she would have, but nobody showed up to accept her surrender, so she clung to that tree, figuring it had to be climbed the way a lawn has to be swept.

Finally, ElizabethAnn ascended to the place where the jagged, rocky cliff face plateaued. Up there, a patch of meadow featured sunny little daisies and shady spots buttered-over with lichen. Beyond the meadow, a second forest grew high and dark and dense and stretched endlessly away.

The meadow's loveliness seemed to invite ElizabethAnn to come explore. As if to facilitate such exploration, a branch angled out from ElizabethAnn's tree, stretching stiff and sturdy across a vast vertical expanse of unforgiving nothingness, toward the plateau, the meadow, and the forest. But the branch didn't quite reach the face of the cliff.

ElizabethAnn sat on the branch, picked a twig out of her hair, smacked a mosquito—this time without apologizing—and tried to figure out what that insect voice had meant by, "Just blip across."

"Just run," said a voice.

"Not you again!" said ElizabethAnn, with uncharacteristic rudeness, to the air around her head. "Francine, I think you've got me into enough of a pickle, thank you very much!"

"Francine? I never thought I looked like a Francine. Do I?" asked the voice.

Peering through the tree's tangled branches, ElizabethAnn discovered the gray, bearded face of an ancient three-toed sloth. Though unfamiliar with sloths, as such, she found the creature, with its large, moist eyes, appealing, nonthreatening, and very nearly cuddly.

"Oh! Hello," replied ElizabethAnn. Then, after an awkward pause while she became accustomed to the idea of talking to such a creature, she added, "No, indeed, you look nothing at all like a Francine."

"What do you think, then?" it asked. "Alicia? Sylvie? Fernando?"

"Dean," replied ElizabethAnn.

"How right you are, my dear," answered the sloth. It pulled a hand mirror out of a matted place in its fur and studied its own face, mumbling, "Francine? Oh, I really don't think I'm a Francine at *all*."

"Would you, by any chance, know how I might get over this gap to that grassy meadow right over there?" inquired ElizabethAnn, of the creature. "They said to blip. Blip across?"

"I told you, darling. Just run!" replied the sloth, preening itself (you never saw anyone preen so slowly) in the hand mirror.

"But … on the branch?" she asked, as fat tears of frustration dripped down her cheeks.

"You know!" said the sloth.

"I certainly do not know, thanks!"

The sloth put away the hand mirror, climbed closer to ElizabethAnn, and inspected her.

"You really don't, do you?" it asked.

"I just got here, sir,"

"Where did you come from, anyway?"

"Through a hole in the ground," ElizabethAnn replied. "This isn't anyplace in No Oaks, is it?" she asked. Briefly, she wondered if she had just traveled through a tunnel into some kind of secluded park or federal recreation area.

"No Oaks? What a dreadful name!"

"That's my home, and I like it, thanks."

"So, you just popped through a hole from there to here?"

"Yes, that's right. I was trying to follow my grandmother, is all. She's pretty spry."

"Your grandmother went first?"

"Actually a monkey went first, and then my grandma … oh, never mind."

"I thought they put a stop to that sort of thing ages ago."

"They? Excuse me but, they *who*?"

"You know, *they*. The queen and them. Well, anyway, welcome to Bumblegreen!"

"Oh. Thank you very much. It's called Bumblegreen?"

"But of course. What else?"

"I heard something like *kedank shooshreek* while I came through the hole. That mean anything to you?"

"A dank shoe tree? What good is a dank shoe tree?"

"No, I …"

"Kids these days!"

"Right, well, where am I, exactly? Bumblegreen? What is that, the center of the Earth or something?"

"Of the what?"

"Earth."

"Whatever is the Urth? Kids these days!"

"Right, well …"

"Here chickadee, now see that branch you're sitting on is an heirloom," explained the sloth. "Magical things, they are. Not many of those left. Just got here, you say? Odd. Anyway, the branch is enchanted, magical, ensorcerized, or whatever you call it, so you can just stand up, run along the branch, and … you'll see."

Something compelled ElizabethAnn to follow the sloth's advice. Who knows what that something was. Temporary insanity? A sudden death wish? Crude animal instinct? Either way, she hoisted herself upright, poised to run.

"Oh, not just yet," instructed the sloth. "Wait for a little breeze. Wind enhances the magic, you know. Stirs the pot, kind of."

"What pot?"

"Magic … don't you know anything? Magic is like a sediment. If it's not stirred up, it kind of settles to the bottom."

ElizabethAnn clung to the tree trunk and nearly lost her nerve, but soon a zephyr tickled the pine needles into a feathery dance, and she felt inspired.

"Now'd be a good time," said the sloth.

Desperate as she was, ElizabethAnn abandoned her usually cautious ways and skittered along the branch, did a little hop, then ran full-out. The end of the branch functioned as a springboard and a little jump sent her flying over to the top of the cliff with plenty of room to spare. She landed a bit abruptly and did lose a tooth, but it had been wiggly.

Once situated, ElizabethAnn remembered her quest to find Grandma and Jackson, brushed herself off, spit out the tooth, straightened her hair bows, and marched across the meadow and through the trees, eyes peeled for clues. Naturally, this behavior didn't seem heroic to her, just logical, for, in addition to being persnickety and dainty, ElizabethAnn, as a true child of No Oaks public schools, grasped logic like a pincer.

ElizabethAnn hiked through the drizzling, dense, dark forest until, in the distance, she spied a second green meadow flooded with sunlight and dappled with daffodils—a sight that filled her with the optimism of a natural adventurer (which she wasn't). She felt grateful to have her feet back on solid ground after all that dreadful tree-climbing, which may have been the very thing that opened up what seems, in hindsight, to have been a secret reserve of courage. In fact, while we're taking the hindsight approach, allow me to suggest that perhaps ElizabethAnn's heart actually secretly beat braver than her slight build and history of cautious circumspection might suggest.

She wove through saplings and stomped underbrush, evaded briar patches and climbed over boulders, and soon, ElizabethAnn noticed a woman in a prim black skirt and white, silken blouse who appeared to be desperately fleeing the green meadow and running straight for her. The woman carried a richly hand-embroidered tablecloth tied into a bundle and filled with bulky items.

Periodically, as she ran, the woman looked over her shoulder, seemingly in a panic. Now and then, items bounced out of the bundle and she had to stop, retrace her steps, and find the items: a golden candelabra, some crystal perfume bottles, and a porcelain candy bowl, for instance. She shoved them back into her bundle. Eventually, the woman, all red-faced and sweaty, ran past ElizabethAnn without saying a word.

Next, ElizabethAnn spied a man, also dashing away from the green meadow dappled with daffodils. He wore black slacks and a white button-down shirt, with a black bow tie hanging askew, and carried a laundry bag overflowing with silken sheets, monogrammed towels, and gossamer dressing gowns. His skinny legs took impossibly long strides as he raced toward ElizabethAnn at top speed.

ElizabethAnn, trying to catch his eye, shouted, "Hello, sir, have you seen my grandma? She's an old lady with white hair, kind of sticking-out-like!" But the man dashed right past ElizabethAnn and didn't bother to answer.

"Can't you stop and talk? Just a second?" ElizabethAnn asked his passing form.

"Whoa!" he answered, not slowing his pace. "'Nother time, 'nother place!"

"I'm ElizabethAnn!" she shouted at him.

"Fast Eddie!" the man yelled over his shoulder. "At your service! 'Nother time, 'nother place, love to chat!"

With that, the man dashed off into the woods, legs like madly scissoring chopsticks. ElizabethAnn paused to watch the two black-and-white-clad figures disappear into the distance, leaving her just as alone as before.

She (mentally) shrugged, forged ahead, and presently arrived at the meadow, only to find it not a meadow at all, but actually a lawn, perfectly manicured and dotted with charming rock gardens, clumps of fruit trees, and flowering bushes resplendent within clouds of colorful butterflies. ElizabethAnn even saw a pond peppered with live swans and surrounded by weeping willows, where a cobblestone footpath led to a scenic wooden bridge. She thought she had never seen any sight as beautiful in all her life and now felt supremely glad she had come to this place of mystery and danger. Incidentally, back in No Oaks, she would have strenuously disavowed any enjoyment of either mystery or danger, even to herself.

In the center of the enormous lawn stood a huge, rambling stone mansion. A shady arbor stretched along the mansion's near side and hosted innumerable climbing vines, heavy with blooms. Ornate columns surrounded the arbor, with potted azaleas nestling around the base of each one. In front of the mansion, a burnished cobblestone driveway stretched away behind a row of stately oaks. On the mansion's portico, a gargantuan brass knocker adorned an enormous set of mahogany doors.

ElizabethAnn looked left and right, up and down, trying to decide which way to go and where to begin among all the delights before her; meanwhile, a squat carriage drawn by four shiny black horses rumbled down the driveway. As the carriage came closer, a murderous screeching emanated from it.

Hearing the screeching, ElizabethAnn wondered if this person might be shouting at her to not walk on the grass, as No Oaks housewives were wont to do (even though their grass was actually indestructible plastic). ElizabethAnn really didn't want to venture back into the dark, wet woods, so when she noticed a little door in the manor's nearest wall, she tried the handle, found it unlocked, and ducked through it.

4

WHEREIN HANK STEALS A DESSERT SPOON, AMONG OTHER THINGS

ElizabethAnn found she had walked right into a sumptuous sitting room. Before her, a velvet-lined box of monogrammed cutlery gaped open on a massive chestnut table. Antique furniture of every kind and description suggested the room had been designed to host numerous conversation circles, some intersecting others.

Curious to learn the identity of the screeching woman in the carriage, ElizabethAnn dashed across an intricately woven carpet, around a Victorian fainting couch, past an art deco lamp, and up to a massive architectural arch, against whose cold marble she pressed her body as she peeked around the corner.

Beyond the arch, a hall ended abruptly in a domed entryway where those mahogany doors stood wide open. Beside them, a butler in a tuxedo idly rocked on his heels and whistled a tune.

The screeching crescendoed and subsided, then a woman (the screecher, herself) leaped from the carriage, dashed indoors, flung her handbag at the butler, kicked off her pumps, and sent them skittering across the mansion's grand foyer.

The butler yawned and said, "Welcome home, Duchess."

The duchess bellowed, "Get me my baby!" and her voice echoed off the marble.

Then, sliding in her stockinged feet on the newly waxed floor, the duchess skidded right past ElizabethAnn, into the sitting room where she fell down in a tangle—hairpins flying every which way, tinkling as they touched down. She draped herself, whimpering, over an ottoman.

ElizabethAnn reached up to check her hair and noticed her pigtails had, somewhere along the way, disintegrated into an entirely unstructured mop, so she licked her palm and used it, as best she could, to smooth the hair flat. Then, with her best enunciation, she stepped forward and asked the duchess, "How do you do?" and curtseyed.

"How do you do, yourself," grumbled the duchess, not in a nice way, glancing over at ElizabethAnn. "Oh, *you*," she said, giving the impression she had been expecting a visitor but not someone quite this terrible. "Hank!" she squealed.

ElizabethAnn heard rapid footsteps out in the hall, and the butler—who was cursed with what can only be described as fish lips—entered, all out of breath. He took a seat at the table, pulled a handkerchief out of his breast pocket, dabbed a bead of sweat from his brow, and commenced polishing silver, saying, "There now, how *do* you do after all, Duchess?"

He winked at ElizabethAnn, as if finding strange children wandering around one's house were perfectly normal. ElizabethAnn curtsied again, in reply.

"Where's the nanny?" asked the duchess.

"Well now, ma'am, I don't want you to be upset, but the nanny's run off, just like the last one."

"Did she? And the housekeeper? With her, I suppose?"

"Yes, Duchess. They both ran off just now, as soon as they heard your, uh, anguished cries from afar."

The duchess sighed and said, "Well, we'll get others. Listen, let me tell you about this meeting I've been at, Hank. I have got to talk it out. I just feel so absolutely humiliated! There's no other word for it. What do you expect? I had to get up in front of this whole room full of creeps and lowlifes and confess to being a kleptomaniac!" The duchess clutched the ottoman like a life raft.

"Goodness!" replied the butler, as he tucked a dessert spoon into his left breast pocket and poured the duchess some tea. "But ma'am," he added, "I thought you were just going for a sort of research or something. I didn't know you were actually a klepto, yourself."

The duchess flung her arm around a nearby chair for support. "My God, man! I'm certainly not!" she said. "I was there *looking* for kleptos—for the thieves that've been making off with every odd bit of finery around this place! I wanted to hear some confessions, I did! But, you know, I was undercover. You have to play their game. Then, boom, they accept you, open up to you."

The butler polished a salad fork and added, "Into the fold, so to speak?"

The duchess gazed out cathedral windows onto exquisitely manicured acreage, resting her chin on an enormous, askew shoulder pad. "Indeed," she agreed. "Into the fold, precisely. I think the whole concept is an import, if I remember my history, but I can't be sure."

"Excuse me," said ElizabethAnn in a small (but not her characteristically tiny) voice. "I don't mean to interrupt, but the thing is, um, I came to see the duchess about a monkey. Is this a bad time?" She held her hands over a new rip in her dress.

"Is that so? Glad to hear it," replied the duchess. "I am, in fact, in the monkey business. Though you should really meet me at my office, or just … I don't know … talk to a representative."

ElizabethAnn cleared her throat and squeaked, "You see, some insects said if I wanted to talk to a monkey I had to go through you, and I've got to find my grandma because she might be in trouble. She might get put into a home, in No Oaks, or else not have a home at all. And I don't know how to get home, myself. Only Grandma knows what to do, and I've got to find her, and she went in after this monkey, you see?"

With the tops of her fists on the dining table and her elbows pointing out like a couple of more-than and less-than signs, the duchess ranted at the butler. "These people were hardened criminals!" She punctuated her speech with an open-handed slap on the tabletop. "It's absurd! And there I was, making up nonsense about stealing an eyelash curler. An eyelash curler, for God's sakes! How many of them even know what that is? Do *you*?" The duchess directed this last question, with a brisk turn of her head, at ElizabethAnn.

"Of course," the child replied, having walked the runway in more than one No Oaks pageant, already.

The duchess ignored ElizabethAnn, rested her forearms on the table's leathery finish, and leaned in, flashing Hank a prodigious helping of cleavage.

"Suffice it to say," the duchess continued, "no one at the meeting said anything about stealing the things I've been missing, like my crystal candlesticks or embroidered linens."

"The thing is," said ElizabethAnn, as she backed toward the little doorway by which she had entered. "I feel like I'm kind of in the middle of something here, and you don't seem like anyone who would really know much about monkeys. Maybe I'm at the wrong place. I should go. Excuse me."

The duchess cocked an eyebrow at the girl, said "Sit *down*," reached out a massive hand, and shoved ElizabethAnn into an overstuffed armchair. "How you do go on," she added. "Listen, little girl, monkeys live in trees and I hope you don't think that's free, after all. *I* own the trees and *I* grant the residence permits on a strict petition basis only, and that's where my expertise in monkeys begins and ends, thank you very much. It's a simple matter of real estate, Real Estate, REAL ESTATE!"

The duchess' hand flew to her forehead, and she collapsed onto a divan. "Oh God, I'm tired of doing business," she said. "Why is it always work, work, work? Hank, get this young lady a form. I'm taking a nap."

"You want me to fill out a form?" whined ElizabethAnn, adding, under her breath, "Can't I just surrender?"

"Listen kid, just fill it out with all pertinent information. Press hard. Keep the goldenrod copy, wait until I'm done my nap, and then boom."

"I don't want to, so I guess I'll see ya 'round," ElizabethAnn said, and turned to go.

"Such hubris!" snapped the duchess. "If you don't want to fill a form, you'll have to go through other channels. That's all I can say!"

She yawned. "Now, Hank, do bring me my baby. I've got to nurse before I nap or these breasts will simply explode!"

As if presenting evidence, the duchess lifted her breasts and cradled them like newborn twins.

ElizabethAnn froze in place, curious to see the exploding breasts.

Hank left the room and reappeared shortly with a squalling, red-faced infant, who proceeded to noisily give suck, tearing the duchess' blouse and biting her nipples with abandon. Between the baby's piercing cries, it slurped hungrily; meanwhile, the duchess sneezed, and sneezed again.

"Oh, the humanity!" she complained, between sneezes, finally adding, "Get me a fan!"

Every time she sneezed, the duchess spasmed so violently ElizabethAnn worried she would drop the baby, so she scurried around the room, looking for a fan. She found one, a moth-eaten antique, and handed it to the duchess with another little curtsy.

"Stop that ridiculous bobbing," said the duchess, taking the wind entirely out of ElizabethAnn's sails as she grabbed the fan, snapped it open, thought better of using it, condensed it again with a smack, and tossed it onto an end table.

ElizabethAnn retrieved the fan, shoved it into her pocket for safekeeping, and inquired as to whether the duchess would like to borrow her handkerchief. After all, she still needed information.

"Oh, well, all right," groused the duchess. She took the handkerchief, sneezed into it a few times, and cast it aside, sopping wet.

"Is it pollen?" asked ElizabethAnn.

"God, no. Pollen! I wish it were only pollen. I'd have it all sprayed or killed or cut down or whatever, and then boom. No dear, it's this baby. Since day one I've been dreadfully allergic to whatever he gives off. His smell or skin or dander or saliva, I don't know, but whenever I'm around him there's a complete racket, and this incessant sneezing, and everyone for a mile gets soggy. Pardon me." She sneezed again.

"Bless you," said ElizabethAnn.

"I've been blessed," said the duchess. "Blessed with a child!" Then, she sneezed some more.

"Now then," began ElizabethAnn. "How is it exactly that you uh, well … uh, know how to find the monkeys, exactly?"

"Oh, my dear, I know them through business. You know, landlordly real estate dealings. Everything around here is mine, mine, *mine,* and I've to manage every blasted thing. The monkeys rent the trees, have their nests, whatever it is, perches or whatever. I get a share of the take: straight percentage or monthly fee, depends upon how it works out with all the pecuniary whys and wherefores, you know. Anyway, I may be having an extra strong fit because of your presence, actually."

"Me?"

"Of course! Don't be stupid. I'm sure you make everyone sneeze. Everyone but the queen, of course."

The duchess sighed, sank further into her easy chair, and threw her head back as if to dislodge thoughts she would rather not think. "We're all allergic but the royalty," she whined. "*Pure* royalty. You know how they are—special special *special*. Both my kids! Even my first! It was the same as this, you know, exactly the same. Listen girl, when you get to The Drone, lodge a complaint on my behalf, would you? This monkey business has been a terrible solution. Terrible! Oh, I remember my first baby, the little beast, I loved him, you know. Of course, I did! Dearly! Suckled him just like this one."

The duchess looked out the window again, and her voice softened. "And tell this to Zade Fandey as well: If I can't name my baby, I shouldn't have to suckle him, either. Fair's fair. Can you imagine the pain when I sent my first off to be raised by monkeys? Boom. Gone. It's the law! Such a dear he was. Is. Whatever."

The duchess followed her complaint with a sneezing fit so profound it blew the butler right into the fireplace.

"But if my boy ever comes back to me, I'll know him by the shape of the swan," the duchess added, once she recovered her breath. "Now, there's something old Zade Fandey didn't plan for: birthmarks."

"The swan?" asked ElizabethAnn, restoring fallen knickknacks to their shelves.

"A swan-shaped birthmark on his sweet little bottom cheek!" the duchess said between sneezes, and that's when she finally dropped the baby itself, who only bounced a couple of times and resumed squalling anew.

ElizabethAnn picked up the squirming infant and carried it through the grand front doors, which the butler had left wide open. She had a vague idea about bouncing it in her arms, like she had seen some mothers do with their infants, away from the hubbub, and that this show of good breeding would win over the duchess and maybe get her a pass home, a chance to surrender, or at least a bubble bath.

The duchess called after her, "Watch out! It's nothing if not a wiggling little mass of trouble! And it bites!"

She said it in such a final kind of way.

ElizabethAnn turned in order to clarify she wasn't intending to run off with the baby, but the doors slammed shut in her face. ElizabethAnn heard *clickety* and *slam* and the sliding of bolts as, with an air of applied athleticism, the butler locked and barred the massive doors from the inside and swished heavy curtains right across the window. ElizabethAnn could see nothing in the window, now, but her own startled reflection.

Using all the strength in her beanpole arms to keep hold of the squirming baby, ElizabethAnn ran down the manor's stone steps and around the corner, but every window and door she approached slammed shut in her face while, inside, she heard someone locking, barring, barricading, and curtaining them over.

"Hey! Don't you want your baby?" she shouted. "Hey! What am I supposed to do with this thing?"

Racing around the building, she found a tiny stained-glass window that hadn't been barricaded. "What about my grandma?" she bellowed into its seams. Someone on the inside shoved a blanket up against it. ElizabethAnn raced on.

Around the back of the mansion, the splendor of its facade abruptly disappeared. Back there, ElizabethAnn encountered a monstrous, tangled field of stinging nettles and thorny weeds containing a collection of what can only be called dilapidated shacks. Their walls looked none too plumb; roofs, none too sturdy.

She didn't want to seek help from the sorts of people who might call such awful places home, so she turned back to the manor. Its solid granite back wall contained only one cellar window, set half underground, surrounded by a drainage culvert.

ElizabethAnn dropped to her belly and carefully placed the baby among some weeds, keeping a grip on its diaper. She pressed her cheek to the ground and strained to see through the pane, though it was coated with a layer of oily grime. Detecting movement inside, she tapped on the glass and heard a little bleat of surprise from within.

"Is someone tapping on the window?" asked a woman's voice.

"Please, please, please, let me in!" replied ElizabethAnn.

"Who's there?"

"It's ElizabethAnn!"

"Am I supposed to know who that is?"

"I guess not. Who are you?"

"Tammy, of course. Who else would be in the kitchen?"

"Tammy, the duchess locked me out of the house! And I have her baby! I just want to give it back!"

"Well, I'm not taking it! You think I want to have a fit? Get it out of here!"

"But it's the duchess' baby!"

"So? Take it to The Drone. No one here wants it."

"To the what?"

"Are you stupid or something?"

"Could you please open this window, Miss Tammy? I surrender and everything!"

"Don't surrender to me. I'm elbows deep in guts. Just whatever you do, don't let that baby out of your sight! Otherwise ..."

ElizabethAnn turned to check on her charge and found herself holding an empty diaper. She jumped to her feet and saw the baby's little naked bottom, off in the distance, as its owner slithered through tall grasses with surprising dexterity.

She gave chase, but her dress caught on thorn bushes, and by the time ElizabethAnn freed herself, the tyke had disappeared. She plunged into the forest, but the baby seemed to have simply vanished: up a tree, down a hole, who knew?

Dashing deeper and deeper into the forest's musty darkness, ElizabethAnn called to the baby, scanned the ground for it, and even made little kissy sounds to attract it, but without result. Soon—her arms and legs scratched by briars, her knees skinned from falling on jagged rocks, and her whole body bruised from tumbling down hillsides—ElizabethAnn noticed birds hovering overhead, as if considering her matted hair a prime source of affordable housing.

Finally, she rested against an outcropping of boulders, shut her eyes, and dropped her tired head in her arms, meanwhile taking in the birdsong and the shushing of the wind. She enjoyed the relief when a passing breeze cooled her skin. She noticed the softness of the dirt beneath her bottom and the hardness of the rock she leaned against, and then ElizabethAnn heard the voices.

"I'm here. I'm here. I'm here." The whispers seemed to come from all around her, from the very wind itself. "Kiddo! Kiddo!" they said.

ElizabethAnn raised her head and looked around. "Grandma?" she asked, feeling foolish. "Are you there?"

Just then, the baby crawled out from behind a twisted vine and looked ElizabethAnn full in the face.

"Kiddo," whispered the baby. "You've got to find Shadooda. Find it for Grandma."

ElizabethAnn lunged for the babe but tripped on a root, fell, and skinned her knee again. She paused to whimper and inspect the damage, and in that time the baby disappeared, once more. No more voices came, except perhaps a sudden, whispered, "Frangipani!" but it might have been her imagination.

ElizabethAnn sighed the deep, warbling sigh of the hopelessly confused and trudged farther along, through the forest, checking every thicket for Grandma, Jackson, a rogue monkey, and now the duchess' lost baby, too.

WHERE THE DUCHESS REVEALS
HER PERSONAL PHILOSOPHY

"Lock it! Lock it! Lock it!" the duchess insisted while Hank attacked the door, shutter, and window, as if they had come alive with ill intent. But even with the house locked down, they could still hear ElizabethAnn's pounding and pleading, so Hank and the duchess ran back into the sitting room and covered their ears with velvet cushions until the ruckus ceased.

Afterward, the duchess said, "Call the fumigator, will you?" and picked up her baby's discarded blanket. She smelled it, sneezed, and hawked up a loogie.

"Yeah, it's lucky that girl finally came along," said Hank.

"But where do you think they found such an odd child? And why wouldn't she fill out the form? It's standard. You fill it, take the kid, and boom."

"Yeah, probably she's a little slow. Let's follow them, shall we?"

Hank and the duchess ascended a steep, winding stone staircase, all the way up to a parapet overlooking the valley. There, the duchess adjusted the eyepiece on a brass spyglass trained on the dense forest to the west.

"Oh no, Hank!" exclaimed the duchess. "I see the girl, but she hasn't got the baby. She's running around this way and that like a fool! How're they training children these days? I swear, each one's dumber than the next."

"The baby probably has a homing device. I wouldn't worry."

"Beg pardon? I birthed that child. I didn't give it any device. Who would have given it a device?"

"In the DNA."

"You think?"

"Yeah, that's how they're engineering them. Zade Fandey gave a press release a while back. It's in the semen. Or the water. Something. It gets into the kid, I tell you. It'll crawl all the way to The Drone by itself, if some wild animal doesn't get it first."

The duchess gasped and exclaimed, "The things you say, Hank!"

"Yeah, sorry."

The duchess turned the spyglass on its smooth, gyroscopic mount, and took in a scene to the south. Through an intermittent curtain of shimmering leaves, she watched the monkey camp and glimpsed various growing children who, by all accounts, appeared healthy and hardworking.

The monkey mamas looked reasonably attentive, but not enough to particularly suit the duchess, who, like mothers the world over, entertained her own ideas as to how she would run the place, if given a chance.

"Did you box up that fruitcake for the older kids?" asked the duchess, adding, "and the scented dryer sheets?"

"The fruitcake, yes, but the dryer sheets, no. Ma'am, they don't have dryers in monkey camps; washers, either."

"Nonsense. How do they dry stuff?"

"Air, ma'am."

"Phooey."

"Fact of the matter, no one in Bumblegreen has a dryer, but you."

"Really? How do they get that clean, fresh scent?"

"Air, ma'am."

"Huh. What'll they think of next?"

"How do you have dryers and fruitcakes and such things, anyway? Imports have been illegal for what? Four years now? Not to pry."

"The basement, darling. So many musty old imported doodads down there: promotional items, toiletries, preserved foods, cases and cases of single-serving boxes of raisins. Acres of things. It's practically endless. Go and see for yourself, sometime. Take home a candy bar."

"Seriously? Acres?"

"Of course, dear. Just in case I run out of things, you know. Theft, natural disaster, looting, lightning strike: anything could happen."

"Boxes of raisins?"

"Sure, why not? Raisins, armchairs, baby dolls, crystal goblets, snow globes. Whatever. To own is to exist. Something you should learn if you're going to be one of us—even if it's part-time or whatever."

Hank's watch beeped, and the duchess jumped in panic.

"Yeah, don't worry. That's just the first alarm," he said.

"So you're not going to … you know? Turn? Right here on the parapet?"

"Not for a good fifteen minutes."

"Thinking ahead. Good man. You'd better hustle and take your medicine."

"Yeah. I'll do it, have lunch, and be back in a little bit."

"Actually, take the rest of the day off, Hank. I'm going straight to bed. But keep an eye out for thieves as you cross the lawn, will you?" suggested the duchess as she shooed Hank down the stairs with a wrist-flicking gesture reflecting equal measures of concern and impatience.

6

In Which ElizabethAnn
Nearly Falls to Her Death

ElizabethAnn found something like a path, although it seemed to appear and disappear at will. It might have only been a sketchy sort of animal track, not a human path at all, but it gave her a sense of direction.

She imagined the path might lead someplace with food, shelter, perhaps answers, perhaps even Grandma, but she lost her way in a swamp. Fog emerged, too. Vines and clumps of damp, hair-like moss hung down from the trees, bringing the forest roof closer in, infringing on her personal space, and making her wonder if she had taken herself someplace wronger than the place she had previously been.

Navigating among downed branches, mud puddles, and hunks of slimy detritus, ElizabethAnn kept going in the general direction of, well, in no particular direction at all, but ever forward.

Finally, ElizabethAnn stopped in a clearing—the sort of clearing that might have once been used for games or meetings or revelry of some sort. The scattering of apple trees growing there looked to have been purposely planted, as they weren't at all in sync with the foggy, mossy, swampy gestalt of the place.

Overhead, an abandoned tree house hovered in the crotch of some large, ancient, maybe-still-alive tree. Boards had come loose and a railing had collapsed. Moss grew here and there, giving the tree house a blotchy, emerald patina. Meanwhile, its quaint, multipaned windows looked out over the top of the settling fog like the eyes of curious crows. Specks of vibrant orange paint still clung to the crosspieces.

ElizabethAnn crossed the clearing, grabbed a ripe apple, bit into it, and held it between her teeth as she ascended a raggedy rope ladder. She wouldn't have been allowed, normally. Too dangerous. But she had done the tire swing, after all. Figured she might as well do the rope ladder, too. No one to see.

Stepping onto what ElizabethAnn supposed might have once been a treetop rocking-chair porch, she tested the floorboards with each step. Some crumbled at the pressure, others held fast, so she made her way to the once-gaily-painted doorway. Inside, she found a sturdy, splinter-free floor and watertight roof. The interior of the tree house, having stayed dry for many years, showed the fine, precise workmanship of agile hands. Clearly, this had once been someone's home. For a moment, ElizabethAnn envied that someone.

A second doorway gave upon a rustic suspension bridge leading to another tree house, similar in construction. In the foggy distance, ElizabethAnn spied more of the structures perched delicately in treetops, camouflaged by branches that had grown over, around, and even through them. A tangle of sagging rope-bridges connected them all.

She tried the bridge with a tentative tap, then a shift of weight, then a few bold steps, but once she got a few steps out, the slats crick-cracked beneath her, and the ropes frayed and threatened to split apart. Frightened, she froze in place, and the decay froze with her.

A rustling sounded, far below. She tried to crane her neck and look down without jostling the bridge, but the creak of complaining ropes warned ElizabethAnn not to push her luck. Then, she heard it: the jingling.

Could have been sleigh bells, if such wintertime entertainments had been a facet of Bumblegreen culture, but no. The jingling didn't sound like wind chimes, nor did it resemble a loop of keys or a jolly jester's hat. It didn't sound like change in a pocket, or breaking glass, or a lot of bracelets tinkling together on a fancy lady's wrist. It sounded, to ElizabethAnn's disbelieving ears, like Jackson's tags.

While she listened, she sensed the rope bridge about to crumble and drop her a very uncomfortable distance, so ElizabethAnn reached for a nearby branch—a living thing, and reliable. Sure enough, just as she shifted her weight to grasp it, the bridge's ropes shrieked in a manner typical of tired, overstretched fibers, and the entire bridge crumbled. Its various parts landed on the soggy ground with the less-than-satisfying *plip plop* of damp things falling into soggy things, but ElizabethAnn, heart racing, clung tightly to the sturdy branch. She wrapped her legs around it and scooted her way to the trunk, hanging upside down, much like a sloth (although ElizabethAnn, herself, didn't comprehend the nature of sloths, as such).

From this strange vantage point, she took a good look around, or tried to. Fog obscured the ground to the point where she wasn't even sure, anymore, just how far down it was. The rustling disappeared; the jingling, too. Whatever had been there a moment before vanished without a trace, just like the duchess' baby.

ElizabethAnn hand-over-handed it along the branch, back to the tree house porch, where she alighted, pressed herself flat against a sturdy wall, and breathed deeply. *This would be a good time for one of those magic winds*, she thought, but no wind came.

The knowledge that she had just escaped a plunge to certain pain, possibly broken bones, maybe even death, swept over ElizabethAnn, and she ducked back inside the tree house to have a good cry. Surprisingly, her fit didn't last long, perhaps because she found the place strangely appealing—something about the quality of the light. Or perhaps she calmed down because of what she noticed next. For there, strewn about the floor, lay innumerable pieces of colored string.

They weren't strings exactly, but rather cast-off pieces of embroidery floss. Purple, orange, chartreuse … the tiny, bright threads stood out against timeworn wood. She gathered them up.

One thing had always been a comfort to ElizabethAnn, as a child. As a younger child, that is. It's a certain game girls play, looping string between their hands and pulling it this way and that, through spread fingers. You can make a cup and saucer. You can make a spider's web, or something like it, anyway. You can make a glass palace, a Caribbean sunset, or a copy of the Sunday *No Oaks Times*, if you've imagination enough. With patience, imagination, and a bit of string, a girl can make just about anything.

ElizabethAnn gathered a piece of thread, tied it into a good-size loop, laced it between the fingers of her two hands, and tried some well-remembered patterns: a roller skate, a blooming flower, a coffee can. Indeed, the activity did calm her. The relaxation it brought on even revived her drive to keep searching for Grandma and, ultimately, survive. Playing with the string reminded her of the fourth thing needed to make the game work: patience, yes, imagination, yes, a bit of string, yes, but also, one needed a grandmother, or a friend, or a sister—someone to agree to the illusion. Someone to say, "Yes! That's a fat man's belly! Yes! That's a crumpled homework paper! Yes! That looks exactly like a bowl of noodles!"

ElizabethAnn descended the rope ladder without incident, stopped in the clearing to grab another apple off a tree, and plunged again into the fog. Venturing into the unknown for the third time that day—in fact, for the third time ever—she felt less apprehensive, more aggressive.

"Grandma!" she called. "Grandma! Little baby! Jackson! Anybody out there?"

Soon, she heard jingling again, like tiny tinkling bells, and called out plenty of hellos and who's theres, but whichever way ElizabethAnn ran, the sound always seemed to come from just a little bit farther on.

7

FEATURING TAMMY, WHO TRIES
TO IMPROVE HER LOT IN LIFE

Perpetually broke, exhausted, overweight, nauseous, swollen, pimply, and cursed with halitosis, Tammy, the duchess' personal chef, had just one good feature: her nose. It was aristocratic with a touch of the exotic, a nose made for someone far greater than she, which might have, in fact, been stolen from its rightful owner and gene-spliced onto Tammy's otherwise undeserving face.

Her mother once told her, "Tams, I ain't given you much. I ain't given you diddly. I ain't even given you that nose. Your father gave you that, the bastard. That's the one good deed he ever done. Try and do something with it besides sniff and blow."

When ElizabethAnn tapped on the kitchen window looking for someone to unburden her of an ill-gotten baby, Tammy was elbow deep into a barrel of goose guts. Having been tasked with preparing these sweetmeats, she could focus neither on the work at hand nor the strange young visitor. It's no wonder: Tammy had just found out she was pregnant.

Anywhere but Bumblegreen this might have been good news, but Tammy was allergic to babies, of course, just like everyone else there. Tammy knew she couldn't raise her baby but didn't want to give it up to the monkeys, either, even though the law required it. So, prior to ElizabethAnn's visit, she had been avoiding thinking about that problem and instead planning revenge against her erstwhile lover Fast Eddie, all in mid-sauté.

The way she envisioned it, the first step of Tammy's revenge would be the hardest. Embodying incredible, irresistible sexiness was Part-One of the plan she'd designed to spur Fast Eddie to a desire to get her back. This would be followed by Part Two, where she planned to ruthlessly spurn his advances until, (Part Three) he died of a broken heart. It was a simple, elegant, satisfying revenge plan. To pull it off, she was going to have to figure out what to do with a face that had never been described more affectionately than as "having potential," even back when Tammy should have been in the full, apple-cheeked bloom of girlhood.

Later, at home in her shack, Tammy stared hopelessly into a piece of broken mirror. She experimented with her hair, with makeup, with various ointments, yet her squinty eyes still resisted enhancement and her lips disappeared utterly into her face. Her hair, with its dull, brown-black shade, hung in a manner neither straight nor curly, not long enough to be dramatic, yet too wispy to hold a style. Tammy called herself a horse's ass for ever imagining she could improve her looks, then proclaimed aloud, "That's it!"

Hours later, Tammy had combed the tail of every black horse in the duchess' stable and made herself a set of horsehair extensions to rival any goddess' tresses. She even devised a technique for weaving them into her hair so that they cascaded to her waist like spilled ink.

The horsehair endowed Tammy with a look so exotic it seemed the perfect frame for her nose. Making her long chin appear even longer, the new hair softly swung to and fro, making Tammy seem wise, noble, and yes, definitely sexy. When Tammy saw herself this way, she swore she could smell it: the scent of a man's annihilation.

With her new weave in place, Tammy crossed the meadow to Hank's shack. When she knocked on his flimsy door, it creaked open at the pressure. The shack exuded a train wreck of scents that could not have left many survivors. Beneath the peppermint top note, rose petals and anise loomed. The sharp scent of persimmon paired with the intestinal smell of jackfruit, and bodily aromas—blood, urine, phlegm, sweat—created a base note, a place to tuck its shoes under the bed, if you will.

Tammy entered the dark shack, waded through the disorienting aromas, heard a pot boiling, then detected murmuring somewhere beyond the not-precisely-rectangular spot of light where Hank's back door stood ajar.

On the back stoop, she found Hank, the duchess' butler, who had cast off his tuxedo shirt and tie. The undone ends of his belt dangled from his waist and clanked. He crouched, extending a handful of plucked grass toward the forest and talking in an unusually high voice.

"C'mon boy, Hank's your friend. I won't hurt you, fella," he said.

"What are you …" asked Tammy, interrupting herself with, "Oh! Oh! Oh! What in the world is that? What in the world!"

"Shh! You'll scare him away."

"But what …"

"C'mon Buster. That's a good boy. Papa has something for you," Hank urged, adding, "Here's some nice grass for the good boy. Here you go."

Then, to Tammy, Hank said, "Look at him. Isn't he cute?"

"What is it?"

"Who knows?"

"Look at those! Are those fangs?"

"Yeah. No, c'mon. The beast is just a big ball of fluff on sticks."

"I don't think so, Hank. It could be dangerous."

"I'm going to trap it," Hank whispered as he crawled across the grass toward a phenomenally shaggy beast that had recently emerged from the woods, looking confused.

The beast cocked its volleyball-sized head to one side as Hank approached and tried to soothe it with nonsense sounds. Then, it cocked its head the other way, flipping open an enormous, floppy ear and exposing the smooth, pink whorls of flesh inside. In the flipping process, the beast lobbed a hunk of hair and a gob of slobber in Hank's direction, then crouched as if to spring.

Tammy gasped. Hank screamed involuntarily and protected his crotch.

The beast (whom you and I know as Jackson, of course) ran in circles, bucking and pawing at the air. Its long, pink tongue lolled out, wagging back and forth with every movement. Saliva dripped from its mouth as if from a loose-lidded pickle jar.

When the beast flipped a blob of slobber right onto the top of its own head, Hank noticed other blobs had since lodged themselves in numerous additional places within the beast's shaggy, mottled pelt.

Hank dove at the animal, grabbed fistfuls of fur, and wrestled it to the ground. In a moment, he had it on its back, four legs kicking the air. But then, Hank's nose got a glob of fur stuck up there, and he couldn't breathe.

The alarm on Hank's watch beeped for a second time that day, as did the kitchen timer in his house. Tammy screamed. Hank shook his head, tried to sneeze the fur out of his nose, but refused to let go of the beast, his conquest. Hank couldn't sneeze, though, and soon he couldn't breathe, either. He could only open and close his mouth, gasping for air that wouldn't come. His body spasmed and his legs pressed together, kicking violently as one. Meanwhile, the beast loomed over him, drooling and clicking its fangs open and shut.

Then, Hank felt his body rising into the air, light as a feather. The world went white, and he could breathe again. He could breathe so well, in fact, it felt as if he were breathing with every pore of his body. The air crisped up, like a comforting blanket of ice. His mind blanked and felt completely at peace, as Hank remembered exactly who he was and his place in the natural order of things. It felt like living the taste of key lime pie, the smell of tanned leather, and the feel of mud between your toes, all at once.

"You stupid ass!" said someone, somewhere.

Hank heard the voice, off in the distance. The sharp, piercing tone of it disturbed his all-encompassing peace and joy.

"What am I supposed to do, now?" asked the voice, which Hank finally recognized as Tammy.

"It's okay," Hank shouted from his swirling white world. "Just wait a few minutes."

Instinctively, Hank moved in circles, round and round, gradually gaining a sense of control. "Do a crossword puzzle!" he suggested.

Then, all at once, along with a splitting headache, the world came into focus again. Hank found himself in his living room, sitting in the white laundry basin he used for washing socks, which was filled with freezing cold water and his own muscular buttocks.

Tammy hopped and jumped, as if with tacks in her shoes, and ran around aimlessly in the manner of someone who knows something very important must get done right away but hasn't the faintest idea what. She looked at Hank, screamed again, clapped her hands, and leaped around in a circle.

"Tammy, listen carefully," said Hank. "Go and get me three-fourths of a cup of that brew on the stove."

She did it. Hank drank it, then heaved himself up out of the basin, grabbed a dry pair of pajama bottoms out of his bureau, and changed into them with no concern for modesty. After what she had just seen, the sight of his soggy underneath parts certainly wasn't going to shock Tammy.

"You saved my life," Hank said, clearing his throat. "Thanks."

"What the hell! What the hell! What the hell!"

"Calm down," Hank requested, quite irrationally, as he covered the iron pot on the stove, turned the gas to low, and set the kitchen timer for another six hours. His watch alarm continued to beep all this time, which explained the piercing headache, so he silenced it.

"I did mention this before, didn't I?" Hank asked, adding, "That I have Zade Fandey's disease? Had it under control, but … got so distracted by that beast, forgot to take my medicinal tea. Sorry. I mean, it's embarrassing."

Tammy's eyes bulged, which wasn't flattering.

Hank asked, "Did you do something with your hair?"

Tammy picked up a paper bag and breathed into it: inflate, deflate, inflate, deflate.

"Tammy, say something."

"I'm sorry, I've just never seen a man turn into a steelhead trout before."

"Never?"

"I have to get back to work," she said then, gathering her purse and coat with jerky gestures.

"At this hour?"

"The duchess is having a garden party, this weekend."

"Oh, that."

"I'll prep all night and take the morning off … and Hank, stay safe, okay?"

"I'll just be here."

"Seriously, though. Don't let that happen again. I nearly had a heart attack."

"I won't. Well, yeah, I mean, I drank my tea, so it's another guaranteed six hours until I turn again. That much I can control. Yeah. No, I just have to remember not to let myself get distracted."

"Yeah," she said, and, "Don't!" and, "Keep that basin full, though, just in case?"

Tammy exited, shut Hank's door, caught her hair in it, opened the door, released the hair, shut the door again, and went about her business, careful to remember she now had that extra body part to manage.

She strolled back to the mansion, experimentally swishing her glamorous new appendage. Meantime, Hank remembered, with effort, how to breathe through his nose.

8

WHERE QUEEN DAHLIA WHISPERS INTO THE FOG

Queen Dahlia seldom traveled with less than a full retinue. Hoisting her palanquin, after all, required numerous servants. Plus, attendants had to comb its fringes, arrange its velvet draperies, and untangle its assortment of tinkling bells. A team of gaily dressed porters had to tote her clothing changes, gourmet food, and emergency first-aid kit, while a stylist remained perpetually occupied with maintaining the queen's elaborate hairstyle. And sometimes, when Dahlia ventured into the misty lowlands, her many layers of taffeta skirts and gauzy accents lost their loft and someone had to fan them dry, by hand. With all her attendants pitching in—respectfully avoiding eye contact and personal conversation all the while—the procedure didn't take too long.

Her regents frowned upon Queen Dahlia's choice of the foggy orchard as a picnicking location but couldn't do much about it. The headstrong thirteen-year-old would have her way.

"It's nothing more than a tame little frolic," she told them that day, before she left the castle. "I'll be back by supper time."

In truth, this picnic was no frolic but a scientific expedition. As soon as she arrived in the orchard—bells a-tinkling and fringe a-swaying—Queen Dahlia gracefully jumped down from the palanquin and set about pacing the perimeter.

Her attendants arranged the royal picnic, as instructed, in the center of the clearing, while the queen walked the perimeter with carefully measured steps. Passing beside a tuft of wild grasses and a soggy old log, she heard the strangest sound, almost like a faint cry of, "Who's there? Who's there?" It grew louder, seemed to come closer, then became faint again.

Queen Dahlia stepped away from the clearing and into the marsh, where the fog lay thickest, and the now-whispering voice seemed to come from someone standing right in front of her, though obscured by fog. She jumped, startled, then reached tentatively into the whiteness. But the next time she heard, "Hello? Who's there?" the voice had retreated far from the orchard's edge.

It's probably just the wind whining through the mangroves, thought Dahlia. She had been out in the misty lowlands enough to know the place could play tricks on your senses.

Dahlia lifted her voluminous skirts, tiptoed around a puddle, and resumed pacing the orchard's perimeter, looking for leaks in her polymer—any place where the dirt failed to meet the ground, any gopher hole that might have been dug, or any odd-seeming wrinkle that might have formed beneath a boulder or a pile of branches, enabling access to the secret portal that lay beneath the orchard.

When she felt satisfied with the clearing's normalcy and the natural quality of the apple trees growing there, she skipped to the picnic blanket and, in a burst of playfulness, twirled until her skirts flew out. The queen next dropped down into that luxurious mountain of embroidered fabrics that were both a privilege and a curse.

Quickly, Dahlia's attendants tamed the flying skirts, flounces, sashes, scarves, and other accoutrements into a decorative circle of royal loveliness. Someone smoothed the feathers in her headdress. Another servant handed the queen a cruller and a cup of tea, careful not to touch her royal fingers, and Queen Dahlia accepted it distractedly. The entire flock moved away, then, to give her royal highness privacy in which to chew.

Alone again and fearful of moving (lest her attendants descend upon her again to fuss, fuss, fuss) Queen Dahlia raised her gaze to the old tree house, quietly rotting at the clearing's edge.

"Looks like one of those bridges finally fell," she said to no one in particular. A few attendants nodded their agreement. A broken rope bridge swayed in a silent breeze. A couple of apples plopped to the ground. Then, she saw it.

A loop of colorful thread hung from a nearby branch. At first, she thought the loop a vision. These being the misty lowlands, after all, such things were possible, but the more Queen Dahlia stared at the thing, the more she comprehended its realness.

She walked across the orchard, and the ring of servants parted to let her through. Gently, the young queen lifted the loop of thread off the branch, drew it between thumb and pinky, then pulled and wove and looped and twisted it. Soon, she had made a cup and saucer, then a roller skate, a blooming flower, a coffee can, and another thing.

"Do you think," she asked her stylist, "this looks like a bowl of noodles?"

"Certainly, Your Highness," the stylist replied, in an obligatory sort of way.

"Maybe not," murmured the queen. "Maybe it doesn't look like anything, I guess."

"If you say so, Your Highness," answered the stylist, spraying back a few stray hairs on the young queen's head. "Its very nice, though," he added.

"Do you think so?"

"Yes, Your Highness," chorused several attendants. Some added curtseys.

Before long, Queen Dahlia climbed back into her palanquin but couldn't fully relax into her silken pillows.

Throughout the long ride home, she peeked at the passing wilderness from between heavy curtains and whispered, "Who's there? Who's there?" into the misty lowlands.

9

In Which Zade Fandey
Makes a Rabbity Sound

"Zade, am I speaking into the right end of it?" asked Grandma, manipulating a hose with a nozzle on one end, a funnel at the other, and a T-connection in the middle that attached it to a pulsating contraption.

"Oh, see, now that's your problem right there, Grams," answered Zade. "You've got the right end, but you have to kind of hum what you want to say, kazoo-like."

"Kiddo! kiddo!" she hummed into the nozzle, then said, "I don't think it's working. How can I even tell where my voice is coming out?"

"Look here. It's simple," Zade insisted. "Well, no, not simple, but for a woman of your intelligence … turn the dial to 'wind,' and you get your voice drifting on the wind. Turn it to 'animal,' and it'll sound like it's coming out of an animal. Turn it to 'dream,' and it'll come through a dream."

"Kiddo!" Grandma screamed into the hose.

"Turn it to 'water,' your voice will resemble the lapping of waves, turn it to …"

"I got it, Zade," Grandma said, and switched the dial from one setting to another. Periodically, she screamed, "Find Shadooda!" into the nozzle.

"Wait," Zade interrupted. "You also have to dial in ElizabethAnn's location. Rain forest floor? Swampy lowlands? Forest canopy? Castle lawn? Field of weeds? Plenty of options here. Pick your location, pick your medium. Then, you're set."

"But how am I to know where my granddaughter's even at?" asked Grandma.

"Right," replied Zade, finger in the air as if to indicate he had already thought of that. "I've a steady stream of monkey spies coming and going. They'll type her locale into a machine upstairs. It comes out this slot, on ticker tape. Oh look, here's one. Says she's in the swampy lowlands."

"Kiddo!" screamed Grandma, wildly turning dials.

"You don't have to scream," said Zade. "There's always some sound distortion, but it's by design. If it's wind, it comes out as a whisper. If it comes out of, say, a bobcat, it'll be a scream, but if it comes out of a rabbit, it'll be a rabbity sort of voice."

"Rabbity?"

"My artistic interpretation of rabbity," said Zade. "Scientists do have fun once in a rare while, you know."

Grandma sighed and placed the hose on its chrome-plated stand. She shoved books and papers aside to lie back on Zade's scarred wooden laboratory table, covering her face with a cool washcloth.

"This isn't going to work, Zade," she mumbled through the fabric.

"It was your idea, Grams!"

"And a 'welcome home' to you, too."

"Welcome home."

"Thank you."

"Just wish you'd come with a plan, is all."

Grandma pulled up the washcloth's corner and gave Zade a look that said, *Don't underestimate me, punk.*

"A grandchild is not a plan. This girl is completely unprepared!" Zade countered.

"Wrong again, friend. My daughter, admittedly, wasn't capable. Sometimes that capable gene skips a generation. But my grandchild is. I can attest ElizabethAnn has the mental clarity my daughter lacks."

"A houseplant has that!"

"I forgot. You've met my daughter. So, you know."

"I remember she's got some kind of block," he said, rapping on his skull with his fist, to demonstrate.

"Indeed, she does."

"My life in No Oaks wasn't so long ago, you know," said Zade.

"It was fun, wasn't it?" Grandma asked. "Being recruited together?"

"A blast," Zade agreed. "It's a shame they made us stop Traveling. We could have been together, all these years."

"You were brave to stay, Zade."

"Brave nothing! It's better here! You were brave to go back to No Oaks!"

"Well, that's true, but I had to groom ElizabethAnn," said Grandma. "And now, I know she can find Shadooda. It's not too late." Grandma sat up and tossed the washcloth into a lab sink, where it *thwocked* nicely against the steel. "Anyway, the wheels are in motion, like it or not, and that's not my fault," she said. "Shadooda made it clear, when I left Bumblegreen, that each portal would still open, but only for a day at a time—just long enough to let in air but prevent Travel. And somehow, when I saw those No Oaks goons coming for me, I knew Shadooda would open ours, today. 'Witches see all,' as they used to say."

"'Magician' is the polite term."

"Really? Not 'sorcerer?'"

"Back in the day, Shadooda did prefer 'sorcerer,'" Zade replied, "but now it's 'magician.' Times change. Anyway, there's no denying the bravery of your return to Bumblegreen, Grams. You're taking a phenomenal risk, but to come here with nothing but your grandchild and your wits … I just don't see how you're going to find Shadooda."

"I'm not, Zade. ElizabethAnn is," Grandma said.

"How do you figure?" he asked, straightening the books and papers on his table with unconcealed exasperation.

"I don't know, exactly, but if she can find that witch …"

"Magician!"

"How do you even have correct terms for them if all the *magicians* have gone underground?" Grandma asked. "I thought nobody talked about them, or to them, anymore?"

"That's true, but linguistics never rest, you know. If anyone *were* to talk about them, which they wouldn't, but if they were to, it would be 'magician,' not 'sorcerer' or 'witch.' I don't make the rules."

"Either way, ElizabethAnn finding Shadooda, alone, isn't going to end your eponymously named disease," said Grandma.

"Ingrates! Naming that disease after me," Zade grumbled.

"Isn't going to prevent the return of the blight, either," Grandma continued, "or the baby allergy, either." She sat up on the edge of the lab table and shook her head as she continued, "If Queen Dahlia doesn't get on board with opening the portals again, all our efforts to find Shadooda are going to be for nothing."

"Queen Dahlia is a child," said Zade, "and not a particularly precocious one. She still thinks the blight was caused by open portals, and who'll prove otherwise?"

"Shadooda? Hopefully?"

"If we find him or her or whatever. If the queen listens to him or her or whatever. If, if, if," said Zade. "I've been trying to please Dahlia, replacing the lost magic with technology, but there are limits, damn it. There are limits!"

"Obviously, Zade baby, nobody's blaming you."

"Talking about tons of people are blaming me!" Zade shouted, breaking some test tubes with a flailing gesture, cursing, and cleaning it up with a whiskbroom.

"Queen Dahlia has to see the big picture, that's all," Grandma insisted. "She's got the power to do good, but the kid needs to age ten years in one, that's all."

"I don't even remotely have an elixir for that," Zade said with a pout, adding, "You'd think if someone explained it to her—the fact that the imports caused the blight, but the way the queen cured the blight, by closing the portals entirely, caused the baby allergy."

"And the baby allergy brought on this monkey technology," said Grandma, "which, in turn, brought on Zade Fandey's disease."

"Stop calling it that!"

"ZF disease."

"That's a tiny bit better."

"So why don't you go to visiting hours," asked Grandma, "and explain it to the queen, yourself?"

"Believe me," Zade replied. "I have."

"And?"

"And she said the scientists concurred that closing the portals would end the blight, and it did, *so there*. She didn't seem to want to think much about Affairs of State."

"She actually said, 'So there?'"

"Yep. She's thirteen."

"But I dissented!"

"Yeah, when she was *ten*. What's a ten-year-old know about dissenting opinions?"

Grandma groaned with the impossibility of it all and finally said, "So this really is in Shadooda's hands. Only a witch, I mean magician, can open the portals against the queen's wishes. And ElizabethAnn is the key to finding it."

"It?"

"'It' meaning Shadooda. Are we still using the non-gender-specific pronoun, or do we honk like a goose now, or something?"

"Oh, yeah, 'it' is still correct for magicians," Zade answered. "But going back to my original issue: A granddaughter is not a plan! The poor kid's alone in a swamp!"

"She'll be all right," Grandma said with, actually, real confidence.

"She's too young," Zade said. "Her psyche is going to be horribly scarred from this."

Grandma ran her hands over the pockmarked table Fandey used for his experiments with chemicals, enzymes, machinery, and monkeys. The mottled surface of the thing alone spoke volumes about the man.

"Scarred?" replied Grandma. "A little frightened, maybe. A little confused. But scarred? Nothing so bad as all that."

10

In Which Tammy First Falls Prey to Seduction

One day, for the first time—this was way back, oh, months before ElizabethAnn came to Bumblegreen—Tammy met Fast Eddie, slouching in the duchess' drawing room. His insolent air made her wonder how the brat ever got an interview with the duchess in the first place. But later that evening, walking behind the mansion, he bumped into Tammy "by chance," and told her he had been hired as a houseboy and assigned to be housed in a certain shack in the nettle-strewn meadow. Would she show him where that might be?

She agreed, and as they walked, Fast Eddie stood tall and proud. All six feet and three inches of him insisted on carrying her bag, though she protested. He now seemed, to Tammy, gentlemanly, solicitous, and trustworthy, though with a hint of badness that made him intriguing. (He knew it did.) While they walked, he spoke of elephant ear and fiddlehead ferns. Of the strangler fig, he exclaimed, "Parasites are the most beautiful flora in the forest!" His sudden waxing scientific-cum-philosophical strangely titillated Tammy. (He knew it would.)

Naturally, on that last stretch of the trail, just when she had warmed up to him, Fast Eddie ceased the friendly banter and became distant, preoccupied. After a brief, old-fashioned bow, he dropped Tammy at her door and walked off without a backward glance. As planned, he left her contemplating his mystery, wanting more, and wondering what dumb thing she had said to make him go from subtly interested to subtly indifferent. Eddie knew how to use unpredictable behavior to make a woman ask, "Is it me? Or is he ... no, it must all be in my head."

Over the next few weeks, romance (of a sort) blossomed, based largely upon Fast Eddie's calculatedly mysterious nature and Tammy's predictable fascination with it.

As time went on, Tammy couldn't help but notice his habit of sticking his head in holes in the ground. He claimed to be looking for portals. Tammy didn't mention the fact that the portals were well known to be sealed off, because stating the obvious around Fast Eddie seemed almost rude, as if it went without saying he had considered such facts from his own unique perspective and rejected them for reasons ordinary mortals simply couldn't fathom.

One day, Fast Eddie did find something interesting: a silver flask stashed in a hole in a tree. He gave it to Tammy as a token, supposedly, of love.

Then, deeper into the affair, Fast Eddie informed Tammy he wanted to tell her something special, in a beautiful place. "Would you meet me on the castle lawn, say about six?" he asked.

Tammy thought the castle a wonderfully romantic spot for a marriage proposal, what with its weeping willows and babbling brook. And with the queen holding regular visiting hours these last few years, it would be easy enough for Tammy and Fast Eddie to stroll into the castle as visitors, then take a detour to the grounds.

Tammy put on a little makeup for the occasion, bought a new dress, and paired it with backless, precarious shoes. But when she met her "boyfriend" there, he stood aloof and said, "Guess what, I've met somebody!"

His jubilant tone implied Tammy should somehow wish him well on his great journey of ... alternative romance ... or whatever.

And the silver flask? He asked for it back.

Dazed, Tammy stared at her reflection in its shining silver side. She watched the fluttering of her minuscule, irregular lashes. She watched the color rise on her otherwise sallow cheeks. She observed her nose from an angle that might not have been its best. She didn't like what she saw, but couldn't stop staring. In the process, she noticed something. A tiny stamp, reading:

Shadooda Majit Goforth
Hindforth and Assoc.
12 Minion Lane

She threw the flask at Fast Eddie's head, but it bounced off and landed in a nearby magnolia tree. He only sighed and walked away, as if to say, *If that's the way you're going to be, I don't want it. It'll only remind me of you.*

11

FEATURING TAMMY'S HEART
OF MALICIOUS BLACK WRATH

12 Minion Lane

Somehow, after bouncing the flask into the tree, Tammy couldn't get the address out of her head.

Hindforth and Assoc.
12 Minion Lane

Where had she heard that address before? The walk home from her humiliation on the castle lawn felt long, tiresome, and pointless. Her sexy dress and too-tight pumps didn't help matters whatsoever. She just didn't feel like being there, anywhere, at all.

Tammy looked down as she walked, wondering if the dainty shoes might have ever led anyone to believe she had shapely ankles. *If one were inclined to believe it anyway*, she concluded, *perhaps they could have been fooled from a distance.*

She walked on and kept pondering that address.

12 Minion Lane

Straying from the castle grounds, she walked right past the road that lead to the duchess' mansion and her own shack, then wandered into downtown Bumblegreen, aimlessly, not realizing what she did, what she sought, why she kept eyeballing the street signs. While Tammy walked the streets of Bumblegreen, she mentally listed all Fast Eddie's promises and revelations and even anecdotes contrasted with his known lies and suspected fabrications and soon understood that everything Fast Eddie ever said to her had been a line, designed to produce a specific emotion or reaction.

Tammy saw the sign she sought—Minion Lane—and walked down the road a-ways, feeling some danger there, what with the endless blocks of lonely, unkempt houses. She enjoyed the distraction of her blisters. She wanted to suffer. The sun gradually set, but still she walked—through swamps and fields and more unkempt neighborhoods—until she came to a spike-topped, wrought-iron fence. A grand arched gate was labeled only "12," and there, an unshaven, portly fellow manned a guard shack.

Tammy approached him and asked, "Um, I'm looking for someone named Shadooda Majit … something." She faltered. The guard turned up his nose and said, "Never heard of him."

"What is this place?" Tammy asked.

"Research facility," said the guard.

"Researching what, exactly?" Tammy asked.

"Nothing interesting," the guard said. "Science. You know."

Tammy walked past the shack, feeling a fool, but then stopped, thought, and returned.

"I must insist," she whined to the guard, who had just opened a rather long and involved-looking novel, "on seeing a Shadooda somebody at Hindforth and something. I'm sure this is the address."

The guard yawned, found a dog-eared page in his book, and, without looking up, muttered, "This isn't a public facility."

Tammy turned away again and walked on, but again, she stopped and reconsidered. This time, she raised her chin, lidded her eyes, and made herself look just as bored as the guard himself.

"The flask said Shadooda Majit Goforth, Hindforth and Assoc. The 'Assoc.' was abbreviated, then, on the third line, '12 Minion Lane,' where twelve was a number, not a word. I held the flask in my hand, and I'm sure it was an heirloom. A *magical* heirloom. This is the address, and I want in," she said, adding, "damn it!" She sniffed just like Fast Eddie would have done in his most haughty mood.

"Hindforth?" asked the guard, giving her a side-eye.

"Yes, indeed. The silversmiths?"

"Silver?" he inquired, shutting his book with a *flumf.*

"Indeed … Hindforth and Associates. I'm a Bumblegreeni, after all, and I have a *right*," Tammy added, with confidence she didn't feel.

In her desperation, Tammy had found a state of profound calm. After all, the outcome of this spontaneous adventure simply didn't matter. If the guard picked her up and flung her into the nearest ditch, it simply wouldn't matter. If he handed her a bouquet of roses, it still wouldn't matter.

"All right," said the guard. In a whisper, he added, "You've clearly seen the heirloom, even if you're not in possession of it. That's the first time, to my knowledge, anyone has spoken the entire password, and thanks for your specificity on that, by the way. They told me no one would even try, let alone get it right." He buzzed the gate open, muttering to himself, "I'm gobsmacked, flummoxed, and impressed besides!"

"Go to Building F," he told Tammy, "but I didn't send ya."

"You didn't send me."

"That's right."

The gargantuan campus of 12 Minion Lane, on its surface, seemed easily navigable. A twenty-minute blistered limp brought Tammy to a group of hexagonal, steel-and-concrete structures. At the heart of the campus, a pleasant, sunlit courtyard enabled visitors to view each efficient building while sitting on a comfortable park bench, contemplating—perhaps the complex's designers had hoped—one's options.

Hydraulic doors shushing in her wake, Tammy walked into Building F and quickly located Hindforth and Associates' fourth-floor office, during which time she neither saw nor heard a single soul. The "research facility" appeared to be a front. She turned the knob on a spring-loaded wooden door that opened upon a foyer manned by a smooth, air-conditioned brunette, sitting behind a smallish desk.

Tammy thought the receptionist looked unfriendly and might be armed to the teeth, or possibly a robot, or both. The receptionist exhibited a too-perfect smile and asked for the password.

"Shadooda Majit Goforth? Hindforth and Assoc. (abbreviated)? Twelve Minion Lane (with twelve as a number)?" said Tammy, trying in vain not to make it a question. The receptionist pressed a button, whereupon a couch, chair, and magazine rack—arranged seemingly for waiting purposes—sunk back into a wall, revealing an ancient granite staircase that descended steeply and uninvitingly into what can only be described as subterranean gloom.

Tammy's pumps clacked on the slippery stone as she walked down into the darkness, childishly pairing her feet on each step. She sputtered and brushed cobwebs from her face, unable to see much in the darkness except the gleam of moist stone. The staircase wound down and down. Eventually, Tammy heard a grinding sound and looked up to see the panel at the top of the stairs closing mechanically above her, cutting out what little light existed.

Tammy tossed away her shoes. She unlatched her fashionably wide belt and threw it somewhere in the darkness, too. Then, Tammy—contemplating her unexceptional life, ignoble aspirations, and lack of upward mobility—pattered down into the dank and musty unknown, eager to learn what horrible thing would happen next. Eventually, she saw dim light emerging from a wide stone tunnel and heard a chorus of hum-singing.

At the base of the stairs sat a thing she had never seen. It looked almost like a machine, yet had seats inside, like a carriage, but there was no place to attach horses in front. Its four wheels looked abnormally fat and small and droopy to Tammy, and the machine's body appeared to be made out of a metal that looked, in the dim light, to have once been painted baby blue. If the machine had ever had a practical use, it certainly didn't have one anymore, except as a haven for bats and a repository for their guano. On the side of the thing, she saw one word: Chevelle.

Tammy made a wide berth around the machine and continued down a tunnel lined with niches—dusty little open-fronted cells set into the ancient, stone wall. The area appeared to be a kind of underground open-air market. Its worn stone floor, broad expanse, and ancient construction of tightly fit granite slabs all attested to once-frequent use.

She padded down the empty, echoing thoroughfare and noticed that within each cell sat a wizened, grubby individual of indeterminate gender singing a simplistic little song, in a whispery hum, into a copper pipe descending from the ceiling. The songs all featured the same nursery-rhyme quality, but Tammy couldn't make out the words. As she walked down the corridor, the individuals each peered at her in surprise and, perhaps, horror. They stopped their hum-singing to squint in her direction through layers of suspended dust. Each one beckoned to Tammy feebly, using gravely tones unused to speech. Still, she walked on.

Finally, Tammy arrived at a cell much like the others, except that over this one hung a jagged wooden sign reading: Shadooda Majit Goforth, Proprietor. Entering the cell, Tammy brushed spider webs off an oily wooden chair and sat in it while she examined the very old person stationed there. It squatted on a three-legged stool and, like the others, hum-sang incessantly into the end of a four-inch copper pipe.

Hey, ho, nobody home
No victuals here, nor a ding-dang tree
Roses grow in summer sunshine
Never do I see, hee

Shadooda finished the song and sniffed in the general direction of its visitor. It didn't bother with pleasantries and made no eye contact. In fact, Shadooda appeared to be sightless as a mole.

"Shadooda Majit Goforth?" asked Tammy, receiving no response.

"Am I right in guessing you folks are magicians? Alchemists? Sorcerers? Witches? Pardon me, I don't know the polite term."

Again, no response.

"I'm happy to meet you!" added Tammy.

Shadooda cleared its throat, ill at ease with this intruder. It returned to hum-singing.

Tammy rubbed her sweaty palms on her dress and said, "If there is actually magic to be had, here, I'm thinking … and I just thought of this, but what I'm thinking right now is … I'm wondering about a spell. I'm in a pretty hard-core situation. I don't think just any old folk remedy would do the trick. I mean, 'black magic' might be the expression you'd use for this. I just thought of it just now, but I like the idea terrifically. Sorry to be so direct."

Preferably, Tammy explained, she wanted to seduce her seducer in return, thus enacting a flip-flop vengeance, preferably of Romeo-and-Juliet proportions, resulting in death (for him), or at least psychological destruction. Though she didn't know the Romeo and Juliet story, as such, she got the idea across with a Bumblegreen tragic-story equivalent.

Tammy felt free saying these things to Shadooda, the way you could confess some small crime, with total ease, to a convicted killer or bank robber, if you knew one. Tammy went on to request the blackest magic imaginable, if anything like that could be obtained by grace, sale, or barter. Also, beyond the magic, she wanted to learn the secrets of seduction itself.

"How can some people know these secrets and others not?" she asked. "Puts us not-knowers at a perpetual disadvantage." She added, "Shadooda? I'm tired of being out of the loop. I really am."

No reaction came from Shadooda, who continued mumbling into the pipe, holding its head at an awkward angle. Finally, Tammy asked,

"So, do you dabble in that kind of thing, or what?"

A resounding cackle emanated from the booths all around, and Shadooda giggled. A magician's giggle is a singular thing, and Shadooda's tee-hees and haw-haws reverberated around its cell, suggesting more voices than one.

"Inquisitive, eh?" mused Shadooda. "Haven't seen your kind at all since I came underground." Shadooda wiped tiny tears of laughter from the corners of its crusty eyes, then added, "Nice outfit. Is that in style?" A burst of belly laughter followed, at which Tammy took offense.

"Just kidding, old girl," Shadooda said. "Been blind as a houseplant for decades. Most of us are, by now, I guess."

"We are!" Echoes of agreement bounced up and down the hall.

"So they're still getting along without us up there in Bumblegreen? Everything still churning?" asked Shadooda.

"Barely."

"Is it time for the revolution?" Shadooda screamed, in a screaming-laughter sort of way. The magicians in the booths all around added their sniggers and chuckles to the uproar, and squeaky echoes crept down Tammy's spine.

"Do you mean … you don't go up? To Bumblegreen? You never go up?" she asked.

"Why would I want to, eh? This place is all mine. All ours. We whoop it up. Have a ball. Square dancing every Friday night!" With that, Shadooda's puckered snout snorted and spasmed in laughter.

Shadooda's merriment caught on with its neighbors and escalated into the charged silence of breathlessness—a couple hundred so-ancient-as-to-be-ageless magicians with their mouths open in simultaneous silent laughter. Tammy experienced a moment of frightened paralysis, until the laughter came back into hearing range and subsided.

"That king and queen, always talking about science and such. We confused them, I guess," said Shadooda. "No use for magic. Just wanted to solve all their problems with imports and science. Big mistake, man."

"I'm a woman," said Tammy, who sometimes had to tell people.

"It's an expression," Shadooda said, adding, "They shoved us sorcerers down here, but, you know, plenty of pinochle and shuffleboard. We love it!"

Again, chilling laughter all around. As crooked as a windshield crack, Shadooda looked barely capable of such entertainments.

"It's over, you know," Tammy told the magician.

"Is it, now? The blight, you mean?"

"Yeah. They closed the portals for good."

Shadooda moaned, then muttered, "That's what they think."

"And the king and queen," added Tammy, "they died."

"Oh! So we can come back up? Yippee," Shadooda deadpanned.

"Yippee!" repeated Shadooda's neighbors, with a distinct lack of glee.

"Who's in charge now, the kid?" Shadooda asked.

"The kid. Dahlia. She's the queen, technically. She's muddling along."

"Weird kid, I always thought, playing alone with her bits of string," Shadooda said. "Too bad for her, but she's got to grow up quick, or we're all toast. Me, I'm toast already, but you and all the above-grounds, you've a teeny bit of hope."

"Little Dahlia?" asked Tammy. "She's harmless."

"She's a royal. They're never harmless. Might be innocent, but never harmless. Too powerful, too young, too stupid."

Tammy replied, "So, I think you're saying ... you'd like to have some influence above ground? And as for me, I want vengeance on Fast Eddie. We could strike a deal, perhaps?"

"You're catching on, kid. I think we could do some serious magic-swapping," said Shadooda, who reached out and read Tammy's thoughts through her face with its thick, calloused, but gentle fingers. "Romance troubles, eh?" it added.

"It's just humiliating."

"Isn't it, though? Awful stuff. Awful stuff. You want to serve up some just desserts?"

"Yes, I do. "

"Good. We'll take care of this naughty Fast Eddie fellow, plus that uppity little queen, all in one fell swoop, we will. How's that for elegant?"

"Whatever it takes," replied Tammy, feeling almost sort-of happy.

"It won't be easy."

"Nothing worthwhile ever is."

Shadooda produced a pencil, sharpened it on its forehead, and handed it to Tammy with a scrap of parchment. "Listen closely, and write this down," it said then, with something resembling a smile, and gave her a very long, very secret, and somewhat evil list of instructions.

Before retreating back the way she had come, Tammy asked, "What did you mean, 'That's what they think?'"

"They think they closed all the portals," Shadooda croaked. "But, of course, if they had, we'd all be dead."

"We would?"

"Sure. Bumblegreen has to breathe. You can't close them all. Open portals the cause of the blight? Bah!"

"So they're open, then?" Tammy asked, disbelieving.

"Just one at a time," Shadooda whispered. "I keep a watchman at the entrance, some woodland creature. Next day, I magically close one portal and open another. Nobody knows. Everybody's happy. Silly queen-child thinks the portals are closed."

Tammy didn't dare ask the obvious questions: who? where? how? why? The strain of not asking showed on her face.

Shadooda said, "Sure I've been mistreated, you betcha, but I don't want everyone to die." It added, "Go on, then! Do your potion. Get your revenge. It's going to take for damn ever, so better get started."

12

IN WHICH JACKSON IS NEITHER
DISEASED NOR ENCHANTED

Upon arrival in Bumblegreen, Jackson, partial to the smell of fish and rotten things, followed his nose to one of several dilapidated shacks standing at the forest's edge, behind the duchess' mansion. As Jackson approached the shack's back door, he spied a muscle-bound, bare-chested man, and the man spied him.

It seemed, to Jackson, as if the man wanted to play, so the dog initiated the typical elbows-on-the-ground invitation-to-play known to all dogs and dog fanciers; however, instead of a romp, a commotion ensued wherein the man disappeared, and a fish appeared in his place.

Jackson approached the fish to investigate.

Someone screamed.

All the commotion overwhelmed poor, gentle Jackson, who fled back into the woods.

After a run through a swamp, a jog up a pine-covered hill, a good piss on an aromatic stump, and a brief nap in a blossoming blackberry thicket, Jackson forgot about the entire bizarre event until he smelled that fishy scent again, whereupon he instinctively, incautiously, made his way back to the cabin. There, he mounted three rickety steps and peered through the open back door, just in time to see the front door shut on a huge hunk of hair.

Tammy opened the door, freed her hair, and left.

Hank (though Jackson didn't know the man's name as such) stood in the shack's kitchenette, wafting steam from a boiling pot up to his nose and adding pinches of herbs to the concoction.

Jackson slunk quietly inside, recognized the shape of a sofa, jumped upon it, and settled into a tight, comfortable ball.

"Hello," said Hank. "I'm glad you're still around."

Jackson tucked his nose under his paw, squeezed his eyes shut, and sighed deeply.

"Would you care for a bite of anything? A drink?" asked Hank.

Jackson viewed the man with one roving eye, then shut it again and fell deeply asleep.

"I don't mean to be rude, but what are you?" asked Hank. "I've never seen anything like … sir? Sir, you're twitching. Oh, I suppose you're about to turn, aren't you? Well, not much to be done about it. Here, I'll make you a nice cup of tea, for after."

Hank took a teacup and saucer from a cabinet and continued, "These herbs I'm boiling are exactly what you'd think, by the way.

I'm sure you've heard of the concoction—keeps you human for hours upon hours at a time.

"You must think me completely out of my mind. *Who'd want that?* you're probably thinking. But, of course, you saw my transformation, so you see the trouble I'm up against! And worse yet—as a man, I can't swim. I've tried, but nearly drowned. What do you do with your arms and legs? They're all over the place!

"I tell you I can read, do a jigsaw puzzle, even cut my own hair, but I can't swim. That's luck, I guess, bad or good. But for you, being a land animal, well, that's not so bad now, is it? I mean logistically— not mentally, emotionally. You don't have to say anything. Buy hey, where did you come from?" asked Hank. "Not around here, I don't suppose?"

Jackson didn't answer, of course. He slept.

After a while, Jackson awoke from his twitchy dreams and remembered his mission to find ElizabethAnn. He looked around the unfamiliar room with its sagging, unmade bed, tattered couch, and brick-and-plank bookshelf where Hank had neatly stacked his folded tuxedos and crossword puzzles. The back door still stood ajar, and afternoon sun streamed through. Sunbeams lit the shabby walls, with their spots of crumbling plaster, lit the dusty floor, and lit Hank, who stabbed a broom at the floor, repeatedly.

"Work, broom! Work!" Hank hollered, then threw the thing down.

Jackson's awakening set the tags to jingling deep inside his world of fur. He leaped up and stretched, then nuzzled Hank's hand.

"Glad to see you up and about," said Hank. "What's your name, buddy? Pardon me, I'm Hank, once a proud steelhead trout. Listen, I'll tell you my story, then we'll be friends, eh? How's that? Establish trust?"

Jackson sat, cocked his head quizzically, and sneezed. Hank took it as a go-ahead.

"I'm swimming along, looking for a bug," Hank began, "the steelhead trout equivalent of a cucumber sandwich. Get me? And I see something in the water. It's fluttery, like a bug, so I snap it. It was sweeter than candy, yet savory, too. I kept thinking, *Is it vanilla? Peach? Nougat?*

"Fact: Fish don't think, and they never have vanilla or peach and wouldn't know a nougat from a hole in the head. Very odd. As I'm sure you know, I was turning into a human: arms, legs, nose hair, ear wax, big annoying brain. Because that bug wasn't a bug at all, but the ear of a dead monkey lying half in the water. Cause of death, unknown. Apparently, even the ear, hell, even a tuft of fur, has enough chemical to give you Zade Fandey's disease, so they say. But you must know that, already, beast. Right?

"I washed up on the bank where I watched a couple badgers consume the rest of the monkey carcass. One turned into a large-bosomed woman wearing a daisy-print tea dress and barbecue apron, and the other, a dwarfish man in his underpants, had a big, strawberry-shaped nose. Don't ask me how I knew what a tea dress was, or a strawberry, or underpants. I can't even begin to sort through all my mental pre-stock. For instance, 'swimming?' No. But 'tea dress?' Yes. 'Strawberry?' Yes. 'Sweeping,' for instance, is a no, so is 'bed-making.' But 'polishing silver?' That's a yes. The list goes on."

Jackson chased his tail, caught it, and celebrated by curling into a ball.

Hank contemplated the notion of an animal that would walk right into your house, jump on your couch, and take a nap in your presence, but which didn't suffer from Zade Fandey's disease. A *tame* animal, a *pet*—though Hank didn't know these terms as such. He did know, however, that Jackson, wherever he came from, was about to be in terrible trouble, very soon. With the animal's innocent, trusting nature, just about anyone could catch hold of it and do experiments. Worse yet, the beast could succumb to temptation, attack a monkey with those magnificent fangs, catch Zade Fandey's disease, and end up one of Bumblegreen's tortured human/animal perversions, so Hank resolved to protect Jackson, no matter what.

A knock sounded on the door.

Hank flung a crocheted afghan over Jackson, just as the front door swung open.

There in the doorway stood a handsome devil whose lean, ropy frame filled the doorway as if the two had been partners for life. The rectangle of the open door framed the triangle of his wide stance, the clean line of his sinuous torso. Here was a man who would have his way and make everyone like it.

"Ha!" said Fast Eddie. "Guess what, fishlips, I got a gift for you!" Fast Eddie followed his ebullient greeting with a grin so irresistible it could have sucked in a county, ravaged the women, pillaged the land, burned the fields, and made the next county over jealous for the same treatment. Fast Eddie tossed Hank a small, corked glass bottle.

"Finally, a way to pay you back! Drink it!" insisted Fast Eddie. "It'll make you permanently human! No more of this fish-out-of-water baloney!"

Hank contemplated the bottle. "Permanently?" asked Hank. "Is this witchcraft?"

"I didn't ask," replied Fast Eddie as he strolled into Hank's kitchen and opened the fridge. "New girlfriend gave it to me, said she got it from some chick with horsehair, said she'd eventually want something in return, bla bla bla, you know how women are. Anyway, she said it's for you! You've got my stuff, right?" asked Fast Eddie.

"I've got plenty," Hank said and retrieved a cardboard box filled with baubles, beads, and silver stolen from the mansion.

Fast Eddie picked a butter knife out of the box, pulled a couple pairs of pliers out of his pockets, and used them to bend the knife blade this way and that.

"This is good stuff. Very soft silver. I tell you what."

"Someone actually got this bottle from a magician?" asked Hank. "I thought they were all dead."

"Yeah. I'm sure they are. Like I said, my new redhead got it from some horsehair woman, or so she said. Probably a bunch of bunk, but she said—let me get it right—she said, 'Don't you want to thank Hank for all he's done for you?' and I said, 'Hell, yeah,' and she said, 'See if he wants this, that's all.' So there you are, if you want it. Up to you. Have you got any food? I'm dying, man."

Fast Eddie loped into Hank's kitchenette in three strides, opened the icebox door, and shoveled things into his mouth.

"This redhead, she said the potion would make me permanently human?" asked Hank.

"Yup. Permanent," said Hank, adding, "The redhead said the horsehair gal said that. She was just a messenger, or something. Man! Dude!" This last exclamation referred to a couple of particularly delicious cartons of the duchess' leftover hors d'oeuvres.

"Okay. Well, thanks," mumbled Hank.

"Thanks nothing!" said Fast Eddie. "You do me favors all the time! The pleasure's all mine, you old salmon! Ha! Quit swimming upstream and drink that bottle. I wanna see what happens! Tell you what!"

"So … the redhead just gave it to you?" asked Hank. "For free?"

Fast Eddie rummaged through the box of stolen goodies with one hand, ate soggy canapés with the other, winked, and talked out the side of his mouth. "Well, not free exactly, but forget about it. She—

kinky little lamb, ain't she?—said the horsehair woman asked her to ask me to do a little something in return for the potion, but it's nothing I can't handle in an afternoon. Ha! C'mon, drink the stuff!"

"I think I'll actually wait," said Hank.

"Spoil sport," replied Fast Eddie. "But listen, seriously, this is huge for me, this stuff. Look at these paperweights, these light bulbs. Look at this gorgeous crap. I tell you what, old Bill Bramble's gonna go crazy over this."

Then, Fast Eddie looked up from the box of goodies, stopped short, and froze. "Hey, Hank? What in holy buckaroo is that?"

Hank followed Fast Eddie's finger, where it pointed, and found Jackson curled up on the couch again, sans crocheted coverlet. He cursed under his breath, wondering how long the beast had been there, out in plain sight.

"It's a beast," Hank said, with pretend nonchalance.

"What kind, exactly?" asked Fast Eddie.

"Don't know," said Hank. "It wandered right out of the woods. Thing is, though: it's vicious. Don't disturb it. And don't mention it. Like, just keep it between you and me."

"Whatever," replied Fast Eddie, carefully cataloguing the information for future use, if any. "I'm going to be man-of-the-hour back at the house, with this box of junk. Bill Bramble's going to love me! That redhead is going to love me! Oh, no. Oh man, dude! I almost forgot the worst thing ever, then Hank, I remembered it!"

Hank raised an eyebrow in inquiry.

"I was in love! I'm telling you I fell in love with that redhead nanny from the mansion. We hit it off! And was she a knockout! Anyway, Hank old buddy, we ran away together, but she turned out to be a squirrel. She was Zade Fandey'd all along! No offense, of course."

"None taken."

"She kept saying, 'There's something I've got to tell you,' but I never listened. I tell you what, all women say that, and it's usually inconsequential. Ha! So I've got her between a set of satin sheets and I tell you what! Suddenly I'm in bed with a fuzzy little squirrel! Says she changes whenever she gets excited! Not much future with a woman like that, Hank. Maybe I should give her a little of this potion, eh? Keep her human forever? You know she'd hate me for it. Bumblegreen's gone to crap I tell you. All the beautiful women are rodents."

With that, Fast Eddie hoisted the box of luxury contraband onto his shoulder and slunk into the woods, bent beneath its weight.

Hank's washbasin still sat there, filled with water. He looked at his watch and knew the medicinal tea would do its job and hours would pass before he turned back into a trout, which was, safety-wise, good, but, emotionally, bad. Very bad.

Hank stood barefoot in the basin, imagining that ultimate relief—wishing to turn, even if just momentarily, into a trout once more. To pass the time, he picked up a crossword puzzle and penciled in some answers. Jackson snored, and the front door hung limply on its half-unscrewed hinges, awkwardly batting against the doorjamb like laundry long forgotten on the line.

13

WHERE DIRT, SOLITUDE, AND DANGER EACH PLAY A PART

Up above ElizabethAnn—far, far above—the forest canopy twittered with bird life, but the forest floor remained a lonely place. ElizabethAnn had managed to hike out of the swampy lowlands and onto higher ground, but her beanpole legs could take her no farther.

Eventually, she stopped calling after the duchess' baby, Jackson, and Grandma, all of them, and conserved energy by resting between the expansive roots of a giant bull oak, meanwhile keeping her eyes and ears peeled for friendly talking insects.

As evening came on, the stillness grew stiller, and the light, dimmer, and ElizabethAnn realized the dense foliage above would soon cut out all starlight and moonlight, and she would be plunged into utter blackness. So, she gathered an armload of fern fronds and dumped them in a cozy corner made by some tree roots. Curling into her nest—accepting it as a tiny new home—ElizabethAnn listened to the strange night birds making their rounds.

Luckily for ElizabethAnn, she knew little enough about forests that she didn't fear prowling tigers or marauding baboons, as she should have, so she enjoyed the warm night air and the wildness. After all, she had just lived the most adventurous day of her whole life, so far.

While she drifted off, ElizabethAnn remembered hearing what could only have been Jackson's jingling tags, somewhere in the forest. *Perhaps the sound of the wind is playing tricks on me*, she thought. *What with the magic sediment it stirs up.* She had never felt so alone before.

Breathing the fresh forest air and feeling a cool breeze ruffling her hair, she realized she should have minded it—the dirt, the solitude, the danger—but, strangely, she didn't. She dragged a couple of enormous fronds over her slight frame to keep the dew off and snuggled into the spongy topsoil of the forest floor. After the day she'd had, it seemed a perfectly reasonable thing to do.

14

WHEREIN FAST EDDIE HAS AN AHA! MOMENT

Fast Eddie's career as a womanizer (or "seducer" or "gigolo" or "mimbo," if you prefer) had, at this point in time, reached a zenith, as far as actual numbers. Yet, his satisfaction quotient hovered at, or below, rock bottom.

As a form of community service, he now taught his most infallible pickup lines to friends and neighbors. Then, when these gentlemen attempted to put the methods into action, Fast Eddie made himself available for consult, free of charge, in case of cold feet, backfire, or other mid-seduction tribulations that can always occur, even to the most suave of practitioners. Despite such benevolent acts, Fast Eddie lived in a state of utter psychic emptiness.

The evening he left Hank's with his box of stolen butter knives, antique salt and pepper shakers, fountain pens, and other luxury detritus, he walked until night, then paused beneath the broad, dewy leaves of a certain rubber tree, where he liked to ruminate, and contemplated his ennui. Briefly, Fast Eddie considered giving up women altogether and taking on real estate, the over-caffeinated soda-pop racket, or a line of Fast Eddie clothing. But then, as a fat raindrop slid off a leaf and down the back of his threadbare T-shirt, he experienced one of those fabled "aha!" moments.

Now, Fast Eddie hadn't received that bottle of potion for free, of course. Shadooda, resourceless as it was, had arranged for the horse-haired woman to give it to the redheaded woman, during which transaction, Tammy (the horse-haired woman) opened a little music box, which played a hypnotic tune, which convinced the redhead to convince Fast Eddie to seduce the queen. Shadooda, being a brilliant magician, had arranged it all just so.

There, beneath the rubber tree, Fast Eddie contemplated the assignment the magician, through Tammy, through the redhead, through a magical music box, had given him.

"All you have to do," the redhead had told him, handing over the brown glass bottle with a shrug, "is seduce that little mimsy, Queen Dahlia. I don't mind. In fact, I think it's hot."

"Seduce a girl? That's it?" Fast Eddie said. "But I'd feel like I was cheating on you, baby!" he added, sounding pretty sincere.

"It's worth it," she replied. (She was bewitched, don't forget.) "Dahlia's the queen of Bumblegreen, after all. Just let me ride your coattails to wherever this leads."

"Sure, why not?" Fast Eddie replied. "Ride any part of me you want!"

"But be sure to make her love you," insisted the redhead. "And be sure to drop her flat on her royal patoot afterward. No mercy. No 'let's still be friends,' or any of that namby-pamby nonsense. That's what the horse-haired woman told me. You have to break her heart into *smithereens*."

"Easy enough, but what good does this do you?" asked Fast Eddie.

The redhead couldn't tell Fast Eddie the good it would do Bumblegreen for the queen to lose her Pollyanna innocence. After all, it wasn't a *good* good. It was a bad good. The redhead couldn't tell Fast Eddie the strength Queen Dahlia would (hopefully, if she had any spunk) derive from the disappointment. The redhead wasn't aware of Shadooda's plan to pump some horse sense into Dahlia through getting her wrung out and hung to dry once or twice. Make her grow up quick. So, she just said, "I dunno."

Shadooda didn't have a whole lot more time left in the world. Even magicians, witches, sorcerers and alchemists have to drop dead eventually, and it couldn't wait for Dahlia to grow up, eventually realize the truth about magic, and the truth about the portals, and get around to saving Bumblegreen from Zade Fandey's so-called wondrous technology. Bumblegreen, and Shadooda, were dying, and the queen had to get prematurely empowered, even before the fruit, such as it was, had ripened on the proverbial tree; hence, the seduction job aimed at turbo-charging the queen's maturity. Dahlia's transformation wouldn't be pretty, but Shadooda never had bought stock in pretty.

When that raindrop slid off that leaf, right down the back of Fast Eddie's shirt, causing a spine-shudder and that now-legendary "aha!" moment, he finally remembered his mission. Not only that, but he saw said mission as the perfect way out of his state of perpetual ennui. Fast Eddie resolved, then and there, to elevate the degree of his art-of-seduction to the pinnacle of mastery, just as any sound criminal, athlete, or entrepreneur would do.

Beneath that rubber tree, on that sultry afternoon, Fast Eddie meditated upon the manner in which he would use the art of seduction to reveal the true depth of his soul. He planned to use Hank's strange and interesting beast to facilitate his scheme.

After a while, a man approached, interrupting Fast Eddie's meditations. Name of Mobius. Just some guy who worked at the castle—a blabbermouth and a fool. Fast Eddie knew the fellow and knew he had probably gotten himself lost, as usual.

Though Fast Eddie normally avoided the graceless, gossiping oaf like a plague, this time he shouted, "Hi, Mobius!"

"What's up, Fast Eddie?" replied Mobius. "What's new with you? Have you heard the duchess' personal chef is carrying your child?"

"I … what?"

"Yup. It's the latest."

"Interesting. I'll do you one better."

"How 'zat?"

"There's a beast abroad in the land—a totally unfamiliar creature. I'm pretty sure it came through a portal," said Fast Eddie.

"Say what?"

"It's true. Now about this personal chef …"

"Don't know much about her," said Mobius. "Fat ankles, that's about it. Also, did you know that good-looking redhead is really a blue jay?"

"No, she's a squirrel."

"She's a blue jay that periodically turns into a stunning redhead, then, in moments of stress, into a squirrel, then, ten days later, into a three-year-old child," said Mobius. "Then back into a blue jay after the sun goes down. She's got Zade Fandey's disease bad."

"That *is* bad," said Fast Eddie. "Are you sure?"

"Nope," said Mobius, over his shoulder, on his way down the path. "Not really, but I heard it from a couple people."

Knowing Mobius' reputation for gossip, Fast Eddie could be sure his news about the beast would race through the castle grapevine by the end of the day. He licked a finger and felt the air, hoping for a little breeze to kick up any latent magic that might help his cause. Even if his idea about the strange beast coming through a portal turned out false, it didn't matter. For Fast Eddie's purposes, the truth, as usual, was immaterial.

Meanwhile, that business about Tammy's pregnancy rattled into the back of his skull and stayed there, under a pile of abandoned inventions.

15

IN WHICH ELIZABETHANN
TURNS A DREAM CORNER

In her feather fern nest, ElizabethAnn dreamt of whispering barefoot down elegant, abandoned corridors. She turned a dream corner, and there stood Grandma, strolling among bamboo groves, wrapped in shades of lavender and saffron, surrounded by others like her.

Grandma and her companions mounted the steps to a pagoda and sat on smooth wooden benches. They conversed without moving their lips and swished long, graceful sleeves against the stone-crafted floor. In the background, a persistent buzzing broke the overall serenity of the scene. Then, Grandma turned away from her companions and looked out, through a dream window, at ElizabethAnn. She beckoned.

"Come, child," Grandma said. "Stroll beneath these blossoming boughs." Grandma breathed a placid sigh of otherworldly contentment and reached out her soft-knuckled hand. She stretched her arm to impossible lengths, but ElizabethAnn couldn't grasp it.

A horse galloped by, and Grandma leapt astride. She laughed as its flying mane tickled her chin.

"Come, child!" Grandma said, again. The horse galloped away, and the wind pulled Grandma's lips into an unreadable grimace. They raced across meadows and stream banks and forests rich in color and scent, then stopped in a rocky place, like a moon. Grandma had traveled a long way in the dream world, and yet the background buzzing persisted. Through the dream window, she spoke to ElizabethAnn.

"Kiddo," she said. "I'm here, in Bumblegreen. But relax! Don't come looking for me. I'm a fugitive!"

Grandma spread her arms wide, letting moon wind ruffle her kimono. "They're watching you, and if you find me, the royal army will follow you and find me, too. See? So forget about me, for now. But know this: There's hidden magic here, and you must find it, ElizabethAnn. You can free me! You can free all of Bumblegreen."

Grandma's sleeves lengthened and her hair grew. Soon, all that tangled fabric and hair filled the dream window.

ElizabethAnn tunneled madly through the window, ripping and tearing at everything between her and Grandma, yelling, "Help me, Grandma! Tell me what to do!"

"Don't look for me, ElizabethAnn," came Grandma's voice from somewhere on the other side of the dark, colorful tangle. A horse whinnied. "You go and find the magic, kiddo. You go and find

Shadooda."

ElizabethAnn heard the skippity-clop of galloping hooves and continued tunneling with claw-like fingers and uncommon strength. She ripped at the strong, stringy mass, more desperate than before.

Awakening from the dream to the stillness of the nighttime forest, she heard sounds of deft scrabbling, as of claws on coarse bark. Rain now fell, and up above, along the expanses of straight and tall, almost endless, pencilish trees, she detected movement and a metallic glint. In a swatch of escaped moonlight, she glimpsed a hint of blue.

A monkey. A blue shirt. A gold watch.

ElizabethAnn popped out of her dream and up to her feet, wiped sleep from her eyes, wrapped her filthy legs around a nearby cycad, and shinnied her slow, laborious way up toward that elusive monkey.

16

WHEREIN THE DUCHESS ENJOYS A
MIDNIGHT REFRIGERATOR ENCOUNTER

In the wee hours of the morning, the duchess threw on a robe. She planned to "grab a little cucumber sandwich" and even rehearsed the words, whisperingly, as she padded down a narrow staircase of ancient stone. In the mansion's kitchen, she encountered a frantic Tammy, standing amid spilled cherries, holding a list.

"Oh! Goodness!" said the duchess, as if surprised. "You startled me!"

Tammy stared, as if at a ghost.

"Tammy, what's wrong?"

"Ma'am, to be honest, I've never seen you in the kitchen before," Tammy said.

"Well, I've just come down in my slippers and robe for a bit of something. A cucumber sandwich, in fact," said the duchess, pretty close to the way she rehearsed it. In truth, she never had ventured into the kitchen before, what with all the staff she employed to do such things, but without her baby, she was lonely.

"I'll get it for you, ma'am," said Tammy.

"Don't trouble yourself, dear," replied the duchess, adding, "My, but those cherries look delicious, actually."

"Oh no, ma'am!" Tammy said. "I mean yes, ma'am, but they've been on the floor."

"That's okay," said the duchess. "I just sauntered down here for a little midnight refrigerator encounter!"

"Did you perhaps mean: 'to raid the fridge for a midnight snack,' ma'am?"

"Oh, yes! 'Raid the refrigerator'—that was the expression I was looking for, precisely," said the duchess, lifting her chin. "You're a wonder at semantics, Tammy! Now, let's see the little dears."

"But I just mopped the floor with an ammonia solution, ma'am," said Tammy, handing the cherries over.

The duchess ate one and did taste a hint of something … Well, it certainly cleared her nasal passages, that was the up side.

"Now then, Tammy," began the duchess. "What keeps you here so late at night?"

"Ma'am, I'm prepping everything for your garden party tomorrow," explained Tammy, who took a mallet and tenderized a steak, making things on the counter rattle.

The duchess yelled over the pounding and rattling. "My goodness! It's lovely to have you here so late! I mean, it's unusual, you know?" (pound, pound) "You know?" (pound, pound, rattle, rattle) "Because you always dash off precisely at eight!" (pound, rattle) "The way you dash off, one might think your house were on fire every day at precisely eight o'clock!"

"I'm sorry, ma'am, what was that?" asked Tammy.

"You must have a wonderful husband waiting at home!" yelled the duchess, over the din. "Kids, perhaps? Or do you go out on the town?"

Tammy pounded harder and pretended not to hear.

"Not that I'm prying," shouted the duchess. "In fact, if you don't want to answer, just tell me to shut my mouth and then boom. You know?"

Tammy placed that steak in a broiler pan and attacked a second one with the mallet.

"It certainly is warm for April, don't you think?" asked the duchess, who sat in a little straight-backed chair and crossed her legs, ankles, and arms.

Tammy pounded harder.

"Well, I guess I'll just lend a hand, then, while I'm here," the duchess said, seizing a bunch of steaks and arranging them on broiler pans, fussing over each one like it was a unique Christmas cookie, or a baby.

Tammy asked the duchess to please wait and let her do it, but the duchess ignored her—fussing, fussing, fussing.

"Ma'am, you wouldn't want to catch Zade Fandey's disease, now, would you?" asked Tammy.

"What a thing to say!"

"Seriously, you should be wearing gloves to handle any type of meat."

"I've done this dozens of times, you silly girl!"

"I hope not, ma'am. Not without gloves, I hope."

"I'm beginning to think you're serious!"

"Quite."

"Only animals can catch Zade Fandey's," said the duchess, "and only from monkeys. Everyone knows that!"

Tammy remained silent.

"Well, I suppose you know best," the duchess finally said. "You're the professional here." She left the steaks alone.

"These are dangerous times, ma'am. It's a shame," said Tammy.

"I guess I'll leave it up to you," said the duchess. "I guess maybe I haven't done this before, after all."

"That's all right, ma'am."

"I was only trying to be helpful."

"Of course."

The duchess left the kitchen and whisked back upstairs, where, thinking of Zade Fandey's disease, she washed her hands three times with cleaning solvents meant for engine blocks, toilets, and high-traffic floors.

17

In Which ElizabethAnn
Appears as a Garden Gnome

The further she climbed, the quieter things became. Wind didn't blow. Birds didn't fly by. The forest's understory—that vast space between the ground and treetops—felt to her like a scary, in-between space where one had to either journey up or journey down, but could never just stay.

Anyone stranded in the understory would necessarily live in a state of perpetual restlessness. It seemed, to ElizabethAnn, like a place where nothing ever happened, where a lone climber could struggle for days, calling out for help, and nobody would hear.

She stopped climbing for a moment and wanted to make a little sound such as "cheep!" or "toot!" or "blap!" just to fill up the stillness. She tried to call her dog's name but only hoarsely whispered, "Jacks?"

ElizabethAnn hugged the tree and tried to peer through the nighttime mist. Something in the darkness brushed her cheek ever so lightly. It could have been a falling feather but felt more like a butterfly giving her little winged kisses. Whatever it was, it gave her the chills, but this was no time for equivocation, so she resumed climbing: steadily, rhythmically, determined against her fear.

Finally, she reached through some leaves above her head—her little hand all scratched and bruised now, with scraped-up knuckles and fingernails broken terribly jagged—and with her last ounce of strength, she pulled herself into a profusion of leaves and branches that grew, all at once, at the tops of the trees.

With the sunrise, so much light penetrated the leaves that ElizabethAnn became temporarily blinded, yet joyfully so, for the sun's unrelenting radiance reminded her of her desert home. Then, suddenly, inexplicably, horribly, and without warning, she was assaulted by the loudest noise imaginable. Eyes squeezed shut against the glare, she clamped onto a branch with her legs and clapped both hands tight over her ears.

It felt like parachuting onto No Oaks Avenue at rush hour.

It felt like trying to relax on a porch swing when all the neighbors started their trash blowers, at once.

It felt like attempting to watch a favorite show in a room full of crying babies.

But it turned out to be nothing more than the sound of the canopy at sunrise. The treetops were filled with life, and not just any life, but the loudest life-forms around. On top of all the noise, the canopy stank. It smelled like wet dog, rotten fruit, dirty birdcage, tootie-frootie bubble gum, and sweaty sneakers, all at once.

A bird buzzed by her head. Another perched on her ear. A caterpillar crawled up her leg. A squirrel tried to make a nest in her armpit, and a rotten, purple, speckled fruit fell and splattered right in her lap.

A thousand birds seemed to call out, "ElizabethAnn! Ann! Ann! Ann! Eliz-liz-liz-liz abet-abet-abet-abet," and a hundred monkeys seemed to taunt, "Looka looka looka looka you you you you!"

ElizabethAnn sat on her tree branch, high in the sky, like a lost garden gnome, and willed herself not to look down. The rotten fruit that had splattered her dress, hands, face, and everything still jiggled there, helplessly. She tasted it, and it wasn't half bad.

Now realizing how very hungry she was, ElizabethAnn scooped up the fruit splatter, shoved it into her mouth, and looked around for more, but as she reached for another, she distinctly heard a voice articulate, "Greetings!"

ElizabethAnn recoiled, lost her balance, and fell. From that height, she could have fallen to her death but instead was neatly caught by one profoundly prehensile tail.

Earl, for that was the monkey's name, still wore his blue golfing shirt with the golden crest over the left breast. But that crest, plus the collar itself, construed all that remained of the shirt. Some scraps of blue knit still hung down, and some twigs pierced the collar here and there, and the golden crest flapped around like a three-day-old bandage. The hazards of the forest—thorns and briars and pointy branches—had rent the shirt asunder just as soon as Earl resumed his typical monkey lifestyle.

ElizabethAnn noticed the monkey still wore the golden watch, but it had lost its luster beneath caked-on mud. Having once looked so civilized, so proper, so well-spoken, so *clean*, Earl was now back in his natural element, having discarded all that human-like pretense.

The fact that Earl had, at one time, actually washed himself remained very much a secret, by the way. No forest creature would ever believe Earl could have tidied up the way ElizabethAnn saw him at the Treacherous Forbidden Stream—except, of course, for Earl's wife, Cupcake.

Cupcake was privy to, and the patient supporter of, Earl's recent—for lack of a nicer term, let's just say "illegal and immoral"—voyage in the name of adventure. She knew Earl did it all for her.

Her savior, Earl stood before ElizabethAnn now, all puffed up and exceedingly proud of his strong and prehensile tail. He enjoyed every opportunity to show it off.

"You look familiar," said Earl.

ElizabethAnn stared, open-mouthed.

"Those fruits will give you nightmares, you know," he added.

She blinked.

The monkey put his smelly, hairy face very close to hers and added, "Unless you like nightmares, Buttercup. Some do."

ElizabethAnn sneezed violently, and again Earl caught her as she fell backward off the branch. He swung her with his tail, cradling her filthy, rag-clad body next to his, for safety.

ElizabethAnn took one whiff of Earl and fainted.

Later, she awoke to a scalp massage. No, that was just Earl picking through her hair for bugs. He found some and diced them with his little razor teeth.

"Just as I suspected," said the monkey, "You've got mites, too. You're going to have to be sanitized."

After a pause—where ElizabethAnn deeply inhaled the monkey's gamey scent in order to desensitize herself to its eye-crossing putridness—she inquired just one thing, emphatically: "Too?"

"Well, Lemon-pie, there's you and also that beast, of course!" said Earl.

"Beast?" asked ElizabethAnn.

"I'm the one being blamed, you know. Me!" complained Earl. "The tribunal's putting me on trial! I plan to argue innocence in the whole matter. How could I help it if I was being followed? How could I evade a hardened, obviously professional, spy like yourself? I'm the victim! I'm the wounded party! How does that sound?"

At the mention of a court of law, ElizabethAnn, who, in No Oaks, had thrived on deadlines and schedules, felt strangely motivated. Now, she had direction, a lead on Jackson's whereabouts, and a living being who seemed to need her help. She felt an urge to take charge that perhaps she had never quite felt before.

"Are we talking about a court of law?" she asked.

"Are we ever!" replied the monkey.

ElizabethAnn's characteristic gawkiness fell away like the husk of a coconut. The shrewd mind that only Grandma knew clawed its way to the forefront, past multiple shynesses and insecurities that typically jostled for dominance.

"No one's going to believe a word you say in that crazy get-up," she told the monkey.

"Not to put too fine a point on it, eh Chickadee?" Earl responded. "What's wrong with this shirt? It has a golden crest from the No Oaks Golf Club!"

"Well, it has a collar ..."

"This is a collared shirt. Business attire."

"A collar and not much else. It's torn to ribbons, if you haven't noticed."

"What are you saying?"

"Listen, why don't you take me to my dog—that beast. That beast is my personal dog."

"You know, you have some nerve insulting my outfit. Look at you!"

"Yes. I'm sure I'm a sight. But, Mr … Mr. Monkey, I'm not the one going on trial."

"Call me Earl."

"I'm not the one on trial, *Earl*."

"Oh, yes, you are!" he replied. "Trial, or else The Drone, or somewhere, anyway. You're summoned! I've got it right here … a summons from the monkey tribunal."

Earl dug into his slabs of matted fur, pulled out a tightly rolled parchment, unrolled it, and, with great dramatic flourish, read, "'To: loose child!' That's you, Custard Lump. 'Said personage, last seen wearing a blue-flowered dress, is hereby summoned to The Drone for a family assignment. Unless the party of the first part is actually a spy, in which case it is summoned to the tribunal for summary execution. Unless the party of the first part is actually a hologram, in which case it is required to return from whence it came, unless the party of the first part is actually …'"

ElizabethAnn sighed and interrupted, "Listen Mr. Earl, will you just take me to my dog, please? If we're going to get you cleaned up before this trial, or whatever it is, that's a lot in a short time. We'd better get the show on the road." It was quite a mouthful for the little squirt, and she lifted her chin with pride.

Earl slung ElizabethAnn onto his back, and for the next couple of hours, he swung, climbed, and crept his way through the loud, wet forest canopy, where macaws guffawed, millipedes dropped right down ElizabethAnn's dress front, and big wet leaves slapped her in the face like so many wronged women.

18

IN WHICH THE DUCHESS CONSULTS THE MONKEY TRIBUNAL

Still restless, the duchess wandered into the nighttime forest, her charmeuse robe billowing in the moonlight, and climbed a familiar tree. At the top, she sat on a platform and rapped on the trunk, which brought monkeys swinging from hither and yon. The duchess' platform, over the years, had rotted through, and now she clung nervously to what was left of it. She told the monkeys she had come to double-check on her baby, but they replied that no new babies had been issued to the monkey camp.

"In fact," one monkey admitted, "we're experiencing a disturbing dearth of babies hereabouts."

The duchess cried. In response, the monkeys only cracked their toe knuckles. "Anyway," blubbered the duchess, as a rotten plank fell from her platform and she clutched another, in desperation, "How's my other kid? Is he eating well? Healthy? Happy?"

"Sure," volunteered one monkey mama. "Nice pink complexion, long legs, weird little button nose, everything a human child should have."

A second plank rotted out and the duchess grabbed at various bits of treetop, asking, "And does he think his mom is some village lady or something?"

"We really don't discuss it, as you know, ma'am. It's not strictly legal, and I *know* you know that." This, from one particularly crass monkey. The lady monkeys gave him the stink eye.

"But when he turns eighteen … I know it's ten, eleven years down the road, but …"

"Oh, right. *If* he turns eighteen," said one monkey.

"What do you mean *if*?"

"Kids these days, they're so willful," replied another monkey.

 "I still want him back, you know!" protested the duchess.

"He does his own thing, mostly—your kid," replied a monkey mama. "He's always off in the forest doing his 'art.'"

"Right. Well, okay. Art, huh?" the duchess said, adding, "I just wanted to check up and make sure everyone's okeydokey."

Having to raise the children of a supposedly superior species when you only want children of your own is a pretty sad life. The monkeys had accepted it with glassy-eyed fatalism, but *okeydokey* wouldn't accurately describe how they felt.

"Right, well, if there's anything you need …" said the duchess, and the last board rotted out from under her. She caught herself on a couple of tree limbs.

"One more thing," she yelled up at the monkeys. "Do you know about this girl in a blue-flowered dress? She's going around fetching babies and refusing to fill out the forms. I think she hasn't been trained. You know anyone like that?"

A few formerly disinterested monkeys swung to the forefront.

"I'm on the tribunal," said one. "Tell me more. This sounds serious."

The duchess told him everything she could about ElizabethAnn. He consulted with some other monkeys and replied, "We'll put out a summons for the kid. She sounds dangerous, wild, and unkempt."

"Yeah," shouted the duchess, "and she's a real allergy-trigger, too!"

Then, without any pardon for their leave-taking, most of the monkeys swung away, through the trees, though a few curious ones remained, staring. That's monkey manners, for you.

"Well, I guess I'll be going then," said the duchess, feeling just as alone as before, maybe more so, and she climbed down the tree—slowly, inexpertly, without an ounce of aplomb, the soiled charmeuse of her robe no longer billowing at all.

19

WHEREIN ELIZABETHANN
SENSES GRANDMA'S PRESENCE

"Are we near a wasp's nest or something?" ElizabethAnn asked Earl.

"No, why?"

"There's a buzzing, a moaning. It's like a humming sound. Don't you hear it?"

"Oh!" said the monkey, "That's The Drone. That's where we're going."

Soon, the pair looked down upon a colossal dome set into the ground. Made entirely of hexagonal glass tiles on a web-like steel frame, it hosted algae growth, condensation droplets, and moss. From it emerged that distinctive droning sound.

Once, the ultra-modern structure might have resembled a gleaming, transparent beehive. Now, it nearly blended with the forest. Enormous plants thrived inside the dome, and their leaves pushed insistently upon the glass. Peering in—past leaves, orchid blooms, and jungle tendrils—ElizabethAnn saw a play of light and shadow that suggested bustling activity. Meanwhile, she felt strangely comforted by the structure's loud, incessant buzzing. *Where have I heard this before?* she wondered.

Earl took ElizabethAnn into the building through a small, well-sprung door. Inside, she could readily see The Drone's sturdy geodesic framework. Densely packed hibiscus and bamboo flanked a central path, but Earl yanked ElizabethAnn into a cane break and whispered in her ear.

"This, my little squash blossom, is what we call The Drone. You can hear why," Earl told her. "It's where I was born, where all the monkeys are born. I'm afraid, in addition to an experimental greenhouse for developing ultra-hardy plant species, it's a lab."

"Something like a monkey hospital?" she asked.

"Not exactly," replied Earl. "More of a science experiment. See, you probably noticed I can talk. Right, well, monkeys don't normally talk, see? We don't normally do a lot of things we can do in Bumblegreen. Like, um, rescue little girls, and wear watches and shirts, and make, you know, complex decisions with multiple non-static factors."

"Multiple wha?"

"We're part of a compromise the queen made when she closed the portals. See, Pudding Pie, that's when all the drama started."

"Drama?"

"You've met the duchess?"

"Oh, drama! No kidding! And the sneezing?"

"The baby allergy," Earl replied. "It's because of the baby allergy that Zade Fandey started his work with us monkeys. You know, *science*. Bumblegreen used to have magic, but now it has science. It's supposed to be better."

"Better for what?" she asked.

"I'd like to say I miss the days when monkeys were monkeys, but that was way before my time."

"Science is better than magic *for what*?"

"Oh, for dealing with the baby allergy," Earl replied, "because magic couldn't cure it. Well, the magicians had actually disappeared by then, so nobody knows if magic could have cured it. But anyway, it didn't."

"Why'd they disappear?" asked ElizabethAnn, remembering what Grandma had told her in the dream: *Go and find the magic. Go and find Shadooda!*

"Went out of style, best I can figure," said Earl, "though some say the magic was banished. No way to know. Anyway, now Fandey breeds us for strong domestic tendencies and nurturing habits. We get injections derived from these plants right here. We come out of tubes, see? There's an artificial monkey insemination process and an arduous routine of being raised in lab cages and special food and … oh, its awful, to tell the truth, but that's what it is. Anyway, Cupcake …"

"Yes?"

"No. 'Cupcake,' that's my wife. She's come back to The Drone voluntarily, sweet thing. We want a child, you see, so she has to undergo fitness testing and so forth—rigorous mental exercises. She's been waiting for an assignment for months, in a cage. It's awful. Seems there aren't enough babies to go around. Me, I think they're hoarding babies, keeping them from us. There's a baby/monkey imbalance or something. I can't figure it out. It's not supposed to work this way. Anyhow, you hide here and I'm going to just pay Cupcake a visit. Won't be but a minute!"

And just like that, Earl left ElizabethAnn alone in a thicket.

She sat and listened to the persistent buzzing and tried to understand why she felt such a fondness for the obnoxious sound, tried to recall the memory it attached to. That's when she finally spied the duchess' baby. It made a slap-slap-slapping sound as it crawled in from the jungle and across the broken and less-than-baby-safe linoleum. Sticky sounds issued forth each time the infant peeled its tiny red knees off the floor and flopped them back down. The baby's skin looked pasty and unwell in the greenish light. It cried, but softly.

A door opened in a wall and a man emerged. His lab coat bore the tag: *Dr. Fandey.*

The fellow's deep, thoughtful eyes brooded beneath a brow so prominent it could have supported knickknacks, for display. A single strip of uncombed eyebrow stretched across it, from temple to temple, and a scanty mustache crawled tentatively over his upper lip, darkening an already swarthy complexion.

Although too young to fully appreciate such things, ElizabethAnn noticed how the man's thick neck, broad chest, and wide shoulders filled out the lab coat and how his lower body disappeared beneath it into a tight little package that meant speed and strength and self-discipline.

With a single graceful motion, Fandey picked up the baby and rocked it against his chest. It quieted, closed its eyes, and fell asleep. Then, Fandey drew aside a palm frond and approached a machine partially hidden by three palms and a monstrous jade plant.

The rusty contraption blinked its hundreds of tiny electronic eyes. Amber, green, and red lights took turns invading the semi-dark, while the thing whirred and hummed. Part of the structure resembled a meat scale, and Dr. Fandey placed the baby there. He stripped it down, changed its diaper, recorded something in a ledger, measured the baby's various limbs, and dressed it in a tiny purple jumpsuit. Fandey looked into the baby's eyes with an instrument and typed numerous notes into a keyboard. Meanwhile, the dewy fronds of elegant ferns dripped steadily, and stems of yellow flowers reached for the doctor's throat.

Holding the baby once more, like a thoughtful chef with a handful of truffles, Fandey wandered into a separate enclosure festooned with orchids. ElizabethAnn made her way through the bamboo—spying, watching, wondering, and listening to the persistent, comforting hum. She watched Dr. Fandey walk along a path, lost in thought. She followed him as he passed an arcade of monkey cages, where expectant monkey mothers (from embittered old veterans to round-eyed, hopeful virgins) chattered and peered out at the babe. Fandey paused in front of each cage, displayed the baby, waited for a reaction, then walked on.

ElizabethAnn crept out of the bamboo and crouched behind a potted forsythia. She watched Fandey take the child into an adjoining nursery, from whence she heard the sound of birdsong. She could see the twinkling light cast by a mirrored mobile and detect the tintinnabulation of wind chimes above The Drone's hum.

Then, it came to her: the importance of the hum. ElizabethAnn remembered the dream of Grandma, every bit of it, but most of all, she recalled the dream's persistent background hum.

"Grandma!" ElizabethAnn yelled, running at Dr. Fandey. "Mister!

Have you seen my Grandma? Lady with white hair, all sticking out! A nice lady! I know she's here, I know it!"

The baby wailed. Zade froze, stared ElizabethAnn full in the face, then pressed a glowing red button on a console.

Gloved hands came from out of nowhere, picked ElizabethAnn up, and shoved her into a tiny crib-like cage with the words 'safety basinet' printed on the side. Inside the crib—much too small for a growing girl with gangly limbs and a beanpole body—ElizabethAnn contorted and peered through the bars, but saw only a sea of white lab coats, each with a stern face perched atop.

"Is this the one?" asked one of the faces on coats.

"I believe it is. Do you have a home, dearie?" asked another.

"Yes, I do!" replied ElizabethAnn. "It's No Oaks, and if you hand over my grandma and dog, I'll go back there, right now. No problem. No questions asked!"

"Sounds like delusional fantasy ideation."

"Affirmative. Some kind of imaginating disorder."

"A place with no oaks? Absurd!"

"She may be delirious."

"Or spastic."

"Is she too old to reassign?"

"Give her a shot of Dixymed."

"Ow! Get that thing away from me!"

"Good idea. Shoot her with Toludrule too. Twenty-five cc's."

"Don't get carried away."

"Whoa! Nervous?"

"Listen, Schvetz …"

"Okay, forget it."

"Gentlemen! The main thing is to reassign her, right away."

"Isn't she too old?"

"How old are you, sweetie?"

"Ah … I'm … ah … hey … wha?"

"Should have asked her before the sedative."

"It's always something, isn't it?"

"Gentlemen! This is a sensitive situation. Dr. Fandey has given strict orders there are to be no new assignments of children."

"And he said not to hurt this one."

"He did? I didn't hear that."

"I thought he said not to let her go."

"I thought he said, 'Just get her out of here.'"

"Someone go check with Dr. Fandey, please."

ElizabethAnn heard running footsteps.

"Regardless, I say she's liable to cause an allergic reaction in the general population."

"Achoo!"

"See what I mean?"

"Affirmative. Anyone have a hankie?"

"There's Cupcake and Earl, they've been waiting a while. Let's assign her there and have done with it."

"What? And go rogue?"

"Cupcake's out of the running. Her tests are sketchy. That female is simply too soft. We need a tough, fanged old broad. Someone threatening. Security, you know."

"Wait 'til Fandey gets here. He's gone downstairs."

"Maybe he'll want to do some tests on her."

"Ah! Ah! Achoo!"

"Chp! Pchp!"

"Don't hold in your sneezes, Sam, you'll burst your spleen."

"I say we assign her right away. We can't have children running around loose, and she's too big for the nursery."

"Roger that."

By lunchtime, the faces-atop-coats remained undecided as to what to do with ElizabethAnn, who had gone unconscious and begun to twitch. The faces-atop-coats had filled a laundry basket with sopping handkerchiefs and left ElizabethAnn locked in the safety bassinet, in the dark, among algae-streaked instruments and faint, amber-colored stand-by lights. She awoke to Earl's urgent whisper.

"Snap to, Twinkie!"

"Uh?"

"Sorry about all this! I'm going to get you out of here!"

"Earl?"

"It's just that the economy is crap, right now. Tree houses are sooo precious," Earl explained.

"The economy? What about me!"

"I'm trying to explain. Cupcake and I, we want you to help us. We don't like the system, Peaches, you know? The Drone, the duchess, the monkey tribunal ... I mean, Cupcake and I, we want out of Bumblegreen. Maybe a permanent move to No Oaks. You know? You could help us!"

Earl unlocked the safety bassinet with a key.

"Where'd you get a key?" ElizabethAnn asked.

"Fandey," Earl replied. "I slipped it out of his pocket. Old monkey trick."

Her cage popped open, and ElizabethAnn stretched and shook the cobwebs out of her head. "I don't think you'd want to be a monkey in No Oaks, Earl," she said. "It's not exactly a wildlife thingy."

"Thingy? Come again?"

"You know, a wildlife thingy."

"Like a wildlife sanctuary?"

"A sanctuary. Yes, that's exactly what it isn't," said ElizabethAnn.

"Listen, we'll talk about it later," said Earl. "There's a security patrol coming. We have to skedaddle."

"My Grandma's in this building," protested ElizabethAnn. "I have to find her. I'm not leaving until I find her!"

Earl indicated she should hop on his back without delay, but ElizabethAnn stood her ground inside the safety basinet, with its top popped off.

"Listen, Cookie," he urged. "We have to scram!"

"I'm not going."

"Oh, Chicken-pie, let's talk about it later."

"No!" ElizabethAnn's shrill yell broke the noontime silence of The Drone, and an alarm sounded. They heard rushing footsteps and shouts in the corridor.

"Okay, okay. I'll help you find her. I promise," said Earl, "but this isn't the time. They'll drug you again and put me in a cage, to boot. Just for now, Pumpkin, please, get on my back!"

She looked down the hall and saw the faces-atop-coats running at her with long hypodermic needles held at arm's length.

ElizabethAnn leaped aboard the monkey's back. Together, they swung through a hydrangea thicket, popped out a ceiling tile with a single swift punch, and disappeared into the jungle.

20

WHERE ZADE COULD HAVE MADE
THE TRANSITION LESS RISKY, BUT NO

"Frangipani!" hollered Grandma.

"What does that mean, anyway?" asked Zade.

"Don't you dare be cute, Zade Fandey," Grandma scolded. "You know it means 'hells bells,' or something to that effect. Did you have to drug her?"

"She was coming to find you. She was right upstairs!"

"So? Haven't you ever dealt with children? I mean, distract her. Give her candy. How hard is that?"

"Grams, you … how well do you know this girl?"

"Frangipani! She's my grandchild! I know her like my own face! What's come over you, Zade?"

"It's just that she wasn't like you're saying. Wasn't easily distracted. She knew you were here. Somehow, she knew it absolutely."

"How could she know that?" Grandma demanded.

"I haven't the faintest idea," Zade replied.

"If she leads others to me, it'll be off with my head!"

"Actually, the guillotine is out of style," Zade responded. "Now, they drop you into shark-infested waters."

"Whatever," said Grandma, sulking. "I want to hug ElizabethAnn so bad I can taste her little pigtails, but this isn't a time for sentimentality. I can only stay cooped up in this lab for so long before I either go crazy or get discovered."

"That's your greatest concern? Going crazy?"

"Or being discovered."

"The thought of a violent coup never crossed your mind?"

"Frangipani! What are you talking about?"

"If you could have just waited a little longer to come back to Bumblegreen, Grams, and somehow let me know you were coming," explained Zade, "I could have gradually reduced the monkey population and made this whole transition a lot less risky."

"I was planning to, Zade, but a pair of goons came for me. I had to make a run for it."

"Good old No Oaks."

"You can be sentimental all you want. Not me. Ever since the time I spent in Bumblegreen, I knew my days back in No Oaks would be numbered," replied Grandma. "I'm just lucky Shadooda opened that portal when it did!"

"Should have stayed behind with me, back in the day," said Zade, with a sparkle in his eye.

"Would have been nice, babe," Grandma said, "but there was ElizabethAnn … remember?"

"And now?" asked Zade. "Will you stay if you can?"

"Truth is, I miss my Scout, already," Grandma mused. "I'd like to wrap my hands around that wheel. Nice leather cover on it. Feels live, that wheel, muscular, like steering a boa constrictor. I love that thing."

"Is that all you love?" Zade muttered.

Grandma looked at him, looked away, didn't answer.

"Thing is," said Zade, measuring vials of solutions and beakers of emollients, "if this scheme of yours works, and it restores the magic in Bumblegreen—and it had better!—the baby allergy will go away and we're going to end up having to take the babies away from the monkeys and return them to their real parents."

"Great!" Grandma said.

"No. Not great. My highly domesticated monkeys will become childless."

"That's the idea, old pal!"

"Grams, we've got a kingdom full of baby-obsessed monkeys. Despite all the genetic engineering and whatnot, don't forget they're still monkeys, with sharp teeth, claws, and such."

"I guess they'll be sad, poor things," said Grandma.

"Grandma, wake up!" Zade said. "They'll be angry! And the monkey tribunal has political power, now. There could be a revolution, a riot, death, mayhem, anything!"

"I hadn't thought of that."

"Why do you think I've been mixing sedatives all day?" he asked. "The monkeys I've got in the lab right now—and I'm talking hundreds—I can sedate them, prevent release into the wild, and prevent assignment of new babies, but only for so long. They'll develop a tolerance, figure out how to escape, how to organize. They're bred for intelligence, you know."

"We could keep those ones in cages and round up all the loose ones?" Grandma suggested. "Put them in some kind of camp?"

"Think about what you just said!" objected Zade. "These are live beings, you know! They have feelings, ambitions, everything."

"What are you going to do?" Grandma asked.

"For now? Yell at you until I feel better!" Zade replied.

"Oh, all right. If it does you good." Grandma grasped a large, greasy gear on one of Zade's unfinished contraptions and went away, mentally, to a world of loud, fast cars that never got caught. She held the gear at ten and two, steered, and remembered zipping into dark alleys to hide while the unclever police, sirens screaming, passed her by.

"Inconsiderate woman! Hot-headed slut! Foul-tempered hag!" Zade yelled, with far more enthusiasm than he really felt.

21

IN WHICH EARL AND ELIZABETHANN
VISIT A FACTORY, OF SORTS

ElizabethAnn and Earl and dusk arrived all at once at the forest's edge. There, the trees stopped abruptly on the border of a tawny meadow sprinkled with columbine.

Earl dangled ElizabethAnn, with his supple rope of tail, four stories above the ground, allowing her to get the best vantage of the castle at sunset. A real fairy-tale affair it was, too, something about which little girls lie abed dreaming.

Weeping willows and shady glens surrounded the castle's high

146

stone walls, and whispering grasses grew on the gently lapping shores of glistening creeks. Tall turrets ascended from the castle's ramparts well up into the clouds, where ElizabethAnn assumed they housed prisoners fed bread and water, or princesses so beautiful the queen couldn't stand the competition. She related these musings to the monkey.

"Sorry, but the whole thing's a cheese factory," Earl told her. "Those turrets? They're actually cheese silos. No barbarous pirates chained to ancient stone walls, in there. No lovely maidens assigned to spin flax into gold, either."

"Is this where the magic lives?" asked ElizabethAnn.

"Magic? Bah, not anymore."

"No? I mean, but it's around here somewhere, right?" she asked. "The magic? And someone called Shadooda? Perhaps nearby?"

"Not that I know of."

"Earl, this is going to sound strange," she said, "but I actually saw this in a dream. Kind of a vision. Something about magic in Bumblegreen."

"Okay, Peachcake, whatever you say. First, we're going in there to free your filth-infested pet. Pardon my candor."

"Oh, yes. Jackson first."

"Full disclosure? The beast isn't here at the castle, yet, but if anyone finds it, they're supposed to bring it to the castle. So, it'll be here, soon. I mean, a war party is out hunting for it."

"Hunting?"

"Hunting! Yes, of course."

"No! Not hunting!"

"That's what I heard, Sugar Lump. That's what I heard."

"Catch-'em-in-a-bag hunting or ..." ElizabethAnn swallowed hard, "*killing* hunting?"

"Couldn't say. Not privy to that level of detail."

A bit more swinging on Earl's part and clutching to putrid fur for dear life on ElizabethAnn's part, and they came to an enormous tree, the tips of whose pendulous branches grazed the wall of one of the castle's many turrets, or cheese silos, as the case may be.

ElizabethAnn stared into the ancient magnolia's cavernous interior. Unlike the long-stemmed forest trees she had shinnied up earlier in the day, to the detriment of her clothing and delicate personal self, this eminent arboreal grandmama supported a profusion of thick, low-hanging limbs that bobbed up and down in the breeze. The branches seemed to reach out gently and beckon the child to climb, climb, climb to her heart's content through a dark and protected world studded with giant milky-white flowers that begged plucking.

ElizabethAnn didn't actually relish the thought of climbing another tree, at the moment. She would have preferred a bubble bath, actually, but understood a bubble bath was more likely to happen inside the castle, than out.

Earl declared his plan a simple matter of his scaling the outer wall all the way up to the chimney, then dropping down that chimney directly into the turret-top chamber. Once there, he could unlock the tower's single window from the inside. Then, he reasoned, ElizabethAnn could climb from a branch of the magnolia tree, right through the window, into the castle.

"You mean, 'blip over?'" she asked, with a grimace.

"It's simple!" chattered Earl, and off he scampered, calling back, "Up you go, then!"

Earl abandoned ElizabethAnn to her tree-climbing task and scaled the castle wall, a feat far beyond the powers of her significantly less-nimble fingers. When she was only halfway up the tree, clinging to bark, she saw Earl appear above, at the tower's window, just as he had said he would.

He screeched down, "Chop-chop little chicken! You're losing time! Forty-five seconds by my gold watch, to be exact!"

Why he didn't climb down himself, take her on his back, and carry her the rest of the way, ElizabethAnn didn't know, but she felt a little grateful, because of the stench. She could smell Earl's putrescence on herself now and had to hold her breath as she climbed. For instance, each time she reached out to pluck one of the tree's gorgeous blossoms, it wilted at her approach.

"Let's play a game!" shouted Earl. "See, I've got a stopwatch on this thing! It's phenomenal!" He gestured at his mud-encrusted golden watch. "I'll set it for three minutes and you see if you can beat it. Ready? Here goes!"

"Wha?" whined ElizabethAnn, who had no intention of racing the hateful little timepiece, but couldn't make herself heard over the blustery wind in the magnolia and Earl's squeals of glee.

Up she climbed, while Earl egged her on like a Little-League first-base coach. Finally, ElizabethAnn found herself climbing directly into the empty nest of some large bird, perhaps an eagle, condor, albatross, or the Bumblegreen equivalent of such a creature.

Finding this snuggly home—albeit someone else's—ElizabethAnn instinctively curled up in the nest as if it were her very own. It might as well have been her bed back in No Oaks, so perfectly sized was it for a gangly ten-year-old well beyond caring about getting poked in the ribs by twigs and bits of straw. So, mere seconds from reaching her goal, ElizabethAnn commenced snoring away while Earl's gold watch's alarm played an up-tempo jazz number.

While ElizabethAnn slept, Earl watched her from the turret window and bemoaned the general cussedness of children. Contemplating this unfortunate delay, he squatted, very on-edge-like, inside a tower where he couldn't the least bit claim to have any right to be, should some possibly armed individual wielding royal authority happen to unexpectedly arrive.

150

22

IN WHICH TAMMY SLAMS
DOWN HER PARING KNIFE

Plush, wine-red upholstery enveloped her in luxury, but Tammy felt uncomfortable, sitting this close to her boss. Hip to hip. Nonetheless, never having ridden in a top-drawer carriage before, Tammy didn't intend to miss a single detail of the experience. She listened to the clip-clop of the horses' hooves, smelled the oiled leather of the harnesses, and took in the occasional "haw!" and "whoa!" of the carriage driver.

Out the curtained window, she watched the carriage's gaily painted wheels crunch through the grass and gravel of the Bumblegreen countryside.

"It was a brainwave, Tammy, it really was," said the duchess. "You must be a genius."

"All I said was, 'Are you inviting the queen to the garden party?'" Tammy replied. "I didn't say anything, really."

"But inviting the queen! Inviting the queen! It's a brilliant idea!" said the duchess. "Of course, I mean, I'm a duchess. I can invite a queen to a party. Why not? Can't I? I don't see any impropriety in that."

"I don't really know, ma'am."

"The truth? Me neither," admitted the duchess. "Trouble is, when, in a case like this, the queen is a thirteen-year-old orphan, what's the protocol? Can an adult duchess invite a pure-royal child-queen to things? Should I go through her regents? All twelve of them? I'd rather not."

"Every child loves a party," said Tammy.

"Exactly!" exclaimed the duchess. "But my mind is whirring. It's asking, 'Should I approach her at visiting hours, like everyone else, or should I make a special appointment?' I don't know. My mind is a-whir, Tammy. It's a-whir."

"Ma'am, I think taking the simplest route is best."

"Yes! You really are a wonder, Tammy. That's wisdom, is what that is. Oh, but don't forget why you're here. This entire enterprise hinges on you!"

"Yes, ma'am," said Tammy. "I know what I have to do. It'll be a piece of cake. No pun intended."

At the castle, as footmen helped the ladies down from the carriage, the duchess gave Tammy a conspiratorial wink before they parted ways. While the duchess headed straight to the throne room, Tammy ducked through a servant's entrance into the royal kitchen, where prep cooks, sauciers, waiters, and sous chefs stood around a large, oval chopping block.

As they chopped, they gossiped, and as the gossip became more interesting, the chopping became more intense. The peppers that were supposed to get julienned ended up diced, the radishes that were supposed to get peeled ended up reduced to shavings, the eggplants that were supposed to be cubed ended up mashed into goo, and then everyone had to start over. Tammy grabbed a green chile and a paring knife and joined the frenzied assembly.

"It's six feet tall and has five arms. That's what I heard," said one cook, who shrugged as she chopped, as if she couldn't help but be a conduit for interesting facts.

"It's hairy," said another cook. "That's the one thing all the rumors agree on. It's hairy as anything. The hair gets everywhere. The thing goes around in this cloud of hair and fur." The speaker's enormous knife, and the smooth way it sliced, gave her an air of authority.

"You're all crazy if you believe anything Mobius says," said a short cook in a dirty apron. "I'll bet it's nothing. The beast is a figment of his blasted imagination, is all it is."

"We'll know soon enough," said a plump woman with a slight mustache. "The queen already sent out a search party! They've got spikes and nets and spears and clubs and things. A blow dart, too. They'll catch the beast, all right, then we'll get to see it before they put it to death!"

"What beast is this?" asked Tammy. Everyone looked at her. For an uncomfortable instant, the chopping stopped.

"Who are you?" asked one of the cooks.

"Tammy, the duchess' personal chef," Tammy responded.

"Oh! Oh! Oh! And you don't know?" replied another one.

"Don't know what?" asked Tammy.

"About the beast?" said the plump one. "The beast that's abroad in the land? The portal-jumping beast?"

"Beast?" answered Tammy, feigning interest in the meticulous peeling of her green chile until everyone returned to talking at once.

"It's a beast! It's abroad in the land!"

"No one knows where it came from!"

"They're gonna catch it!"

"They're gonna spear it!"

"It's broken the Universal Portal Compact! It's come through a portal!"

"There's no other explanation!"

"They're going to cook it on a spit!"

"Oh, my!" said Tammy, trying to conceal her growing panic. "When did the search party go out?"

"It's going out now! Right now!" replied the shrugger.

"They're loading the carriages with slingshots!" said the plump one, adding, "and cannons! And those pointy things you set on fire and shoot!"

Tammy peeled the chile's flesh off until only seeds remained. She gathered the seeds, separated them into equal piles, then arranged the piles of seeds into spirals. In the meantime, she listened to the queen's cooks describe Hank's beast as everything from a hairy, man-like snow-beast to a sharp-toothed, mouse-like rodent with a broken wing.

"What I heard," said the plump one, "was it was over there near the duchess' place, hiding out in the forest." She asked Tammy, "Have you seen footprints? Anything?"

"Oh!" Tammy answered. "That reminds me! I'm on a secret mission! The duchess is having a garden party, see? She's inviting the queen, and I'm to find out the queen's favorite dessert."

She spoke the truth, but also, Tammy hoped to distract the cooks from their discussion of the beast. It worked. The assortment of cooks—on its third go-round of vegetables, the diced and mashed remnants of which accumulated in a festive mound in the center of the chopping block—latched on to the new topic like gymnasts grasping at rings.

"White chocolate ganache!" yelled the plump one.

"Applesauce!" said Big Knife.

Tammy grabbed a pen and wrote their ideas on her arm until she ran out of flesh. All the while, she worried herself sick about Hank, who could be in imminent danger if caught sheltering the beast. In her anxious state, Tammy hopped from one foot to the other.

"The restroom is down the hall," offered the shrugging chef, who shrugged again, as if she couldn't resist the urge to be helpful at all times.

Tammy ran down the hall, found an exit, dashed through it, and found herself in the midst of the castle stables. Before her, a cavalcade of war chariots departed, weapons piled high on their roofs. Sergeants-at-arms leaned out the windows, huzzah-ing with excitement.

She ran after the last chariot, which had a cannon as big as a sofa strapped across its rear. Its horses slowed in order to navigate a deep pothole, and that extra couple of seconds gave Tammy a chance to leap astride the weapon. In this manner, she rode along with the search party, clinging to the cannon's cold iron while concocting a plan.

Tammy's first idea involved dressing in warrior garb and, once they'd found the beast, pretending to kill it, but really letting it go somewhere in the woods. Her second idea involved walking up to the soldiers out of nowhere, looking like some troubled peasant woman, and declaring she'd seen the beast, then pointing them in the opposite direction from Hank's shack. The third idea involved committing some kind of very public crime in order to draw the war party's attention away from Hank and his beloved beast. Mind you, she was aware that all these plans were far-fetched and deeply flawed.

The carriage Tammy rode, which followed behind ten or twenty others, rounded the castle's corner. There, momentarily, Tammy caught sight of a monkey leaning out a turret window, above a magnolia tree, like some hideous, unwashed Rapunzel, screaming, "Chop chop, little chicken! Chop chop!"

She put it out of her mind, thinking, *No, no, that couldn't have really happened* and *Focus, Tammy, focus on the task ahead.*

PART TWO

THE CUMBERSOME OUTRIGGINGS

OF QUEENLINESS

THE CUMBERSOME OUTRIGGINGS OF QUEENLINESS

23

FEATURING A WALKING FLOUNDER

Long before ElizabethAnn ever dove through a portal, before Jackson ever smelled monkified air, and before Grandma's daughter called the goons to take Grandma away to a home, Jimothy Schrank —a wide, flat man secretly known to many as The Walking Flounder —called to order an emergency stockholder's meeting at an old barn he considered the Favra Watch corporate headquarters, in Bumblegreen.

Huffing, puffing, and sighing excessively as he spoke, Schrank began, "I've called this meeting to talk about rejuvenating the Favra

Watch Company!"

Among those on the board, not one facial expression changed.

"It's pretty good, already," said a woman in a green gabardine pencil skirt ten years out of style.

"Is this going to require an investment?" asked a stork-like gentleman in a blue serge jacket.

"If it ain't broke, don't fix it!" exclaimed a bald man with a lisp, a stutter, and an issue with spitting when he spoke.

Schrank cleared his throat and continued, "I don't mean to rock the boat …"

"Then don't," interrupted Green Gabardine, who picked up her briefcase and stood to go.

"Ah, but there's trouble on the horizon," said Schrank, who knew his audience.

"Projections of doom? Why didn't you say so!" said Blue Serge, and Green Gabardine sat back down.

"Bumblegreen is getting tired of Favra watches. They've become commonplace," Schrank said.

"They're a time-honored tradition!" said Baldy. "That's what makes them commonplace!"

"Sales are down," Schrank blurted out, and everyone gasped. "It's true," he continued, "so we need to rejuvenate, rethink, re-invigorate the company!"

The board members slumped in their chairs and pouted.

"Don't worry," said Schrank. "I've got it all worked out—a new product and a new market."

"Go on," said Baldy, with caution.

So, wide, flat Jimothy Schrank explained to the now-interested gathering that the Favra Watch Company would soon introduce a brand-new luxury watch to stand head and shoulders above any watch ever made and even, "redefine the very meaning of the term 'luxury.'" Schrank asserted (there is really no need to quote his every hyperbolic word) that the success of the new product would be guaranteed. An absolute slam-dunk.

"But practically everyone in Bumblegreen has a Favra already," said Green Gabardine. "Parents hand them down to their kids, who hand them down to their own kids, and so on." She rolled her eyes like one does when stating something obvious, adding, "That's the very meaning of quality."

"Quality, yes," Schrank said, "but what about style?"

"What's that?" asked Green Gabardine.

"Style is the thing that makes quality not good enough," said Schrank.

"If it ain't broke," grumbled Baldy.

"How you gonna get rich with that attitude?" Schrank yelled, now impatient with the old fuddy-duddies, adding, "Do you want to become Major Players in Finance, or not?" He followed this statement with more of his sigh-like breathing or wheezing and the sound of his own feet nervously shuffling beneath him, seeming to belong to someone else. "And now," he said. "I'd like to introduce you to our new board member."

"New board member?" complained the executives, in unison. They groaned and whined about this horrible surprise, until Georgie walked in.

Tall, with broad hips and shoulders, Georgie topped off her look with a short but stylish haircut that seemed to say, either, *Let's get down to business* or *I'm too cool to care if we do or don't.* Sauntering into the room, she absentmindedly blotted trail dust, with an embroidered hanky, from her thick tangle of lashes. On the way to her seat, she barked, "Okay, Schrank, update me."

Schrank explained that with the technology now available, certain information programmed into Favra's new luxury watches would enable a particular style of travel. "That's travel," stage-whispered the big man, "with a capital T."

The board members sat up straight at that—some with expressions of interest, others with outrage. Georgie merely leaned back in her seat and tented her fingers.

"I intend," said Schrank, "to enter certain coordinates into the specialized 'global positioning system' inside the timepiece." Here, he hesitated, "Let's not call it a timepiece. It's so much more. Let's simply call it 'The Favra,' to be understated."

"Show me it!" said Baldy.

"Ah, well, I will, see, but there's a glitch. The watch kind of disappeared. I don't exactly have access to it right now, but I'll have it for you, soon."

"You better!" said Baldy.

"Soon? You're the one that called the meeting, Schrank, why don't you have the prototype, now?" asked Green Gabardine.

"You won't believe this—funny story, actually—but a silly little monkey stole it off my wrist one night while I was sleeping."

"Oh, brother," said Blue Serge.

"We'll get it back," barked Georgie, "Don't worry about that. I know monkeys. I can get it. But Schrank, tell them about the coordinates."

"Anyway," said Schrank, "the coordinates will enable, as I said, certain windows on other worlds to be accessed. Certain thrills, let us say very simply, that will be exclusively available to the new Favra watch owners of Bumblegreen."

"Global positioning system?" asked Blue Serge, "For traveling purposes? I don't see the point. Where would somebody want to go?

And why?"

"Ostensibly," said Georgie, now casually picking her teeth, "to travel through portals, I assume. For fun."

"Call the police," replied Baldy, who slouched in a way that indicated either intense self-protection or total surrender to fate. He made no move to call anyone.

"This is outrageous," said Green Gabardine, who covered her face with her hair. "Portal travel ended years ago. Speak not of it!"

"Bumblegreen is changing," said Schrank. "People want to explore, they want to be free …"

"Its against the law!" said Blue Serge, "and it'll ruin everything!"

Schrank shrugged and said, "Well, it was just an idea."

"A dumb one!" said Baldy.

"Well I, for one, would love to Travel," said Georgie, "and get out of this crap Bumblegreen."

"Imagine!" said Green Gabardine, almost agreeing.

"Oh, well, it was just an idea that could make everyone millions," Shrank mumbled.

"Millions?" asked Green Gabardine. "How?"

"Portal travel isn't just for tourists, you know," Schrank whispered, forcing them to quiet down and listen. "It's for importers, too."

"Imports, eh, Jim?" asked Blue Serge. "Fun idea, sure. Folks are dying to get imports back. Dying to. It's illegal, of course, but they're dying to."

"But gee," Georgie prompted, "the only way you could program the correct global positioning coordinates into that watch is if you had *The List*." She raised an eyebrow.

"Prindal's List, you mean," Schrank replied, as planned. "Well, as you know, that list is desperately illegal to use, plus impossible to find." He said it with a shrug, as if those were just fun facts.

"What's Prindal's List?" asked Green Gabardine, and everyone gasped. Had she been raised by wolves? No, just the victim of a sheltered childhood.

Schrank did his best to explain the nature and origin of Prindal's List, but his version of the story wasn't anywhere near as detailed as the one that follows.

24

WHEREIN, LONG AGO, A BLIGHT RAVAGED BUMBLEGREEN

It all started when a local farmer found every one of his chickens tits up, red in the face, mangy, and dead. Then, scavenger types discovered hundreds of field rabbits just the same: feet in the air, stiff as boards, and dead as Fred. Next, large game became thin on the ground. Hogs wouldn't fatten. Badgers disappeared, leaving large holes gaping and uninhabited. Monkeys seemed to be the only animals immune to Bumblegreen's deadly blight.

Wherever entire villages had fallen prey to the blight, mass graves peppered the landscape. Homes, mills, shops, and saloons lay abandoned: morbid ghost towns from which passing gypsies shielded children's eyes. The same gypsies spent chilly nights without fires rather than scavenge planks from the rotting shacks thought to be cursed. Dead farmers' relatives burned bodies along with crops, food stores, and homes, with great, weeping finality. The massive pyres sent up inky plumes, dry-brushing history, blacking out hope.

With the blight's source unknown, superstition flourished in this once-educated land. Bitter accusations flew among family members and former friends, where every soul sought a spook to take the sharp end of his sorrow and fear. Villages in the north emptied out as peasants attempted to travel to blight-free provinces in the south; meanwhile, southerners hiked north. Everyone wanted to be someplace else, but all this traveling seemed only to spread the deadly blight itself.

During their reign, Dahlia's parents, the king and queen, funded a barrage of undertakers, coroners, and gravediggers to travel the kingdom autopsying bodies and performing burials both sacred and sanitary. They ordered teams of experts to inspect crops all over the kingdom, and where anything appeared suspect, they burned whole fields with a free hand.

Of course, the monarchs put every intellectual, scientist, deep thinker, and even crossword-puzzle expert in the land to the task of discovering the cause of the blight. But, ultimately, these experts made little progress in determining even a single plausible explanation for the sweeping disease, whose deadly appetite didn't discriminate between human, animal, or vegetable. Indeed, a map of the lands ruined by the blight portrayed it taking on a polka-dot pattern and striking with sudden ferocity wherever least expected.

"The blight is caused by imports, you know," Shadooda told those beleaguered monarchs, back when rulers used to have monthly meetings with magicians, way back when.

"Pish-tosh," said the queen. (That's how queens talk.)

"Alligator shoes, dishwashers, paperclips, all that stuff," Shadooda added.

"Nonsense," said the queen, adjusting her crown of imported crystal.

The king shifted on the imported velvet seat of his throne and said, "Some say the blight is actually caused by magic!"

Shadooda said, "Your Highnesses, magic is the fundamental force that keeps Bumblegreen ..."

"Utter nonsense," said the queen.

"Technology is!" said the king.

"Technology is an import! It doesn't even ..." Shadooda couldn't finish because the queen rang a bell just then, and a couple of guards dragged Shadooda away. The monarchs didn't bother to end conversations, anymore—too much trouble, what with all the back-and-forth. Working parents have to save time somehow.

Finally, the king and queen had spent so many late nights inspecting blighted regions, consulting scientists, and pondering horrible developments that, exhausted, they caught the terrible blight themselves and died tragically on a would-be-beautiful spring day. On their deathbeds, rather than appealing to Bumblegreen's magicians (all of whom had, like Shadooda, mysteriously disappeared), the monarchs, using imported bullhorns, separately croaked appeals—neither to God nor sorcerer, but to science.

25

IN WHICH PRINCESS DAHLIA
RUINS HER POUFY COIFFURE

As a very young child and the last of the royal line—back when her parents were still alive, of course—Princess Dahlia learned the royal knack of greeting people with polite disinterest, which was handy for practicing queenliness. However, her privileged situation as the last of the royal line had its drawbacks, too. For instance, she had never been thrown into a swimming pool by a big brother, dandled on one knee by a kindly grandfather, or chucked beneath the chin by an adoring uncle. Nobody had ever even played this-piggy-went-to-market with her toes. And, of course, the princess had never moped about the castle in footy pajamas, dragging an old worn blanket, sucking her thumb. In fact, she had never even dressed herself without at least three attendants.

With such limited life experience, it's understandable that young Princess Dahlia never ventured outside the castle grounds. Oh, and also, she didn't have any friends. She thought the teenaged duchess was her friend, but she wasn't.

Mostly, Princess Dahlia played alone games, like cat's cradle with a piece of string. As mentioned before, she could make all kinds of things with her little loops of string: a thing she called a mouse's bed, a tangle that looked like a clump of trees, a thing with a peephole in the middle, and a twisty thing to catch your finger in.

Throughout childhood, she took instruction in needlepoint, which was supposed to teach patience, diligence, and concentration. Also, she had her lessons on Affairs of State, taught by handpicked advisors (handpicked by her, of course). Being a child at the time, she handpicked the ones whose methods of instruction relied heavily upon doing arts and crafts and consuming cookies and milk. Who wouldn't?

The day Princess Dahlia ventured as far as the swampy lowlands, she had been playing alone, or thought so, anyway. She snuck through the castle's massive oaken doors and along its stone veranda, then dashed across the castle "lawn," which, due to the blight going on at the time, amounted to little more than a few patches of weeds in a broad expanse of dust and mud puddles. Princess Dahlia looked back once, just once, at the massive stone fortress that rose up into the sky with a combination of whimsical romanticism and austere majesty. Then, she ran off.

The teenaged duchess, whose name was really Iris (though only Dahlia called her that), had been telling Princess Dahlia elaborate tall tales about the swampy lowlands for years. Now, Dahlia wanted to see if a village of tree houses really did thrive deep within the bog, with rope bridges joining them each to the other. She wanted to see the homemade flags representing hitherto unknown states of being and parallel worlds (or so the duchess had told her), flapping in the swampy breeze. And what about the blazing campfires the duchess had described? And the gypsies that danced in circles by starlight? Princess Dahlia felt curious about those, as well.

Princess Dahlia didn't know if she should believe Iris' fanciful stories but wanted to. Living, as she did, in her rarified royal world, she hadn't heard the rumor that the tree houses in the swampy lowlands were actually abandoned, if indeed they had ever existed. But even if she'd known, Princess Dahlia would still have liked the duchess' version of reality better, what with its flags and campfires and notion of a simple-but-happy gypsy subculture. So, with little else to do on a dreary, cloudy day (long ago, now), the princess set off toward the fringes of the castle lawn, where things turned even browner and soggier.

Unknown to darling Dahlia, who wouldn't even suspect a fly of buzzing, the duchess crouched nearby, behind the bronchial twigs of a blight-killed shrub, spying on the princess. While Dahlia snuck toward the swampy lowlands she scampered from dead bush to downed branch to clump of droopy trees, trying not to be seen by the gypsy-like reclusive badger hunters (who may or may not exist). The duchess snuck right behind her, one thorn bush away, tracking Dahlia's every move.

Princess Dahlia approached the place where the swampy lowlands began. The ground squished beneath her feet, and the vegetation changed to horsetails, mangrove trees, spooky swinging vines, strangler figs, and dew-covered, broad-leafed ferns. A mist, with its rotten smell of birth and death, encompassed the region, and rain sprinkled down, ruining Princess Dahlia's poufy coiffure.

Undaunted, she crept farther into the swamp. When, in her travels, the terrain changed again, the princess found herself wandering among tall, densely packed, and perfectly straight trees. Finally—somewhere in the middle of these misty lowlands—her shoes filled with squishing mud, her gown sodden, and her trembling lower lip tasting teardrops, the little lost princess finally spied one of those fabled tree houses. There was even a toothless gypsy hanging his laundry on the handrails of a rope bridge.

Still tailing the princess, hiding just one thorn bush away, the duchess saw the scene, too, and wondered if she herself was actually psychic, since she had really made up all that stuff about the toothless gypsies. Yet, there they were, in the flesh, hanging laundry in the rain.

Friendly Princess Dahlia ran into a clearing and waved up at the gypsy and his clean, wet underthings, intending to make friends. The gypsy spied her, and his eyes opened wide and white as beacons. He waved his arms back and forth overhead in the commonly accepted worldwide symbol for either *Look, here I am, lost on a desert island!* or *Stop! Stop! Don't go any farther!*

Wondering what was wrong with the man, or if he was simply trying to air out the socks still clutched in both hands, the princess waved back and ran directly into the center of the clearing, where a badger hole swallowed her up.

She fell, at first thinking she would probably end her adventure with a nasty sprained ankle. But after disappearing into the badger hole, she heard an earsplitting, disturbing sound of mechanical malfunction—*kedank*—followed by a windy, ghostly sound:

shooshreek. The princess felt herself being pulled forward, as if by a high-powered magnet, only with her teeth uncomfortably more magnetic than the rest. Then, she experienced the undignified sensation of being thoroughly taken apart and meticulously reassembled. Finally, she fell through the end of a large drainpipe, onto a hard, stone surface—the floor of a belfry—where church bells blasted her eardrums.

Little Dahlia covered her ears with both hands and looked down from the belfry into a street full of half-dressed people dancing in a manner both mathematically precise and gleeful. Thrilled, she waved at the dancers below and shouted, much as the toothless gypsy had just waved and shouted at her, trying to get someone's attention. However, before Princess Dahlia finished her first wave and shout, a hand gripped the back of her dress, another pressed firmly over her mouth, and she was whisked right back up the drainpipe.

Dahlia heard the clanking and whooshing again, felt the uncomfortable magnetic pull, and experienced the serious discomfort of becoming, for a few moments, little more than a rattling box of loose puzzle pieces of herself. This time, though, the experience took place within the arms of someone else—someone smelly, yet soft.

A moment later, Princess Dahlia popped right back up through the badger hole into the clearing in the swampy lowlands, one very frightened and confused little girl, indeed. There, she found a tremendously long rope tied around the waist of the toothless gypsy, who now panted on the ground beside her. Three more gypsies coiled the rope onto a giant spool. Their ragged, sweat-soaked shirts did little to improve upon a look of general toothlessness.

Panting all the while, the gypsy on the ground asked repeatedly after the princess' health.

Dahlia said she guessed she felt fine, but when pressed, shouted,

"Actually, I like to dance an awful lot!" (not realizing this was rude). "Can't we go back?" she queried the gypsies, one by one, insisting, "Let's go back through that hole and dance, shall we?"

The gypsies smiled but ignored her entreaty while exchanging meaningful looks with one another, the way grown-ups sometimes do. Then, once they finished coiling the rope—breathless, relieved, and generally flushed from exertion—they invited Princess Dahlia up the rope ladder, into the tree house community, for tea.

The young duchess, of course, watched this entire scene (minus the bit on the other side of the portal, about which she could only guess) from behind a berry bush, beside herself with envy. The duchess knew full well the unspoken rule that made it very much against a type of spies' honor to try to join the fun upon which one was spying. So, she watched Dahlia climb up to the tree house and talk for hours with the swampy lowland gypsies. She watched the gypsies light oil lamps to brighten their simple chamber for the princess, and then she watched some more as, slowly, more gypsies crossed rope bridges to filter into the room: wives, children, aunts, uncles, grandmothers, and so forth.

The duchess squinted between the parted leaves of a scrub oak and cursed Dahlia six ways from Sunday. If she could have made some noise, she would have hollered at the heavens, "Why does that brat always get the breaks? Why!" Instead, she just punched her left fist into her right hand and yanked on her two damp pigtails until it hurt. Meanwhile, the gypsies assured Princess Dahlia that due to an infinite number of dangers, the future queen of Bumblegreen (and last of the royal line) should really not engage in what they called "portal jumping."

"But," said Prindal, the man who had rescued little Dahlia, "if you'll be a good girl and steer clear of that badger hole, well then!" He exchanged glances with his fellow gypsies while they all doubted they could manifest any bribe valuable enough to influence a spoiled princess intent upon adventure.

"We'll be your friends for life!" suggested one of the spool-rollers. At this, the princess brightened considerably.

"And we'll tell you all about our adventures!" added the other spool-roller. He received a quick elbow in the ribs from Prindal, who whispered such stories might not be appropriate, but the flickering lamplight revealed an excited smile spreading over Princess Dahlia's face. *Friends? Really?* the smile suggested. The gypsies locked eyes in agreement: yes, they would commit to this promise of friendship.

"And I," replied Princess Dahlia, "will be your friend, also. And I will ..." Dahlia wracked her brains for something such a sheltered little girl could offer such mysterious and worldly adults. "I will teach you to embroider," she finally said. This unexpected bonus brought raised eyebrows, wondering frowns, and approving head nods around the gypsy circle. Thus, the gypsies and the princess struck a deal that, in the end, would change Bumblegreen forever.

As dusk came on, the teenaged duchess trudged home alone, despondent and vengeful, while Princess Dahlia enjoyed a jubilant piggyback ride in the singing, dancing company of new friends.

26

In Which the Princess Has a Horrible Realization

The day she looked through a certain keyhole, Princess Dahlia had been playing alone, again. Despite ideal weather, blue skies, and gentle winds from the northeast, the castle lawn, that day, lay dead as an overused loofah, just the same as years before, when Dahlia ran off on her secret adventure to the swampy lowlands. It always looked like that during those years of the blight, which is why the princess seldom played on the "lawn."

Throughout childhood, Princess Dahlia (much like the duchess herself) loved sneaking and spying. Castles present immense opportunities for such amusements, so, over time, the princess got eyesful of chambermaids bemoaning lost loves, scullery maids flirting with the landed gentry, stable boys sneaking cigarettes behind closed doors, and other giggle-worthy tidbits of naughtiness.

On one particular blight-decimated spring day, the princess tried out a new method for spying through keyholes. The idea was to shake her head rapidly back and forth in front of the keyhole instead of pressing her eye to it. She wanted to test the idea that a wider swath of inner room would be visible this way, if a bit blurry. Little Dahlia practiced her new technique by peeking in on a couple of her parents' advisors in a private chamber.

She heard urgent whispers on the other side of the door, but, through her keyhole vantage point, could detect only flickering light. Such a flicker typically indicated someone pacing fretfully in front of a window and made her wonder if she might have come across a juicy situation. Soon, Dahlia heard muffled voices and a croak-gasping that might have been sobs. Despite the potential for real intrigue that would otherwise have made this a prime spying adventure, Princess Dahlia suddenly felt sick to her stomach. She didn't like the sound of those sobs. Not at all. Intending to run outside and watch clouds in the birdless sky, she backed away from the door but tripped on the hem of her gown, fell on her royal behind, and gave out a little involuntary cry.

The dress was made from a simple (if high-quality) cotton fabric dyed a deep mineral red and printed with images of roses and carnations. The scattered flowers, with their long stems, appeared to cascade, the princess sometimes thought, from a bouquet whose ribbon had come undone. When Dahlia fell, she saw her gown spread around her and fixed the floral pattern in her head forever. Those roses and carnations would visit her nightmares.

Dahlia righted herself, and, unable to resist, took another peek through the keyhole. This time, she saw two gentlemen standing there, in dark suits, with entirely unreadable expressions, looking at the door, specifically at the keyhole through which she, in turn, gazed back at them. Princess Dahlia turned to flee once more but tripped over her gown again, lost her balance, and bumped the door, jiggling the latch. Its metallic sound rang out like a ladle hitting the bottom of an empty soup cauldron in a room full of hungry, desperate people.

A special silence seemed to blow right through the keyhole. As the door creaked open, the princess prepared her most contrite expression. Yet strangely, the gentlemen opened the door all the way, revealing nothing to hide, as was the custom where royalty and doors were concerned, but certainly not as pertained to little children. The men, dressed in double black, as if for a double funeral, kneeled before the young princess, bowed their heads, and solemnly murmured, "My Lady."

She knew this to be inappropriate treatment for a mischievous nine-year-old, princess or no, but didn't know what to do, except squirm. The men remained on one knee until, finally, one looked up at her with wet, red eyes. In that moment (because she was a bright child, after all) Dahlia put two and two together.

With a sharp intake of breath, Dahlia realized a tragedy had occurred, and she, being the last of the royal line, had just become both orphan and queen.

Tears rolled down her rosy, unprepared cheeks.

27

WHERE THE REIGN OF QUEEN DAHLIA (THE FIRST) BEGINS

Sitting on the throne on coronation day, looking out over hundreds of expectant faces, nine-year-old Queen Dahlia resolved to become a revolutionary monarch. She decided to adhere, like her parents, to science, since the magicians had already disappeared from Bumblegreen, anyway. Yet, due to her aforementioned unique experience in the swampy lowlands, Dahlia would take an unusual path. She felt the kingdom needed an influx of new scientific expertise. Unlike her parents, the new queen actually knew where to get it. So, right after her coronation, Queen Dahlia called a meeting.

"We'll begin the reign of Queen Dahlia the first by instituting a think tank!" she proclaimed. The room's silence only seemed to amplify the swishing of her countless layers of taffeta skirts. (The royal costumer had earlier presented these to the girl as the first of many cumbersome outriggings of queenliness.)

"We'll get all the best minds together in one room," Dahlia said, "to create a place where real thinkers will think their brains into applesauce coming up with a solution to the blight."

"I see," said the bravest of her new regents, a tolerant half-smile on his bewhiskered face, "and from whence will we procure these intelligent persons?"

Queen Dahlia understood the gentleman's lack of enthusiasm. After all, the most intelligent persons in the kingdom generally considered themselves to be assembled right there, at that court, in that room, at that moment. Dahlia's suggestion, she knew, came as a bit of an insult, but she hoped the sting would fade with the success of her mission. While speaking, she had been stirring her tea and now, suddenly, smacked the damp spoon against her palm with a firm *thwack*.

"From other worlds!" she declared.

Queen Dahlia snapped her fingers, and before the inevitable condescending tut-tuts and don't-be-sillys could escape the lips of a single regent, the meeting room's door swung wide. Four rugged strangers trundled in, dressed in heavy boots, helmets, bass-fishing vests, and hip waders. They each carried bulging backpacks with mysterious gear strapped to the sides.

In truth, the outfits the lowland gypsies wore had nothing whatever to do with the work they were to perform. Their "gear" was nothing but scraps from a local blacksmith's shop, but Dahlia felt the costumes projected a sense of cautious optimism, intellectual earnestness, and leathery experience that would win over skeptical court conservatives. (Though, at her age, she wouldn't have known to put it into those words, exactly.)

"Portal exploration, gentlemen! These fine men and women are seasoned explorers of Bumblegreen's well-known portals," Dahlia said. She waited for a reaction, positive or negative, but received only silence.

She cleared her throat and continued, "Disguised as rabbit burrows, squirrel's homes, and other natural hollows, these portals enable us to examine life outside our little 'paradise.'" (Her clear discomfort with the word suggested the sarcastic quote marks in the minds of her more linguistic-oriented regents.) "More importantly," Dahlia added, "the portals enable us to meet new people and find fresh talent. Of course, if you know anything about portal travel, you know these other worlds can sometimes be as blank as moons, yet some of the portals lead to worlds rich with wonders!"

A pause here.

Dahlia raised her teacup to her lips as she let the speech's introduction seep in. She did not actually sip. In fact, she could hardly breathe for fear her regents, who had been her parents' cronies—stooped pessimists and close-minded codgers, to a man—would burst into laughter and dismiss her idea with careless waves of their gnarled hands, but Dahlia's audience sat transfixed, as hoped.

She set her teacup down on the wooden conference table, rather than in its saucer, lest a shaking hand expose her fear with the telltale rattle of china.

"Some of these worlds can be vibrant with astounding technology, buzzing with inventive activity," she explained.

"Yes, yes," answered one of the regents, "of course. We know about the portals, sweetie. I mean, Your Highness." The old man plunged his head into his crossed arms in tired embarrassment.

The queen's financial advisor took up where the old man left off, a bit too loudly, covering for his associate's gaffe. "It's where all our imports come from: furniture, lab equipment, office supplies. From other worlds, of course. But the sort of people who Travel are ... what's a way of putting it? ... not exactly risk-averse."

He cast a dubious glance at the four rugged strangers, Dahlia's lowland gypsy friends.

"Hello! Fine crystal? Hello! Immunizations? Hello! High-end microbrewed beers?" ventured a certain political strategist whose rudeness had always been pardoned because of it being such a consistent and essential part of his overall being. "Who makes these in Bumblegreen? Nobody! We get them from the gypsies, the so-called Travelers, but so what? What's that got to do with the price of peas?"

"Besides valuable imports," continued the queen, "really smart people can be found in these other worlds. And technology. And machinery. And ... and things you can't even imagine! We've used up all our own resources trying to cure this blight, including even your own brain power, if I can say that. Can I say that? Well, I did. So now, I think, I believe, I insist, I mean ... I *command* that we explore other lands, not for luxury goods, but for brilliant minds. We'll bring back experts from these places—advanced doctors and scientists—and maybe they'll know how to end the blight."

Young Queen Dahlia looked out the castle's high, arched windows at the bleak and ruined landscape beyond. Her arm gracefully rose and gestured at the barren, dust-blown acreage that had once been a verdant hillside.

Growing bolder, she picked up her cup and slammed the thing right in the center of its saucer.

WHERE QUEEN DAHLIA
MEETS THE LONE DISSENTER

Brought hither in strange clothing, scientists from other lands spent hours upon days upon months upon years of professional rumination trying to find the cause of Bumblegreen's blight. Of course, said scientists also spent many of those days quite confused and jumbled up by all the jumping-through-portals-to-other-worlds business, what with time changes, barometric pressure adjustments, occasional motion sickness, and so forth. Nevertheless, these scientists turned out to be very intelligent—the cream of the crop. The cream, in fact, of several crops, as they'd come from quite a few different worlds, which Prindal and his merry band canvassed thoroughly for the famously intelligent and terrifically wise.

Once begun, the intensive research process required ceaseless dedication from both scientists and gypsies, who worked tirelessly with microscopes, posthole diggers, astrolabes, butterfly nets, and respected texts in Latin. Meanwhile, all parties involved traveled back and forth to the different worlds, what with the need for delicately calibrated equipment, trips to specialized libraries, and holiday vacations with loved ones. Yet, during a full year of study and investigation, the blight did not abate one bit. Folks continued dying left, right, and center, all over Bumblegreen.

The queen had turned ten by the time Bumblegreen's united coalition of multi-world scientists finally reached a consensus as to the blight's cause. They told Dahlia the blight was caused by infectious mites that seemed to come from nowhere at all. Specifically, no breeding grounds for the mites existed in Bumblegreen, so they could only be classified as Visitors from Another World.

The scientists duly signed and notarized the confoundingly brief report, stamped it with official sealing wax, and delivered it to the ten-year-old queen during a throne room ceremony. Standing in a disorganized mob, the imported scientists wore expressions that could only be described as "stricken," or even, in severe cases, "palsied with anguish."

Eyes downcast, feet dragging on the hand-woven carpet of fine imported silk, the brave cadre had to admit to young Queen Dahlia that they themselves had brought the mites into this world. In their travels through the portals, they had, for a year now, been unwittingly transporting blight-carrying insects microscopically embedded in their hair, skin, and clothing. This was the prevailing belief.

"But what about before you came to Bumblegreen?" asked the queen.

"Before us," began one of the imported researchers—a particularly fearless and intelligent lady—"the mites were (supposedly) carried by the Travelers. I mean, the lowland gypsies, Your Highness. Our research tells us they were the only ones known to portal-hop, as merchants, importers, and adventurers."

The lady rested her slender wrists upon her tousled white hair, as she was wont to do in moments of anxiety, "Even so, the mites aren't the real problem ..." the wise woman added, but just then, a hubbub in the throne room drowned out her words, and Queen Dahlia became distracted.

So, to sum up, the gypsies themselves were believed to have caused the blight, which, over many years, had killed thousands and orphaned the queen. Indeed, it seemed the gypsies—unknowingly, mind you—had decimated the kingdom's crops, wild game, domestic livestock, citizens, and royals. The gypsies: Dahlia's only friends. What could she do? Ever since taking on the mission of finding learned persons from other worlds, the gypsies themselves had toiled earnestly for a cure to the blight, only to prove themselves guilty of causing it.

The evidence proved the gypsies ought, strictly speaking, to be thrown in a cage and dropped into shark-infested waters, batches of stinging nettles, or a vat of boiling oil: all standard Bumblegreen execution techniques. As soon as this news got out, townspeople clamored for gypsy blood, but Queen Dahlia wouldn't give it. Instead, she pardoned the gypsies and burned their supposedly mite-infested clothes in a symbolic bonfire. Then, Dahlia thanked the imported researchers and sent them back through their respective portals, thoroughly shampooed so as not to infect their own worlds with Bumblegreen's native insects.

Before they parted forever, Queen Dahlia said a special goodbye to that outspoken lady scientist, the one with the slender wrists and tousled white hair. After all, she had been immensely helpful, what with her audacious suggestions and courageous experiments.

"Now, remember," Queen Dahlia admonished the lady, "we're closing these portals for good, so don't try to come back through!"

"I won't!" the lady said, with a gleam in her eye. "With a new grandchild on the way, I'll be too busy anyway!"

"I have to ask you to sign this, the Universal Portal Compact," said the queen. "Says you won't try to come back under penalty of death." (All the scientists had to sign it.) "Bumblegreen can't survive any more traffic coming through, what with the mites," the queen added. "You understand?"

"Sure, I understand," the lady said, signing the paper with a flourish. "Frangipani! I wouldn't want to cause you any trouble! But Queen Dahlia, keep in mind what I said, please!"

"What you said?

"Among the scientists, I was the lone dissenter to the final analysis."

"There was a dissenter?"

"No one tells you anything, poor dear."

"Please, tell me," pleaded Dahlia.

The lady stepped closer to whisper in Dahlia's ear. "The real problem isn't the mites, but the imports ..." she began, but just then she slipped in the mud and slid right down into the badger hole that would send her home again. Some say she was pushed.

"Wait!" yelled Queen Dahlia. "What's the real problem? And anyway, I never learned your name!"

"Your Highness," screamed the lady as she disappeared down the hole. "Soon, everyone will just call me Gra…" and she disappeared, leaving behind nothing but the faint clang and hiss of *kedank shooshreek*.

29

IN WHICH PRINDAL'S LIST
FINALLY RETURNS TO THE STORY

The gypsies bemoaned the scientific verdict, their own irreparable guilt, and the loss of the portals—the emotional center of their now-meaningless world. They mourned with drum sessions and blues guitar and the singing of dirges, then commenced, ceremoniously, with shovels, to fill in the portals. But every badger hole, rabbit warren, and hollow log they tried to fill just swallowed the dirt, transported it to another world, and remained open.

The gypsies consulted a chemist, an ecologist, a physicist, and a general contractor. It would have been more effective to use witchcraft, but all they had was technology, so, together, and with the aid of science, the group invented a special polymer. Then, workers cleared a large area around one portal, rolled a sheet of polymer over the land, and used glue, a heat gun, and spikes to bond the film to the ground.

From a royal observation booth adorned with velvet swags, young Queen Dahlia watched these goings-on through imported opera glasses. Trying to get a good view of the proceedings, she fell from her booth. No one noticed, so she clambered back in among her draperies and covered her skinned elbow with a decorative flounce.

Men with shovels next spread topsoil over the polymer, making a hillock. Then, they planted bushes and saplings and wild grasses into it, scattered armloads of twigs and leaves to camouflage the new plantings, and declared the portal permanently closed, concealed, and obliterated. Dahlia jumped down from her stuffy booth, this time on purpose, balled up her excess skirts, approached the worksite, and asked one of the shovel-wielding men if everything was going to be all right, now.

"Yes, Your Highness," he said. "Forest detritus will accumulate here. Trees will grow over the spot, and this portal will be rendered gone from Bumblegreen for good. But you shouldn't, I mean, Your Highness, if you don't mind my saying, you shouldn't be barefoot in a construction site. For your own safety, and all."

Queen Dahlia dropped the lifted skirts to hide her feet's habitually unshod condition. Then, satisfied with the man's explanation, she declared the experiment a success and decreed all the portals must be sealed in just such a manner. Extensive research and development hadn't actually been conducted on the polymer yet, and she knew it, but Dahlia hadn't slept properly in weeks and wanted the thing over with.

So, the gypsies, chemist, ecologist, physicist, and general contractor closed all the portals in Bumblegreen, just so. Meanwhile, Shadooda, in its underground lair, listened to these goings-on through its copper tube and cackled that utterly amused cackle of witches-observing-science-at-work. It could roll back that hillock with a snap of its magical fingers, if it wanted to.

After that, things grew quiet down around the swampy lowlands. The gypsies' bonfires wouldn't burn as high anymore, and they lost that dedication that used to get them down on their knees, feeding in the kindling, stick-by-stick, blowing on the coals, and gently coaxing. What's worse, they lost their motivation to gather, sing songs, and look forward to another day. In fact, the gypsies' once-jolly attitudes —due to changes in humidity, passing low fronts, and barometric pressure adjustments caused by the closed portals—quickly and fundamentally changed. The now sad, bored, blameful, miserable, toothless, lowland gypsies finally felt the dampness, which they hadn't noticed before, in their bones.

Slowly, slowly, not all at once, the gypsies wandered apart. Rumor had it some went south to tell bogus fortunes at a traveling carnival, while others took up trades as farriers, grocery clerks, even letter carriers.

By the time young Queen Dahlia finally settled all her blight-related affairs and got up the guts to petition her regents for permission for a play day, many months had passed since she had seen her gypsy friends. Down in the swampy lowlands, where she finally ran, one day, in a tiny, allotted speck of free time, hoping for some long-missed merriment, Dahlia found none of the camaraderie she expected. In fact, only one gypsy remained: Prindal, the fellow who had rescued her from the other-worldly belfry. An old man now, Prindal lay on a bed of straw, as was his wont, and when Dahlia peeked into the tree house, having awkwardly climbed its rope ladder in a bejeweled gown, Prindal felt her presence and opened an eye.

"Princess …"

"I'm the queen now, remember, Prindal?"

"Your Highness," he rasped.

"Where is everyone? Where are the fires? The singing? The music?"

"Gone … gone," groaned Prindal.

He reached beneath his pillow and pulled out a ragged, soiled cloth that might have once been the front of a barbecue apron, covered in straw dust. Prindal offered the scrap to the queen, who opened it to find an elaborate pattern of amateur cross-stitch.

"We started this for you, all of us, but they left me alone to finish," Prindal said. "I finally got it all down. Mind, don't prick your finger on the needle. It's still in."

She turned the embroidery one way and another and found it to be a list of very long numbers with the odd letter thrown in and a few symbols, as well. Not perfectly spaced, not evenly sewn, not an expert job, but a person could read the cross-stitched numbers without too much trouble.

"Prindal? What is it?" she asked.

"Latitude and longitude," he croaked. "Global positions, Your Highness, for the portals, all of them. Just in case someday you want to find them again."

Poor Prindal fell back upon the straw, and the queen noticed his fingers, bloodied with pinprick dots. Then, Prindal left this world—not via portal as he had planned long ago, but the ordinary way, leaving behind a cold carcass.

Despite objections from every advisor, the queen gave Prindal a formal state burial, a majestic monument for a tombstone, and a thirty-one-gun salute. No one came to the funeral except Dahlia, thirty-one lazy, depressed soldiers, and a hired preacher. And what a dreadful preacher he had been—couldn't stop sneezing during the whole ceremony, while someone's baby wailed in the background.

All the bummed-out peasants holding placards outside the cemetery gates proved a pathetic protest, indeed. Their signs read,

Prindal was a ratfink!
The queen likes portal jumpers!
The gypsies caused the blight!

and so forth.

During Prindal's funeral, these picket signs listed sideways and flopped in the wind while the signs' undernourished owners summoned just enough vim to direct their anger at the nearest authority figure but not enough vigor for any real follow-through. Peasants wandered erratically outside the cemetery's wrought iron gates, starting fistfights, flirting with guards, and herding children into unmanageable groups.

On the second-greatest day of mourning in her life, the queen gazed through her tears, past the wads of black tulle and charcoal velvet with which the royal stylist had saddled her, and over a sea of distant faces distorted with unfocused rage. She knew the disgruntled peasants were disorganized, unsure, and pathetic, for now, but there were a lot of them, and they probably wouldn't remain that way for long.

Her gut, the gut of a royal, told Dahlia *deposed rulers don't walk away with a pink slip, a severance package, and a footprint on their royal behinds.*

Deposed rulers, said her gut, in gut-language, *don't walk away at all.*

30

WHEREIN BABIES BECOME
THE NEW PROBLEM

During the blight, when people thought the end of the world was nigh, they did all kinds of things for no good reason, creating an atmosphere in which the duchess could be herself without the least shame. For instance, when she was sixteen, a drunken carnie proposed to her spontaneously in a supermarket aisle, and she went for it. The marriage lasted about as long as the cabbage in her basket, but it produced a son with a swan-shaped buttock birthmark. The tyke charmed everyone with his precocious smirk and (like his father) an advanced instinct for pleasing women.

Even in infancy, the duchess' son possessed a certain way of giving women exactly what they thought they wanted in return for a piece of themselves they never knew they'd miss. He was the duchess' pride and joy, sole focus, and eye-apple until, one day, she convulsed with sneezes in his presence, and it wouldn't stop.

The sneezing became so tremendous it knocked holes in walls, smashed crystal, shattered china plates, dislodged linoleum tile, and even brought down small outbuildings. At first, the duchess thought what appeared, inexplicably, to be an allergy to her own child must be entirely psychosomatic, so she exposed her thoughts and feelings to a psychologist. He told her she was right. To confirm this finding, the duchess brought her baby in to see him, and the psychologist promptly sneezed his clipboard right through a window.

"See?" was all the duchess could say to the startled shrink.

The duchess next hired a nanny who cared for children in her own home, but the nanny sneezed off both doors of her ramshackle house and shattered the bare bulb that illuminated the place. Then, she sneezed a hole in the tarpaper roof.

The duchess took her baby away, with apologies, but the nanny said, "No, ma'am. No apology needed. This ain't the only child done this to me. They all seem to, now. I'ma hafta give up my profession, and where will I be then? Ollem babies done this to their mommas, daddies, me, and jest about everbody. Allus been sneezin' the town down!"

Carrying her boy from the nanny's Minion Lane home to her awaiting carriage, the duchess saw evidence that the nanny spoke truth. Roofs on the homes there undulated strangely, walls tilted out at odd angles, fences posed in bent and twisted arcs. Even the mailbox posts stood off-kilter. Once considered ripe for gentrification, the neighborhood now looked slummy, to say the least. In fact, soon after the duchess' visit, property values on Minion Lane hit bottom. Local families, who had once hoped to sell out for big bucks, hid their sad situations behind closed window blinds, taking their allergies to their offspring as a personal shame.

The problem quickly developed into yet another pandemic.

At that time, the queen—just ten years old—held the highest office in the land, even if only by her fingernails. So, when any Bumblegreen resident came to her with a problem, it meant all logical methods of solving the problem had been exhausted, and the petitioner was hoping for the careful application of magic, which used to be possible.

Back then, magic was among the powers of the royalty—not to do magic, per se, but to control those witches and magicians and alchemists who could do it. The magicians used to live on the royal grounds, here and there, in little bungalows tucked away in groves and small forest clearings, but they didn't just give charms away. They constantly studied their craft. Call it professional development. You couldn't just walk up and disturb these people. You wanted magic, you had to go through the queen, and that's exactly what the duchess finally did.

"Dahlia, honey," said the duchess, one day, long ago, between sneezes. "Entertain this kid, would you? While I put some cheese on a couple crackers for us both?"

Unthinking, Queen Dahlia held the boy. The duchess was surprised and a bit alarmed to notice the queen didn't sneeze when exposed to the baby's dander or saliva or essence or whatever it was. Actually, more than alarmed, the duchess was furious. Here stood yet another thing perfect little Dahlia held over always-second-best Iris. The cruel, barbed fishhook of resentment found purchase (yet again) in the duchess' heart.

"All I can think of is putting magic on it, Dahlia," said the duchess. "All Bumblegreen's parents are blowing their doors down, sneezing! Roofers are having a field day, and hey, good for them, but the peasants can't afford new roofs, only to sneeze them off in a week! My own roof is next, I'm sure of it. What do you think?"

Dahlia tickled the duchess' little boy, played patty-cake with him, and paced the room with a grounded, thoughtful step that belied her years. She pulled up one of her many underskirts to wipe a spot of jelly from the tyke's pudgy face.

"Iris, I have to tell you a secret," Dahlia began. "Those magicians? Last time I saw one, I was just a kid. Now, the bungalows are empty; the cabins, abandoned. Iris, the magicians have disappeared!"

The duchess' baby crawled across the room, slipped on something, and fell down boom. Dahlia comforted him while the duchess looked on, helpless and sneezing.

"Disappeared?" asked the duchess. "Even Shadooda?"

"That's what I'm telling you," Queen Dahlia said. "I keep quizzing the regents, but they just shrug and tell me maybe the magicians died or something. What a lot of hooey! But don't tell anyone about this. It'll be the end of Bumblegreen. People will lose whatever hope they have left!"

The duchess did lose hope (of rescuing her relationship with her son) but she also gained hope (hope of getting some of Queen Dahlia's mojo). She now knew two things: that Queen Dahlia was the only adult in Bumblegreen not allergic to children and that she had a secret she wished the duchess to keep. A vague sense of unrealized power surged in her.

"Dahlia," asked the duchess. "What are you going to do?"

The queen rubbed her temples, took a deep breath, ate a piece of cheese, looked out the window, slumped, turned to the duchess, and said, "There's a man named Zade."

"You're going to marry him?"

"Gross. He's one of the imported scientists."

"I see. I thought you sent them all home."

"Yes and no. I asked Zade to stay. I just worried we might need a scientist, at some point in the future. Well, the future is here, quicker than expected, but thankfully, Zade has developed an experimental technique, using science. You know: artificial magic."

"Can he cast a spell to end this sneezing?" asked the duchess. "Because I'll volunteer to be the first subject. I swear, I will!"

The duchess' boy tried to climb up on a sofa but couldn't get his little legs up. The queen helped him, while the duchess—safely across the room—stewed.

"Not a spell, no," answered Dahlia. "Zade proposed an idea that I absolutely hate, but it's the only solution I've got on the plate. He proposed … well, he proposed that he take monkeys and inject them with this formula. It's not magic, but it's magic-like. It's science."

"Monkeys?" asked the duchess. "What, you mean monkeys from out of the forest?"

"Monkeys, exactly," said Dahlia. "It would make them almost like people. And then people, like yourself for instance, could actually …" Dahlia couldn't finish. She gulped and wandered to a window in a far wall, where she gazed upon hundreds of acres of green, fertile acreage that had finally recovered from the blight.

"What? What?" asked the duchess. "I could do what?"

"You could send your child away to be raised by the monkeys," said the queen softly, not looking at the duchess.

"Are you crazy?" asked the duchess.

Dahlia kept her eyes trained on the distance, on the green hills rolling away to bright, distant mountains. As she gazed, the thought of this new baby-allergy problem destroying all she had repaired since her parents' death became more and more intolerable. She breathed the deep breath she had taught herself to use when she needed queenliness. She held it in. She let it out.

"Are *you*?" answered a now-haughty Dahlia. "Who's going to take care of your child, Iris? What are you going to do? Hire villagers to run in and do thirty-second shifts with your kid? I assume he spends most of his time alone, as it is. Doesn't he? Is that a way to raise a child? Does he eat off a tray that gets passed through a slot, like a prisoner? I mean, what do *you* recommend? Because think what'll happen to the next generation of Bumblegreenis—neglected children with allergic parents. They'll be roaming the streets, forming adult-free societies of their own. Iris, think ahead!"

Offended, the duchess picked up her boy and attempted to march out the door with him, but that act alone caused her to sneeze a triple whopper. The door bowed out, then recovered. Some plaster crumbled from the wall, and a rafter crashed down, barring the way.

The queen tilted her head and raised one eyebrow.

The duchess hugged her child tightly.

The world went silent except for bits of plaster and wooden beams finishing their apocalyptic tumble.

"All right," said the duchess. "I don't have a choice. I guess I'll have to let my son be … raised by monkeys, for lack of a better term. I can't believe I'm saying this. But if this is the case, Zade Fandey hands his monkeys over to me. I want to be their manager, or boss, or whatever."

"Fine with me," replied the queen. "Someone has to."

"Where will they live?" asked the duchess.

"I hadn't thought about that," answered Dahlia.

"They'll need real estate and plenty of it," said the duchess. "Let me manage that, too. And they'll pay. Oh, yes. Nothing's free."

"I suppose if they're so humanlike, they ought to be able to pay," said Dahlia.

"Indeed. They'll pay," grumbled the duchess.

"Iris, you can't be serious," said the queen. "You want to make a profit off this? That's sick."

"Dahlia baby, I know you've lost the magic, don't I?" asked the duchess. "I can keep a secret, can't I? Or not. Whatever I choose."

"Oh, blackmail, is it?"

"Let's call it a friendly arrangement," said the duchess. "You need to solve the baby problem. I need to survive my toxic parenthood, and also, by the way, save my mansion from debtors. Hurry and say yes before I bring the roof all the way down. I feel another sneeze coming on."

Dazed, Dahlia extended her pale, aristocratic hand. The duchess grabbed it with her meaty, sticky one, and the two shook on the deal.

Within a week, the duchess' son called a monkey mama.

31

WHERE QUEEN DAHLIA GOES
ROGUE, IN HER NIGHTIE

"There's a handhold off to your left!" shouted Horace, the queen's chief of security, bobbing and weaving for a better vantage point. Several pages and aides held taut a massive fishing net for safety purposes. With her many skirts tied into a highly complicated series of knots between the legs, the agile, eleven-year-old queen herself had volunteered to scale the stone barn's interior wall. As she climbed, she clenched Prindal's cross-stitched list of portal coordinates between her teeth.

Now that they couldn't anymore, everyone in Bumblegreen wanted to dive through a portal. Forethought (in Bumblegreen, as in most places) wasn't so big among the masses. In fact, as soon as the queen had closed the portals and signed the Universal Portal Compact forbidding Travel with a capital *T*, exploration of other worlds became a sudden, Bumblegreen-wide obsession. `

By the time the portals had been closed a full year, and the dearth of imports had forced an unwelcome lifestyle change, many were desperate to go abroad just to grab armloads of the soft and shiny and new and dazzling items that would make them feel whole again. Treasure hunters reasoned that if only they could find Prindal's List, they could locate where the portals lay beneath the soil, loosen the polymer with shovels, picks, and jackhammers, and ultimately dive through the portals to other worlds. They'd have to find the latitudes and longitudes by the stars, but the intrepid would-be-Travelers figured they could do it, somehow.

Some further reasoned that maybe if they took more baths they could kill more mites and prevent the blight from coming back when they hopped between worlds, because—like most, but not all, of the imported researchers—they believed mites, not imports, to be the cause of the blight. It didn't matter what they believed, though, because they just wanted to get stuff they wanted and fulfill desires disguised as needs.

Ever since the closing of the portals, safes, strongboxes, and armed guards had proven no match for the queen's portal-obsessed subjects. They'd drilled, blasted, and sawed through walls to try to lay hands on Prindal's List, although they had, so far, been unsuccessful. *But,* the queen kept asking herself, *how long can that luck hold out*? That's why, along with Horace, her chief of security, the queen decided stealth would be key.

There'd be no more lockboxes and safes and formal changing of the guard. The location of Prindal's List would have to be a mystery. First, Dahlia had just tried keeping The List in her underwear drawer, but somehow a thief, hiding behind the royal bedroom draperies, had been caught in the nick of time by loyal sentries. That's when the whole changing-of-the-hiding-places thing began, which periodically involved secret nighttime forays to all kinds of rummy locations, like the castle's ancient barn.

Straddling one of the barn's oaken rafters, young Dahlia panted with the effort of her climb but stayed game, always game. She folded the sampler neatly and affixed it with thumbtacks to the top of the ceiling beam. Her subsequent shout of "whee!" and free fall into the safety net below made her chief of security visibly blanche and sweat, but he knew Dahlia, so he wasn't exactly surprised.

Later that night, lying in bed, thinking, Dahlia decided she had grown sick of scaling gritty cliffsides, crawling through damp drainage tunnels, and climbing, as described previously, up to rafters to find new hiding places for Prindal's List. Its location never stayed secret for long, as the sentries stationed nearby usually gave the location away, no matter how well they were disguised as fruit sellers, farmers, or shepherds. Dahlia concluded the only logical solution would be to steal the sampler herself, secretly hide it where no one would ever look, appoint no sentries at all, and not tell a soul.

So, young Dahlia snuck out in the morning's wee hours and retrieved the sampler—no mean feat. This time, she scaled the rock wall on her own, without a backup plan, a belay, or even a lookout. She grabbed the tattered scrap of cloth that had become a kingdom-wide fixation and stuffed it right in the bosom of her nightgown, which, considering the hour, was the attire she naturally wore. In just such a well-stuffed state, the queen climbed back down.

Subsequently, she retired to the castle's cheese factory, where, all alone, in the dead of night she stirred Prindal's List into a freshly made vat of gouda. There were no witnesses but the bats in the eaves overhead and a bunch of mice who thought Dahlia, in her voluminous white nighty, must have been a specter.

During the blight, the masses had been starving and the kingdom didn't have many resources, but it did have caves, and caves are good for storing cheese, and milk could always be got from one source or another, be it cow or goat or dog. Yes, dog cheese, that's real. The cheese-factory idea made perfect sense to Dahlia, back during the time of the blight. Let's not forget she was nine, then. Young Dahlia, when she first became queen, didn't know anything about anything, but she had heart, so she went ahead and overhauled the castle's vast drawing rooms, unused bedchambers, and superfluous offices. All those rooms had always seemed like wastes of space anyway to the dreamy little girl, with her ever-present loops of string.

Soon, Dahlia found she liked making cheese a lot better than reading Affairs of State files. Her regents never liked the cheese factory idea, of course, but Dahlia was queen, so she got what she wanted, and now the castle was full of vats and beakers and Bunsen burners and strange machines and red waxes. And that's where we find the queen at this point in the story, age eleven, in her nightie.

Dahlia put the gouda through the typical cheese-making process and made it into a nicely waxed wheel, just like any other. Next, she donned some too-big boots she found in a worker's locker, grabbed a brass ring heavy with skeleton keys, opened the cheese-factory door, breathed the cool evening air deeply into her lungs, and trudged into the forest by moonlight, gouda tucked under one arm. Finally, she arrived at a certain cave on the outer reaches of the castle grounds.

This particular cave, forgotten by most, had long been used as a curing cave for cheeses that would age a good ten years or more. The wooden doors across the cave's entry had been hammered into place, centuries ago, by somebody's nephew who needed a job, it looked like—none too sturdy, their construction. The lock on the door looked a bit rusty as well. *It might actually be better this way, all dilapidated,* thought the queen, *as who would suspect?*

Inside the cave, Dahlia unburdened herself of the heavy, List-containing cheese, placing it, randomly, third from the left on the center of three shelves.

Now, all this business with the duchess' first baby and Zade Fandey's monkeys and Prindal's List happened long ago, long before ElizabethAnn came to Bumblegreen, long before Jackson was ever called "the beast," and long, long before the duchess ever visited her own kitchen for "a little cucumber sandwich."

PART THREE

THE UNDERSTATED ELEGANCE

OF IMPOSSIBLE TASKS

THE UNDERSTATED ELEGANCE
OF IMPOSSIBLE TASKS

32

WHERE ELIZABETHANN RESEMBLES
A PSYCHIC SUPERHIGHWAY

ElizabethAnn, awakening in the magnolia tree's nest, noticed an enormous blue butterfly flap twice around her head, then settle on one of the tree's waxy leaves. The way it let itself be blown around on the wind and flapped its graceful, paperlike wings just enough to imbue its flight with purpose, she thought it the most beautiful thing she had ever seen.

Next, a couple of small, pink ones came around, flitted in and out of the branches, circled twice around her head, and fluttered off.

Soon, hundreds more butterflies of all sizes and colors spun, drifted, and danced inside the sun-dappled cavern made by the magnolia's arching boughs: small white ones like bits of tissue, enormous jungly green ones, tiny deep-purple ones, and multicolored butterflies with stripes and spots and unusual edging, like escaped tassels from velvet draperies.

When one rather large yellow and pink fellow perched on her nose, ElizabethAnn stared it straight in the eyes until she went cross-eyed, which served to open up her back-brain storage unit. By popping her ears and knuckles at once, making a kissy face, and tapping a very special rhythm with her toes—a rhythm that just seemed to come to her—she received her first vague telepathic message from the butterflies. She sensed distress.

With this new intuitive ability, she understood the need to raise her eyebrows as high as she could and cluck like a leghorn rooster. Using this technique and finally remembering why she had climbed up to the nest in the first place, ElizabethAnn telepathically asked the butterflies if any of them had seen her dog or grandmother.

From the butterflies, ElizabethAnn sensed, or heard, or intuited, a distinct "yes," as well as something about Grandma being imprisoned, imperiled, and in need of rescue. The butterflies then offered to take her to Grandma.

Knowing Jackson wasn't even inside the castle yet, she abandoned Earl's plan of sneaking inside to wait for her dog's dead-or-alive delivery. Instead, she allowed the butterflies to land on her shoulders, legs, and arms. Thousands of them squeezed ElizabethAnn with their tiny little feet, picked her up, and lifted her into the air. As she rose out of the nest, she noticed a glint, a gleam. A silver flask. *How did that get in there?* she briefly wondered, grabbing the flask and stuffing it in her pocket.

The butterflies gently lowered her all the way to the ground. As she drifted down, she remembered the painstaking climbing she had done just hours before and lamented that it had all been for nothing. Then, that big blue, the first one she'd seen, flew ahead, guiding the way to the lair of the very, very evil who-knows-what that had, according to the butterflies, imprisoned her grandmother.

As she stumbled down the path, sandwiched by butterflies fore and aft, ElizabethAnn became aware of a familiar humming carried on the wind, but The Drone was a day's travel away. This humming differed from The Drone's persistent buzz in that it felt more musical, like singing, and soon she deciphered it:

Run free, run free
Food nor drink nor money have I none
Find me in an ancient chamber
Skipping merrily hee

"Francine?" ElizabethAnn asked. "The other guy? You insects, are you there?"

"We're here," answered the butterflies, psychically, in unison.

"No, no, I'm talking to a bunch of mosquitoes, or gnats, or they might have been dust mites, I guess," ElizabethAnn replied, but this was confusing, so the butterflies didn't answer.

She ran down the path, and the hum-singing continued, though it faded in and out. In fact, the sound seemed, to ElizabethAnn, to waft on the wind, unconnected to anything or anyone. Then, suddenly, it ended, as if she had passed through a zone and left the sound behind.

ElizabethAnn tried to stop in her tracks and look back, but she couldn't. The butterflies gathered around her ears, clouded her vision, pushed her onward, until, with little choice in the matter, she continued down the path. Finally, the big blue butterfly in the lead stopped short in a forest clearing and hovered in midair.

There, ElizabethAnn noticed a tiny house, the size of a doll's house, set among patches of bare dirt, rotten logs, and a variety of wild grasses growing unchecked. Nearby, a pile of black and white clothing had been tossed into a heap among dirt, twigs, and decomposing matter, and a bow tie dangled helplessly from the edge of a jutting boulder.

The tiny house's rooftop reached just up to ElizabethAnn's elbows and shone in the evening sun, seeming to be encrusted with some sort of crystalline glitter. Tiny flagpoles surrounded the house, and ribbons attached to their tops flew proudly in the breeze. Rose petals had been wrapped around each and every picket of the tiny fence around the house's tiny front yard, constructed from mismatched patches of moss and pretty tumbled stones.

Colorful leaves made a walkway across the moss to the little front door, offset by a patio paved with bright berries embedded in polished, dried mud.

Orange polka dots, made from tomato seeds, decorated the tiny door itself. Little windows had been cut into the house's walls, and the framing around the windows, well, it looked like chips of gold. Real gold!

In fact, every square inch of the house's exterior glittered or shone with one colorful ornament or another. The strange dwelling caught the light from every direction, emitting a prismatic glow. It was, in short, the sort of thing no little girl could take her eyes off of under any circumstances, whatsoever.

Then, ElizabethAnn realized the flag posts around the house were actually silver candlesticks stuck into holes filled with dried mud, and the flags flying from them were actually hair ribbons—the very same ones that had long-ago fallen out of her own hair. Her ribbons!

A lanky man, whom she recognized as Fast Eddie, crouched at the side of the house, pounding Orange Slush bottle caps into the ground with a ball peen hammer, creating a tiny footpath through a tiny hedgerow bordering a tiny moss-lawn that appeared to have been clipped to a perfect barbershop trim with the very scissors that stuck out of his overalls bib pocket.

In the background, that same redheaded woman ElizabethAnn had seen running from the Duchess' mansion, so long ago, wore the same sassy black skirt, which was now sweat-stained, untucked, and strained at the seams. With a sledgehammer, she pounded a cut-crystal vase, which she had earlier wrapped in banana leaves and placed in a nest of twigs.

Shards of crystal, sparkling prettily with delicate rainbow reflections, flew with deadly force all around the clearing. When a dagger-like sliver whizzed past her ear, ElizabethAnn dove behind a fallen log. From there, she peeked through a tangle of branches to safely observe the unusual, and potentially deadly, scene.

Fast Eddie completely ignored the whizzing shards of pointed glass. He reached through the house's tiny windows with special tweezers to adjust a love seat made of canary feathers, place a fireside urn made from a carefully reshaped golden thimble, and glue in a mantel made from a matchbox.

Soon, the redhead tired of wielding the sledgehammer, abandoned her glass-smashing project, and commenced embedding golden chips in the clay of a tiny dining patio, just off the little house's back door.

ElizabethAnn approached Fast Eddie and crouched down to look inside the wonderful little house. There, she found emerald jewelry embedded in gold-leafed walls and translucent beads threaded on a tiny banister made of a twig, which ascended a stairway made of stacked, imported, breath mint tins. She passed her fingers over the house's strange textures and glittering designs.

Fast Eddie used a shish kebab skewer to reach through a window and hang a tiny framed picture over the tiny living room's tiny matchbox mantel and seemed not to notice ElizabethAnn at all. The redhead at the far end of the clearing now swung a pickaxe to reduce a golden candelabra to golden smithereens.

"Fast Eddie?" inquired ElizabethAnn, "I sure do admire your painstaking, um … This little house is, well, it's … I sure do like it, is all. I'd like a home like this myself, one day—only, life size."

Fast Eddie grunted, and she understood him to be deep in an artistic trance. He handed ElizabethAnn a pair of tweezers. She discovered a dish filled with tiny forest flowers that appeared to have been pressed flat between the pages of a rather comprehensive dictionary. Being a proactive girl, she got busy gluing the flowers to the house's few as-yet-undecorated walls.

The fact that ElizabethAnn's butterfly escorts whizzed in manic circles around the meadow and buffeted her body with aggressive little weightless sneak-attacks didn't distract her for a moment. Whatever they wanted from her, she figured, could wait. Little girls don't come across fantasy dollhouses of this nature too often; most, never.

Reaching through windows into the house's various rooms, Fast Eddie arranged furniture made of bent spoons and hurricane glass, each piece expertly upholstered with a scrap of embroidered tablecloth. Instantly, Elizabeth understood the anything-goes concept of the thing and set about constructing a credenza from slivers of broken crystal and swaths of linen napkin. In fact, she, too, fell deep into an artistic trance. That's when she heard the voice.

"I want you to know, I'm fine!" it said, directly into ElizabethAnn's head's interior space. Could have been Grandma's voice, but it could also have been a chipmunk with acorns stuffed in its cheeks. "Don't try to rescue me!" it said.

ElizabethAnn, at the moment, wasn't trying to rescue anyone. She had never been deep in an artistic trance before, had never felt the peace. So, for once, she forgot all about Grandma, Jackson, the summons, Earl, and the monkey tribunal itself, whatever that was. She felt at home, for once. Not in Bumblegreen, exactly, but in her skin. She had gone deep—to a deeper place than even Grandma could reach.

Leave me alone, ElizabethAnn thought at the voice. *Go away, you illusion of Grandma.*

"It's me, kiddo. It's really me!" said the chipmunk Grandma voice.

Grandma? thought ElizabethAnn. *Can you come back later?*

"Not really! I've got instructions for you!"

Whatever, thought ElizabethAnn. She didn't mean to think it at Grandma. She just did.

"Is this thing working right?" she heard Grandma say, faintly. "Is the dial on dollhouse? Is the toggle set to butterflies?"

ElizabethAnn sewed a tiny mattress, stuffed it with feathers, and set it up in a tiny bedroom along with a tiny headboard made of mushroom tops. The world had disappeared for ElizabethAnn, for the first time, which made her realize how *there* the world usually was.

"ElizabethAnn?" asked the voice. "Are you there?"

I'm here, thought ElizabethAnn. *I'm more here than ever.*

"Everything hinges on you, kiddo," said the voice, "it's an important mission!"

ElizabethAnn reached through a window and wallpapered a tiny bedroom with fresh green leaves. She debated the use of each of a variety of available resins for the purpose. She tested them, experimented, evaluated.

"I don't think I'm getting through to her," she heard Grandma say, and ElizabethAnn remembered how important *Important Missions* used to seem, but only faintly.

"I've broken a law, ElizabethAnn, called the Universal Portal Compact," said Grandma. "I'm a fugitive."

Now why would you go and do that? wondered ElizabethAnn.

"Actually, you've broken it, too," Grandma said, "but no one knows you. No one knows you came through a portal. Me, they know. Me, they could arrest, imprison, drop into a pool of angry sharks, or whatever."

A cloud passed slowly over the meadow while Fast Eddie perfected his mantelpiece. The redhead, off in the distance, smashed something. ElizabethAnn ran out of green-leaf wallpaper.

The sun emerged again from behind the cloud, the tiny house sparkled and gleamed anew, and ElizabethAnn thought, *Okay, let's go home then, Grandma. Where do I surrender?*

"Have you forgotten about the 'home'?" asked Grandma's voice inside her head—now, a bit more emotional and chipmunky than before.

A vision of a bright room came to ElizabethAnn, then: swirling colors and desperate voices, a room both light and dark at once, a place both wonderful and evil. Overwhelmed by the vision, ElizabethAnn sat on a log and shut her eyes. She knew the room she saw wasn't Grandma's 'home,' but someplace else.

"Find Shadooda, ElizabethAnn! Only Shadooda can prove my innocence, restore Bumblegreen's magic, and let me come out of hiding!" said the chipmunk Grandma voice.

ElizabethAnn stood, stomped her feet, hummed a tune louder and louder, and marched around the field: anything to rid her mind of the chipmunk voice, the butterfly entreaties, and the confusing images. But the one voice she wanted to get back—the silent voice of nothingness she had found in her artistic trance, her own voice—she couldn't find again. ElizabethAnn's mind felt like a psychic superhighway. That's how she learned about the elusive nature of momentary inner peace, and it made her sad … sadder than a little girl should ever have to be.

33

IN WHICH THE QUEEN MANAGES
TO SOUND VERY GROWN-UP

"Your Highness!" squealed the duchess, after the reverberations of the traditional gong and trumpets had died down.

The duchess' cook, Tammy, whom the duchess had recently declared a genius for suggesting she invite the queen to her garden party, had scampered down to the castle kitchen to learn the queen's favorite dessert. Meanwhile, the duchess entered the throne room thinking she and Tammy about the cleverest party planners on the planet.

"Iris? Is that you?" asked Queen Dahlia, sounding less than thrilled but more than bored. She had snuggled into the cushions of her throne, tucking the royal feet up, as any thirteen-year-old in a wistful moment is wont to do. "Mind those Affairs of State files and just skooch past the firewood," she said, gesturing broadly at the active workshop her throne room had become. "Sorry about the mess."

"Sure, it's me!" replied the duchess. "How you doing, honey?" Their bond as childhood playmates allowed the duchess' overly familiar tone.

"Oh, I'm fine, I guess," the queen said. "Did you come with complaints? Not sure I can handle any more complaints today, Iris. If it's not the cheese, it's the portals. If it's not the portals, it's the harvest. If it's not the harvest, it's someone's livestock got loose. Oh, and if it's not any of those, it's this 'beast' nonsense. I don't even think there really is a beast, but I sent the war party off on a mission, anyway. Keep them out of my hair."

"Beast?" queried the duchess.

"Just a silly rumor!" Dahlia said. "Tell me some good news, Iris. Anything at all will do."

"I'm having a party, darling!" gushed the duchess, "and you're invited!"

The queen smiled graciously, but her eyes held a shadow that didn't surprise the duchess. After all, the duchess hadn't always been the best of friends to young Dahlia, who, in her youth, had been the type of odd and lonely child likely to suffer abuse by cruel children and thoughtless adults alike. Of course, being a princess, a protective royal bubble had saved Princess Dahlia from ever knowing her status as an unhip, uncool loner, but the duchess, who hadn't enjoyed such a bubble, had always profoundly resented this fact. Even though she stood ten years Dahlia's senior, the duchess' resentment of the princess was deeply rooted, especially since that day, long ago, in the swampy lowlands.

After inviting the queen to her party, the duchess made small talk, then threaded her way out of the throne room, past various piles of accumulated junk left in the corners and aisles.

As the duchess exited, Queen Dahlia silently congratulated herself on doing a good job of neither accepting nor rejecting the invitation. Dahlia had said she would be delighted to come if she could find the time, which sounded very busy and grown-up to her, very *I have so many better things to do*, even though she didn't, actually.

Immediately, a regent announced the queen's next visitor.

"Send him in," sighed Dahlia with a grand, sarcastic wave of her jelly-limp arm.

The widest, flattest man she had ever seen shuffled in, wearing a bedraggled toga made from a velvet curtain. One of the queen's regents had wrapped it around the fellow in propriety-conscious haste.

Queen Dahlia insisted upon seeing anyone and everyone who wanted an audience, which of course caused this never-ending and highly annoying onslaught of visitors, but, being a conscientious child, she felt awfully bad about all the years it had taken to cure the kingdom of the terrible blight. She felt awfully bad, too, about the baby-allergy problem that had ensued as soon as she closed the portals to stop the blight, and also about how everyone had to have their babies raised by monkeys, because of that. And, of course, she had Zade Fandey's disease to feel bad about, too—an entirely new problem resulting from the technology that had solved the baby allergy.

Dahlia felt bad about everything that had happened in Bumblegreen pretty much since she took office and thought perhaps her destitute subjects might feel better if they could come and talk to her in person. Giving her subjects an audience seemed like the least she could do.

Sometimes, it was also the most she could do. And sometimes, frankly, she just wanted the company. With the gypsies gone, she hadn't friends anymore, poor thing. Of course the young queen heard no end of complaints about her come-one-come-all policy from her heartless regents, who would have liked to cast most of the scruffy visitors down the nearest well.

Dahlia watched the bedraggled man shamble in on cut and bloody feet—the absurd length of velvet wrapped around his wide, flat torso, mummy-like. Curtain loops hung off his shoulder like ceremonial fringe and periodically bounced and swung as his feet shuffled nervously beneath him.

"Your Highness," the wide, flat man said. "I'll get right to the point."

"Oh, please do."

"I ask only for a chance to leave this world behind me. My wife was killed by the blight. My little girls … well, I never had a chance to see them grow up … The blight, you know."

The wide, flat man shed a tear and didn't speak again until the droplet had traced a clear path all the way down to his chin and disappeared in the folds, there. He continued, "My farm was burned by the sanitation police, and now I have no place to even lay my head."

"Dear man, dear man, there must be something worth living for," she dutifully replied.

"With respect, Your Highness, you misunderstand," he said. "It's not that I want to die. You see, I've heard of these portals to other worlds, and I'm respectfully asking to descend through one. I just want a single portal to be opened so I can dive out of Bumblegreen. I don't know, maybe I'll get lucky and the parallel world I find will be a nice one. Anything would be better than this … surrounded by memories of my girls.”

The man let out a wail and a sob, which frankly seemed contrived to Dahlia. She had seen this sort of thing before.

"And maybe if you could leave the portal open for a bit,” he continued, "just in case the other world is maybe not so great … waddaya say, Your Highness?”

The queen thought his large, expectant eyes and pleading tent-shaped brow gave him the look of a hungry macaque and suppressed a giggle before shaking her head.

"I should lecture you,” she said, "on the irresponsibility of introducing Bumblegreen germs—your germs, and I daresay you seem to have your share—to another world. It'd be unconscionable, you know. But I'm not going to bother with all that. Here's a chit for five wheels of cheese. You can sell them, eat them, use them for a bed pillow, if you want. That will be all.”

Then Dahlia, feeling utterly queenly whenever she did it, licked her finger, deftly swiped a chit from a stack, and offered it in her upturned palm.

An aide announced, "The bedraggled man may approach!”

Schrank took the chit, careful not to touch the queen's flesh, then changed his mind, grasped her hand, fell to his knees, and sobbed.

Dahlia looked down at him, wanting to feel his pain, wanting to care just a little, wanting to shed a tear on his behalf, but she had had her fill of pathos for the day. Her mind wandered, wondering if she had already seen too much to feel anything anymore for anyone. Except embarrassment, she knew she could still feel that but didn't feel it, now. In fact, she felt nothing and sighed at the lack.

On his way out, the man tripped over his curtain toga and went sprawling, which Dahlia politely pretended not to see.

The queen figured she ought to report this last visit of the day to

Horace, her chief of security. The wide, flat man, with his desire to break the Universal Portal Compact, could make trouble if he somehow found a portal and somehow opened it … but no, that was impossible … but still. So, Queen Dahlia gathered her enormous collection of billowing skirts into as tight a ball as possible and padded, happily barefoot, past the detritus stacked here and there in the throne room and down a stone hallway lined with grandiose oaken doors.

Various staff members and petty nobility ever-so-helpfully pointed her down branching hallways, past mysterious alcoves, and up winding staircases, until she finally found the castle's security chamber. Dahlia could never remember where anything was anymore, since the extensive castle-to-cheese-factory renovation. In the chamber, Dahlia addressed Horace, her chief of security, a dwarfish fellow who spent his idle time working out with a set of rusty free weights.

"Horace! Man!" she said. "We've got to move your office! I can never find this place!"

"It's because of the castle-to-cheese-factory renovation, Your Highness," Horace replied. "Whuff!" He did a bicep curl.

"Now, listen here," she protested. "How else were people supposed to eat during the blight? I mean really, Horace. I had to do it!"

"It's okay, Your Highness," he replied, pumping a barbell once, then twice. "I know. The people … needed … cheese." He dropped the barbell onto its stand with a harsh, metallic clang. "They needed it, then. Whuff! But now? I don't know." He commenced another set of curls.

"But what else can I do for them?" the queen whined.

"You've got a big heart, Your Highness," Horace said. "No one can say different. But at this point, we could actually convert it back to a castle. The blight's long over. You know? Whuff!" In a single motion, he jerked a barbell overhead.

"Yes, yes, I'll think about it," she said. "Anyway, a remarkably wide, flat man approached me about opening a portal, today. That's what I came to tell you."

"A wide, flat man?" Horace repeated.

"Yes, the widest, flattest man I've ever seen," she said. "Have the guards keep an eye out, would you? I've a feeling he could start trouble."

"Yes, Your Highness," Horace said. "Would that feeling be your royal intuition at work?"

"Oh, I don't think so, Horace," she said. "It's probably just the regular kind."

"Whuff!" he said. "I'll spread the word."

34

In Which Georgie and
Schrank Concoct a Scheme

Georgie powered up her homemade flying machine, bounced down a runway, and rose into the crisp, autumnal air. By the time she arrived, dappled with goose poop, at the old barn Shrank had set up as a makeshift headquarters for the until-recently-dormant Favra Watch Company, she found him halfway through the contents of a coffee thermos and pacing.

"I had a meeting with the queen, today," Schrank said, "and tried a certain technique to convince her to open a portal, so we can get this

Favra thing off the ground, but no-go. She didn't buy my act for a minute."

"Perhaps," Georgie suggested, "we could frame the idea of opening the portal as a 'temporary' maneuver deemed necessary due to some 'national emergency' situation."

She then proceeded to discuss a scheme whereby a scientist who had, shall we say, a little self-interest in the project, would be hired to write out a plausible 'environmental catastrophe' scheme.

"In the meantime, though," Georgie added, "we need that prototype back!"

Schrank groaned and said, "I thought that was your job."

"It is," she said. "I'm working on it."

"It's hopeless," Schrank muttered, covering his face, "You'll never find that monkey. He might have thrown the watch in a river by now or smashed it or gotten killed and eaten by a bear. I mean, he's a *monkey*!"

"That wasn't just any monkey," said Georgie. "It was a Bumblegreen monkey. A Zade Fandey technologically advanced monkey. Pretty sure he's figured out how to use the watch by now. In fact, he's probably already trading stocks and checking his blood pressure."

"Great," said Schrank. "So now I have to worry about the ape reverse-engineering my invention?"

"Possibly," Georgie replied. "They're supposed to be domestically oriented, the monkeys. They're not businessmen, but things go awry a lot around here. An awful lot, in fact."

"What have you done to me?" Schrank hollered.

"I'm not the monkey, remember?" Georgie said, patiently. "I didn't steal the watch. All I did was tell you I could get it back. And I can. I'm sure I can. You'll see. I'll get you that watch and we'll both soon be rich beyond our wildest dreams."

"We better!" Schrank said.

"It's just a matter of thinking like a monkey—something I'm quite used to, in fact," said Georgie with a wink. She strode to the barn's open hayloft, leapt from it onto a branch of a tree, and disappeared into the foliage.

35

WHEREIN DAHLIA SHIVERS
AT A DREADFUL THOUGHT

Completely oblivious to the fact that over the weekend Earl, Grandma, ElizabethAnn, and Jackson, in that order, had breached the seal between worlds and begun a universe-altering course of events that no amount of magic or science could undo, Queen Dahlia indulged in a leisurely garden walk. On her walk, she mused on yesterday's meeting with Horace and her regents, where they discussed this strange beast that was supposedly abroad in the land.

"It seems," Horace had said, in-between tensing and releasing his right and left pectoralis majoris muscles, "a rumor has taken hold. Something about a strange and horrible beast being abroad."

The regents had then quizzed Horace as to the nature of the beast while Queen Dahlia sat on her throne, fighting off her costume's bejeweled accents and stiff bows, which constantly interfered with even the most basic motor functions. Horace had then suggested a war party be sent out in search of the beast, so Queen Dahlia, unthinking, approved the mission with a lazy wave of a heavily beringed hand.

Afterwards, the queen forgot all about the beast business; that is, up until she mentioned it to the duchess the next morning. Still, she figured the rumor nothing but a hoax. Imagine, then, her surprise when, as she strolled the garden, Queen Dahlia saw her war chariots galloping off, banners streaming and coaches gleaming. Oddly, she also spotted a lone figure running behind the last chariot.

Dahlia almost yelled out, "Hey! Wait for that guy!" but caught herself just in time, realizing such impulsive behavior wouldn't befit her queenly stature. Dahlia guessed she was probably supposed to pretend she didn't see that lone figure, or maybe she was supposed to not care. Actually, most of the time, Dahlia had no idea what she was supposed to do or say, but whatever it was, it was surely the opposite of her natural inclination—that much she had learned about queening in the last four years.

While she pondered these mysteries of etiquette, the lone figure leaped aboard the cannon strapped to the back of the last chariot. *See*, Dahlia thought. *Sometimes these things resolve themselves.* That seemed a very queenly sort of thought, so she plucked a violet and tucked it behind her ear.

By the time the queen returned to her private chambers, she was overcome with the sudden inexplicable melancholy to which every

Bumblegreen royal is prone. She collapsed on her mammoth canopied, curtained bed, eased the heel out of one slipper, and dropped the shoe soundlessly onto a sheepskin rug.

She picked up her favorite import, a Magic 8-Ball, and watched the edges of its answer cuboid bobbing and swirling in a mysterious blue liquid. When the Magic 8-Ball finally displayed its message, she read, *discover whom you can trust.*

"Interesting," Dahlia mumbled as she rose, changed her earrings, and absently rifled through a file labeled *Affairs of State* that some well-meaning staffer had slid under her door. Tucking it under her arm, she sighed, stood, and wiggled her foot back into the slipper.

The queen left the royal bedchambers and wandered out into the castle's grand gallery, where wrought-iron chandeliers loomed overhead, suspended from a true cathedral ceiling with a peak well up in the stratosphere.

A stained-glass window cast eerie blood-red reflections on the ancient room's enveloping stone. Propped slightly open, the window let in a merciful, magical breeze. A thread of sunbeam carried the scent of moist forestlands beyond. The corridor, with its cold stone and enormous expanse, made a joke of little Dahlia, so alone, like an ant that had lost its trail.

As she padded along through the grand gallery, the queen idly wondered what these latest Affairs of State were all about. She noticed someone had compiled them into a set of collated manila folders with varicolored tabs all along the edges. While she walked, her voluminous taffeta skirts rustled incessantly, creating the only sound in the vast, empty place. She finally reached a pair of giant wooden doors, muscled the latch back, and leaned into them until they squeaked open just enough to let her squeeze into the throne room.

At one end of the cavernous room, a stage stretched from end to end. Embedded in the stage floor lay a trapdoor whose rusty hinges attested to ages of disuse. At the stage's center sat the jewel-encrusted throne where the queen received her visitors. Beside the throne, a giant gleaming lever stuck out of the floor. Carved walls reached up, up, up, to a ceiling so high it vanished behind a series of crisscrossed beams, where pigeons roosted now and again and where the queen often heard mice squeaking their high-altitude lives away.

In the walls, doorways led to stairways, which led up to magnificent box seats, one on either side of the stage, designed to keep the royals in safe isolation from the masses. The room had been built, of course, for grand occasions such as coronations, weddings, and the like. For any such occasion, laws stated one percent of Bumblegreen's population must be present, so the room stood prepared for standing-room-only crowds.

Nowadays, Dahlia used the throne room for visiting hours and storage, but she never forgot it was also designed for another, quite-unpleasant purpose. Right smack in the middle of the room's empty floor, an iron cage stood, bolted to the ground. This way, the people crowded around could look a prisoner in the eye, hear his last words.

The lever beside the throne, if pushed, would set into motion a series of gears, pulleys, and belts that would drop the floor beneath the cage and dump the cage's inhabitants with great screaming drama down a twenty-foot free fall into an underground chamber that could, at royal discretion, be stocked with alligators, boiling oil, a forest of cactus, stinging nettles in flower, swimming hungry sharks, or whatever. In all her five years of queening, she had never pressed that lever and never planned to.

A dozen rusting pikes lay toppled like pickup sticks in one corner of the throne room, and the east wall now served to keep stacks of firewood out of the rain. Balls of moth-eaten yarn occupied another area, and years' worth of disintegrating cardboard boxes labeled *Affairs of State* listed against one another along the south wall.

The queen scampered across the room, dropped the file she carried, unread, into one of the *Affairs of State* boxes, then drew an elegant sleeve up over her face as a puff of dust emerged upon impact. Thoroughly relieved to be rid of the fussy, grown-up-ish document, she squeezed back through the heavy throne-room door, and, with steps so light she nearly skipped, returned to her royal bedchambers to be dressed for another day of avoiding responsibility.

36

In Which ElizabethAnn Finds a Source of Internal Light

ElizabethAnn tried to remember peace of mind and recall its characteristics, but the voices of both the butterflies and Grandma assailed her—asking for help, asking for someone named Shadooda, warning about dire fates awaiting, and insisting she, ElizabethAnn herself, must be the savior of them all.

She cared … but, oh, she didn't care as much as she thought she ought. Mostly, ElizabethAnn wanted to get back to her work making miniatures for the tiny house in a field in the middle of the

Bumblegreen woods. She felt, somehow, that that might actually be the key to finding Jackson, freeing Grandma, and discovering the whereabouts of this Shadooda person.

While she worked, she came to realize how much she, too, needed a home. Going back to life with her parents, the Von Earps, didn't seem possible anymore. What used to feel like real life, for her, would now be little more than a placeholder. She fantasized that she could fit inside the tiny house, live there, and bring Grandma and Jackson, too. ElizabethAnn picked up some golden shards, bright leaves, beads, baubles, silver cutlery—various of Fast Eddie's raw materials—but didn't return to her work just yet, because of a sudden thirst.

"Check your pocket," said a butterfly voice, inside her brain.

She reached into the pocket of her stained, ripped, rumpled, blue-flowered dress and fetched out the mysterious silver flask. She shook it, heard sloshing, and unscrewed the lid. Hoping the flask contained something fruit-punch flavored, ElizabethAnn took a swig.

All of a sudden, the tiny dollhouse was no longer tiny. It loomed before her, life-size. The surrounding forest loomed as well, giant size. The butterflies circling overhead looked like dragons, now, and she could see the caterpillariness of their hairy, meaty bodies. *Oh,* she thought, *that's awfully unattractive.* The world hadn't become bigger. It was just that ElizabethAnn had shrunk, and she figured this out pretty quickly.

Viewing the dollhouse from this new vantage point, she thought it looked even more beautiful and inviting than before. She walked across the now-life-size moss lawn, along the bottle-cap walkway, past a grass-stem forest, and up to the formerly tiny door. She knocked and heard footsteps inside go ticker-tack, ticker-tack. Then, the tiny door swung open.

Before her stood a smartly dressed bird in silver vest, tiny slippers of gold, and a puckish cap made of a brilliant green leaf. He was so decorated, in fact, and strutting in such a proud manner that, at first, ElizabethAnn didn't actually realize he was a bird, but then she noticed his beak, tail feathers, and round beady eyes.

"Hello there," she said. "I'm ElizabethAnn."

"Pleased to meet you, little girl! Bill Bramble!" said the bird, adding, "And, goodness, but you are beautiful!"

ElizabethAnn went all soft inside, until the bird added, "I'd like to have you for my collection!"

"I don't know about that," she replied, "but may I come in?"

"Oh, certainly not," said the bird. "No, no, I never let anyone in. This house is a work of art, you see. A very private work of art and I … oh no, no, no, no."

The butterfly voices inside her head instructed ElizabethAnn that she must, under any and all circumstances, get inside that house, and quickly.

"In that case, I'd like my hair ribbons back!" ElizabethAnn yelled, as if upset. She stamped her tiny foot and marched right over to one of the candlesticks serving as flagpoles, at the top of which her lost ribbons fluttered in the breeze. She kicked at the mud around the candlestick's base, then clawed at it with her hands, as if intending to upend the entire thing. The act was just as provocative as she had hoped.

"No! No! You mustn't!" screamed the effete little bird. "You mustn't! Hands absolutely positively OFF!" He twitched as if having some sort of fit, pecked at ElizabethAnn's hands, and screamed, "You're ruining everything!"

"What? Ruining this collection of junk?" ElizabethAnn taunted.

"What kind of fool are you?" countered the bird. "I've every kind of perfectly bright shiny little thing in this house you can even imagine. It's perfectly lovely in every way and much better than any old ordinary house made of sticks and bricks!"

"I don't think it's so great," ElizabethAnn said, goading the bird, "I mean on the outside, sure, but in there … I bet the inside's just as plain as this mud!"

"Plain as mud! I … well …" Bill Bramble blustered and fumed. His feathers turned red and pink and purple. He hopped on one leg, stuck his head beneath his wing, ruffled his tail, and made some very strange, unbirdlike sounds, finally adding, "I'll show you, you rude little thing! I'll show you something no one's ever tried before!"

"Hmph," ElizabethAnn replied, standing now on the seemingly normal-sized lawn of the (to her newly tiny self) normal-sized house, noticing hundreds of now-dragon-like butterflies waiting in a nearby tree, rather conspicuously, for her to do something-or-other that involved getting inside that house. In the meantime, Grandma's faint voice echoed in her head, saying, "Find Shadooda!"

Just as she had hoped, Bill Bramble ushered ElizabethAnn inside and took her on a tour of the place: east wing, west wing, the works. One wall was covered in snakeskin, another with toucan feathers arranged in zigzag patterns, and up near the ceiling, a molding of what looked like golden beads extended all the way around a room.

"Golden beads!" gasped ElizabethAnn, then caught herself. "Oh, they're probably not real golden beads. They're probably only pebbles painted with a golden paint you made from smashing up yellow bugs or something and adding a little passionflower paste or something. This is the jungle, after all, and you're only a bird, I guess, or whatever."

Bill harrumphed, stuck his beak in the air, and led her down another hallway, where ElizabethAnn saw a pedestal, all pink and white. *Perhaps,* she thought, *it's a table, a bed for a bird … a desk? A tap dancing stage?* It was decorated with rows of pearls and tiny pink blossoms, and ElizabethAnn, who dearly loved pink, thought she may never have seen anything so beautiful in her life.

"And these pearls?" she asked. "I suppose they're not real, are they?"

He didn't answer but strutted and keened around the pedestal, obviously full of pride but anxious about something.

"They must just be pebbles painted with the sap of a tree, or bleached in the sun, or something," she said.

"Actually, my dear, these are real pearls," the bird whispered dramatically, adding, "Yes! I'm connected! I have birds … uh, bird 'friends,' let's call them, who fly far distances for me. You see, I can't fly anymore because of, *you know*. I might be up in the sky and then suddenly turn. That's a nasty fall. Nasty! So, these birds make it their business to get things for me. I have *needs*," he stated in reply to numerous additional unasked questions, including the one that goes, *So, what's the point of all this?*

"I have to have certain things," he added. "I get these ideas, visions really, and I have to make them. HAVE TO MAKE THEM! I'm an artist. I don't know if you know what that's like."

ElizabethAnn wasn't listening anymore, as she had found an arch that opened upon a newish wing of the house, where a source of internal light shone through from the other side.

"There's nothing there," said Bill, but ElizabethAnn saw rainbow reflections and heard a voice whisper, "Frangipani!"

She walked down a dark tunnel, toward the source of light.

"No! No!" Bill Bramble cawed. "The tour is over! That's the end! Thanks for visiting! Off-limits! Off-limits!"

ElizabethAnn wandered farther, softly calling, "Grandma?"

37

WHEREIN THE QUEEN PRETENDS TO BE A REGULAR GIRL

Dahlia returned to her bedroom, where a chambermaid armed with a powder puff whisked every speck of residual throne room dust from her royal person. Meanwhile, Dahlia felt mighty pleased with herself for dispensing of this last Affairs of State file so handily. The chambermaid subsequently outfitted Dahlia in a charming navy-striped milkmaid outfit, with a baby blue apron all down the front. And no, that's not your typical queenly attire.

The queen's milkmaid outfit had been carefully designed (by

herself) as a clever little get-up for cheese making. It wasn't majestic, regal, or imposing in the least, and gave Dahlia a break from all those billowing skirts, bejeweled ornaments, and elaborate headdresses. In fact, people seldom recognized Queen Dahlia when she wore the disguise, which she didn't mind at all.

When Dahlia made cheese, she wanted to be a worker, a commoner, an ordinary girl. She didn't look one bit the royal in her calico farm dress, apron, and thin cotton slip, even to the point where she pulled her shock of dirty blonde curls back into a bonnet—an ugly bonnet, too.

Dahlia imagined other commoners surrounding her, one day, ignorant of her true identity, acting perfectly normal. She imagined going out among them and making friends. Perhaps, she dared to dream, she could even catch a beau in an ordinary dress like this. In this dress, Dahlia imagined, she could talk with other milkmaids of typical girlish pursuits … one day, perhaps. A queen could dream, anyway.

"Off to make the cheese, then," she sang to her attendants.

With that, Queen Dahlia dashed down some stairs, emerged in the sitting room, passed through the armory, and ran up a winding staircase to the rooftop coop of royal pigeons, where she stopped for a visit with her avian pets (another of Dahlia's secret pastimes). Specifically, she enjoyed naming and renaming the pigeons as they molted and changed nesting places and she lost track of who was whom.

Upon the parapet—surrounded on two sides by sheer drops and on two other sides by the high stone walls of turrets with their tops in the clouds—Dahlia cooed to Samuel and Djem-djem and little Katerina, her favorite pigeons of the moment.

That's when wide, flat Jimothy Schrank, wearing a tight, sweat-stained T-shirt, suit pants, and what he thought was a very real-looking lumberjack beard, blundered through a door and approached unsuspecting Dahlia, who busily babbled at her birds in the addlepated manner some people do with pets.

"Where's the queen?" Schrank demanded.

Startled, Dahlia spun to face him. "Who's asking?" she replied, in her gutsy milkmaid persona. She didn't recognize Schrank, even though he had, the very day before, confronted her during visiting hours wearing a velvet curtain as a toga. The voluminous fake beard threw her off, as did the lack of a toga—also, Schrank never turned to the side, so she couldn't notice his odd dimensions. Meanwhile, Schrank himself didn't recognize the queen without her usual headdress, face paint, and layers of skirts and gauzy accents.

Schrank's glued-on beard bounced merrily as he pulled out a business card that read, "Favra. Read my face," then, "Jimothy Schrank, CEO."

"Yeah? So?" asked the queen, as milkmaid, after reading the card.

"I have an appointment with the queen. Please go and fetch her at once," Shrank replied.

"I see," said the queen. "So the queen should be expecting you? You're telling me the queen should be expecting you, at this hour of the morning, at, I mean, the royal pigeon coop, of all places? How did you get past security anyway, you, you, you ..." She gestured wordlessly at his indecent attire, seeming to imply a dearth of grammatically acceptable phrases to describe it.

"I beg your pardon, miss," said Schrank. "I made an appointment through the Affairs of State office, you see, just yesterday. There were boxes to check on the sixteenth page of the form, you see, that allowed one to request various meeting places. And, in an impulsive moment, I actually checked 'pigeon coop,' thinking it'd be very private and out-of-the-way. And there were times of day, and one could check a preferred time, so I checked ten a.m., you see, because I go for a jog at noon, before a lengthy lunch. And, you see, the form continued in this manner right down to the day of the week requested, alternate venues for rain, acts of God, and suchlike and also a whole next-of-kin page, in case, I suppose, the queen threw me in the big iron cage consequent to the meeting.

"Ha ha," he added, mirthlessly.

Schrank spoke the truth. He had done all those things and filled out all those forms. He had actually picked the pigeon coop as part of his Plan B, hoping to catch the queen off guard, which he had indeed done. But this time, thanks to Horace's vigilance, the castle guards had recognized Schrank as he entered the grounds. He glanced back over his shoulder as he spoke.

"I expected the page at the desk to recommend a more appropriate venue, you see," Schrank said, "but he just took the form, looked at it front and back, like he'd never seen one before, then took this big stamp and stamped it. I believe the stamp said, 'confirmed,' or 'definite,' or perhaps 'irrevocable,' or something else with a similar sense of dire finality. Then, the young fellow—with cheese on his face, I remember, Camembert, actually—seated behind the desk, he said, 'Well, oooookay, then,' which I took as a kind of hip, modern form of official confirmation. So, yes, I do believe I have an appointment," which was, in fact, true.

"Oh," said the queen-as-milkmaid. Her face fell considerably. "I'm afraid I can't help you. The queen's gone out riding."

"Riding? Oh, dear! You see, it's rather important," replied Schrank. "Of course, I described the unusual circumstances of this meeting in the form itself, and there should have been a report issued by an environmental commission as well, based upon research, you see. It's very important research. It's dire. It's dire! Of dire importance to the kingdom, environmentally, having to do with a certain polymer. But anyway, that's confidential, dire and confidential. I need to know the queen's decision about this. Its … well … as I mentioned, it's … it's dire," Schrank concluded, running out of adjectives and shuffling his feet beneath him as if trying to destroy an infestation of small bugs.

"It's rather an urgent, some might even say 'life and death' Matter of State. I do hope the queen has decided to meet with me," he grumbled. "Otherwise, oh … I just don't know."

"And why, may I ask—not that it's any business of mine—didn't you just pop in during visiting hours like everyone else?" asked the queen.

"Visiting? Oh. There's … visiting hours?" Schrank bluffed. "I could … you mean that long form and all the next of kin and twenty-five pages wasn't … absolutely … necessary? Oh, dear. But I do have a special appointment! Can't you run and find the queen? I'm sure she'll come, I mean if she knows what it's about. It's official State Business and of serious environmental import. I represent an agency, you see. It's research we do."

"What agency?"

"Impact. That's what we're called."

"I thought it was Favra," said the queen, who finally thought she recognized Schrank.

"It is. I mean, that's one of my … I also represent Impact, an environmental agency."

"Do you have a calling card from Impact?" she asked, still unsure whether the man's story was legitimate.

"Oh, no. Not at the moment," Shrank improvised. "You see it's a very complex, difficult-to-explain situation with the two agencies and their relationships. You wouldn't understand."

"Wouldn't I?" asked the queen-as-milkmaid, batting her oh-so-peasant-looking lashes.

Dahlia heard the sound of many running feet, then a banging on the door through which the man had just come. The queen now saw that Schrank had barred the door behind him. His sweat-stained shirt broke out in fresh spots of moisture, and he darted a fearful glance toward the door. Clearly, its old boards could only hold out so long against the repetitive banging.

"As you see," he said, "there are those who would have this information kept from the queen! There are those who profit from keeping it well hidden, if you get my meaning. As you see, I'm being pursued! I have information the queen needs, and I, frankly, need the queen's protection terribly. As you can see, these pursuers have already ripped my sport coat and dress shirt from my back, but I evaded them and kept on!"

The pounding on the door grew louder, with more and more fists, and was joined by voices raised in alarm. Dahlia tried to decide whether Schrank was really a base criminal using a highly unusual subterfuge to mislead her with cockeyed theories about her precious portal polymer (which would have explained his being chased by castle guards) or a bona fide scientist who actually filled out those absurd forms to get this special audience, and his mission really was an important Matter of State. If that were the case, then the people pursuing him could be her regents, who were always trying to keep things from her.

Either way, Dahlia figured that Affairs of State file, which she had, just moments ago, carelessly tossed into a dusty box, probably held the answer.

One thing was sure. The queen-as-milkmaid wasn't about to reveal her true identity to this strange bearded fellow. Furthermore, she was too embarrassed about her ignorance in this supposed Matter of State to simply go over and speak through the rapidly splintering slats of the door and find out why her security personnel (or whomever) pursued the man so avidly.

Plus, she thought, *who knows if the enraged castle guards will even tell me the truth? They could be "protecting me," as my stupid regents usually demand.*

Dahlia concluded there was only one way to figure out if the bearded man could be trusted, and it was to go back and read that Affairs of State file.

"Well," said the queen to Schrank, "it *is* the weekend, you know."

"I know," said Schrank, hanging his head in the abashed manner of one aware of how much red tape lies between himself and that which he seeks.

Dahlia acted casual. She opened the pigeon coop's door and made a show of checking water dish and food levels while allowing several of the birds to perch on her arm. She hummed a wistful tune as she imagined a peasant might. Then, she flung her arm in Schrank's direction.

Djem-djem, Samuel, and little Katerina flew in his face. Shrank fell backward in cursing shock and outrage, sneezing violently at the assault of down, dander, and dust, while the queen ran back through the door by which she had entered, barred it behind her, hot-footed it down the spiral staircase, and dashed back the way she had come.

"Affairs of State. Affairs of State. Affairs of State. Affairs of State," Dahlia chanted as she raced down one hallway and another, gradually becoming lost in the castle's labyrinthine passages, seeking a route back to the throne room.

Many dead ends later, the queen exited into a courtyard and leaped an iron gate with inches to spare. Intending to cut through the royal equestrian center and reenter the castle from the west wing, where she knew her way around much better, she charged into the quagmire of amber and umber horse-piss-saturated mud that stood between herself and those Affairs of State files.

Soon ankle-deep in muck and fighting its sucking pull, she shoved a horse's hindquarters out of the way and charged thickly forward through the mire. "My kingdom for a pair of galoshes," she muttered, as she trudged.

Each step through the paddock's stinking squish brought the queen's shoes closer and closer to meeting their makers. The nails got sucked out of the soles, and bits of leather flapped around in places they didn't used to. Every time Dahlia thought she might have found an old board, a rock, or a hunk of hay to step gingerly upon, thus evading the quagmire, that board, rock, or hunk would itself sink into the very bowels of the earth. (And bowels were definitely a theme, there in the horse yard.) The queen tried not to think about where she was and the possible ill-boding to her health from such general ickiness.

By the time she reached the center of the paddock, the damage to her dress, certainly, was irreversible; to the shoes, unspeakable; to the dainty handmade lace of her thin cotton slip, lamentable; and to her personal psyche … well, there's no telling. Yet, the determined queen forged ahead, pursued by a looming fear of total humiliation, which, to tell the truth, loomed more often than most of her subjects, regents, and acquaintances could ever know.

She charged through the equestrian center with prize-winning single-mindedness and eventually reached the split-rail fence at the end of the paddock which, somehow, as if by magic (although magic was ever so out of style) delineated an impossibly perfect border between the filthy paddock and a fresh, grassy meadow studded with black-eyed Susans and Queen Anne's lace, which stretched out before her like a content dog after dinner.

Dahlia so wanted to collapse upon the grass and give up, lamenting that it was all too much for her, that her inbreeding was kicking in and her dainty ankles could carry the weight no longer. But, in the act of tumbling over the fence, the queen got a whopping splinter jabbed into her thigh. She stopped to pull it out with a pinch of her dirty nails, which she didn't even know she could do, and the jolt of pain spurred her just enough to send her crawling across the grass, leaving a muddy wake across its emerald surface while tearing the dress even further.

Eventually, she gained her feet again and limped, loped, jogged, and finally ran. After all, Dahlia now anticipated the additional humiliation she would endure if found in a ripped dress with the pearlescent skin of a royal thigh showing through, so she got vertical and made tracks. As she zipped across the meadow, she looked back over her shoulder; meanwhile, the bearded man, she assumed, in his sweat-stained T-shirt, waited on the parapet, either confused, afraid, panicked, and desperate, or scheming, conniving, manipulating, and plotting with a vengeance.

The queen charged on: out of breath, out of shape, weak in the knees, and at her wit's end. To preserve her dignity, she headed for a secret entrance that she knew from childhood, which enabled a certain special way for a secretive little spy (or a dung-smeared queen, as the case may be) to enter the castle without being discovered.

Approaching a familiar turret, she grabbed the lowest branch of a spreading magnolia nestled against the castle wall and swung herself up into its familiar embrace.

38

WHERE BEAUTY AND EVIL
ARE DEEPLY INTERTWINED

Faced with ElizabethAnn's pouty intransigence, Bill Bramble did a furious dance, jumping and spluttering and making more of those very un-birdlike sounds, until finally he said, "Okay, then. I'll show you! I'll show you something! The most magnificent room in all the world!"

"Oh, please," replied ElizabethAnn, with a calculated sneer. "What could ever be so special as all that?" Snootiness wasn't her style, but she needed to get down that dark hallway and into the room at the end, with its strange internal light, or it felt like the persistent psychic butterfly voices would explode her brain.

Bill hopped farther down the tunnel, and soon they arrived in what was, indeed, a most incredible room. The walls undulated with glow-in-the-dark colors of blue, pink, orange, yellow, white, puce, you name it. But the atmosphere in there felt terribly, terribly dark. In the center of the space, Bill spread his wings wide with pride. He even crowed, which was quite out of character for his species.

A closer look revealed the truth of the matter: The walls were covered with butterfly wings. No, not wings sadistically ripped from dead butterfly bodies, but wings still attached to real living butterflies, whose feet were cemented in the walls' dried mud. The trapped butterflies flapped their lives away, hour by hour, in this beautiful butterfly hell, stuck hideously in the mud until death. Shuddering, ElizabethAnn heard more psychic transmissions here than she had heard yet, and Grandma's voice joined in the cacophony. She said, "Find Shadooda! Prove my innocence!"

"Isn't it magnificent?" shrieked Bill. "Isn't it the world's most elegant creation! Isn't it the epitome of wonder and a celebration of life! Couldn't you just faint!"

"Now, see here," said ElizabethAnn. "There is a limit, you know."

"LIMIT?" protested the bird, "I'M AN ARTIST!"

ElizabethAnn, by now, had had enough of the entire blasted space/time continuum and Grandma's vague instructions and missions and urges toward heroism. ElizabethAnn didn't want to save Bumblegreen just at that moment (not that she would have known how). She just wanted a bubble bath, and, more than anything, to not have any more messages coming into her brain unbidden.

"Grandma!" she yelled, much to the consternation of Bill Bramble. "I'll do it, all right? I'll do it, but get out of my head! Let me alone, or I'm going crazy!"

Faintly, in the background of her mind, she heard. "Zade? Is this thing working? This doesn't sound like ElizabethAnn anymore ..."

All the while, the trapped butterflies flapped their lives away, gradually slowing their wing beats. Some sagged off the walls and seemed to have lost their spunk altogether. Finally, ElizabethAnn heard, "All right, ElizabethAnn ... I guess I'll ... if that's what you really want." This was followed by a hiss and a buzz and then nothing—nothing but ElizabethAnn's own blessed, blessed, private thoughts.

"Listen, Bramble, you can't just keep these butterflies imprisoned here," ElizabethAnn told the bird. "And for what? Forever? That's not right."

"I'm an artist! You don't know what it's like!" replied Bramble, fluffing his feathers self-importantly.

"I certainly do!" ElizabethAnn replied, simultaneously realizing that she certainly did. "But you've gone too far. That's all there is to it."

No one had ever spoken like this to Bill Bramble, either as a bird or in his human guise. Meanwhile, it was awfully hot in that close little cavern, and several butterflies had already suffocated. Their bodies drooped lifelessly from the walls, bumping deadly back and forth between desperately flapping neighbors.

Hot as she was, ElizabethAnn remembered the duchess' delicate fan, retrieved it from her pocket, and fanned herself while considering what to do next.

Now, as you can imagine, this was no ordinary fan, but a magical heirloom. Like the magical liquid in the silver flask, which had made her shrink, the breeze from the fan actually made ElizabethAnn grow larger again. In a few flaps of the fan, she towered over the bird.

At this new, safe height, ElizabethAnn pondered her options anew. She considered folding up the fan and beating Bramble about the head and neck with it until senseless, but that might alter its magic, and she might be left at her current in-between height forever. So, instead, she punched a hole through the ceiling. Plaster rained down, as one might expect, and sunlight stabbed down through the hole.

Bramble jumped and leaped and flapped and uttered all kinds of demands for ElizabethAnn to cease and desist in the destruction of his private property. But this was all to no avail, naturally, as ElizabethAnn, despite her excellent breeding and manners, discovered she could be a very stubborn little dickens when she wanted to. She tried pulling the butterflies gently off the walls, with the intention of setting them free through the hole in the roof, but their legs were stuck fast in the hard, dried mud, and their psychic screams pierced ElizabethAnn's mind like so many needles.

That's when she got a brain wave and thought, *I'll spit them free.*

Who? Delicate, polite, persnickety ElizabethAnn? Surely the child had never spit before in her life, except toothpaste, of course, but that's not projectile spitting. This was hawking and spitting for distance. Things had happened in Bumblegreen: she had climbed, she had blipped, she had clung to rancid monkey fur for dear life. She had swung through a forest canopy and slept in a bird's nest. She had eaten rotten fruit, consorted with butterflies, and ridden upon a smelly wild animal's back. ElizabethAnn wasn't the same particular, pleasant, ever so timid, delightfully tidy child she had once been.

So, she spit—all over the room, in fact, and soon, her saliva dribbled messily down the walls in great gobs and streaks, softening the mud as it did so. Moments later, freed butterflies flew from the walls—up, up, through the hole in the roof, and into the sky.

By the time all the butterflies had been freed, ElizabethAnn stood ankle-deep in mud and covered with spit and slime from head to toe. In fact, she existed now so many mental miles away from the prim, proper little girl she had once been, that she barely remembered No Oaks. Mr. and Mrs. Von Earp had, by now, faded into dim images in her mind, and the endless acres of plastic grass, and the dust blowing in the wind, and the scorching persistent sunshine, and the police on every street corner—these recollections seemed now like half-remembered dreams. But Grandma, with her shock of white hair, her lips pulled back in a crazed fast-driving face, her slender wrists resting atop her head in her thinking pose—Grandma's presence felt stronger than ever.

Bill Bramble wept, tore at his feathers, stomped his feet, and cried out in a manner half human, half bird. "I can't believe it. I can't believe it. I shall never create another work of art in my life! I shall devote myself to monk-like simplicity!"

He stalked through the house, out through the back door, and instantly turned into a freckle-faced four-year-old boy—a grouchy, despondent boy, but a human boy nonetheless. His footstep crushed a corner of his tiny tennis court, and he didn't even care.

ElizabethAnn stepped through the hole in the ceiling, then fanned herself up to something approximating normal size, at which point she discovered things in the meadow had become very different, already. A freckle-faced boy, who hadn't been there before, now sat on a log and moped. Also, thousands of butterflies filled the skies.

The redheaded woman seemed to have disappeared, but a cinnamon squirrel with a bow in its hair crouched in the grass, watching ElizabethAnn intently. Fast Eddie sat, slumped, in the middle of the meadow, mouth agape.

The four-year-old boy Bill Bramble was now sulked on his log while watching the butterflies make vast, colorful clouds of themselves. Then, he lowered his gaze to ElizabethAnn.

"Mama?" he asked. "Mama, is it you?"

ElizabethAnn was ten, and nobody's mama, nor did she feel that obvious fact needed to be stated. She just looked at him in a way that said all that.

Young Bill shook his head with sudden vigor, like a dog repelling water. "Nothing," he said. "Nevermind. Nothing. Nevermind."

After having swung along for miles through a forest canopy on the back of a talking monkey, then being forced into heroism by butterflies, ElizabethAnn had pretty much achieved a state of total acceptance of fate and resolved not to be surprised by anything else that might happen in Bumblegreen. So, if sadistic, grown-up birds now turned into motherless, human children, she'd just file that under Miscellaneous Unexplainable Phenomena and move on.

Intending to reconvene with Earl, whom she assumed to be still waiting in the castle's turret (and further intending to run all these recent events by him for clarification and some general Bumblegreen reality checks), ElizabethAnn dashed through the meadow and back to the path from whence she had come, but a cloud of butterflies flew ahead and created an absorbing picture of storybook beauty before her.

They flitted around, alighting on branches and doing loop the loops. Soon, the air filled with them to such a degree that ElizabethAnn couldn't see her way forward. Through the colorful cloud, she stumbled along, barking her shins on downed branches and tripping over rocks, until finally she realized, with a growing sense of panic, that she had utterly lost the trail. For the second time since this entire adventure began, ElizabethAnn prepared to sit down and have a good cry, but, just then, she received another psychic transmission.

Follow us! the butterflies said, collectively.

I want you out! replied ElizabethAnn. *Out of my head, for good!*

Follow us! they insisted, as if they knew better, and ElizabethAnn, being a sucker for people (or beings, generally) who threw around that I-know-better attitude, went along with it. While following the butterflies blindly, she pursed her lips and opened up her back-brain to get a message across: *Do you know Shadooda? That's all I want to know*, she asked, psychically.

There was a pause accompanied by a buzzing—a buzzing in a different language, if that makes sense. Then, she received another message. *Yes*, the butterflies said. *We know. Follow us.*

ElizabethAnn realized poor Earl would have to wait a while longer, and poor Jackson was probably going to get kidnapped and imprisoned at the castle in the meantime. But she just hoped that with fistfuls of magic from this Shadooda character, she'd soon remedy these wrongs.

Thousands—who knows, maybe millions—of little insect bodies led ElizabethAnn along. They flew into formations, creating in one moment a path of violet butterflies surrounded by whites, in another moment, the illusion of a bouncing ball for her to follow. Blues and greens crowded behind her, forming a wall that made it impossible for her to turn around and run back.

ElizabethAnn, gradually growing suspicious, followed the butterflies deeper and deeper into the forest until she became so tangled in vines and undergrowth that she simply couldn't go on. She doubted the butterflies, now. Their psychic transmissions had ceased.

ElizabethAnn yanked the vines from her legs and the bramble branches from her hair, turned around, and tried to run back. She flapped her arms and shooed the insects away but couldn't make progress, couldn't outrun them. The butterflies landed on her, thousands of them, and clustered around her head, threatening her breathing, so she did as they insisted and hiked farther into the ever-darkening forest. She hadn't any choice.

39

FEATURING THE THINGAMAJIGS OF YORE

Your typical monkey, your natural monkey, doesn't get bored. Animals don't. They sniff the air, lick their privates, sleep, dream, listen to the world. On a moment-to-moment basis, the absence of stimulus doesn't bore them in the least. Earl, however, up in the castle turret, was not a natural beast, in any way. Distracted by clouds, fantasies, and, of course, his fascinating golden watch, he didn't notice ElizabethAnn had long ago left the nest in the magnolia tree, so he sat in the turret and waited for her. But after an hour or so, he got a little stir-crazy.

At one point, the turret-top chamber might have been some lucky knight's luxury apartment. A deep fireplace with a stone chimney dominated the decor. An arched doorway, with its engraved keystone, added pizzazz. The tower's wrap-around windows framed panoramic vistas. Elegant, iron candelabra stood affixed to the walls. The burnished oaken floor suggested leisurely comings and goings, lingerings before leavings, and fireside lounging. The room must have made quite an elegant *pied-à-terre* at one time, but now the room simply stored somebody-or-other's cast-off belongings.

Earl, being Earl, had to go and start snooping, had to go and get curious. He finally turned off his golden watch's bleating chime, which seemed to have done nothing to rouse ElizabethAnn from her rest in the nest of some large, possibly angry, potentially sharp-beaked bird. So Earl looked to the room itself for amusement.

Wooden boxes, upholstered couches, stacked chairs, and mismatched chariot wheels comprised the base of a deep pile of castle detritus. In among all that rested a carved, inlaid, bejeweled, child-sized bed frame. *Must have taken a special kid to sleep in that thing, back in the day,* thought Earl. He circled the pile, looking for a place to start snooping, then climbed up into the precarious stack of oddments. One foot on a pile of planks, one hand steady on a parade baton. Then, he did see something interesting.

Just out of reach lay a chocolate tin with an unlatched top, looking like something someone might occasionally visit and open and peek inside. *This object, among all these others, might actually see action once in a while,* thought Earl. *It might even still be loved, in some small way, by a child, somewhere.* The tin sparked his curiosity.

A monkey foot grasped a clanking tangle of disassembled machinery. A monkey hand felt cold iron, which could have been a cook pot, a bedpan, a rusty sewing machine treadle, anything.

Faltering, the monkey foot reached for a pile of velvet cushions. A monkey tail wrapped around a coat rack. Another monkey foot felt around blindly until it felt something soft, imprinted with roses and carnations.

Finally, a monkey foot grasped the edge of a battered old bucket and advanced Earl a little closer to his object of fascination: that chocolate tin. Earl could see the tin now, marked as it was with colorful paints and pencils from some child's free hand. Words were written on the side, but he couldn't quite make them out. Earl's legendary curiosity increased, and he felt he simply had to read those words. He had climbed so close by that point, almost close enough to see, but squinting wouldn't bring the letters into focus.

Up went the sash and in went the queen, tumbling through the tower window, ass over teacups, landing in an awkward heap on her head and right shoulder, where her muck-covered boots dropped blobs all over her precious royal self. From that ungainly position, she took a moment to appreciate the sight of her childhood treasures—keepsakes that brought back memories of simpler days. Her eyes scanned the pile from her topsy-turvy position and remembered that little chocolate tin and how much she used to enjoy sneaking up here for a few idle moments with it and its contents.

Dahlia righted herself and looked left and right, searching for the tin amid the thingamajigs of yore. She saw it. She also saw a furry hand near it—wiggling, straining—and wondered to whom that hand was attached.

Perhaps, thought Earl, *if I switch my right hand to that crystal figurine and grasp a bedpost with the left? If my foot could find purchase on that wooden crate ... Yes!*

Earl craned his neck to read the tin, with its mysterious label. But the crate upon which he stood had been yearning, for years, to touch down to the floor in deference to gravity's immutable law. It chose that moment to do so.

The crate fell, and with it a broke-bottomed chair, a bedstead, a coat rack, some velvet pillows, a crystal figurine, a bouquet of parade batons, some wooden planks, a clanking tangle of disassembled machinery, some mismatched carriage wheels, a sewing machine treadle, and that soft thing imprinted with roses and carnations.

The queen heard a noise and reacted accordingly, protecting her head.

An avalanche of ancient things slid through the room, toward an unlatched door that burst open when assaulted by the fists of iron and crystal and ceramic and velvet and wool, releasing an avalanche onto the tower's winding staircase.

All those things slid down the stairs in a great and spiky wave of obsolete comforts that had once held magic and mystery for a child— a child who, on a single fateful day, lost all access to the luxury of childhood.

The things tumbled and dove headlong out of exile and into a cheese-infused modernity they knew nothing about. With them tumbled Earl and, jumbled up in the mess, the queen, as well.

While getting knocked and bruised every which way, Earl did manage, once, to bring his head above the tumult, to think for one bare-bottomed second that he might save himself. That idea was over as soon as a broken credenza swept down the stairs and engulfed him in one of its gawping cabinets, but in that fleeting moment he got a glimpse of the tin that had inspired him so.

The tin surfed the avalanche, bouncing from chair to mattress to flowerpot to floor lamp, and as it did so, Earl could momentarily read the label a royal little girl had once scrawled in crayon, reading: *Bits of String Too Small to Save.*

Earl grabbed for the tin, but it dipped into a chasm between some tumbling casks and a flip-flopping duffel bag filled with old clothes.

The queen herself fell into the open jaws of a stuffed and mounted hippopotamus head and, with legs and arms akimbo, slid downstairs inside the massive jaw of the thing, as if on a cramped toboggan, until the questionable vehicle rose higher and higher toward the crest of the wave of tumbling objects. A bouncing, splintering, hope chest goosed the hippo head, and the head caught air.

The hippo went flying. The chocolate tin did, too. Atop the wave of her childhood keepsakes, the queen clung to remnants of hippo teeth, her face a rictus of apocalyptic disbelief. In a single involuntary motion, her hand shot out, caught the flying chocolate tin, and used it to protect her face when, mid-air, her body skidded into a rattling rack of hand-painted bone china.

Happily, the china had been well-packed for storage and transport purposes, so while the queen's body reduced the shattered china to infinitesimal smithereens, the padding protected her shoulder, hand, arm, right hip, left foot, and all the stuff attached to those parts from being completely reduced to minuscule shards of bone.

The credenza Earl rode bumped and wobbled, shuddered and flew, and, in one pristine moment of aerial acrobatics, sent Earl flying into space just before it crashed into a wall and shivered into one hundred and twelve unrecognizable pieces.

Poor, curious Earl. He landed smack on top of the bone china, too, or its padding, anyway. And, as such, he also landed pretty much right on top of the queen, who had essentially merged with the padding as if it were some new kind of royal attire and she, resplendently dressed.

A long silence ensued, during which one or another of the long trail of random, fallen, broken things fell farther down, or broke even more, or settled farther into the endless avalanche of detritus, making various tumbling and bumbling sounds that interrupted the moment's overwhelming post-apocalyptic hush.

Though still in shock, the queen gradually extricated herself from her awkward situation and determined that she and the monkey were somehow both still breathing. She found the soft thing decorated with roses and carnations. Having grown far more practical than sentimental by all these recent travails, she tightly wrapped the bloody monkey in the well-remembered dress.

Amid the commotion, the queen forgot her mission to forestall profound embarrassment in the face of this Schrank, the interloper on the parapet. What had, only a moment before, seemed so important as to be worth wading through a stinking quagmire to get to, now seemed like some dream problem from a dream world.

Dahlia blinked twice then limped down the hallway in a serpentine fashion, cradling poor Earl, unsure where to go or what to do with the monkey, or even from where the beast had come. A vague memory of her desperate race to the throne room, for some supposedly important reason, jiggled through her brainpan, but Dahlia couldn't remember the point of that journey at all anymore.

Castle guards came running, or rather fast-walking, to be truthful— maybe not even fast. More of a cautious tiptoeing action was really what they were doing. They'd heard the commotion, thought the roof had caved in, and hadn't wanted to endanger themselves. They didn't know the queen was involved, naturally, so when the guards saw the queen tottering toward them, looking wraithlike, milkmaid-like, injured, and somewhat bloodied, they screamed.

Queen Dahlia screamed, too, and then everyone screamed, on and on. At first, the guards screamed in sudden horror and shock, but then, once they recognized the queen, their screams turned to the higher pitched, electrically charged screams of horrified embarrassment.

For her part, the queen screamed her shock at the guards' screaming, but that soon became her screaming in general dismay and anger at not being helped at all. Then, when the guards' screaming continued unabated and, in fact, rose in intensity, the queen's screams took on the throaty, warbling affect of a more aggressive-type battle cry. At that point, she wondered if she might somehow not be in her own castle at all, but in some lunatic asylum.

Soon, a more sensible guard came running along, heard the screaming, and slapped everyone involved. Of course, he thought the queen was a cheese-making wench and gave her the old one-two, one-two, with the back and front of his hand, until she slapped him back, at which point he realized what he had done.

He first blanched, then blushed, then covered his face with his shirt and screamed himself, until the queen said something about an infirmary, and everyone snapped to.

The guards made a chair of their hands and carried the queen, monkey in arms, to the infirmary, where medics bandaged and sedated and medicated and restrained the two of them until the important missions they had both been on faded into oblivion. And what a wonderful feeling it was, for Dahlia and Earl, who completely forgot Jackson was being hunted, ElizabethAnn was looking for Shadooda, Schrank was waiting on the parapet for the queen, and the duchess was throwing a stupid garden party.

40

WHERE ELIZABETHANN IS DELIGHTED, AT FIRST

Stumbling into a clearing in the woods, ElizabethAnn found herself in what can only be described as a butterfly headquarters, where thousands of chrysalises hung from boughs in a forest grove. There, millions more butterflies flitted around, again alighting on branches, again doing loop the loops, and generally appearing beautiful and innocent and delightful and guileless.

ElizabethAnn was not impressed. She clucked, crossed her eyes, tapped her toes, and popped her ears as hard as she could. *Where is this magic? How do I find it?* she psychically demanded.

You said you could help me find Shadooda!

A cloud of monarchs swirled tightly around itself in some sort of whirling, tumbling dance, or collective seizure or ... *could it be a meeting?* thought ElizabethAnn. In fact, it was. It was a summit meeting among the rulers of the butterflies who, at that moment, debated what to do with ElizabethAnn. Telecommunicating on a grand scale, members of the hurly-burly, hectic, mid-air crowd—none other than the grand-poohbah butterfly grandmamas and granddaddys of the forest—gossiped, made general observations, and rumor-mongered as they decided ElizabethAnn's fate. They conducted their meeting kind of like, well, if you can imagine a corporate board meeting held amid the chaos of a children's birthday party, where VIPs might have worn both cone-shaped hats and patterned silk ties.

Some of the butterflies suggested keeping ElizabethAnn and using her for a variety of projects that needed a human touch. Others discussed the possibility of bewitching her to stay in the meadow with them forever. This occasioned a prudent question as to what the child ate, and how she relieved herself, and whether or not her basic needs could be attended to by butterflies, working solo or in teams.

What's the magic word? Magic pill? Magic potion? Where are the magicians! How do I find Shadooda? ElizabethAnn continued to psychically transmit, with growing anger at the butterflies' silence.

As to the question of what she ate, one big blue registered concern as to whether or not she ate insects, raising the question of whether or not they had just invited a predator into their midst. Then, as to how she relieved herself, great questions (very difficult to translate from the butterfly) emerged, resulting in the butterflies' near mental exhaustion and a unanimous agreement to get rid of ElizabethAnn as soon as possible. Not mental-marathon runners, these butterflies.

They concocted a strategy and broke for nectar. Then, the cloud of butterfly sentries standing guard over ElizabethAnn danced a dance of unparalleled beauty, which featured patterns and moving images and great swaths of color weaving in and out, forward and back, in mesmerizing rhythmic patterns. As intended, the lovely dance gradually weakened ElizabethAnn.

Growing sleepy, she tried to cling to her mission, psychically insisting, *You ... said ... you ... knew ... Shadooda ...* but weariness came upon her like a cloudburst.

We lied, the beady-eyed insects answered back.

ElizabethAnn fell backward onto a soft mass, where, in inexorable tiredness, she curled into a ball. Soon, the mass grew and formed itself around her while she remained just conscious enough to see the pure whiteness of it, hear the sticky, gooey sounds it made, and wonder how it, and she, got in this position in the first place.

Though barely conscious, ElizabethAnn kept her eyes open just a peep, just enough to see enormous caterpillars at work— horrible-looking beasts, with their mandibles and constant regurgitation of silk. The caterpillars' many little arms molded the silk of the cocoon they built around her like a team of potters and weavers working as one.

The sleep felt so good, she knew it was a trap. Panic rose in ElizabethAnn, and she tried to scream, but nothing came out. The white walls of her cocoon closed in and forced her to curl up tighter, as the mass closed around her sleepy self. Finally, the hideous face of one last caterpillar puked up a snowy glob that closed off her final, tiny peephole.

Inside the cocoon, translucent silk walls glowed so beautifully that her new prison soothed ElizabethAnn even further. She was so sleepy, she didn't even notice the walls hardening like ultra-smooth plaster. Didn't even notice she would never be able to claw her way out of there. Never, in a million years.

41

WHEREIN DAHLIA POINTS
OUT SCHRANK'S WRONG MATH

"Now then," said the queen to Schrank, whose voluminous red lumberjack beard was gradually coming unglued. (As soon as the sedatives wore off, she awoke in the infirmary, remembered her mission, called this meeting, and met the concerned parties in a room that conveyed some semblance of dignity.) While attempting to be royal and officious, she slapped back doctors and nurses and various worried-looking individuals who hovered over, under, and around her like so many ants trying to hoist a potato chip.

Dahlia's royal stylist squatted nearby as well, adjusting part of an elaborate dress he had managed—thanks to a great deal of manipulative eye-rolling and hair tossing on his part—to convince Dahlia to wear, only minutes before the impromptu meeting.

"I've read your report," Dahlia began. "I've seen your data … Stop it, will you? I can't stand these ruffled collars, anyway!"

Dahlia tore off the itchy, beaded-and-feathered collar her stylist had been meticulously fluffing up for the past five minutes. It clattered to the floor, threads breaking, crystals rolling this way and that. The stylist gasped and skidded to his hands and knees, scooping up the supposedly infinitely valuable beads with tensely cupped hands. The bandages all over Dahlia's neck and arms showed now, but she didn't care.

She told him, "In an attempt to put to bed this ridiculous portal-opening nonsense you've been bothering me about, I've followed your unbelievably inaccurate timeline …

"Oh, would you stop it with the thermometer?" she shouted at a nurse. "How am I supposed to talk to this man with a damn thermometer in my … I'm sick of being babied! I'm not hurt worth a damn. A couple of cuts and bruises! Big deal! I just got a little dazed! If you people don't mind, I have a meeting to conduct!"

The doctors and nurses hovered and bandaged and poked and prodded and measured her bruises slightly less. Then, as soon as she was distracted, they recommenced their work, just as before.

"You really shouldn't have left the infirmary, Your Majesty!" said one.

"To run off like that, you worried us so!" said another.

"And to find you later in the throne room! Agh! So dusty, that place!" said a third.

"Completely unsanitary!" added a medic.

"I had business to deal with, you sops, now give me back that file!" the queen said and snatched the long-sought Affairs of State file from a castle guard who was attempting to spray it down with some type of primitive sanitizer hardly more effective than the "cootie spray" of a No Oaks school child.

"I've parsed these pie graphs," she said to Schrank, who had been dragged downstairs from the parapet after being attacked by a legion of clerks. (While Schrank waited for the queen at the royal pigeon coop, they had finally burst through the old door and pummeled him with bureaucratic stamps leaving permanent scars that read, "irrevocable," "non-deliverable," and "expunged.")

Dahlia opened the Affairs of State file to one of its carefully tabbed pages and turned it so Shrank could examine the supposedly highly scientific information found there. She pointed out the wrong math, grammatical errors, and severely defunct logical fallacies blizzarding around on the page.

"I'd like to know," she said, "what exactly you think the problem is with my polymer?" Dahlia swatted one doctor who reached for her with a stethoscope. She stamped on the foot of another who approached, tentatively, with an ice pack disguised as a throw pillow.

Schrank—quaking, hopeful, determined—having practiced his lies upon lies for hours upon hours, had convinced himself that the young queen would easily acquiesce to his "scientific superiority" and his insistence that the polymer be removed from the portals immediately, for community health purposes.

"The polymer is insecure, you see. It's got to be removed!" Shrank declared. "It's raising havoc with amphibious mammals and sea creatures and also, well, it seems to be peeling up in places … Your Majesty."

"Does it?" she inquired.

"Absolutely!" He ad-libbed, assuming the young queen hadn't had the sense to check on the portals, hadn't visited a certain familiar badger hole and used its vicinity as her personal thinking place, hadn't periodically examined certain hollow trees, woodpecker holes, and small caves, just to ensure the polymer on the more unusual surfaces still held true. But she had. Not every day, mind you, but she had.

"I'm terribly sorry," replied Dahlia, "but we're going to have to back up a bit. Now, I forgot to ask, silly of me, but why don't you start by showing me your credentials?"

"Credentials?"

"Get that damnable thermometer out of my face, you cretin! … Sorry. Now, about those credentials …"

"Um, credentials, credentials, let me see …"

A large guard entered, unannounced, and rumbled, "Your Majesty …"

"I'm busy!"

"I'm sorry, Your Majesty. I humble myself at the feet of your all-seeing gaze and infinite powers of worldly dominion …"

"Oh, shut up. What do you want?"

"The monkey is awake, Your Majesty. What should I do with him?"

"Sakes alive! Throw him in the cage. I'll question him later. It's just a stinking monkey."

"Right, Your Majesty!"

"Yes, Your Majesty!" parroted a guard who stood off to the side, wanting to be included.

"Who are you?" asked the queen.

"No one, Your Majesty," he mumbled.

"Now," Dahlia said, turning again to Schrank, who, at this point, was trying to slink out of the room through a side entrance, "about those credentials."

"I've got them!" he said and gulped. "They're with my associate, though. I have to get them from Georgie. She'll know exactly what to do."

The queen declared the meeting adjourned and also a complete waste of time on everyone's behalf.

42

WHERE HEROISM GOES UNREWARDED

Ever-ambitious Georgie swung through the forest canopy, where she often went to improve her holdings in the treetop real estate market. It was her habit to climb up into the trees, make like a monkey, hide in leafy places, sneak from branch to branch, and generally keep an eye out for monkeys preparing to abandon their roosts. Once they did so, Georgie squatted in the spot until some new, young monkey couple came along, then she made the newcomers "a great deal on a double-wide tree limb."

Typically, Bumblegreen treetops buzzed with monkey families

eager to do right by their little human charges, so Georgie tended to find this adventure a teensy bit fun, especially due to its refreshingly immediate payoff. But lately, there had been a dearth of young monkey families to exploit, creating a situation that often left her muttering, "How did I get myself into this pickle?" "There's got to be a better way!" and, "I'm too old for this crap!"

This particular day, Georgie climbed and shinnied and creeped and crawled through the treetops for a different reason entirely: she needed to find Earl and his purloined watch. After hours and hours up there, though, she didn't have any luck, and now—long after the stars had come out—she was stuck in the tall, pencilish trees without any way back down. In the meantime, she came upon a wondrous and unexpected sight. Down below, on the forest floor, what looked like a thousand lanterns softly glowed around the edge of a meadow. Really, they were chrysalises made by giant caterpillars.

Then, Georgie saw millions of sleeping butterflies adorning tree limbs around the meadow, looking like a child's finger painting—the colors so beautiful in their random unmatchedness. Georgie settled onto a branch and leaned down for a better look at the phenomenon, where she noticed one of the lantern-like pods (an especially large one) swaying violently and unnaturally. She feared whatever creature might someday emerge from it.

Faintly, Georgie heard pounding, as of tiny fists upon impenetrable cement. This accompanied cries for help in rhythm with the swings of the lantern-like pod. A moment later, the wind picked up and drowned out the sound of the faint cries. Georgie wondered if she had actually imagined them all along. She listened to the wind whistle through the canopy in that distracting way that sounded like a singsong nursery rhyme and heard:

Live long, not strong
Rats nor bats nor toadstools beside me
Mumbling in the ever-gloaming
Longing to be free-ee

Thus distracted, Georgie climbed farther through the forest canopy, away from the lantern-lit meadow, following the wind's musical whistle from treetop to treetop, until she lost her grip and fell, screeching hideously, through the layered branches like a badly thrown ninja star.

As she fell, Georgie tried to grab onto this branch and that, slowing her fall just imperceptibly, minutely, but enough, as she went, to catch herself just before the understory, where about a mile of long, branchless nothingness invited her to fall to certain death. There, she hung from a branch, both arms clutching bark, ten fingernails dug in deep. Cursing her life, fate, and overly ambitious nature, Georgie screamed for help.

When Georgie grew hoarse, she tried to kick her legs back up onto the branch, skin-the-cat style, but didn't have the strength or agility. Then, more tired than ever, she considered just going ahead and falling to her death. Didn't see a lot of other options. But, the very next moment, a moon ray illuminated what appeared to be a man, down below.

"Hey, you!" Georgie yelled.

The man's uniform suggested he had recently made a horizontal career move from something involving transportation to something involving security and had got the two outfits hopelessly confused. In order to see, he kept pushing his too-big, feather-crested helmet to the back of his head and getting choked by the chinstrap. Finally, he cocked his head at a funny angle until he could look up to where

Georgie hung in the shadows of the canopy.

"Now, what in the …" said the fellow, whose toes hung out the ends of a pair of badly broken boots. It was Mobius.

"Can you get me down from here at all? Get a ladder, maybe?" Georgie screamed at him.

"Mile-long ladder?" Mobius mused. "Well … I suppose I could go and look for one." He shrugged, turned, and walked away in a manner that indicated this would be one more pointless, fruitless venture in a day, and now an evening, filled with nothing but pointless, fruitless ventures.

"No, wait!" screamed Georgie. "Don't go!"

"Okay," replied Mobius, turning back and re-cocking his feather-crested helmet so as to peer up at Georgie.

"Could you catch me?" Georgie whined. "I mean, if I let go, could you catch me, because I can't hang on much longer. I'm falling! I'm falling!"

Mobius squinted, twisted his feather-crested helmet to the other side, loosened his collar, which wasn't buttoned straight anyway, and tried to remember the last time he had caught something that big falling from a distance that high and couldn't. He opted out.

"I think," he said, "the best option for you would be a trampoline."

"A tramp? Do you have a trampo … will you pretty-please go and get me one?" Georgie pleaded, adding, "Oh, I'm losing my grip!"

Georgie dug her nails into the bark of the branch. Tucking her chin awkwardly, she could just barely see Mobius below, busily engaged in some manner: zipping this way and that, stopping, going, thrashing around, then dashing here and there. In the moonlight, she saw flashes of pink, down there. Didn't know what that was. Pretty soon, she lost her grip for a final time. The fingernails just broke.

"Should have taken that calcium supplement. Doctor always said

..." Georgie muttered, as she fell.

and fell

and fell

and fell

and selected a death of regal, dignified silence for herself. She didn't scream or flail but simply tried to enjoy the crisp, clean air, the flashes of greenery, and the scent of pine, as she experienced the last moment of her life in the glorious freedom of unfettered descent.

She landed in a surprisingly bouncy manner.

One bounce, two bounces, then a sound of *rrrrrrip*, which she figured was her skin bloodily zipping off, then a sound of *crick-crack*, which she figured was her femurs snapping in two, then a sound of *ooph*, which surprisingly came out of her own lungs and didn't sound like a death rattle at all.

In the end, she found herself tangled in a wad of distinctly unwashed laundry.

"How ya doin'?" asked Mobius, who stood before her, naked as a bullfrog.

"Sorry that shirt ripped," he said, "but them pants held fast, dint they? Used m'scouting knots!"

"Am I in the land beyond?" asked Georgie, who didn't feel well at all, having landed on her side, where her arm now hung strangely.

"I dunno? Am I?" asked Mobius.

"I mean am I dead, you dolt," Georgie snapped. "Obviously not. No one this stupid would be in the land beyond."

"Nope, yer not dead," he replied. "Ya landed in a trampoline made o' m'clothes. Them clothes was too big fer me, anyhowz!"

Then Georgie saw it: the shirt and pants tied to each other and then to a couple of tree branches, the shirt sleeves stretched in opposite directions, the pants legs affixed to tree trunks with vines. Mobius' underpants tied one end of his undershirt to a tree trunk. A sock tied the other end to a sapling.

"Not bad, kid … not bad," Georgie said, just before the pain of her broken arm whooshed over her like a typhoon, and she passed out cold, eyes wide as saucers.

Mobius didn't notice the nearby profusion of sleeping butterflies, nor the wildly swinging chrysalis from which a little girl's voice begged for freedom. He had a life to save, after all (Georgie's), so he picked her up and carried her, fireman-style, his dingle a-danglin', back to the castle, which wasn't far. There, a cheese maid screamed in alarm, doctors came running to Georgie's aid, and various individuals set about striking Mobius soundly on the head and shoulders for his offensive nudity.

Mobius shrugged it all off as one more thankless adventure among many.

43

IN WHICH EARL COMES
CLEAN, BUT UNDER DURESS

Georgie awoke to moonlight leaking through the castle infirmary window, adding an eerie glow to the light of a single flickering candle. Finding her arm in a cast didn't shock her nearly as much as discovering a monkey in the next bed over, wearing the long-lost Favra prototype watch-of-the-future.

It's a little-known fact, but monkeys tend to get quite a bit of dirt in their claws from time to time. It can become compacted and uncomfortable, especially after the numerous adventures that tend to befall them, so they have to stop now and then to pick their claws with a twig. Such an activity is, to a monkey, as drinking water is to a giraffe: one of nature's goof-ups, a supremely vulnerable moment. When Georgie awoke, she found Earl—head bandaged, three fingers taped together, tail in a brace—sitting on the edge of his bed, wearing the shredded remnant of a No Oaks Golf Club shirt, and attempting to pick his claws in just such a way.

Wincing from a constellation of all-over bruises, Georgie rose and approached the monkey in the calm, assertive stance she had learned in some long-ago self-defense course. She asked his name.

Earl sized Georgie up, answered her in the bored but obedient manner of your typical Bumblegreen monkey, then returned to picking his claws with a twig.

Georgie stated her status as a shareholder of the Favra Watch Company. Earl simply continued picking his claws. A clod of mud shot out, past Georgie's ear.

"As a principal shareholder of Favra Watch, I'd like to know just how you happen to be wearing our secret prototype watch," Georgie said, then added, hopefully threateningly, "Answer up, monkey!"

"Well," said Earl, looking over his shoulder, making plans to enjoy the luxurious castle interior to his heart's content and maybe look for Jackson, too. See if the beast had been caught, yet. "I stole it off Jimothy Schrank while he slept, if you must know," he told her.

Georgie raised her eyebrows and loomed over Earl with all the threatening humanity of her humanness (constellation of bruises notwithstanding). Earl attempted to run away, but with that clunking wooden brace on his broken tail, he didn't get but a few steps.

With her good arm, Georgie applied firm but steady pressure to his scrawny monkey neck and asked him to kindly elaborate.

"It was the duchess!" he admitted. "She told me where to steal it! She just wanted me to use the GPS feature to find a portal, and jump through, and pick up some dumb old antiques!"

"What antiques?" shouted Georgie, illogically. (I mean, does it really matter?)

"A crystal chandelier and a pair of Louis-the-fourteenth end tables!" screamed Earl, from inside an increasingly uncomfortable headlock.

"The duchess? The DUCHESS?" Georgie hissed as she unlatched the Favra from the monkey's wrist and fastened it to her own. "Show me the portal!" she insisted.

"Just press the button," he said. "The watch has the entire list of GPS coordinates programmed right in."

"Which portal is open?"

"I just chose one at random and followed the watch's map to find it. Don't remember which one it was."

"Well, where the hell was it?"

"In the forest, someplace. I dunno."

A nurse entered, saw the battered monkey splayed on the floor, and whistled for help. At the sound of rapid footsteps, Georgie dove out a window, ran across the castle lawn, ducked into the shadows of the forest, and crept away through the night.

With her arm in both a sling and a cast, and Georgie's various other body parts bandaged to the point of near immobility, and with her overall self still dressed in her infirmary gown (whose boxy, brief design hardly suited her figure), Georgie limped through woodlands, down highways, and across byways, through the long chill of night.

When she finally arrived back at the old barn serving as Favra Watch headquarters, she slumped, exhausted, against its barred double doors framed by ancient oaken beams. Georgie knocked, but nobody came. So, she sat in a shaft of moonlight, nursed her injuries, and waited.

44

In Which Tammy Intimidates
Somebody, for Once

Georgie awoke, with the first rays of the sun, to a bugle call and a bullhorn's announcement.

"Company arise and prepare to depart! Beast sightings so far: zero!"

All around the Favra building, cobalt military tents squatted like one-eyed beetles. Men bustled around, periodically stopping to strap gear to fat, gray packs—tin cups and plates clanging together as they did so. Georgie heard a whisper.

"Don't turn around," said the voice. "Just tell me if you've seen a four-legged beast, smaller than a horse."

Georgie jumped, then peeked around the side of the barn, where a woman hid behind a wild rose bush.

"Who are you?" asked Georgie.

"Shh!" replied the woman, partially concealing her face behind an abundance of straight, dark hair and glancing in the direction of the decamping army. "Just between you and me: Have you seen it? The beast?" the woman whisper-yelled. (It was Tammy, the duchess' personal chef, of course.)

"I've seen a monkey," said Georgie.

"No, not a monkey," Tammy replied.

"I've seen a glowing lantern in the woods. Lots of them, actually," Georgie offered.

"That's interesting," said Tammy. "But no, I'm talking about a furry, four-legged beast. If you saw it, you'd remember. Something you've never seen before, I guarantee."

"I can't say I have," said Georgie. "What's this all about?"

Tammy looked over both shoulders twice, saw no one watching, and emerged from hiding. "I'm Tammy," she said. "I'm traveling with the war party. We're in search of this beast. It's official royal business."

Tammy's waist-length, jet-black horsehair extensions and daring attitude, born of a post-getting-dumped nihilistic worldview, intimidated Georgie, who felt cowed at the end of Tammy's sharp nose.

Since joining the war party and traveling over many a dusty trail, Tammy had become brazen, confident, and kind of mean; meanwhile, she had convinced the soldiers that she belonged to the expedition, as part of the cook staff.

"What I really need to know," whispered Tammy, "is how far are we from the duchess' mansion? I've a need to get to the mansion vicinity lickety-split, before the rest of these fellows. Any idea?"

"Sure," said Georgie, pointing. "It's down this road, straight that way, then a left at the crossroads, and a right at the big rock."

Georgie had just described the exact direction the war party planned to go. There wasn't much hope of Tammy sneaking ahead of the soldiers to Hank's cabin. Well, maybe if she ran. Maybe. In the background, soldiers rolled their tents, shoved them into canvas bags emblazoned with royal seals, and loaded them upon carriages. Others brushed down their horses and harnessed them for travel.

"Travel time? If I run?" asked Tammy, eyebrow raised.

"Couple hours, maybe. Maybe more, though," replied Georgie.

Tammy had to get to Hank's cabin before the war party sniffed Jackson out. She knew how much it meant to Hank to save that beast. She wasn't exactly physically fit, but she steeled herself for the task ahead. Taking off without so much as a by-your-leave, Tammy fast-walked right into the forest. She found a trail bordering the road, with a veil of trees in between, so she could keep an eye out for the carriages, should they catch up to her. As she fast-walked, Tammy developed a new style of locomotion that was sinuous, one might even say lithe. It involved hips describing circles and long active reaches with the legs, thighs working, ankles trying to stay steady in non-sensible shoes.

The shoes' well-tanned leather made her look at once tough and high-maintenance. As Tammy marched, she realized that, in a grand reversal of how things are generally supposed to go, Fast Eddie's love had made her feel ugly and insecure, but his rejection had, ultimately, made her confident.

As she walked, Tammy recalled her erstwhile lover: the slender arms that seemed to hang so easily as if they were but doll arms hooked over pegs in his shoulders. That free. That loose. She hated him for those arms. Then, she remembered that nasty habit of his: gum popping. Fast Eddie used to feed himself a stick of gum just after Tammy had said something clever. Then, instead of remarking upon her cleverness, he just made his gum go *Pop! Pop! Pop!*—weirdly erasing her intelligence and wit with each explosion.

Racing to find Hank and the beast before the queen's army did, Tammy didn't let these thoughts slow her pace. She used them as fuel and remembered the elaborate black-magic rituals Shadooda had given her. Yes, as soon as she returned home, revenge against Fast Eddie would return to its rightful place first and foremost on Tammy's to-do list, but for now, she concerned herself only with saving Jackson.

She hoped Hank still had the beast under his protection but understood it could be living anywhere by now—alone and unsuspecting—just the way Fast Eddie had long ago found Tammy, herself.

45

WHERE EVERYBODY WANTS TO
AVOID A NEST OF ELECTRIC EELS

"My watch! My baby!" Schrank said, kissing his stupid watch like a long-lost child.

"I told you I could find it!" Georgie crowed from her perch in the hayloft.

"Good job, Georgie!" Schrank replied while preparing coffee. "I'm going to make you chief head executive of everything!"

"Whatever," she said. "I'll be long gone through a portal to a better world before anyone notices that."

"About that," said Schrank. "I'm afraid I failed, once again, to convince the queen to open a portal. I just don't understand why she didn't buy our story, what with all those charts and graphs."

"I don't want to hurt your feelings, Jim," Georgie said, tucking her infirmary gown around her thighs, "but that crap wouldn't have fooled a junior-high dropout, let alone the queen of Bumblegreen."

"But it nearly had *me* convinced!" he protested

"Well, you're a fool, then, Schrank, and I don't suspect the queen is one."

"All royals are fools and illiterates," Schrank said. "Everyone knows that."

"Dahlia's different," said Georgie. "We're not going to be able to trick her. Not easily. Anyway, it doesn't matter because one of the portals is already open."

"Already WHAT?" asked Schrank.

"The monkey told me," she said. "He went through a badger hole to a place called No Oaks and has a shirt to prove it. The deed is done! All we've got to do now is find the damned portal."

Schrank was silent a moment, then said, "We're that close to getting out of Bumblegreen? Really?"

"And making a million in the process, don't forget," said Georgie.

"So," asked Schrank, pressing buttons on the watch, peering at the coordinates that popped up, "which portal did the monkey go through?"

"I don't know," she said.

"Wait, what? There are hundreds!" Schrank complained. When Georgie shrugged, he added, "No matter. We can go from one to the other and check them all. We're getting out! We're getting out!"

"Slight problem with that idea," said Georgie. "No doubt there're sentries watching over the portals: monkeys, I'd bet. You start going through Bumblegreen trying to jackhammer portals open, the queen's going to find out, and whoops! There you go! Dropped from the cage into a nest of electric eels! Bye-bye!"

"Crud."

"My feelings exactly."

"Though I always envisioned execution by sharks, instead."

"I'm sure Dahlia'd be willing to accommodate your special execution needs."

"Okay, taking execution off the table, how can we find the open portal?"

"Wrong question—question is, 'Who opened the portal in the first place?'"

"Who did?"

"A magician!"

"How do you figure?"

"Because the portals are scientifically, hermetically sealed. No one can open them. But magicians can do anything; ergo, they can open portals."

"Admittedly, a shot in the dark, but okay. What do we do now?"

"I have a lead. The duchess' mansion is full of old heirlooms, and whenever I'm there, lately, I can smell magic, literally smell it. Smells like old pennies. Anyway, I think if I scour the place, I'll surely find an heirloom or something that gives a clue as to how to locate a magician."

"Now, that's *really* a shot in the dark."

"Got a better idea?"

"No, I don't, except couldn't you just ask the duchess? Save all that time?"

"Oh, no," replied Georgie. "So much directness could send her into fits, or worse: get me exiled from the mansion. The duchess is the type where you don't just ask. You cajole. You sneak. You wheedle. As long as nothing's said outright, everything's okay."

"So," asked Schrank, "how does this cajoling and wheedling work, exactly?"

"From that old pennies smell alone, I can tell the duchess, or someone in her mansion, has access to a magician," said Georgie. "I'm sure of it. So, all I have to do is snoop around and find the magician, or the magical heirloom, or whatever she's got."

"As if," said Schrank.

"As if what?" asked Georgie.

"As if magicians were blowing on the wind like box-elder bugs," he said. "They're hidden someplace. They're gone. They're private royal property. Nobody can find them. Maybe they're all dead!"

Despite a total lack of surveillance in the Favra barn, Georgie felt the need to whisper: "I really don't think so!"

"You're freaking me out," replied Schrank.

"Give me a couple of days," she insisted. "I know I can find a magician, witch, sorcerer-type person. The answer's there, in the mansion, somewhere. Right. Under. My. Nose."

Schrank gave Georgie the old squint-eyed look of a co-conspirator and evil-doer and nodded his head ever so imperceptibly. Thus, the pair made their agreement in the way of spies. This made the act of opening a portal—which they believed would (but didn't care if it did) destroy Bumblegreen permanently—seem somehow glamorous and benevolent, rather than just plain wrong.

46

In Which Tammy and Hank
Submit to the Inevitable

Hank and Jackson sat together on the couch, enjoying what had become Hank's afternoon routine: contemplating his unopened bottle of magical potion while folding laundry and soaking his feet in a basin of water, waiting to turn into a trout. Hank's medicinal tea concoction burbled on the stove while Jackson gnawed away on the wooden arm of the sofa.

"Bah! I tell you, beast, being human's unbearable," prattled Hank. "I'd do anything to be a trout again. Oh, why won't I turn? This water's freezing! Beast, listen, if I turn and end up on the couch instead of in the basin, you'll flip me into the basin, right? With your nose? Right? We're buddies, right?"

Jackson looked at Hank with the peaceful but unknowing eyes of a dumb beast.

"Oh, how I envy you!" said Hank.

Jackson shook his big head and jingled his tags.

"I love it when you make that sound!" said Hank, who briefly considered holding his nose and chugging down that potion Fast Eddie had brought, in one gulp. He could stop all this unpredictable back-and-forthing from human to fish and turn into a human forever, for safety's sake, but Hank couldn't do it. The cost-benefit analysis kept coming out even. After all, becoming a human was its own type of torture. Just then, the front door swung open, and there stood Tammy.

"Where's that beast?" she hollered, before collapsing in the doorway.

Hank ran to her side, as did Jackson, whose tongue lolled out in the usual way.

"He's right here, Tams," said Hank. "Why? What's the trouble?"

"We've got to hide him!" she panted, then passed out.

Hank fanned her awake with the crossword puzzle section of the *Bumblegreen Gazette*, then massaged her ravaged feet, asking, "Who is it? Who found out about him?"

"Queen Dahlia herself!" replied Tammy, upon awakening.

Jackson turned a circle, jingled his tags, and found a new place to curl up on the floor.

"Hide him!" Tammy shrieked with enough vibrato to scare the front door off its one remaining hinge. "A war party's coming! They're searching every house! They're supposed to take him if they find him, dead or alive!"

"Crud," replied Hank, as his wristwatch beeped. "Bad timing."

He turned suddenly, blissfully, inexorably into a trout.

Tammy sprang up and chased Hank's wildly flopping fish-self around the room, finally caught him, and dumped him into the washbasin.

"Sorry," said fish-Hank as he swam in tight, washbasin circles. "Not much to do now but wait, I guess."

Looking out the window, Tammy watched the war party arrive at the duchess' mansion and assemble on the lawn among the patio furniture, statuary, and decorative tables the duchess had set out for her garden party.

A division of soldiers stomped across the field of thistles and weeds toward Hank's cabin. Quickly, Tammy considered hiding the beast, but where? She could run it into the forest, but Jackson was so friendly, he'd surely dash right back out and into the soldiers' arms. So, she stood there, holding the basin filled with Hank, in his trout incarnation, and the soldiers drew closer.

"Hank," Tammy said. "I don't know what to do."

"There's nothing to do, I'm afraid," answered Hank, gawping his fish mouth. "My poor beast. My poor, poor beast."

"If we don't put up a fight, they might take him alive," Tammy supposed. "Better than dead, don't you think? Best of the two evils?"

"Dead?" asked Hank, with alarm.

"They're armed, buddy," Tammy replied. "Spears and dart guns and long things with spikes."

Hank gasped as only a fish can do.

Tammy kissed Jackson, tentatively, on the top of his big furry head, hoisted the basin containing fish-Hank, and walked out the back door. She couldn't bear to watch. As she exited, Hank's front door burst open. and the panicked sounds of amateur dogcatchers at work soon echoed through the valley.

Tammy didn't look back as she carried the basin next door to her own shack, which had already been ransacked by another detachment of soldiers who broke her two kitchen chairs and left dresser drawers dumped upon the floor.

"Some war party," said Tammy to the fish, who seemed to be crying fish tears. "More like a bunch of ruffians on the loose."

Hank gawped helplessly while Tammy complained about the damage to her shack, just to distract him from what was going on next door. When she ran out of complaints, she remembered a folk song and sang it at the top of her lungs, trying to drown out the crashing, smashing, and exclaiming.

Despite all that, they could both hear, loud and clear:

"Get the spear!"

"Get the net!"

"Look at its fangs!"

"Why's its tongue hanging out like that?"

"It must be diseased!"

"Load the gun, you idiot!"

"Can't you see it's vicious?"

Tammy sang,

> *Live long, live long*
> *Food nor drink nor money have I none*
> *Longing for the rainy weather*
> *Once I did make merry-ee*

She couldn't remember where she first heard the little tune. It almost seemed as if it had been drifting on the wind, in and out of her consciousness for years, waiting to come to mind.

Eventually, the hubbub next door died down. Hank continued to gawp and swim in circles in his basin, and Tammy slumped at her window, watching disheveled soldiers drag away a large, unwieldy bundle wrapped in canvas. They loaded the bundle into a carriage, looking utterly spent.

As they left the premises, the soldiers defiled the duchess' pristine lawn with carriage tracks, knocked over a fountain, and smashed an ice sculpture Tammy had personally ordered for the party. In the distance, Tammy saw the duchess run outside, throw up her hands, and, presumably, rebuff the oafish soldiers as the war party drove away, banners gaily streaming. Some soldiers leaned out the windows to apologize, others to cheerfully huzzah.

Once the royal train of carriages had become but a dot in the distance, Hank popped back into his human self.

"Hate to say this, Hank, but we're supposed to report to work at the garden party in about an hour," said Tammy as she walked him back to his shack.

"Oh, that thing," replied Hank. "What about my beast?"

"I'm trying my best to distract you, Hank," she said. "Go along with it, for once."

"Just give it to me straight, Tams," he asked.

"Let's just talk about something else," she said. "Tea. Tea is nice. Tea is pretty, almost. Tell me, this tea you make, is this some kind of witch's brew?"

"What? No, no," he said. "It's just an herbal remedy for staving off the effects of Zade Fandey's. Only works for about six hours at a time, though. What happened to my beast? Where's my beast? Did he survive the raid?"

In his shack, where the soldiers had left everything broken and disheveled, Hank sighed, removed his wet clothes, wrung them out, and put on his tuxedo. Tammy pressed her nose to the window, watching carriages disappear in the distance.

"I get it," he said. "You're trying to tell me I don't want to know."

"Yup," answered Tammy. "Let's talk about tea. Or we could talk about the duchess' party. Your choice."

"Well," said Hank, going along with it. "On the subject of my tea, I have this to say. It's nothing magical. Witchcraft, I think, would be more efficiently distilled. This stuff is just a folk remedy. In fact, I need some now, to make sure I don't change again for another six hours."

While speaking, they both noted an absence of blood stains on the floor, which gave them some measure of happiness. The beast had disappeared in a canvas sack. That was all they really knew.

"But speaking of witchcraft, this is witchcraft," said Hank. He showed her the still-unopened brown bottle Fast Eddie had given him. "Fast Eddie got this from somebody who got it from somebody who got it from a magician, or so he says. Says it'll turn me human for good. What do you think?"

Tammy took the bottle from him with great care. She held it up to the light streaming in through the shack's back door. "That's quite a claim," she said.

"Don't I know it," he replied.

"Worst-case scenario, it's swamp water and you get an amoeba," said Tammy.

"Yeah. No!" he replied. "Worst case scenario is it actually works."

"Hank, buddy," she said. "That's the best-case scenario."

"Babe, you don't know," Hank replied. "You've never been an animal. You've never known peace."

"Never known peace? That's very true. I never have known peace," she agreed. "Maybe I should try and contract Zade Fandey's disease, eh?"

"Sure, if you don't mind being a fish literally out of the water," he said.

"Yeah. Too risky," she said.

"By far, Tams," he said.

Tammy settled deep into Hank's saggy couch, dropped her head back, and stared at the ceiling. Hank sat beside her and put his hand on her growing belly.

"So, I've been meaning to ask … whatcha got in here?" he asked.

"A baby, Hank. I can't hide it anymore," Tammy said, and cried.

Hank fetched her a handkerchief.

"It's Fast Eddie's," she admitted. "He did this and then left me!"

"Oh, sorry," was all Hank could think to say.

"I should have known better," Tammy said.

"Apparently he fell in love with a …" Hank began.

"With that nanny!" Tammy wailed.

"I was going to say with a squirrel," he said. "She's really a squirrel."

"She is?" Tammy asked.

"Yeah. It's over between them. Maybe you can get him back?" Hank suggested as he stroked Tammy's horsehair tresses with growing fascination.

"I don't want him back," she said. "I want to destroy him."

"Oh. I guess that's a human thing," Hank replied.

"Yeah. Vengeance," she whimpered through tears.

"Oh," he said, without understanding.

Finally, she said, "I have a way of getting my vengeance. Witchcraft that I know about. But it includes a laundry list of herbs and incantations and instructions and all these funky rituals I have to do."

Black magic, after all, is tricky stuff.

"For vengeance?" asked Hank.

"Yeah," she whispered. "It's real black magic!"

"I hate to see you like this Tams," said Hank, retrieving the potion from her wildly gesticulating hand and replacing it on a shelf. "I'm used to gathering herbs, though, what with the tea. So, maybe I can help."

"Could you? I have to get a couple kinds of mushrooms and grind them into paste and … let's see," said Tammy, as she drew a folded parchment from her pocket and squinted at it. "I think I have to catch a skink." She looked up, inquiringly, almost shyly, from the page, through her cascading ebony curtain.

Hank drew the hair aside and tucked it behind her ear.

"They're not so clever, skinks," he said. "You can just grab them by the tail, if you know how."

"I'm sorry, Hank. About your beast," she said. "I tried to save him. I did."

"Do you think there's a chance they let him live?" he asked.

"You really loved him, didn't you?" she replied.

"To the extent that I understand love, yeah," he explained. "What do you think they'll do to him? I mean, if he's still alive?"

"Probably drop him in the tank with swimming, hungry sharks. He's a portal jumper, after all," she admitted.

Hank stared at the floor. "If I'd taken that potion, I would have stayed human and could have fought them off."

"Not really," said Tammy. "It was a whole, entire war party."

Hank leaned against the back door's jamb and stared out at the patchy grass where he had first found Jackson. Tammy came up behind him—intent, still, upon distracting her friend from his morbid, worrisome thoughts—and put her chin on his shoulder.

"Look," she said. "I think I see a skink."

Hank sighed.

"Let's catch it," she said.

Hank (wishing to be a fish now, more than ever) reluctantly agreed, "Yes, let's catch it, then head up to the mansion and help the duchess with her stupid party."

"Something to do," answered Tammy.

"Yes," said Hank, deftly catching the skink by its tail. "Something to do."

PART FOUR

THE HUE AND CRY

OF A BLOODLETTING MOB

THE HUE AND CRY
OF A BLOODLETTING MOB

47

WHEREIN THE QUEEN GOES INCOGNITO

Queen Dahlia sat on the dusty throne-room floor, her back against a collapsing cardboard box full of Affairs of State files, her skirts billowing like a crashed hot-air balloon deflating in the sun. She watched the iron cage, where Jackson sat panting. Dahlia could barely believe her own eyes. There he stood—the strangest creature ever to walk on four legs. And if that beast hailed from Bumblegreen, Dahlia would eat her petticoats poached. With a silken hanky, the queen dabbed at tears of frustration and groaned. The idea that this strange beast could have come through an open portal served as the catalyst for the umpteenth doomsday scenario to play out in her royal head in less than a week.

While she watched Jackson, he watched her. More specifically, he watched the cheese and roast beef sandwich the queen had brought along for lunch. She ripped off a hunk of sandwich and tossed it to the dog, who eagerly gobbled it up, tired as he was of the bitter lizards and fatty rodents he had been snacking on these last couple of days. Glad to see someone, anyone, happy—even if it was the very beast that would probably cause a kingdom-wide blight, her own overthrow, and the end of civilization as she knew it—Dahlia tossed the rest of the sandwich to the sloppy, fanged, and stinking animal. She had to admit he was kind of cute.

When Dahlia made a kissy noise, Jackson cocked one ear. When she made a clucking sound, he swirled around and adorably wrapped one paw over his nose. The queen fell a little bit in love with the funny old beast and poured out her troubles to it. She confessed to Jackson her general unsuitedness for queening, her love of simple gingham, and her affection for running barefoot in the castle's cold, stone corridors. Jackson's moist, long-lashed brown eyes seemed to emit understanding.

Dahlia told the beast he was doomed. He seemed fine with that. She told him the peasants were liable to violently overthrow her when folks got wind of his existence. He took an unconcerned stance on this as well. In Dahlia's opinion, the beast had the right attitude to life.

Jackson (though Dahlia didn't know his name, as such) ate the sandwich greedily, then rolled around and scratched his back on the hinges of the terrible trap door that could have opened at any moment to drop him screaming down a twenty-foot freefall into certain doom. Dahlia informed him that, due to resentments regarding her unpopular leniency with the gypsies a few years back, the only way she might possibly keep both her job and her head, once the news about Jackson got out, would be to send him to his death in a very public manner.

Jackson licked his paw without comment.

Gazing at the obviously otherworldly beast, Queen Dahlia wondered how a portal could possibly have opened. She knew Prindal's List was safe in its hiding place in the gouda, so she could only conclude the polymer on one of the portals must have failed. *That Jimothy Shrank must have been right about my polymer,* she thought. *But how could he have been? His science was utterly unsound!*

The horror and confusion of it all had driven Dahlia to her current state of crouching in the dark, in the dust, talking to a dumb animal, fearing for her life. The plucky gal, with her turbulent mind, storm-tossed head of curls, and explosion of layered silken skirts, knew eventually she would have to take some kind of very public action about the beast and shuddered under the weight of it.

Dahlia, at this point in her short queening career, was utterly sick of people, especially her subjects, with all their requests and entreaties. She was sick of schemers trying to undo all her hard work in sealing the portals. (Hard work that had, she believed, saved Bumblegreen from certain doom.)

"Now, *who,*" began Dahlia. "If you could talk, Beast, perhaps you would tell me *who* was that long-legged, lanky, weirdly grinning, sort-of handsome-ish man who came out of the woods just as the soldiers presented me with you, all trussed up inside a canvas sack?

"And sorry about that, by the way. I mean, that guy, the way he jumped up and basically took credit for your capture, what was his deal? He said he had told someone about you, and that someone told the duchess, who told my security chief, who told me. Rather a roundabout manner of claiming responsibility, don't you think? And anyway, wasn't it especially odd when the lanky man said—oh, what was it? I remember it as a sort of half-compliment, half-insult that disturbed, yet kind-of intrigued me."

Jackson chased his tail. Having caught it, he wagged it. He didn't know Fast Eddie was trying to seduce the queen any more than she did.

Talked out, and now sandwich-less, Dahlia left Jackson in the cage. She squeezed out between the throne room's monstrous oaken doors and ran past pages and regents and subjects demanding autographs and meetings and lengthy explanations of utterly mind-boggling things. She ran past several nursing mothers sneezing at their babies, and past the cracks in the wall plaster where, as a child, she had hidden secret notes, turning the whole castle into a child's time capsule of life's trivialities. Finally, she dashed through a side exit and right onto the castle lawn, where she threw her sad, confused, and half-seduced self down on a hillock of grass.

48

IN WHICH HANK DISCOVERS A NEW TALENT

"Am I early?" asked Georgie, looking around the duchess' lawn and noticing the full trays of hors d'oeuvres, brimming bowls of punch, and hundreds of empty seats.

The duchess wore a brave smile, but had to work not to blink, so the tears wouldn't fall. Tammy and Hank stood at attention, holding rigid smiles and trays loaded with food. No guests were in attendance.

"Not really," answered the duchess.

"But I'm here! *We're* here, aren't we? And that's all that matters," Georgie gushed. "Now I, for one, am starved for entertainment.

Duchess, did you know Hank tells the most intriguing stories? Go ahead, Hank! Tell the duchess about … you know … something interesting." Georgie gave the surprised butler a wink.

"Hank? Oh, Georgie, don't be silly. He's the butler!" replied the duchess.

"And only the best butler this side of the castle!" replied Georgie. "A butler's got to entertain, you know. It's an oft-overlooked part of the job description."

"It is?" chorused Hank, the duchess, and Tammy.

"Most definitely!" sang Georgie as she eased her slender posterior into one of the duchess' imported wrought-iron garden chairs, just as if the party were in full swing.

In reality, Georgie didn't know Hank, didn't know if he could tell stories, tap dance, or what, and only chose him to distract the duchess because he wasn't Tammy, who might tell a certain disturbing story about seeing Georgie traipsing through Bumblegreen in an infirmary gown and make things worse for her. Grasping at straws, Georgie was trying to distract the duchess in order to fulfill her promise to Jimothy Schrank. The first part of her plan involved keeping the duchess entertained. The total absence of guests at the party made that tough, though.

The duchess lay on a chaise lounge ensconced in a patch of tiger lilies. Hank stood nearby, holding his platter of cucumber sandwiches, looking down at the grass, holding back tears, biting his lip, and shifting from foot to foot.

"Go on, Hank!" said Georgie with one of her trademark full-lipstick grins. "Tell us a story!"

Tammy looked, puzzled, at Hank. He winked a red-rimmed eye and shrugged, as if to say, *Why not? Things couldn't possibly get worse.*

He put down his tray and gently grasped a piece of garden statuary

—a simple but elegant female figure in a demure pose. As Hank concocted a story, he rubbed the figure gently and rhythmically with his thumb. Before long, this tender gesture fascinated the duchess.

"I guess," Hank began, glancing at Tammy, "this is … a love story."

"Oh, splendid!" said the duchess, clapping her hands, lying back on the chaise, and closing her eyes.

Hank cleared his throat, thought a moment, and commenced: "You see," he said. "I was once loved by an enchantress."

"Wonderful!" Georgie exclaimed.

"You know," Hank added, "this story is from the old days—the days when portal travel was a perfectly ordinary thing. Nothing to it. Does that shock you ladies?"

"Oh, no!" exclaimed the duchess. "Those were the best days!"

"It all happened," he continued, "in the sultanate of Gimran, in another world, back when men were men and travel was Travel, with a capital *T*."

Tammy tried not to laugh. She could tell this newfound storytelling skill delighted Hank, even as he discovered it. His tears over Jackson stopped flowing and a half-smile played upon his fishy lips.

"There was a problem, however. Our love was forbidden," said Hank, with gravitas.

"Of course it was!" agreed the duchess.

"This girl, she was too young. A decade my junior, actually," Hank lamented. "Ah, but ladies, her beauty was unsurpassed. Now, of course, when I saw her on the street, her whole body was covered discreetly in the traditional voluminous orange cloak that women wear in Gimran."

"An orange cloak?" the duchess asked. "Oh, that won't do at all. Very unfashionable!"

"Nevertheless," said Hank, with authority. "That was what they wore. What can I do about it?"

"Oh," replied the duchess.

"But, you see," added Hank, "when her black-rimmed eyes peeked slyly from above that orange veil … oh! I used to go mad with desire! This girl was nothing less than an enchantress; and I, a helpless victim of her charms."

Georgie's glee practically jumped around the garden like aphids. She had planned on somehow distracting the duchess for hours, and now Hank played right into her hands. With the duchess thus distracted, Georgie planned to sniff out that certain subtle magic she had promised to find for Schrank. Georgie could already sense the fresh, strong, old-pennies aroma of magic that seemed to permeate the duchess' mansion.

"This particular young woman was actually an orphan," continued Hank. "And, although she wasn't a little girl any longer, the law of Gimran decreed she must live in the orphanage until marriage. Gimran wasn't the sort of place where young ladies struck out on their own, you know, and rented apartments, and that kind of thing."

The duchess and Georgie laughed at that: the duchess, at the absurd notion of living in an apartment; and Georgie, at the funny notion of not striking out on her own.

"But, in secret," Hank continued, "the curvaceous and unashamed lady used to embrace me generously. Oh, I probably shouldn't admit the truth …"

"Admit it!" ordered the duchess, giggling.

"Well, all right, but it might offend your delicate sensibilities, Duchess," said Hank.

"Delicate? Delicate my hat!" Georgie exclaimed. The duchess gave her friend a playful swat and continued giggling. By now, she was well into her second glass of champagne.

"My enchantress cared nothing for social conventions," continued Hank, still dutifully holding aloft his platter of cucumber sandwiches. "When the elders at the orphanage scolded and beat her for her carefree ways, she only laughed. Her name was …" Hank paused, stuck.

Tammy's effort to hold back her mirth resulted in an involuntary snort.

Hank looked around the meadow desperately, seeking inspiration, then found it in Tammy's eyes. "Hazel," he said.

Georgie breathed a sigh of relief, and the duchess giggled like a lunatic.

Sensing the "party's" descent into informality, Tammy put down her tray of gouda and crackers and looked at the woods' edge, where she had stashed a wicker basket containing a skink, some mushrooms, a batch of herbs, and three wildflowers Hank had helped her gather for her black magic recipe. *No time like the present,* Tammy thought. Clutching the parchment Shadooda had given her, she snuck into the woods, retrieved her basket, and got busy doing black magic.

49

IN WHICH DAHLIA DOUBTS
HER VERY PURPOSE IN LIFE

Dahlia, on her hillock of grass, gazed up at the clouds and contemplated the venerable Favra Watch Company, her meeting with Schrank, Prindal's List safe inside its gouda, and the wide assortment of criminals who had been after The List for so many years. She contemplated just letting people go, one at a time, through the portals. Over and out.

They want to leave Bumblegreen? She thought. *Why am I keeping them, anyway? What's so wonderful about the place? After all, we're overrun with Zade Fandey's disease, always in danger of getting the*

316

blight again, and utterly paralyzed—economically and progress-wise —without the imports we used to depend upon. The magic that used to keep this place afloat has disappeared entirely, thought Dahlia, *so what's the use?*

What bothered Dahlia the most was the way the magicians had utterly vanished. *Perhaps,* she thought, *they disappeared through the portals themselves.* She didn't know where they had gone, and no one else seemed to know, either. The thought of investigating the mystery gave her a headache. The notion used to be that with magic, anything was possible. But without it, how could Dahlia insist life in Bumblegreen amounted to something even a little bit special? *Maybe it's time to abandon the place, after all,* she thought. Bumblegreen had been fun for generations, but this world was getting to look and feel like a failed experiment.

Ever since she had been crowned, at the tender age of nine, Dahlia had asked herself these questions weekly, daily, even hourly, and still didn't have any particularly good answers. Despite everything, it just didn't seem right to abandon a world her family had ruled for as far back as anyone knows—not just for her own sake but for that of all the peasants.

We're all Bumblegreenis, she thought, further asking herself, *Does history count for nothing? Can the peasants even survive in other lands?* Then, she wondered, *Won't folks, after they've Traveled, eventually want to come back?* Because if they did, all that Travel back and forth would cause the blight to return (so she believed), and then Bumblegreen would be in the soup again.

In her mind's eye, Dahlia saw Bumblegreen's population dwindling to nothing and its landscape, polka-dotted with open portals, becoming a blight-ridden dustbowl. Bumblegreen! This Bumblegreen! The willow that weeped over her, the daisies that wiggled in the breeze, the nearby magnolia tree spreading its elegant branches, the castle's green lawn stretching to evergreen woods—this picture of perfection.

Of course, thought Dahlia, *these are the castle grounds, not the* real *Bumblegreen.* She had heard about starvation, and destruction, and ugly buildings built far from plumb. She knew such things were out there, somewhere in Bumblegreen, but hadn't personally seen them.

Out on the lawn, chewing on a grass stem, it occurred to the young queen that she might just go out into the world and have a look—see how bad life really was for non-royals, if indeed it was bad at all. While chewing, she noticed a particularly low-flying cloud in the sky. Dahlia stood up, toes buried deep in the soft, luxuriant grass, and watched the cloud moving across the lawn, unnaturally fast. It headed out there toward the "real" Bumblegreen.

She looked back at the castle's grand entrance, its parapet, its tiny slits of windows.

No one was watching her, so Dahlia locked eyes on the cloud and ran after it as it ducked into the woods and seemed to float along, just under the trees' extensive canopy. She found a path into the woods and scampered after the cloud—her eyes up and feet running blind.

After she had run a good distance, the young queen marveled at how the forest's vegetation changed, becoming more tangled and brambly. She marveled at how much farther into the forest her long legs took her, now, than in her childhood days of dashing after wild hunches. Then Dahlia stopped, caught her breath, and realized just how dark and lonely the unkempt woods can really be. In light of that, she thought about all the enemies she had made, not the least of them this Schrank fellow from Favra or Impact or whatever it was.

One thing bothered Dahlia about Schrank. Favra Watch Company —that venerable old Bumblegreen institution—had money, power, and pull. She wondered if she hadn't made a deadly mistake by sending Schrank away so curtly. There were assassins about, after all. Probably. Maybe. In the dark and wet, surrounded by strange and pointy leaves, Dahlia became acutely aware of her vulnerability. She imagined stealthy figures in all the shadows. Just then, Dahlia felt a tickling all around her head and face and caught her breath, figuring she had been caught in a net of some kind.

This is it! she thought. *Assassins have got me now!* But then, Dahlia saw the butterflies.

Before her eyes, the cloud she had been following simply dissipated into bits and pieces—pieces that flitted and floated on their own, like picnic napkins loose on the breeze. Each piece turned out to be a single white butterfly. The butterflies, with their gleaming whiteness, surrounded her.

She marveled at the butterflies' delicate tissue-thinness and the delightful fluttering of their graceful wings. The queen forgot her troubles and danced among them, taking the butterflies' presence as a good omen, until they flew off into the darkness of the forest, teasing their way above a slender, seldom-used path.

Queen Dahlia felt as if she were about to leave castle grounds. She didn't know exactly where the boundaries lay, but it didn't look too castle-ish back there in the woods. It sure didn't. Didn't look too royal. A few too many thorny branches and too much darkness and too many hanging, swooping vegetative things for that, but she had to either follow the brightness of the butterflies or stay in the creepy shadows.

The path she had come in on lay clear of underbrush. She could still run back home. Dahlia looked back at the castle's fairytale beauty, then peered the other way, into the darkness of the forest, into shifting shadows. She couldn't fathom walking back home just yet. In fact,

Dahlia got it into her head she might actually run away. Yes!

Some regent or other will surely take over ruling Bumblegreen, she figured, and *he'll probably do a decent job, too. In fact, I could,* she thought, *hide out in the woods forever.* She imagined some little abandoned cabin she could make into a home … start a little garden … get a dairy cow. Yes! Yes!

Dahlia lifted voluminous skirts and charged headlong through the underbrush after the butterfly cloud. While charging, she fantasized sewing a couple of her petticoats together to make a sheet for some little peasant-sized bed. Another layer of skirts could be stitched into curtains for the window of her cabin. She couldn't wait to find an abandoned cabin and set up housekeeping. She would use pieces of her feather headdress as fishing lures, melt down her jewelry for money, and start a little apple orchard out in the middle of nowhere.

Oh yes, young Dahlia had it all figured out as she gracelessly crashed through the saplings, yanked tangled creepers from her arms and ankles, and spit out the gnats that flew into her hurrahing mouth. But never mind that. Truth was, Dahlia hadn't the faintest beginning of an idea how to cook a meal, tie a shoelace, or make a bed, but we won't dwell on such details at this important moment of self-actualization.

50

WHERE GEORGIE TRIES A COUPLE
OF ENTHUSIASTIC LOGROLLS

"Hazel believed in love and only love," said Hank, pacing the duchess' lawn. "She even told her young friends that to love one another was to worship the creator. What blasphemy! But I'm Godless, myself, so I didn't mind a bit."

Hank glanced between Georgie and the duchess, looking for sign that he had gone too far.

"Oh, so am I!" said the duchess.

Georgie nodded and smiled, thinking: *perfect, perfect!* She knew real estate was the duchess' only deity. Hers, too.

"Hazel prayed three times a day, as was the Gimrani custom," Hank continued, "but she claimed each time she made love that counted as one. Hey, sometimes two!"

Tammy, sneaking behind a bank of oleander bushes, was surprised to hear such racy subject matter coming from her old buddy, Hank. *What does Hank know of making love?* thought Tammy. *Fish lay eggs!*

Tammy crept into the forest, grabbed her wicker basket, and circled around to the mansion's service entrance, confident that, due to Hank's captivating story, no one would notice her absence.

Before long—with the duchess in thrall to Hank's tale of love and adventure—Georgie snuck into the mansion. There, she ransacked the sitting room for heirlooms, trying to sniff out the magic she knew was present. Through an open window, Georgie could hear Hank expounding away.

"Of course," he said, sadly, "Hazel was shunned by proper society girls in Gimran, but also secretly envied. I was a younger man then, you see, and working as a nurse."

"A nurse?" asked the duchess with a touch of alarm.

"Oh, yes," replied Hank. "You see, as you know, I enjoy being of service. This is my gift. "

The duchess liked that, and relaxed into her lawn furniture in something like a coquettish pose.

Inside the mansion's sitting room, Georgie opened a china cabinet and carefully removed each decorative plate and whisky decanter from its shelf. A gentle breeze swayed the room's gauzy curtains as Hank's words drifted across the lawn.

Georgie turned the plates and decanters upside down, spun them on their edges, pressed them to her forehead. She made up magical sounding words and uttered them, feeling foolish but determined to activate any magical properties that might be hidden in the heirlooms. So far, no luck. She moved on to an old credenza, where she found silver cutlery, serving spoons, tablecloths, and the odd salt-and-pepper shaker. She clicked the items together, juggled them, spoke to them, and shook them. So far, nothing. Yet, that magic smell grew stronger.

"At first," continued Hank, his voice drifting through the drawing-room window, "Hazel mocked me mercilessly. She dogged my footsteps and hid behind pillars, watching me, in order to mimic me for the amusement of her friends. Ah, cruel youth!"

The duchess gazed up at the perfect blue sky. Hank's story fed her imaginings, like winged dragonflies to a sticky-tongued toad.

"But all the while, I knew Hazel was there," said Hank, "and I was thrilled by the attention. I welcomed my unusual admirer!"

Georgie had, by now, ransacked the china cabinet, a credenza, and an oaken chest filled with moth-eaten woolens, but she hadn't found a single heirloom. The magic smell tickled her nose, though, growing stronger by the minute, and soon, Georgie was nearly drunk with the essence of the stuff.

The very rug Georgie stood upon could have been an heirloom, for all she knew. *A flying carpet?* she wondered. To test it, Georgie did a dance, tried some calisthenics, and even lay down and tried a couple of enthusiastic logrolls. Nothing.

She wondered if the silk settee could be an heirloom. *Would the magic come through my rear end, or what?* she wondered. She sat on it, bounced on it, then tasted a corner. She actually licked it. She was running out of ideas.

Throughout all this, Hank kept the duchess enthralled, but who knew how long before she noticed Georgie's absence? Anything could break Hank's spell, so Georgie worried as she searched.

"Now, I could have made certain overtures to Hazel, of course," Hank continued. "I could have seduced her, to put it crudely, but," he added with a wink, "I was in no hurry to get embroiled in a, shall we say, 'indelicate social matter.'" Hank's storytelling skill amused him just as much as it did the duchess. For the first time, being human started to seem almost fun to Hank, what with discovering new talents, and all.

"What happened was," he continued, "one day, Hazel followed me down the back alley of a bustling market, but tiptoeing down some steep steps, she tripped and fell and sprained her ankle. She cried out in pain, so, instinctively, I turned to her."

"Because you were a healer!" suggested the duchess.

"Indeed. Indeed!" Hank agreed. "So, I finally faced my pursuer. She lay helpless on the ground, eyes wide with fear!" Hank paced the lawn, allowing the suspense to sink in.

Georgie ran her hand along the marble wall of the mansion's foyer, pressing here and there, looking for secret panels. Then, she inspected the dining room's candlesticks, the silver bowl centerpiece, and each of the chrysanthemums floating in it. She pulled out all the drawers in a sideboard and dumped their contents on the table. As the scent of magic grew, Georgie got sloppy. And angry.

Georgie opened a window and heard Hank's voice carry across the lawn, past ornate wrought-iron chairs, untouched cucumber sandwiches, and unpoured glasses of punch; past hillocks of violets and patches of daffodils; past the swans floating serenely on the lake; and past the little wooden footbridge.

"I gently manipulated Hazel's ankle," continued Hank, "but she screamed in pain! I could see the ankle was sprained, and badly, too. The girl would have to be carried through the city streets to the orphanage hospital. You see, for a girl like her—any Gimrani girl, for that matter—to be touched by a man in public … well, it could bring irreparable disgrace. Of course, I offered to leave her and go in search of help, but poor Hazel cried and begged for my protection."

Tears sprang to the duchess' eyes and Hank noticed this with amazement. The storytelling, for him, was like sneezing and having rubies fall out of one's nose—an unexpected, hidden talent.

"She was more afraid of being left alone and helpless on the street," he said, "than of being touched by me. You can see her predicament."

"Oh, yes, I can!" exclaimed the duchess.

"Hazel grasped my sleeve and said, 'You must carry me, Hank. But not a single soul can see us!'" Hank added, "So, that is exactly what I did."

Inside the mansion, Georgie riffled through packs of gum, rusty watches, expired tubes of silver polish, makeup compacts, boxes of hairpins, tools used for small repairs, and even a bunch of old bicycle chains. The sideboard drawers seemed to function as a repository for every type of small-sized junk imaginable, but none of it was magical, as far as Georgie could tell. She grabbed a vase of tulips, flung the flowers to the floor, and carefully inspected the *objet d'art* for an imprint of any kind, but found nothing.

She put her ear to the vase and tried to listen for … *what?* she thought. *Am I expecting the cries of a trapped genie? The sound of witches cackling?* Georgie felt more foolish than ever, but that scent of magic had become so strong it made her delirious. Her need for the magic, and its source, made her grind her teeth.

"I cradled Hazel's slight form," continued Hank, "and then, like a common criminal, I carried her down a nearby alley, where overflowing garbage receptacles gave off the most horrendous stench."

"Oh!" interjected the duchess.

"Indeed!" he said, "But she told me, 'It is nothing! Just please be quick and keep close to the walls!'"

When Hank spoke for Hazel, he took on a husky but feminine contralto that painted a picture of a young girl with wisdom beyond her years. "Her attitude," said Hank, "was conspiratorial, not commanding. She used to wrap me around her little finger, she certainly did." Though Hank really ought to know nothing of such romantic ideas, they tumbled into his story, unbidden.

Mentally, the duchess took note: *So that's how it's done. Seduction.*

Hank could see the wheels turning, that female machinery grinding along, see the duchess' mind traveling down each psychic road, just as soon as he paved it for her. Now he understood, actually, how Fast Eddie felt. A surge of power accompanied his lies. He didn't like it.

Georgie wandered down the marble hall, inspecting each piece of statuary she passed. She peeked into an office and chewed a bunch of erasers, sharpened some pencils, pounded rubber stamps. Nothing doing. No magic.

All she sought was an imprint or some slight hint as to the location of a magician. She felt sure these kinds of people—these shaman types, these magical types—they wouldn't be immune to bribes. Just the coordinates for that one open portal into No Oaks—that's all she needed to get the hell out of Bumblegreen and make a million to boot, but her lengthy search produced nothing. Eventually, Georgie felt ridiculous. She left the duchess' office a shambles—lamps knocked down, desk drawers overturned, books strewn about the floor—and headed farther down the hall.

"She clutched me boldly," said Hank to the fascinated duchess, "Meantime, I carried her through those unfamiliar back alleys." Hank powered up to the story's climax. "You see, I kept my direction by looking above the walls of the city and navigating by the stars.

Finally, we arrived at the hospital's servant entry. I placed her on the stoop."

"You left her? No!" exclaimed the duchess.

"Oh no, Duchess," Hank continued. "I instructed her to beat her fists violently upon the door while I watched, hidden behind a wall. She did as instructed, and a doctor came. Oh, this doctor! He demanded to know how she had ended up in such an out-of-the-way place."

"Oh! Doctors! They can be so …" the duchess said.

"Indeed!" Hank agreed. "And Gimrani doctors are the worst. Are they doctors or private investigators? Right?"

"Right! Right!" the duchess agreed.

By now, Georgie had rummaged through a game room, a conservatory, a library, a study, a storage closet—still, not an heirloom in sight. Down a marble hall she wandered, then off through a magnificent drawing room that led to a parlor, and, from there, through a ballroom that led to a receiving chamber that led to a banquet room. She wasn't stopping and looking for heirlooms anymore. She was just exhausted and following her nose.

Indeed, the scent of magic became stronger by the minute.

51

WHERE ELIZABETHANN, AGAIN, ASSERTS HER WORTH

At one point, ElizabethAnn, locked tight inside her silken cocoon, heard voices—those of Georgie and Mobius. That was back when the whole trampoline incident occurred. She yelled for help and used her last remaining ounce of strength to set the cocoon in which she was, in fact, cocooned, to swinging. But Georgie and Mobius had troubles of their own, if you'll recall, so, eventually, ElizabethAnn managed only to rock herself to sleep. As she drifted off into the center of a deep cottony cloud of mental nothingness, she wondered vaguely if she would awaken with wings. Her dreams, however, didn't let her rest easy.

Grandma came to her again, saying, "Wake up, ElizabethAnn! Find Shadooda, kiddo! Don't succumb! You've got to fight!"

Each time she heard the voice, ElizabethAnn half-woke, struggled against the butterflies' spell, pounded on the walls of her prison, then sunk back into troubled slumber. Finally, in the most vivid dream yet, Grandma came to her in the form of a badger waddling its way through an underground tunnel. In the dream, ElizabethAnn marveled at the comfort enjoyed by badgers, something at which she never would have guessed.

"Lizzy?" asked the badger.

"What?" answered ElizabethAnn.

"I said, Lizzy!" shouted the badger.

"No one calls me Lizzy," answered ElizabethAnn.

"Why's that?" asked the badger.

"Because I'm five syllables worth of girl!" replied ElizabethAnn, just the way Grandma had taught her, and she saw a toothy smile creep over the badger's furry face.

"Just checking," said the badger, whom ElizabethAnn now recognized as Grandma.

"Grandma?" asked ElizabethAnn. "Is this where I surrender?"

"Who said anything about surrendering?" replied the badger.

"But how're we ever going to get back to No Oaks?" asked ElizabethAnn.

"Kiddo," replied the badger, "we're never going back there. Nothing awaits us there but a 'home.' Me, in the very near future, and you, for sure, eventually."

"But why are you hiding from me?" asked ElizabethAnn.

"Kiddo, listen," said the badger, polishing its whiskers. "I've broken a thing called the Universal Portal Compact. I can't explain the whole thing to you now, but if you can reveal the truth about Bumblegreen, the truth about the portals, the magic, and the blight's real cause being imports, you can set me free. I can come out of hiding. Otherwise the queen, when she catches me, will … I don't want to say."

"Tell her the truth!" shouted a voice at the distant end of the badger tunnel. Grandma looked, disapprovingly, in that direction.

"Zade, don't pester me," she said. "All you think about is your monkey coup."

"If this girl is so smart, Grandma, she had better get on it and release that magician," said the voice. "Otherwise, I'm letting all these monkeys go free. They're already starting to rebel and I don't think I can prevent a war much longer—a toothy, claw-slashing, monkeys-versus-humans war. I'm not kidding."

"See, ElizabethAnn," said Grandma-as-badger. "This isn't just about setting me free anymore. Basically, if you can do this thing, you can kind of end the power of the monkey tribunal forever. And if you can't, well, it's too late to go back to No Oaks. I mean, if you can't, then … I don't know."

"I know!" said the distant voice. "If she can't get those portals opened I'm going to have to release this batch of monkeys, give them the human babies they're clamoring for, and resume the entire thing just as it's been! Nothing will change, and you two will have to go back to No Oaks, if you don't get captured and executed first. That's it! That's all! Tell her that!"

"I'm not telling her that. She's just a kid!" shouted the badger, down the tunnel.

"I heard it anyway, Grandma," said ElizabethAnn. "Who's at the other end of the tunnel?"

"Damn," said the badger. "It's Zade. Zade Fandey. He's grouchy, but he's a good man. He just doubts us. Me, anyway. You too, a little. He doesn't think we can do it."

"I don't think so, either," replied ElizabethAnn. "I haven't found any magic or any Shadooda person. I don't even know what he looks like. Or she."

"Just follow your instincts, ElizabethAnn," said the badger. "You've got a good head on your shoulders. That's what I've always believed."

Then the badger galloped, as well as a badger can gallop, down the length of the tunnel. As ElizabethAnn watched its twitching tail retreat, she felt that feeling again—the soft cloud of mental nothingness.

Soon, she awoke, still inside the chrysalis. Feeling a little refreshed this time, she resumed pounding the walls, swinging the pod, and screaming for help.

52

IN WHICH GEORGIE FINDS THE
SOURCE OF THAT OLD-PENNIES SMELL

By now, Georgie couldn't hear Hank's story anymore, so deeply had she explored into the depths of the mansion. She had rummaged through a game room, a conservatory, a library, a study, a storage closet, and still, there wasn't an heirloom in sight. Down a mahogany-paneled hall she wandered, then off through a parlor, which led to a ballroom, which led to a receiving chamber, which led to a banquet room. She wasn't stopping and looking for heirlooms anymore. Exhausted, Georgie just followed her nose, now. The scent of magic became stronger by the minute.

"Oh, Hazel replied to the doctor with vagaries," said Hank to the duchess, training his gaze on the distance. "With each sentence she uttered, the doctor furrowed his brow more, but Hazel only howled with pain and clutched at the ankle. So, finally, the doctor called an assistant to fetch a stretcher and carry Hazel inside, to safety."

"Thank goodness!" exclaimed the duchess.

"Her great acting job really made me laugh!" said Hank. "And I admired her determination, her boldness, the overall level-headed way she handled the situation."

While Hank spoke, the duchess resolved that she wanted to be level-headed like Hazel, especially now that she knew it was sexy. She didn't know how, but she wanted to be that.

"I knew then that I was in love with her," Hank said. "That was the moment, and what a golden moment it was! So what I did was follow them into the hospital. I wasn't on duty that day, as a nurse, but I pretended to be, and I managed to get myself assigned to have Hazel as a patient. During her convalescence, we got to know each other thoroughly," said Hank, raising an eyebrow. "Thoroughly," he repeated.

Exhausted by her search, Georgie slumped into an armchair in yet another grandly furnished room—some kind of formal breakfasting area, where geraniums bloomed on a cheery window ledge. Out that window, Georgie saw the duchess and Hank, still on the lawn. Now, they strolled together. The duchess tossed her hair like a girl, and that made Georgie happy, but the feeling surprised her. Georgie didn't know she could feel gladness for another, so she catalogued the feeling, much like an archeologist would do with some strange bit of statuary.

Georgie's chair swiveled, so she swiveled it, and that's when she swiveled around and noticed the slender stone staircase that wound down and down. She crept over to it, and the brio of magic she smelled there fairly made her hiccup. Cautiously, Georgie descended the stairs.

Hank and the duchess strolled past a little garden fountain, in silence.

"So that's when Hazel fell in love with you?" asked the duchess.

"She?" replied Hank. "Oh, she was young. Who can ever know if the young truly love?" With his sad eyes still secretly remembering Jackson, and with his plump lips pursed in their characteristic fishy manner, Hank declared most solemnly, "It was I who loved."

The duchess pondered his statement. It pierced her heart, really—the pathos of it.

Meanwhile, down in the mansion kitchen, Tammy performed the purification rituals required by Shadooda's black-magic spell.

She boiled a certain tree fungus and rubbed her gums with its juice. She ground roots into powders and sprinkled them into her hair. Certain flowers had to be dried and desiccated in a limestone mortar while she muttered incantations in forgotten languages. In the midst of this, she heard footsteps in the shadows. Tammy dropped her herbs and roots, and gasped.

Georgie stood before her—tall, willowy, with her piercing gaze, pale spiky hair, and dangling watch-fob loop.

"Got any snacks?" Georgie asked.

Tammy pointed at the refrigerator, trying in vain to hide her strange ablutions behind a linen napkin. Uninvited, Georgie took a chair at the table and sat, backwards, in it.

"We meet again," said Georgie.

Tammy laughed nervously and said, "Odd, I guess!"

"Odd," said Georgie, "or destined."

Tammy wished the redly lipsticked woman would go away and leave her to her business.

"If you don't mind my saying so," said Georgie, "you seem to be performing, may I be bold enough to say, some kind of witchcraft. I don't know what all you're into, but I sniffed it out. I have a nose for magic, see," Georgie added, pointing at her prodigious honker. "Now, I don't need to know your business, but I was just wondering … thing is, I have some needs myself, magic-wise. I take it you have a connection? I mean, with a sorcerer or magician, so-called?"

Georgie chewed her broken fingernails and thought about all the awkward moments of her life, like this one, and wondered how she had lived through each and every one of them. She even considered giving up her quest and letting the whole idea of leaving Bumblegreen fade away. *Maybe, with her magic,* Georgie thought, in a sudden panic, *Tammy can turn me into a toad!* Sitting backwards in that kitchen chair, Georgie worried she had taken things too far. But Tammy simply shrugged and said sure.

She told Georgie where to go: twelve Minion Lane. Told her those three special words: Shadooda Majit Goforth. All the while, Tammy tried to figure out why the magician's location should be such a secret and awkward thing. *It's just a magician*, she thought. Tammy figured probably bunches of people were doing it, seeing magicians. But they weren't.

Ascending the staircase, Georgie added, "So, would you say, speaking generally, based upon whatever you know about her, him, it … Would you say Shadooda is … This Shadooda Majit Goforth, would you say its witchcraft is entirely white, or … does it dabble …"

"A bit off-white, I'd say, frankly speaking," Tammy unblinkingly responded. "Nearing to gray. Not exactly black magic, I mean, but not exactly white, either, if you really want to know."

"Oh, I do," said Georgie. "I definitely want to know"

53

WHERE DAHLIA TURNS OUT TO BE A TOUGH MARK

The deep, dark woods weren't quite as empty and abandoned as they had at first appeared to Dahlia. As she picked her way down a little-used path, Fast Eddie appeared, splashing on cologne, in a grove of saplings. Seeing the queen, he leaped upon a vine and swung into her path with hearty machismo. The handsome fellow, with his wild hair and brave demeanor, cut an imposing figure in there amid the things of jungly darkness.

The queen recognized Fast Eddie as the tall man who had tried to take credit for the capture of the beast.

He opened with a simple compliment, something about her fabulous clothes.

Queen Dahlia wasn't sure whether or not Fast Eddie knew to whom he was talking, whether or not he actually recognized her, as he hadn't called her "Your Highness," done obeisance, or voiced any of the expected salutations to which a queen becomes accustomed. If, indeed, he didn't know she was the queen, Dahlia didn't want him to. But if he already knew, she didn't want him to know she was running away from home. That's why she didn't quite know what to say, so she said, "Oh."

"Fair maiden," said Fast Eddie. "May I have the honor of escorting you to your planned destination? I wouldn't want any ill to befall you. Your daintiness inspires me and your beauty enslaves me."

Now, the queen of Bumblegreen was as used to being complimented as a flower is to blooming, as a cockroach is to scuttling, as monkeys are to swinging. Compliments infused Dahlia's atmosphere like incense. She really didn't notice them, so she simply took his elaborate request at face value, sized up the fellow, and decided she wouldn't mind his company. Company or no company— it didn't matter much to her, either way.

She replied, "You may," thinking it a normal thing for a girl to say.

Along the journey, Fast Eddie tried out a selection of his practiced charms on her, but Dahlia had her mind on the imagined cabin, the cloud of butterflies, and her new life as a non-queen, so she wasn't listening. He began with some run-of-the-mill compliments, then gradually slid into his trademark system, where the compliments were actually backhanded, insecurity-generating, faux flattery.

Dahlia merely ambled along in distracted silence, so Fast Eddie added, "I adore your sense of humor!" It was supposed to make her confused, since she hadn't made a joke.

"Huh? What?" Dahlia replied, then, "Oh, if you don't mind, you're stepping on my gown." Never mind that the gown was already dragging in the mud and the dirt and the brambles and the sticks, Fast Eddie *was* stepping on it.

Frustrated, Fast Eddie swung away on the nearest vine. Dahlia barely noticed his absence, just as his presence had been but a minor amusement.

Clearly, his typical insouciance wasn't the right approach to take with a queen, but what was? Fast Eddie would have to cultivate a new technique—an approach to seduction fit for a queen. He wanted so badly to reach that next pinnacle of success in the art of seduction. So far, he had learned one thing only, and that was that despite her youth, Queen Dahlia was no easy mark.

54

IN WHICH TAMMY DELEGATES HER DIRTY WORK

After her visit to Shadooda, Tammy took on a great deal of work—overnights, day shifts, whatever she could get—at the duchess' mansion. Shadooda had made an extraordinary demand of Tammy in exchange for the black-magic vengeance formula, and in the desperate, highly emotional condition Tammy was in at the time, she saw fit to acquiesce. So now, in addition to giving a certain magical potion to the redhead so that she would give it to Fast Eddie and get him to promise to seduce the queen before giving the potion to Hank … and in addition to gathering herbs and mushrooms by the full moon all damn night long, and in addition to memorizing a variety of archaic incantations, Tammy had promised to depose the queen of Bumblegreen or at least give it her best effort. Now, she was stuck.

A promise to a magician isn't something one breaks on a whim, so, over the last few days—even as she planned the garden party, unsuccessfully attempted to save Jackson from the queen's war chariots, and served a canapé to Georgie, the duchess' single party guest—Tammy had also been scheming on how to get the duchess herself to fulfill the most difficult of Shadooda's requests.

After her initial visit, the duchess lost her fear of the kitchen, with its mysterious silver doors, and took to visiting regularly. The duchess even saw her little jaunts "for a cucumber sandwich," as she kept insisting, as a way to develop a sort of secret friendship, or clandestine meeting of the minds, between a highborn woman and a simple peasant lass. *Something storybooks would romanticize,* the duchess thought. She wanted to see if such cross-cultural alliances would turn out to be as fascinating as they were forbidden. She viewed her developing friendship with Tammy as a social experiment.

The failure of the garden party turned out to be the perfect stroke of luck Tammy needed. The very next evening, the duchess came down to the kitchen for a chat, and Tammy, while crushing garlic for a soup, asked, "Duchess, how many people were supposed to come to your party?"

"Hundreds!" said the duchess. "Including seventy to eighty individuals of the highest social standing. But oh, how I do despise people of the highest social standing, dear. Perhaps it's best they never came. I prefer to be here, with you, in the kitchen."

"That's nice," lied Tammy.

"It's true! Peasants are just as pleasant and forthright as they're rumored to be."

"Listen, though, ma'am," continued Tammy, chopping carrots. "Wouldn't you love to have a gathering of, say, more than a hundred? Like five hundred, for instance? Or a thousand? And what if it were guaranteed that they would all show up? What would you think of that?"

"Oh, my goodness," replied the duchess. "My dear silly adorably innocent girl. One doesn't have such gatherings in Bumblegreen."

"Never?" asked Tammy.

"Never? Well, never say never," said the duchess. "I mean, I suppose that many people would come to … to a beheading or something. Or a coronation. There were that many at the queen's coronation, certainly. And … if there were a catastrophe or something, I'm sure that many would show up, just to see it and all. I would. I know that."

"Catastrophe?" asked Tammy, finally getting somewhere. "What kind of catastrophe?"

"Just speaking theoretically?" replied the duchess. "You know, like if the queen were deposed or something. I mean something insanely major like that. You need one percent of Bumblegreen's population to witness it, to make it official."

"Wouldn't it be grand to have a large gathering like that?" asked Tammy, peppering the soup. "I mean, think of the clothes you could wear! All eyes trained on you! I could serve canapés. It'd be grand. I mean, really grand!"

"Oh! Wouldn't it, though?" replied the duchess, falling right into Tammy's trap.

So that's how Tammy planted the seed that the duchess herself should try to depose the queen. Tammy, of course, had no investment whatsoever in removing Dahlia from the throne, but Shadooda had insisted she try, so, like all great women, she delegated the job.

Check that off the list, thought Tammy.

"I do believe a political rally would have a certain amount of social pull," mused the duchess, down in the kitchen, that night. "You know, perhaps that's what Bumblegreen's people really need. A cause. A garden party isn't inspiring enough, perhaps, to draw a crowd."

Tammy flattered the duchess: "I know it, ma'am. And perhaps you have more influence politically than socially? A massive occasion like that would prove, I think, your importance to the kingdom at large, too. It's an idea, anyway."

"Yes, darling," muttered the duchess. "Just a silly little idea."

"Silly," said Tammy, adding sugar to some cookie batter.

"Indeed," said the duchess, "but there's no cause to depose the queen."

"No, none," replied Tammy, adding butter.

"None," replied the duchess.

"No, none," said Tammy, chopping nuts, "except for the beast, of course."

"Beast?" asked the duchess, with real innocence, for once.

It wasn't that Tammy hated the beast or Queen Dahlia. Goodness knows she had risked everything to try to save Hank's furry friend. More than anything, she didn't want to hurt Hank. It was just that, well, the beast had already been captured and was quite possibly even dead, by now. Being a portal jumper, it might be carrying otherworldly mites, which could potentially cause a recurrence of the blight, which could be considered the queen's fault, in a way. The situation turned out to be awfully convenient.

After all, don't forget that nothing, really nothing at all, was more important to Tammy than getting revenge on the man who had made her carry a baby whose allergic potential could kill her in her sleep.

Tammy continued the conversation by explaining the reason for the war party that had chewed up the duchess' lawn and broken her ice sculpture. She detailed how those soldiers had captured the portal-jumping beast

"Obviously, Duchess, the polymer has failed," continued Tammy. "Queen Dahlia's mission, as queen, more than anything, is to protect us from another blight. She told us to have faith in that polymer. Innocently, we did, and now look! Not just any creature, but a hairy creature, probably full of mites, has come across from another land and re-infected Bumblegreen! It's reason enough for a vote of no confidence, I think."

The duchess sad down, hard. "Oh my God," she said. "What have I done?"

"Done? Nothing yet, Duchess, but if you manage to depose the queen …" Tammy began.

"No, Tammy! You don't understand! This is all my fault!" cried the duchess.

Now, it was Tammy's turn to sit down hard. A paring knife dangled, forgotten, in Tammy's hand, as the duchess related some vital information.

"I had this housekeeper named Fast Eddie. He's gone now," began the duchess.

Tammy gritted her teeth and said simply, "I remember him."

"I sent him to the market one day," the duchess said, shrugging as if to imply everything had seemed so routine, until things went awry. "I gave him a shopping list. Nothing special: salami, cheese, bread, whatever. He came home with this wheel of well-aged gouda. I like the well-aged cheeses."

"Of course," answered Tammy, who knew exactly what the duchess liked.

"I don't know why, but I kept it aside," continued the duchess. "I sent all the rest of the groceries down here to the kitchen. I was hungry at the time and thought I'd just put the gouda there on the sideboard and fix myself a snack."

"Yes?" answered Tammy impatiently.

"Hank was at home, on his break," said the duchess. "You know how he needs his breaks."

"Yes," said Tammy, waiting, with extra patience, for the point of it all.

"So, I took a knife and sliced the cheese," said the duchess. "I can slice a cheese, you know, I'm not totally helpless."

"Of course not, Duchess," Tammy said.

"And lo and behold," said the duchess, "there was something in the cheese."

"In the cheese?" asked Tammy, finally interested. "You mean, besides cheese?"

"Yes, something besides cheese!" exclaimed the duchess. "I had to break apart the entire gouda to get at it. At first, I thought some careless soul at the factory had dropped a cleaning rag in there, and I was going to return to the store and complain!"

"Of course," agreed Tammy. "One doesn't want to find things in one's cheese."

"But then I took a closer look and realized what it was," whispered the duchess.

"What was it?" Tammy whispered back, beginning to think this story hadn't been worth waiting for after all.

The duchess dropped her head into her hands and paused, seemingly suspended in angst.

Something sad was in the cheese? thought Tammy.

The duchess walked upstairs in silence, leaving Tammy in a state of consternation. Shortly, she returned with a cloth wadded up in her hand. The duchess laid it out on the chopping block, smoothing it flat so Tammy could catch the full import of the thing.

Tammy saw the even rows of cross-stitch, the faded colors, and the worn bog-country linen. In pop-eyed wonder, she pondered Prindal's List, with its carefully needle-pointed list of numerical coordinates. Tammy blinked again and felt suddenly as though she would faint.

"Don't faint," said the duchess.

"I'm not! I'm not!" screeched Tammy, whose lips had gone rubbery.

Her hands suddenly felt newly discovered, like out-of-place items of endless wonderment, and she dropped her paring knife. She was looking at information so secret, so coveted, such a matter of kingdom-wide security, that its very presence felt nothing less than terrifying. Tammy's eyes fixed on the cross-stitched list as if it were not a dirty, cheese-smelling scrap of linen but a pulsating neon sign making titillating promises in an adult bookstore.

The duchess should have tucked the offending scrap into her pocket. After all, no one can handle exposure to a thing like that without invoking some kind of celestial, otherworldly, or all-powerful being for guidance. Tammy grabbed a kitchen rag and blew her nose, then untucked and retucked her blouse, then loosened her belt, then jingled her keys.

"It's the real thing," said the duchess. "Prindal's List."

"I see that," said Tammy, who had dropped her head between her knees to take deep, calming breaths.

"I've been wanting imports for so long," explained the duchess. "You know how I crave them!" She hung her head. "I went to the monkey camp and recruited a particularly energetic little simian. Told him I had an adventure for him. He couldn't resist, of course."

"So you opened a portal? You ... you're the one who let the beast in?" asked Tammy.

"Not exactly. Not exactly," replied the duchess. "You see, one of the portals was already open."

"But duchess, how did you decode these numbers to find the portals in the first place?"

"Oh, that. Well, yes, that's another thing," said the duchess. "It gets worse."

55

WHERE MOBIUS FOILS HIS
CRUEL-HEARTED COWORKERS

On the day in question—long before Fast Eddie had impregnated Tammy and even before Grandma had been threatened with being sent to a 'home'—a shipment of gouda was scheduled to go out from the castle's cheese factory to some local shops, and it turned out to be one wheel short. Who knows how? Dress maids skim, attendants pilfer. One expects such things from one's staff, here and there. So, a foreman dispatched a servant for a replacement cheese, and that servant happened to be Mobius. Yes, Mobius of clothing-trampoline fame.

Ironically, Mobius happened to hail from a town in the castle's outlying regions, off in the direction, actually, of that cheese cave. As a boy, he had played in the cave, very naughtily of course, feeling quite clever for having a secret clubhouse in a long-forgotten cheese cave. His parents may or may not have known, but even if they had, it was one of those things where—what's the harm, after all? Much later, in adulthood, due to a shortage of cheese-factory workers, Mobius eventually found a job at the castle. He was an all-right kid.

On the day in question, the workers putting the village's cheese order together found their allotment one wheel short. Thinking they'd play a good joke on the new guy, they sent Mobius off to find another wheel of gouda. A wink and a nod among the workers served as complicit agreement that they could all use a smoke break that might extend, who knows, maybe all day, if Mobius turned out to be as dense as they predicted.

The castle grounds, of course, were terribly labyrinthine, and if one didn't know one's way around, it was nearly impossible to get from one place, predictably, to another. In fact, if a man had the time, he usually found it much more logical to wander at random around the campus and simply hope he ended up where he wanted to get by luck.

So, as the lazy workers lit up their pipes, joints, and cigarillos, Mobius, always eager to please, wandered off in search of cheese storage. Now, he may have been a little dense, but the thing was, Mobius knew he was dense. So, immediately, he schemed for a way to appear less dense than circumstances were sure to prove he was, all to the mirth and general hilarity of his cruelhearted coworkers. Remembering that cave from his childhood, and knowing it stood about a thirty-minute sprint from castle central, Mobius gambled that an hour spent fetching a cheese that was guaranteed to exist versus an hour spent wandering aimlessly in search of cheese storage nearby (which could end up being behind locked doors, for all he knew) would be an hour well spent.

On the day in question, Mobius aimed his bowlegged stems in the direction of that outer-limits cheese cave for very well-aged cheeses, ran like the dickens, broke the rusty lock off the cave's door with one blow from a rock, entered the cool darkness with all its secret childhood memories, and grabbed the third gouda from the left on the middle shelf, randomly selected. Then, with the ten-pound wheel tucked beneath his arm, Mobius hotfooted it back to the castle's cheese loading dock.

Mobius' success in fetching a gouda surprised his smoke-enwreathed cohorts quite a bit, but they grumblingly added the wheel to the stock and delivered these wheels to maybe ten or twenty simple corner shops in various outlying villages.

Another stroke of fate might have delivered that wheel to some good-hearted farm lass, who might have, in blissful ignorance, used Prindal's List for a dinner napkin. But, as dumb luck would have it, Fast Eddie happened to buy the innocent-looking gouda on an errand for the duchess.

What happened was, when the duchess cut open the cheese and discovered the list, she panicked and told her one and only friend Georgie about it (in confidence, of course). Georgie then borrowed the list for a day, turned around and traded its coordinates to Jimothy Schrank for a share in the Favra Watch Company, then returned the list to the duchess with little fanfare.

The rest, as they say, is history.

56

IN WHICH DAHLIA HEARS
MUFFLED CRIES FOR HELP

Dahlia had been tromping through the woods for a good hour, and by this point, a bit of the charm of running away had worn off. She still felt determined, but not sure to do what, and she was disappointed that she hadn't yet found the abandoned cabin of her fantasy, nor did she know where her next meal was coming from. That's when the queen came to a clearing and saw an astounding sight.

Thousands of butterflies flitted around a sun-dappled meadow.

Tiger-colored monarchs covered the trunks of trees. Small yellow butterflies flew this way and that and alighted on the meadow's abundant purple calendula. And those big, tissue-like white ones, with their raggedy wings that seemed so ethereal and cloudlike—they flew at top speed, like a swarm of hornets, right into a multicolored mid-air gaggle of more butterflies. The way the butterflies intermingled, the way they flew around one another, never seeking nectar, never alighting on tree branches, it looked to Dahlia like they were communicating. Indeed, she was right.

Though she didn't speak butterfly, nor could she detect their supersonic psychic communications the way ElizabethAnn could, the queen still understood herself to be the subject of their gossip. She didn't want to be. She was trying to go incognito, after all, so she hid from the butterflies by squatting on the ground and flipping the top few layers of her skirts right over her head. It felt so cozy in there, with the fabric above and so many layers below, that while waiting for the butterflies to forget she was there, Dahlia fell asleep.

When she awoke, it was dark, and the butterflies slept on branches and leaves. Queen Dahlia flipped down her skirt tent only to gasp at the sight of enormous caterpillars building silken sacks and hanging them—all delicate, pendulous, and sleek—from branches. The giant chrysalises hung serenely, swaying in the gentle night breeze and catching the moonlight in a way that made them glow like so many lanterns. Dahlia walked through the spectacle—silently creeping, delicately stepping, feeling like an interloper in someone's boudoir.

The giant caterpillars worked through the night, building their oddly shaped cocoons—works of art as tall as men, with walls as thick as Dahlia's fist.

The queen found an abandoned, broken cocoon hanging from a tree branch and curled up in it to sleep. She found it terrifically cozy, like a perfect silken hammock, and snored away to the sticky, liquid sounds of large caterpillars building extreme cocoons in the distance. She didn't sleep long, though, for a disturbance awakened her. Wiping sleep from her eyes, Dahlia heard the initial sounds of ElizabethAnn's struggles and saw gigantic caterpillar craftsmen retreating into the shadowy woodlands. Subsequently, she noticed the erratic swinging of a cocoon in the moonlight and heard the muffled calls for help.

Curious as ever, Dahlia tiptoed over to ElizabethAnn's wildly swinging, fresh, new, still-sticky, still freshly slightly reptile-smelling chrysalis. Awkward, yet unfailingly polite, she knocked on its plaster-hard exterior, almost expecting an answer.

Nearby branches unwittingly attacked the queen's elaborate costume as she rustled around the forest clearing, searching for an L-shaped stick. Meanwhile, Dahlia batted down her various skirts and petticoats, aprons and bows, as they snagged on every twig, thistle, and climbing vine she encountered.

Having found what she wanted, Dahlia placed the long end of an L-shaped stick on the side of the cocoon and used the short end to crank it around and around, drilling a hole in the hard, yet resilient substance. This work was no small feat, and when she finished, the queen found herself (perhaps for the first time ever) covered in dripping sweat. Plus, her outfit's gauzy accents now drooped— sopping, filthy, and wadded-up.

Dahlia peeked through the hole she had made and found ElizabethAnn inside.

Though not at her best, ElizabethAnn surprised Dahlia by being unmistakably human.

"Hello in there! Hey!" Dahlia shouted.

ElizabethAnn saw the hole, and through it, a mouth with teeth. She prepared to scream, but then saw the mouth replaced by an eye—the eye of a girl much like herself.

"Hey, you!" ElizabethAnn heard. "Why are you in there?"

"I've been kidnapped?" she replied.

"Weren't you calling for help, before?" asked the queen. "I thought I heard a scream and a struggle."

"Yes," replied ElizabethAnn. "Can you get me out of here, please? I have an important mission."

"I don't know," replied the queen. "Who are you, anyway?"

"My name is ElizabethAnn," said ElizabethAnn, "and I have to save Bumblegreen, I think."

"Is that so?" asked Dahlia. "That's great, because I thought it was all up to me."

Dahlia was reasonably uneducated and knew it; nonetheless, she was willing to go out on a limb and assume the combination of human child and insect cocoon did not normally occur in nature and that foul play was afoot. So, she wiped a gob of sweat from her brow, threw what was left of her headdress aside, and set about drilling another hole in ElizabethAnn's cocoon. Between the holes, she punched a crack in the weakened cocoon substance.

Dahlia tried to poke her head through the crack, but with the force it took to do so, her whole body tumbled inside, headfirst, falling right on top of ElizabethAnn, who grunted.

"You look human," commented Queen Dahlia.

"Thanks?" replied ElizabethAnn.

"Where are your monkeys?" asked the queen. "Your parents?"

"Monkey parents? No, no, you don't understand," replied ElizabethAnn. Then, she described her tumble through the portal from No Oaks (pointedly not mentioning Grandma's role in the whole thing). The queen Mm-hmmed and Aha-ed throughout ElizabethAnn's jagged story, with its enormous gaps of reason and mixed-up order of events.

"We have a problem. Oh boy, do we have a problem," said Dahlia, adding with a sigh: "I guess my days, make that hours, as a fugitive from duty are over."

The queen explained to ElizabethAnn who she was and what she was doing there. It took some time, as she had to carefully spell out the fact that Queen Dahlia wasn't just a weird name, but an actual royal title.

ElizabethAnn rubbed her eyes and made a sleepy sound that meant, "I'm really not a typically problematic child."

So, it's true, thought Dahlia. *There really is a problem with my polymer.* Her portals had become porous. And this crumpled, whimpering, sleepy child, this awkwardly named "ElizabethAnn" creature, represented the beginning of the end for Bumblegreen.

Dahlia felt tempted to seal up the chrysalis somehow, from the inside, and stay in there with ElizabethAnn, hiding from the world, possibly living on small grubs and stray bits of lichen forever. But, with a deeply felt sigh and an even deeper sense of duty, the queen stuck a leg out the crack in the cocoon, grabbed ElizabethAnn by her scrawny bicep, and dragged the kid, blinking, out into the world again.

Queen Dahlia and ElizabethAnn shuffled, hand in hand, through the darkness of a forest lit only by the subtle lantern-like glow of hanging cocoons reflecting moonlight. Queen Dahlia told ElizabethAnn she would have to watch the ground, since Dahlia herself had to keep her eyes on the sky while she tried to remember the fundamentals of starlight navigation from her few lessons in childhood.

To keep them both awake as they struggled through the forest by night, Dahlia asked ElizabethAnn to talk about her home, her hobbies, her friends. ElizabethAnn eagerly complied. She told Dahlia all about roller skates, how they laced up, how difficult it could be to get the tension of the laces just right, and how once you stood up, you had to use the toe break to push off. Then, you could sail around and around the streets and sidewalks of No Oaks, just gliding, gliding, gliding.

ElizabethAnn told Dahlia how she had fallen once and skinned her knee, and how it had started out red and oozing, turned dark and crispy, then got all greenish and yellow around the edges, then one day the injury had simply been gone! And she could skate again! How wonderful that day had been. ElizabethAnn also babbled on about how exertion such as this made her want to eat cheese and crackers all the time, like it was a phenomenon.

At the mention of cheese, Dahlia dropped her eyes from the sky, stepped over a pile of animal dung (which ElizabethAnn had helpfully pointed out) and raised her eyebrows in yummy agreement. Dahlia told her young companion all about Bumblegreen cheese and how she herself knew just how to make it. She said she could produce a block of cheddar, a slab of gruyère, or a wheel of gouda in her own personal factory.

Dahlia admitted to being a connoisseur of brie and havarti and even salty farmer's cheeses. ElizabethAnn asked what sort of crackers the queen typically paired with these delicacies and the queen listed the brands of preference, which of course meant nothing to ElizabethAnn, until she described their tastes of caraway, of rye, of parsley.

ElizabethAnn told Dahlia all about typical No Oaks plasti-lawns, with their borders of real (sometimes) marigolds, nasturtiums, and peonies. Dahlia described the darling crocuses that popped up all over the castle grounds throughout the spring, and how in childhood she used to lie on hillocks and watch the clouds. ElizabethAnn concurred that even in No Oaks, children watched clouds. She added that sunsets were another popular no-cost entertainment.

The hapless pair picked their way through the forest—holding hands, watching the stars, and turning this way and that. ElizabethAnn described No Oaks weather, and how you could see a storm coming from far away, watch it rain across the desert, across the golf course, and, finally, right across the street, before it got to you. She described the vast banks of storm clouds that came crawling over the land, casting profound shadows and roiling past like some living thing late for an appointment with the horizon. She talked about sleet and how it made a sound like a thousand tiny cymbals crashing. Dahlia liked hearing that.

Dahlia told ElizabethAnn about the world of half-naked dancing people she had visited once, so long ago, after her fall through a certain portal into a certain belfry. She also told ElizabethAnn the sad story of the toothless lowland gypsies, and how, when they had been Travelers, they were social outcasts but also her own secret friends. Then, briefly, they became heroes, then, finally, villains, and she told ElizabethAnn how the group had entirely disappeared just when she, Dahlia, needed friends the most.

Finally, ElizabethAnn and Dahlia were both surprised when they stepped out of a thick barrier of broad-leafed trees and shrubbery, right over a curb, and onto a street. Lit by the glow of a public lamp, this street of irregular stone blocks lay flat and clean before them. Across the street, forest mist settled on the front door of a bakery, the shingle of a shoemaker, and the squinty windows of the office of a notary public.

Around the corner, ElizabethAnn recognized a barbershop, not that different from those in No Oaks, and a deli, and a candy store, and a bridal boutique. All were closed for the evening, of course. All looked abandoned and spooky and locked up tight.

The queen trudged up one lonely street and down another, trying to get a good fix on the stars above despite the dim light of several streetlights.

ElizabethAnn pointed at a sign designating Queen Street. She asked, quite logically, if Dahlia knew the road—if, perhaps, she could get some navigational bearings by it, follow it to some familiar place. Since, after all, if Dahlia was the queen, it must be her street, more or less.

Dahlia didn't want to admit she had never actually left the castle grounds before, but she did, her head bowed in shame. "You know, though," Dahlia added, in her own defense, "keep in mind the castle grounds themselves really are quite extensive. We have meadows and forests and swamps and bogs and even shops … and now a cheese factory!"

ElizabethAnn pointed at another sign. "What about this one?" she asked. "Minion Lane."

"Intriguing."

"I have kind of a feeling about it."

"Do you? Like an intuition?" asked Dahlia.

"I suppose its something like that. I feel like this road might go someplace that's sort of good and sort of bad. Kind of like Bill Bramble's house."

"Who?"

"This boy that lives in the woods and he turns into a bird."

Queen Dahlia shrugged at the thought of that and took ElizabethAnn's hand again. The girls entwined fingers. They looked into each other's eyes, briefly, as a way of gathering courage, then peered down the long, dark lane and walked on.

57

WHERE ZADE FANDEY WALKS INTO A TRAP

Long ago, before ElizabethAnn got involved in any of this, Grandma signed the Universal Portal Compact and returned from Bumblegreen to No Oaks, while Zade Fandey stayed behind. Soon afterward, Bumblegreen newspapers splashed Fandey's great strides in monkey breeding all over the front page, while the business section filled up with Jimothy Schrank's commercial breakthroughs in household implements, athletic footwear, and, of course, watches. Being that they were clearly a couple of clever fellows, Zade got it into his head that he and Schrank could work together. Schrank agreed to meet him.

"Fandey, Fandey, Fandey. Zade, Zade, Zade," began Schrank, leaning back in his executive chair, exuding confidence. "What exactly can I do you for, old chap?"

Zade heard the conference room's door click shut behind him and knew, even before he sat down, he had walked into a trap.

"Jimothy, what I'm looking for is some delicate timekeeping machinery," replied Zade. "It's a scientific matter, a thing for the lab. You know how it is with science, always so exacting."

"Indeed, indeed. Always so exacting," replied Schrank. "Is that what it takes, Fandey? To save the world from sneezes? Exact timekeeping?"

"Ah, well, partially, yes," said Zade. "I won't attempt to explain the entire monkey breeding process. It's rather complicated. Plant extracts are involved, you know. We develop an organic compound, but there's a fermentation process, as well. Of course, the radiation, though, is the main thing, and it takes a very exact amount of exposure, you see. It's … you know how it is."

"No, Fandey. I don't know how it is," said Schrank, on that long-ago day. "Why don't you tell me all about it?"

Schrank's mocking tone didn't impress Zade, but he got the drift—he was being asked to divulge his secret monkey-breeding process so Schrank could copy it and attempt to profit thereby.

"Listen, forget it, Schrank," said Zade. "I changed my mind. I'd rather count the seconds on my fingers than rely on one of your damn watches!" He added, "One would think you'd provide the equipment out of patriotic duty, just out of your love for Bumblegreen and its future. But I guess you're not the 'love' type."

"No need to get testy, Fandey," replied Schrank. "I mean, seriously, love anything? I'm insulted. I love plenty. For instance, I really really love the timekeeping technology I've spent my entire career creating. And I'm sure you can understand I'm not about to just hand it out to everyone who comes sauntering along. It's very advanced, you know."

Shrank pulled up his coat sleeve to display the Favra watch prototype, and said, "See?" He added, "This baby tells ultra-mega-accurate time. Down to the milli-willi-silli-second."

"There's no such thing as a silli-second," replied Zade.

"Okay, you win!" announced Schrank. "You're smarter, Zade! But trust me, this baby would even hold its own among imports, and I mean the *best* imports."

"Yeah?" asked Zade. "Let me have a look at it—this ultra-special watchamacallit of yours."

"Certainly!" answered Schrank, with pride. He slid the watch across the conference table. Fandey took a very careful, very scientific look at all the Favra watch's functions. All.

"Nice watch," said Zade. "How much do you want for it?"

"Well, I can't sell you this one, exactly."

"You're wasting my time. C'mon, Jim, I have things to do today."

"Because, my friend, it's a prototype! But I'd be happy to take an order for a couple hundred. What do you say?" asked Schrank. "We'll produce them right here in our factory, 'specially for you."

"Oh in the name of … I'm not a retailer!" objected Zade. "I'm a scientist! I want one watch. One. Sell me one. I've the budget for it. Or else, no deal."

"So sorry, Zade," responded Schrank. "Don't want to let down my beloved Bumblegreen and all that, but I'm looking for a distributor. Someone with cred, with clout, a trusted name. More trusted even than Favra Watch. That'd be you, old boy."

"That's nonsense."

"Oh, all right, all right. There's one other thing you could do for me, though. Just one little thing."

"Like pay a fair price for a simple consumer product? I could do that, just fine."

"Come on! Be a sport!" objected Schrank. "All I want you to do is endorse it. Give us your name. Let us call it the 'Zade Fandey Scientific Watch.' That's all I want to do. With your name on it, this baby could really fly off the shelves. Waddaya say?"

By this point, Zade was too furious to care about exact time anymore. And for Zade, that's pretty furious. He stormed out of there and back to the lab, where he continued to work with substandard timing equipment, only now he felt righteous about it.

58

WHERE THE DUCHESS TRIES
TO DEFLECT THE BLAME

Zade Fandey's monkeys started coming out cross-eyed, flat-nosed, and short-tailed. Eventually, the duchess complained. Zade had to admit the problem was with the timing of the monkey-humanization process, and he told her how Schrank's mega-accurate watch could have been, but wasn't, the solution to all this. In fact, Zade admitted there might follow a whole generation of cross-eyed, flat-nosed, short-tailed monkeys, unless he got better timekeeping equipment. As part of this conversation, he told the duchess all about Zade Fandey's golden watch, of course, including its bonus feature, its GPS finder.

So, when the duchess put together the finding of Prindal's List (by her), the loaning of it to Georgie (by her), Georgie's friendship with Jimothy Schrank (longstanding), Schrank's golden watch with a GPS feature (as described by Zade), and the fact that Schrank had programmed Prindal's List's GPS coordinates directly into the watch (which could only have resulted from a combination of the above factors), she felt that she herself deserved something in return for her contribution to creating the Favra, so the duchess decided, on her own, to borrow the watch for a while.

Talking to Tammy that night in the kitchen, while she peppered the soup, the duchess explained it like so: "When I realized the watch could let me actually use Prindal's List to go and get more imports, I was too scared to try it myself, so I found a monkey that'd work for me, and I just told him to go and steal the watch. He's good, this monkey. A natural."

"Steal it?" asked Tammy, incredulous.

The duchess watched her own feet shuffling nervously and said, "Don't judge me, peasant girl."

"But Duchess … stealing?"

"I'm no better than anyone else, okay?" insisted the duchess. "I'm weak. I want my things. To own, you know, is to exist. What do you own? Nothing! So there!"

Tammy stopped chopping her peppers. "Don't take it personal, Duchess," she said. "I didn't mean it that way. Actually, I'm glad."

"You're not going to turn me in?"

"Oh, hell no! I think you've got guts, Duchess. I really do. Guts enough, for instance, to depose the queen. After all, you have Prindal's List. You might as well depose Dahlia. In fact, you might as well take her place."

"I hadn't thought of that."

"Don't go by half-measures!" urged Tammy. "That's what I say! Take this all the way to the top! Sure, you may be the one who opened that portal but … how'd you get past the polymer, anyway?"

"The monkey told me the portal was just open," said the duchess, shrugging. "He didn't even have to dig a hole. I still haven't got my set of Louis-the-fourteenth end tables out of him, though. Damn it."

"Okay, so Queen Dahlia's polymer isn't so stable after all!" reasoned Tammy. "That's bad news for the queen, and perhaps (in another way of looking at it) you didn't even open the portal for selfish reasons. Perhaps you opened it as a test. You could spin it like that. You had to test the polymer for safety, after all, didn't you? Someone had to, eventually."

"Yes, that's right," agreed the duchess. "You people really are clever, aren't you? It was a test, and Queen Dahlia and her precious polymer failed the test!"

"Exactly," affirmed Tammy, eyebrow raised.

59

In Which Bits of String Play a Critical Role

"Let's be friends," said Queen Dahlia, "and you can just call me Dahlia."

It's not every day a girl makes a new friend, and she's a queen from an enchanted kingdom and a sophisticated thirteen-year-old besides, so ElizabethAnn felt quite pleased at this offer. She responded with a smile, and asked, "Dahlia? Where does this road go, anyway?"

"I don't know," moaned Dahlia. "I don't know where I'm going, and I don't know how to save Bumblegreen." She marched doggedly down Minion Lane and finished, "I don't know anything!"

"Save it from me?" asked ElizabethAnn.

"Not you exactly. Don't take it personally," answered Dahlia. "It's just that the portals weren't supposed to break open. And when I get my hands on that monkey, that Earl, whoever he is, oh man, I'm going to wring his neck."

"Because he might have those mites on him?" asked ElizabethAnn. "The ones that destroy everything and cause the what-do-you-call-it? The blight?"

"Yes. That's true," replied Dahlia. "The mites are a gigantic problem, but why did that monkey have to go and break the Universal Portal Compact? Now I have to put him to death, you know. I have to!"

"Oh, no! Not Earl!"

"No one's supposed to breach that polymer, ElizabethAnn. It's against the law. It'll cause the blight to return, and we've just gotten over it. I mean *just*."

"Do you think ..." began ElizabethAnn. "I've been meaning to ask you, Dahlia ... do you think a furry animal might carry a certain amount of those mites? Would that be a problem if, perhaps, I had a companion who was on the shaggy side? Or no? Not really? That'd be okay, wouldn't it?"

As she awaited the answer, ElizabethAnn watched the scuffed toes of her once-shiny patent leather shoes shuffling along Minion Lane, in the darkness and chill. She thought fondly of her beloved, loyal Jackson, who, as it turns out, might have become a possibly unwitting pestilence-carrying fiend.

The queen stopped, gasped, described to ElizabethAnn the beast imprisoned in the throne room's cage, and got a nervous nod of assent from her new friend. That's when Dahlia realized ElizabethAnn and the beast had come through a single portal together, which was an enormous relief, as she had been thinking the two were unrelated catastrophes from separate worlds.

"What I need right now," Dahlia said, stopping to rest on a boulder, "is I need to find Shadooda. It's the only way."

"Shadooda? Yes! I need to find that, too! What is it?"

"You? Why do you need to find it?"

"My grandma said I had to! Oops."

Queen Dahlia covered her eyes, as if that might make some portion of her new troubles go away. "Don't tell me," she said. "Please, please, please don't tell me there's a third portal jumper."

ElizabethAnn sat on the boulder, too, and looked up at the stars for a while. "Let's put it this way," she said, carefully. "I have a reason to believe that something called Shadooda, which has to do with magic, has disappeared from Bumblegreen."

"I'd say that's correct, yes."

"And I have a reason to believe, also, that I'm supposed to find it. That I was actually sent here, or even possibly groomed my entire life, for the purpose of finding it, for some very good reason."

"Oh, yeah? What reason might that be?"

"I don't know, but there's a reason, and a good one," said ElizabethAnn. "I'm just saying I have it on good authority. If I find this magic, everything is going to be okay for you, and also for me, and it's going to cure this baby allergy."

"Really? Cure the baby allergy? Well, this is getting really mysterious."

"Seriously, it's true."

"So, you're saying if you can find Shadooda, you can cure the baby allergy and save Bumblegreen?"

"Yes."

"Without the blight coming back?"

"Yes."

"What's the catch?"

"I get to live here," answered ElizabethAnn, "and so does ... somebody else."

"Somebody else, huh? Who might that be?"

"Just someone," said ElizabethAnn, and somehow, for the first time, she felt like she really could make a home here with Grandma and Jackson—with Dahlia, too.

"All right," said Dahlia. "Let's do it. Why not? How do we find Shadooda?"

"Okay. You say the magic's disappeared, so who'd know where to find it?"

"No one. My ancestors, that's all. And they're dead."

"Dead, huh? All the way dead?"

Dahlia gave her a funny look.

"Seriously, do these ancestors live on in any way?" asked ElizabethAnn. "Like in dreams or clouds or shadows in the corner of your eye?"

"Funny you should say that."

"Why funny?"

"Ohhh," Dahlia mused, as she lay back on the boulder and gazed up at the night sky. She reached into her pocket and pulled out the loop of string she had found at the tree house, strung it between thumb and pinky, then wove it here and there until it made a shape.

"Cup and saucer," said ElizabethAnn.

"You say cup and saucer? I say crown."

"Oh, sure! A crown! Same shape!"

"I don't play with these strings anymore. Since I've become queen, my regents don't let me. It's unsophisticated and all."

"I won't tell."

"But when I used to do it, this game used to give me a tickly feeling," said the queen. "They say Bumblegreen royals have this thing: royal intuition."

"What's that?"

"Like a thing where your ancestors speak to you and you get this kind of mojo. Royal mojo. It tells you what to do in a moment of crisis and all. As a kid, I used to get it when I played that string-loop game. I never told anyone."

"Do it now."

"I did it already."

"And?"

"Do you know what?" replied Dahlia. "I think we should continue walking down this road. It might be a ways, but we shouldn't give up. Just keep going all the way down."

The girls walked on, through the starlight and shadows, in silence.

A chill shivered ElizabethAnn's tender shoulders and Dahlia stopped, ripped off a petticoat layer, happy to be rid of the cumbersome thing, and gave it to her friend for a cape. ElizabethAnn rubbed its silken texture against her cheek and felt comforted. Wrapped around her shoulders, the petticoat kept off the chill of night and cradled her in just the sort of luxury that makes it suddenly seem that, despite all odds, everything's going to be okay.

When the girls finally arrived at twelve Minion Lane, way out there in the hinterlands, they approached the dark, foreboding guard shack. The queen, unused to having to introduce herself, simply stated, "Hello. I'm Queen Dahlia. I believe I'm supposed to be here, now."

The obese guard, who sat inside in a swiveling chair, blubbered doubt through a handful of corn chips, donned a pair of reading specs, and squinted at Dahlia's face. By now, she had received her share of scratchings from branches and dirt specks from gusting wind. Her face didn't necessarily have the royal look about it.

"Where's your entourage, then?" asked the guard.

"I'm incognito," replied the queen.

"Why would a queen go incognito?" asked the guard.

"I don't think that's a question you have the right to ask," the queen answered back, in a perfectly haughty manner that assured the portly guard she probably was, actually, the queen. He opened the gate and gave Dahlia a flyer about safety protocol. She laughed and tossed it into the bushes.

"Littering!" protested the guard.

"It doesn't matter," she said. "The world is ending, I'm sure of it."

The guard watched Dahlia walk down the long promenade, multiple skirts and gauzy layered accents swirling around her like a cloud and a mist. ElizabethAnn scampered along behind.

Dahlia and ElizabethAnn approached the campus, entered the courtyard, found Building F, opened the office door, confronted the brunette who may or may not have been a robot, and the queen explained she intended to see Shadooda or "heads will roll." (A pretty old-fashioned but still effective threat.)

The receptionist pressed a button.

The couch, magazine rack, and coffee table slid away, and the set of stairs, somehow oddly familiar to Dahlia—or to her ancestral memory, at least—appeared. The queen eagerly descended. ElizabethAnn followed along.

The girls reached the bottom of the stairs, with its stone gallery and dim light. They passed the rusting Chevelle and bat hotel. They walked past the little alcoves on either side of the wide hallway, each one housing a wizened crone of some kind.

The magicians gave the girls the old fish-eye while sing-song-muttering endlessly into their copper tubes. As they walked down the corridor, ElizabethAnn noticed little signs posted outside some of the cells, even though they were so greasy and drab as to be almost indistinguishable from the rock walls themselves. They said, for instance: *Criminey Finchforth, Magic Maker* and *Dame Sninkletter, Sorcerer*.

"Dahlia," whispered ElizabethAnn, "Shouldn't we stop here and inquire? These folks seem to be magicians."

Dahlia pulled her friend aside and whispered, "My intuition is, it's been a rather long while since there's been any ongoing training for their craft. Those folks, well, advanced magic is nothing but a memory for them."

Dahlia further opined that most of these old ex-magicians just kept themselves busy with their little singsongs because that was all they had in them anymore.

"There's only one magician in this place that's going to be any good," she said. "A particularly talented one, name of ..." Dahlia took out her loop of string and made that cup and saucer shape again. She stared at the shape a while, then crumpled it back into her pocket. "Name of Shadooda Majit Goforth."

Shadooda's sign looked like it had been scratched with a claw out of a rotten plank from a shipwreck, but there it hung, outside its little stone booth, just like the others. To ElizabethAnn, Shadooda looked like just another crumpled magician squatting on a three-legged stool, joining the chorus of mumblers with its face inside a four-inch copper pipe. But Dahlia understood this person was special.

"Shadooda Majit Goforth," Dahlia said, "you can stop your singing, now. I'm here."

Shadooda did stop. It shuffled asymmetrically up to Dahlia, put its face about an inch from her royal nose, and said, "Don't be smart with me, missy. These songs are the only hope we've had for a decade! But, what the hell, it's time for my break, anyway. Five minutes per hour! Fifteen minutes per shift! Union regs! Legal requirements!"

The magician burst into great cackles of laughter at that, and those in booths up and down the hallway joined in, like grisly mockingbirds.

60

IN WHICH THE QUEEN ALTERS
THE POPULATION OF THE DUNGEON

Why a couple of dedicated capitalists like Georgie and Schrank couldn't get a break for love or money (although they seldom used love) remains a mystery. Usually, that much determination and focused intent yields some inkling of a beginning of a clue as to how to get a perfectly genius moneymaking scheme off the ground.

After all, they had investors, a business plan, a spreadsheet, and a worthy product; yet, so far, the hapless pair couldn't seem to take their scheme from idea to reality. Despite their possession of an electronic invention of unspeakable value, despite the good name of Favra Watch, and despite their doggedness in the face of obstacles, the pair still lacked one thing: knowledge of which GPS coordinate corresponded to that portal to No Oaks, which they assumed was still open.

That's why, once Georgie (thanks to her rendezvous in the kitchen with Tammy) finally did manage to name a magician—Shadooda Majit Goforth—and tell Schrank the address on Minion Lane that Tammy had provided, she and Schrank jumped into her homemade aircraft, flew out over the high-tech complex, circled it twice, touched down inside the gates where the guard couldn't stop them, explored the campus at length, found the Hindforth and Assoc. office, and endured an interaction with the receptionist. Eventually they, too, descended the long, dark stone steps into gloom.

When they approached Shadooda's cell, Georgie and Schrank heard something they didn't expect: little girls' voices.

"So, you see, there's a portal somewhere that's open, Shadooda, and I need you to fix the polymer and close 'er on up," one little-girl voice said.

"I'm the evidence," the other voice said.

"Yes, she's the evidence of foul play," the first voice said. "This is ElizabethAnn, and she came through a portal from another world."

Shadooda sniffed the air and rubbed its hands together, making a shushing sound much like dry grass in a breeze. The potbellied, crackle-skinned, bewhiskered lump of a person slapped its hobnailed boots idly against the flagstones, tapped out a little rhythm on the wood of its stool, and whistled long and shrill, up toward the ceiling, as if summoning a ghostly flock of gulls.

Shadooda finally said, "Girls, we're not alone," and stepped, with surprising agility, into the shadows of the hall.

Before they could run, hide, or think fast, Georgie and Schrank felt themselves being hoisted by their shirt collars. Shadooda pulled the pair close and smacked its lips at them. It blinked rapidly and groaned in a deep, painful-sounding way. It squatted, stood, cracked its joints, snorted, and released them.

"So many visitors, and I'm hardly dressed for company," it said. The crones up and down the hall cackled at that, and the sound of their dry laughter pinged off the rock walls like bullets. "What do you two want?"

"Us?" asked Schrank.

"Are you Shadooda Majit …" asked Georgie.

"Of course!" chorused Shadooda, ElizabethAnn, and Dahlia.

"You're the magician?" asked Schrank.

"Of course!" chorused the three again, clearly anxious for Georgie and Schrank to get their business over with.

"Actually, I heard you talking about something about a portal," said Georgie, "and that's kind of what we wanted to inquire about, too."

"Let me guess, now," said Shadooda. "These girls want me to close one, and I'll bet you two want me to open one. Would that be it?"

"Open one?" exclaimed the queen. "No! No one can open one! That's treason!"

"Treason? Phooey," said Georgie, not recognizing the queen in her disheveled state. "This is business, little girl. Pure and simple."

"I like business," Dahlia replied. "What sort of business would that be?"

Before Schrank could stop her, Georgie whipped a business card out of her jacket pocket. "Favra. Read my face. That's our tagline."

"Favra, huh? Favra Watch Company? THE Favra Watch Company?" asked Dahlia, adding, "Hey, mister, come closer. Yeah, you! Don't I recognize you? You're the wide, flat man with no credentials!"

"Oh, no," Schrank said and dropped quickly to one knee. "Your Highness, I can explain!"

"Schrank, what are you doing? That's just a little girl, that's no … oh, dear," said Georgie, right before Schrank grabbed her belt loop and hauled her down to her knees.

"Beg your pardon, Your Highness!" Georgie said, suddenly remembering that the queen herself was a little girl, yes, about the age of this one.

"Long live the queen!" Georgie added, then grimaced out of embarrassment, then cowered out of fear.

Queen Dahlia considered the pair.

"Normally," Dahlia said to ElizabethAnn, "I'd have my security personnel haul the both of them off to the cage. I don't know if you realize how bad this is, this attempt to open a portal. See, another open portal could cause an even bigger blight. Just like …"

"Just like me and Jackson could?" ElizabethAnn said, finishing the thought.

"Very good. Yes," Dahlia replied. "You catch on quickly, don't you?" Dahlia put her hands on her slender, thirteen-year-old hips, and said to Georgie and Schrank, "You two are under arrest. I don't know how I'm going to arrest you with my bare hands or anything, but consider yourselves under arrest."

"We're entitled to a trial!" whined Georgie. Schrank elbowed her.

"Sure, but consider this," said Dahlia. "I'm the judge and also the star witness for the prosecution; so, good luck with that."

"With respect, Your Highness," said Schrank, with very little respect at all, "The monkey tribunal has a say in things now, too, and the Favra Watch Company has done a great deal of outreach to the monkey community. We're going to fight this, with respect, Your

Highness. We have rights."

Queen Dahlia rolled her eyes at Shadooda, as if to say, "Kids these days!"

"I've heard about this monkey tribunal," said Shadooda.

"As if I didn't have enough trouble with seven regents, now I've got a bunch of hoity-toity apes constantly second-guessing me. Never mind an open portal. It's too much!" said Dahlia.

That's when Georgie and Schrank made a run for it. They put an awful lot of effort into their mad dash, considering they were merely running from two little girls and a hobbled old magician.

With a great deal of huffing, puffing, slipping, sliding, and a sincere attempt at rapid acceleration, the two sped away down the gloomy corridor.

"They're getting away!" announced ElizabethAnn.

"Get back here, you miscreants!" shouted Dahlia.

Shadooda cocked its head in the style of an inquisitive puppy and laughed softly. "Little girl," it said, "do you even know where we are?"

"Underground?" answered Dahlia. "In a … a hallway … a tunnel … a subterranean flea market? I give up."

"It's a dungeon," said Shadooda. "Say it: *dun jun.*"

Dahlia gulped and looked around the place with new eyes.

"So," said Dahlia, "I don't suppose there's any way out?"

"Nope," replied Shadooda.

"For them, or … for you, either?" added Dahlia.

"You got it, Bright Eyes," Shadooda replied. "On top of that, tell me, what do you see all around you? Don't answer, I'll tell you. You don't see much, do you? Because its stinkin' DARK. Dark as the inside of a cow! And what happens when people live in the dark?"

Dahlia couldn't answer. She was still digesting the fact that this was the Bumblegreen dungeon—that Bumblegreen even had a dungeon.

"They go blind," said ElizabethAnn.

"Aren't you a pip!" responded the magician. "That's right, little alien, they go blind, like me."

Dahlia looked around the fetid place with new horror.

"So, if this is a dungeon, where are the prisoners?" asked ElizabethAnn, stupidly.

Shadooda looked at her long and deep, as did the magicians across the hall. "Queen Dahlia's parents, the old king and queen, they put us here," answered Shadooda. "Science was the rage at that time. Magic was out. You know how fashion is, so fickle."

"But, who feeds you?" asked Dahlia.

Shadooda cackled, as did the magicians up and down the hall. "Insects are a lot more nutritious than they look, you know, and we've rat-catching contests, too," it said. Then, raising its voice to be heard from afar, it added, "Some witches are real champs at it! We've got one can wrestle a greased rat in thirty seconds, can't you Sninkletter?"

A distant reply came screeching down the hallway, bouncing off stone—a yelp of either delight or panic.

"We used to walk on the land, you know," added Shadooda. "Used to brew herbs and cure the ill. Help lovelorn girls find beaux and all that. Used to bring the rain, too. Life was a bit lighter then, eh, old bats?"

A chorus of giggles reverberated up and down the hall.

"Shadooda," said Dahlia, "I don't know what to say, except you're certainly free to go now, if you'd like. I'd like to have this whole place blown up, I honestly would."

"Yeah, thanks for that," said Shadooda. "Ever hear the expression, 'too little too late?' None of your problem, of course, but I'm dead blind, you know. What good would aboveground living do me? This is my home, now, so I think I'll stay."

The general hum of magicians mumble-singing into their tubes filled the ensuing silence like the drone of bees.

A wail slowly built at the far end of the gloomy corridor, and finally Georgie and Schrank raced back past ElizabethAnn, Shadooda, and the queen, running fast as their legs could pump, this time with faces frozen in panic.

"Raaaaaaaaats!" Shrank and Georgie yelled as they zipped past Shadooda's cell.

A moment later, ElizabethAnn, Shadooda, and the queen heard the sounds of two people trying to ascend the very steep and slippery stone stairs. A ticky ticky ticky ticky sound of rapid footsteps mixed with dull thuds, curses, and whimpers, as the pair knocked into each other and the walls.

"They are rather large, the rats," Shadooda said, and sniggered.

"It looks like I'm going to need some dungeon space for two new inmates, Shadooda," said Queen Dahlia.

"Need the space?" replied Shadooda. "A minute ago you didn't know we were here, and now you're evicting us? Just like royalty!"

Dahlia peered down the corridor to where Georgie and Schrank could be heard banging on the rock, on top of which sat the couch, coffee table, and magazine rack overlooked by the blow-dried brunette.

"I can't exactly let those two criminals go, can I?" Dahlia asked.

"Good point," said Shadooda, "and all the cells are full."

"Someone would have to double up, I guess," Dahlia said. "Maybe you and Sninkletter."

"Don't know about that," said Shadooda. "Snink sings off-key."

"What else to do?" asked the queen.

"Wouldn't want those two as neighbors, exactly," Shadooda

admitted. "That Georgie and whatshisname. Unpleasant types."

"Likely to whine and complain a lot," said Dahlia, "and not much good at singing nursery rhymes, I'll bet."

"Likely to bring in a conversational element, too. Yech," replied Shadooda, with a sigh of defeat. "If they're going to stay, be better for us to go topside, I guess."

A low hum of approval, from the other magicians, reverberated up and down the hall. It became a hiss—a hiss of yeses.

"What about the magic?" asked ElizabethAnn, in a tiny voice. "The magic we came here to get? To save Bumblegreen?"

"Save?" asked Shadooda. "What save? Bumblegreen's doomed. Forget about it. The blight's coming back, either way. People can't control themselves, that's the real reason."

"But Shadooda, you've got to shut that open portal!" pleaded Dahlia. "It has to be magically and completely shut! Sealed forever!"

"Sure, Chickadee. No problem. Except for one thing," said Shadooda. "Those portals? They aren't meant to be shut. Open, they invite the blight, but closed, they cause the baby allergy and will, eventually, suffocate us all. The portals are prehistoric and essential to Bumblegreen. They're meant to remain open. So, no, I'm not shutting the open portal, or any others that fall open, and open they will, over time. Bumblegreen has to air out. There just isn't anything I, or you, or anyone can do about it."

This news was too much for Dahlia, who collapsed in a faint on the stone floor. ElizabethAnn stood over the queen's inert body, wondering what in the world she was expected to do about any of this.

"It's the beginning of the end, you know," said Shadooda, to rumpled little ElizabethAnn.

"But Grandma said I had to find you and get you to bring back the magic," ElizabethAnn explained. "She said the magic would save Bumblegreen. That's what she said. The magic would save …"

"Grandma?" asked Shadooda.

"My Grandma. From No Oaks," said ElizabethAnn. "She's in hiding, a fugitive, unless you can bring back the magic. Or I can. Or someone!"

"So Grandma returned, did she?" Shadooda said. "Great old gal! Maybe there's a chance for us, after all. Slap that queen awake. I want to tell her something."

ElizabethAnn shook Dahlia, who awoke with a sigh as deep and lonely as only a soon-to-be-deposed ruler can sigh.

"Cripes," Dahlia said, "but it's a long walk back, only to tell people it's the end of the world."

"End of the world?" Shadooda said, pulling a small, tattered suitcase out of a cobwebby corner. "Not quite." The magician shuffled to a corner of its cell and felt around until it found a greasy porkpie hat with a hole in it. It fondled the hat before placing it gently inside the suitcase, saying, "There's only one thing that ever kept Bumblegreen alive, you know. Queenie, don't you know the real cause of the blight?"

"The real cause? The portals? The mites coming through the portals?" answered Dahlia. "We spent years figuring that out. That's the one thing I'm sure of. Those portals get opened again and Bumblegreen's doomed!"

"You sure about that?" asked the magician.

"Sure? Sure, I'm sure! Everyone agreed!" replied the queen. "Researchers imported from other lands! Scientific experts! Everyone!"

"Everyone?" asked Shadooda.

"Every … oh, well, maybe not exactly everyone," said the queen.

"There was one dissenter, I think."

"Ah, a lone dissenter. And who might that have been?" asked Shadooda. Its gnarled fingers placed a tin cup in the suitcase, next to the hat.

"She was an eccentric old gal, that one. Didn't catch her name," replied the queen. "Didn't catch her reasoning, either. She slipped through a portal before telling me much. Anyway, the woman's long gone, now."

"Was it Grandma? Was it Grandma?" asked ElizabethAnn.

"Indeed," replied Shadooda. "That was Grandma."

The magician shuffled around the edges of its cell, feeling its way past inhabited spiderwebs and rotting furniture. It found a soiled handkerchief lying on a bench and placed it, gently, into the suitcase, before latching the lid and telling them, "Grandma knew something no one else wanted to face."

"There's more to know?" asked Dahlia, righting herself and sneezing from the dusty floor. She brushed off her flounces, petticoats, ribbons, bows, peplums, and sashes. "Out with it, Shadooda," she said. "I haven't got all day. There's a kingdom going down the tubes, as we speak. What's the secret?"

"The open portals never were never the problem, Queenie, nor were the mites that came over on the Travelers. What the real problem was was the imports. Bringing physical objects across the space/time continuum? Never a good idea," Shadooda said, as it took the frayed suitcase in hand, shuffled into the hallway, and felt along the wall.

Shadooda reached out with its free hand, beckoned, and said, "ElizabethAnn, give me your hand. Dahlia, all you need to do to save Bumblegreen is open the portals and bring back the magic, the magic your parents hid from the world. They didn't mean any harm. They didn't know what they did, sending us down here, but Bumblegreen needs us. What you can do with your oh-so-precious laws is make it so imports can't go through, but people can. If they bring imports along, then wham!" Shadooda said, making a guillotine-like gesture with its hand.

"Actually, now we drop criminals into a pit of ..."

"Like I care."

"Never mind."

"They'll still import, mind you," Shadooda grumbled. "People can't control themselves around temptations, but they have to, that's all."

"They can't!" said Dahlia, thinking of her own weaknesses for soft, shiny, glittery new things.

"I know," Shadooda said with a sigh, "but they have to."

It looked back, bared its surprisingly intact teeth, and whistled in a way that went up, down, warbled, trilled, and came to a nearly symphonic crescendo.

A great "Ahhhhh" resounded from the chorus of other prisoners, followed by the shuffling and bustling of hundreds of magicians packing their own small suitcases. Blind, arthritic, or both, they made their slow, laborious way down the hall, behind Shadooda, ElizabethAnn, and Dahlia, toward the gloomy end of the corridor— the end that Shrank and Georgie had so recently fled.

Dahlia looked back at the encroaching, wizened army of crones, whose feet shuffled along like the half-dead, and whose shoulders hunched like they had been taken apart and put back together wrong, but whose eyes, though hopelessly blind, shone with the first sign of hope in years.

"Where are we going, Shadooda?" asked Dahlia. She distinctly remembered the entrance being at the other end of the corridor; the rats, at this end.

"Up. Up. Up! Don't tell me you came the long way?" Shadooda

said.

"Long way?" the girls chorused.

"This is the way to the shortcut. Oh no, no, no! Don't tell me you came the long way!" Shadooda said.

The magicians in the corridor laughed cruelly at this, their guffaws vanishing into the blackness at the end of the hall, where rat's eyes gleamed in unblinking red pairs.

Walking farther into the gloom, Dahlia heard rodents scuttling. She clutched ElizabethAnn, who, in turn, clutched Shadooda. The old magician chuckled and took the girls deeper still, the ancient army of magicians following silently.

Finally, Shadooda stopped at what appeared to be a completely nondescript spot in the center of the hall and looked up. There, above them, loomed a hatch in the ceiling, with a lock on it. On the floor lay a sledgehammer. Dahlia and ElizabethAnn picked up the sledgehammer and, with all four of their beanpole arms working together, managed to smash the rusty padlock. Its jagged pieces rained down.

Opening the hatch, Dahlia pulled down a metal ladder. It led up, up, and up through a narrow stone compartment. She put her foot on the first rung.

"Wait," said Shadooda. "Queenie, you're tougher than I figured on."

"Me?" answered Dahlia, unused to being called anything other than Your Highness.

"I have a confession to make," said Shadooda. "I was in a position recently," it croaked, "to set certain, er, ah … wheels in motion. Wanted to toughen you up a bit. Make you grow up, quick. I haven't much time left, see, and I thought this idea might, uh, what-do-you-call-it … hasten the arrival of your royal mojo. Give you a few tribulations to navigate. Forgive me! What I'm trying to say, Queenie, is that there's probably going to be some trouble in store when you get back to the palace."

"Interesting theory," said Dahlia. "Can't say it was a good one."

"Beginning to regret it, actually," said Shadooda.

"So, what should I expect?"

Shadooda cleared its throat. "Well, let's just say keep your big-girl pants on. There might be an insurrection of sorts. Not sure. But if so, it'll do you good in the long run. It really will. Not that that's much consolation."

Dahlia giggled (at the notion of wearing pants) and ascended the ladder.

"Other girl, you follow her," Shadooda commanded.

The old metal rungs, though bent and wiggly, held. The queen climbed up, toward a distant rectangle of light that seeped in around the edges of a second trap door. ElizabethAnn followed.

At the top, Dahlia pushed open the trapdoor and climbed through, into the light. Then, she reached down to take ElizabethAnn's hand, but strangely, her friend wasn't there. Dahlia only heard a terrible scream as ElizabethAnn fell back through the chute, onto the hard stone of the dungeon floor.

The hatch slammed shut, seemingly of its own accord, leaving Dahlia in a room chock full of people staring directly at her.

61

IN WHICH CERTAIN PURPOSES MUST
BE DESCRIBED AS NEFARIOUS

ElizabethAnn tried not to cry. Instead, she sucked on her fingers, raw and swollen from having slammed against the ladder when she fell.

"That hatch is enchanted," said Shadooda. "Royals only allowed."

Hundreds of magicians gathered around poor, bruised ElizabethAnn. She looked up into their glassy eyes.

"Why didn't you tell me?" she asked.

"Forgot," said Shadooda. "I'm old."

"So, I'm stuck down here?" asked ElizabethAnn.

"Oh no, you can still get out, alien child. Just go the long way."

Shadooda pointed down the corridor, toward the stairs by which ElizabethAnn and Dahlia (and Tammy, long ago, and Georgie and Shrank, more recently) had first entered the dungeon. The sea of sorcerers parted to show her the way. At the end of the corridor sat Georgie and Schrank, exhausted, on the dusty floor.

"What about those two?" asked ElizabethAnn.

"Not them. They're stuck here, now, by Queen's orders. Woe betide the rest of us!" Shadooda declared. "You can get out, though. Only, you've got to go and find Grandma for me."

ElizabethAnn smiled and nodded, having no idea how to find Grandma, but not wanting to let on. Nursing a turned ankle, she limped back the way she had come. She walked the gauntlet of magicians, then passed Georgie and Schrank who were curled into fetal positions against a cold stone wall. She felt she should say something.

"I'm going to get Grandma," she said, "and get us all out of here."

"Who are you, anyway?" Georgie asked.

"Did you really come through a portal?" Schrank asked.

"Just tell us where the portal is. Just tell us, please! Just whisper it!" Georgie pleaded.

"I don't know," said ElizabethAnn. "In the woods, somewhere. If I knew, I would've returned to No Oaks long ago." This last was a lie. She only said it because she enjoyed giving the impression she still had a home, somewhere.

ElizabethAnn limped past the wrecked Chevelle and up the long flight of stairs to where the rock slab magically drew aside. She climbed into the office, greeted the receptionist, walked through Building F, traversed the lengthy driveway, sauntered past the guard shack, and trudged down creepy old Minion Lane, back the way she had come.

Abandoned by Dahlia and shouldering the impossible burden of finding a Grandma who didn't want to be found, ElizabethAnn felt profoundly alone. Images of those hundred sorcerers dressed in filthy rags, their blind eyes shining with hope, flashed through her mind. ElizabethAnn cried and snuffled with despair as she walked along, not caring who saw. She wandered unfamiliar cobblestone streets, wretched and lost, until she came upon a woman with a prominent, fascinating nose and the world's longest, thickest black hair.

"Are you lost, little girl?" asked the woman. It was Tammy.

Tammy took ElizabethAnn to her shack, fed her, and let her nap on a cot while she mended the hem of the girl's torn, rumpled, blue-flowered dress. Tammy decided this little urchin would do perfectly for the last, but most crucial, segment of her black-magic revenge and seduction scheme. Black magic being the dangerous medium it is, Tammy feared to take the scheme to fruition all by herself. She wanted some type of trial run, and ElizabethAnn looked, to her, like the world's most perfect guinea pig.

On the fateful day of her own visit to the dungeon, long ago, Tammy had learned from Shadooda that seduction was nothing sexual but merely a matter of creating fascination—a mystery, a riddle, an invitation to look deeper—and a suggestion that a lot of interesting "otherness" would be found just beneath the surface.

"Fascination," Shadooda had said, on that long-ago day, "can turn into any type of love: sexual, parental, platonic, and, yes: obsessive."

Tammy reasoned that a child could apply the black-magic seduction technique just as well as she could, and that way she could see how it worked. So, Tammy rousted despairing, confused, and overtired ElizabethAnn and guided her out onto the streets for some "fun."

"Little girl," asked Tammy, "what is your deal?"

"Deal?" asked ElizabethAnn, who had sunk her head down as far as it would go between her shoulders, determined to disappear, one vertical inch at a time.

"Look," explained the new Tammy—nose forward, long coarse hair hanging, arms swinging from her erect frame like hooks on pegs. "You have to try to make someone fall in love with you instantly. Try anyone. In fact, try everyone you meet. Every single one." The pair hid, by now, in an alley in downtown Bumblegreen.

"I'm supposed to be finding my Grandma," whined ElizabethAnn. "I have to save people." Tammy looked at her funny, and funnier still when ElizabethAnn added, "I have to save Bumblegreen itself, supposedly."

"You're really a nut, you know?" Tammy said. "It's cute, but come on. Now, just for Auntie Tammy, try and seduce someone. Anyone you see."

"That's impossible. Plus, inappropriate."

Tammy yanked the child behind an earthen wall that hid them from the street. "No, it isn't," she said. "It's only logical. You just look them in the eye and let them see your face."

"See my face?"

"Placement of the eyes, the nose, chubbiness of the cheeks, lip shape, ears. *You* know. It's phrenology," Tammy said. "People read your face, intuitively, and if it's good, they just like you, and boom, they want to do things for you. Plus, I'm rubbing your head with a magical ointment that should attract people to you. Stop squirming! It'll make them fall in love with you, in a certain manner of speaking. I mean, an age-appropriate type of love. I'm not some weirdo. Here, have some more. If you do this, I'll take you to your beast. I know exactly where he is. But nothing's free, you know."

"I know where he is, too! Yech!" protested ElizabethAnn. "He's at the castle! Now, let me go!"

"Okay, fine," said Tammy. "Just test out this love potion for me, then I'll take you there. Or I'll let you go, and you can find your old grandma or whatever you want. Come on! Be a sport! Just seduce somebody for me. Go out there and see if this stuff works."

"Why don't you just do it yourself?"

"Are you kidding? What if I made the potion backwards? What if it's deadly? What if it turns me into an old hag? I got enough problems. Now, go."

"If I seduce them, would they buy me a cruller?"

"Who?"

"The people I'm supposedly going to seduce with my supposed charm."

"More than that! A custard-filled éclair!"

"But I want a cruller."

"Try this guy, right here," said Tammy, "crossing the street with the blue backpack and grocery sack."

"Him? No way!"

"Why not?"

"His arms are full. How could be buy me a cruller?"

"You'd be surprised."

The pair walked on.

"This hotel concierge," Tammy said. "Dead ahead. White gloves, bowtie, spats. Bet he loves children."

"He's on duty. He can't buy me a cruller."

"Have more faith in humanity, child!"

The pair walked on. "There," said Tammy, pointing.

"Where?"

"Raccoon coat at one o'clock," said Tammy. "Carrying a pet ferret with a bow on its head and appearing to be late for something. Smeared lipstick, wrinkled brow, cruel shoes. Do it!"

Tammy pulled the child's hair back in a quicky bun and shoved her out on the sidewalk, right in front of the malcontented woman.

"Phrenology!" Tammy hissed, by way of egging her on.

"Excuse me," began ElizabethAnn, catching the harried woman's eye. At first, the lady just kept walking, the way city people do, but ElizabethAnn held her gaze relentlessly.

"Uh, yes? Yes? What is it?" replied the lady.

ElizabethAnn said nothing, did nothing, just kept her face front and center, unavoidable-intelligent, but devoid of any specific thought-message. The woman hesitated and shifted her ferret to the other arm.

"May I pet your ferret?" asked ElizabethAnn finally, not like an eager child and a stranger on the street, but as if the lady and she were old friends, and this, an ordinary, casual, mid-conversation request.

"Certainly," said the woman, and lowered the pampered beast to the child's eye level.

ElizabethAnn petted the ferret, but looked the woman in the eye and let the slightest smile of innocent pleasure play across her lips, saying nothing.

A pause, then … "Would you like a cruller, little girl?"

A handclap sounded! It was Tammy's, as she jumped and clapped and ran into the street with unconcealed glee, then ran back behind the wall and hid in the alley. ElizabethAnn walked away with the lady, holding fast to the raccoon coat and looking over her shoulder at Tammy, who gave her a thumbs-up and pointed at a pastry shop.

It's time, thought Tammy. *T minus everything.*

Tammy waited until ElizabethAnn had finished her cruller, then ran into the bakery, grabbed her by the ear, and dragged her off in a castleward direction, making some hasty excuse to the bewildered ferret lady, who, in the meantime, had fallen so deeply in love with ElizabethAnn that she was even then mentally redecorating her spare bedroom in pastels and zoo animals. When ElizabethAnn vanished as quickly as she had come, the normally stodgy, humorless woman burst into a brokenhearted torrent of tears.

62

**WHERE THE DUCHESS
ARRANGES A RE-LOVE-LUTION**

When Dahlia climbed up through the trapdoor in the throne room's floor, the duchess froze, glancing over her shoulder, and her face seized in an expression of pure shock. Bent at the hips as she was, it looked as if the duchess had been just about to sit upon Dahlia's throne. In fact, the extravagant train of the duchess' low-cut velvet gown had actually tangled itself around the throne's bejeweled legs. The duchess hesitated, then straightened up and settled her weight, inelegantly, on one haunch, as if all along she had merely been

394

searching for a more comfortable standing position.

Dahlia looked up and saw, in the box seats flanking the stage, her regents peering down at her from one side and Zade Fandey peering down from the other.

The din in the packed room subsided in a wave. First, those closest to the stage clammed up. Then, those further back in the audience took the cue from the others, and, eventually, the population of the entire cavernous space—teeming with sweating, hollering, impatient humanity—figured out something was up. The townspeople assembled on the room's vast floor even stopped swatting one another with leather hats and squabbling about lost items. By the time the trapdoor clanked shut behind the queen, a profound hush had swept over the entire room.

In the midst of that shimmering moment, Queen Dahlia became keenly aware of her disheveled condition. She reached up to adjust her headdress, but it had fallen off hours ago, so she groped the air, as if hunting for a halo, and stood there feeling naked, utterly perplexed, and frighteningly surrounded.

As Dahlia looked on, the duchess seemed to deflate, and the regents —a moment ago so full of pomp and bluster—also gradually slouched into crumpled positions of embarrassment. The duchess avoided meeting the queen's eye and made as if to tie her shoes, though they were stilettos. Nobody spoke. Also, nobody explained the presence of the large crowd, seemingly a random sampling of Bumblegreen itself.

Next, the velvet curtains flanking the stage swung and swayed, twisted and jostled, as monkeys climbed down the curtains from their perches in the ceiling beams. Molting, gray, and weary, twelve monkeys—the monkey tribunal itself—gathered into a semicircle around Dahlia. A spokes-monkey stepped forward. The foot-long whiskers descending from his nostrils and ears didn't seem to impair his speech or hearing much. He informed Queen Dahlia that she was being deposed.

"Deposed?" the queen asked, incredulous.

"Ahem," began the monkey, "The duchess, your regents, and one-percent of the entire population of Bumblegreen just now voted, practically unanimously. They called us in to make the final decision."

Dahlia blinked, unfamiliar with the concept of voting and unsure of its import.

"It's a revolution," continued the monkey, unabashed. "The duchess arranged it."

"Wait a minute," said the queen. "The duchess? But didn't Iris just invite me to a party?"

"Hi there, Dahlia!" said the duchess, with manufactured cheer. "Darling, don't think of this as a revolution," she said. "It's not meant in that spirit, at all! It's meant as a re-love-lution! It's in your best interest!"

"No, it isn't!" yelled Zade Fandey, from his box, high above. "People, the queen's the only one who can save Bumblegreen! Things aren't the way they seem! The open portals aren't even what caused the blight!"

"Good God! A mad man!" shouted the duchess. "Who is that?"

"It's Zade Fandey," barked the spokesmonkey. "He's holding hundreds of monkeys prisoner in the lab! Not releasing them into the wild! We're putting him on trial, next!"

"Listen here, Fandey," shouted the duchess. "The queen's sheltering hostiles! Look at these mite-infested portal jumpers!"

She pointed at Jackson and Earl, who cowered together inside the iron cage with the trapdoor floor.

"I know what I'm doing!" yelled Zade Fandey at everyone below.

"I'm a scientist!"

"Pshaw!" yelled back numerous members of the monkey tribunal.

"Don't forget, I made you!" Zade said, pointing at them.

"Don't forget this tribunal has power," yelled the monkeys. "And this time, Fandey, we're going to get our way!"

"Queen Dahlia won't even let respectable citizens Travel! It's unfair!" shouted the duchess to all and sundry. "When I'm queen, you'll get so many imports your only problem will be storing all that stuff!"

The crowd chanted, "Du-chess, Du-chess, Du-chess," then, "Im-ports, im-ports, im-ports."

"Iris? You arranged all this?" asked Dahlia.

"Well, it wasn't my idea, per se, exactly on my own," explained the duchess.

"Somehow, I thought that," answered the queen.

"I was working in tandem, you know. I was inspired by ... well, I was inspired," said the duchess. "A little fairy whispered in my ear, and boom. I mean, it's so necessary, Dahlia. You simply aren't suited, darling. You know that!"

The duchess made a grand sweeping gesture whose meaning was unclear, and the crowd let out another roar. She grinned with the pleasure of her newfound popularity and made a mental note to spearhead more peasant uprisings in the future.

"You shall address me as Your Majesty, thank you very much." Dahlia sputtered, adding, "...a little fairy?"

Never before having been described as anything as adorable as a little fairy, Tammy would have enjoyed this exchange, if she'd been present.

"Leave the queen alone, you ruffians!" boomed a voice from somewhere high above. Sliding on a rope suspended from the unknowable recesses of the room's elaborate structure of rafters, down came Fast Eddie—his clothing in tatters, his shirttails torn, his shoes absent, his face scratched and bleeding. His once-white shirt showed signs of having been chewed by rats, and indeed a small rat still clung to his back, attached to the fabric of his shirt, seeming to want to nest there.

Pigeons flew out of the dark, shadowy rafters as he descended. Three perched on his shoulder, hip, and pant cuff in an entirely too-familiar manner. Fast Eddie slowly, but ever so slowly, slid down the frayed and knotted rope until he hung in midair, well above the heads of the townspeople.

"Fair and innocent maiden, I will defend you!" said Fast Eddie, rather overdramatically, to the queen, then coughed up a wad of something and released it on the unfortunates below. "I've been here all along, witnessing this treasonous spectacle, watching and waiting for you. Fair maiden, Queen Dahlia, I've gone countless days without food, without daylight. In my sordid hiding place, I've been attacked by vermin, but all this is of no import to me, for I care only for your love!"

"Huh?" inquired Dahlia. "Hey, didn't I see you just yesterday? In the forest?"

Overall, Fast Eddie's act was a grand one and would have taken in any lady, at all. Any normal lady, that is. How much he had suffered for her, what he was willing to sacrifice, the humiliation he would endure for this love that had vanquished him—he made all that apparent.

How many hours had he been waiting in the vermin-infested rafters, just for the chance to spy on this terrible betrayal?—the lady in question was meant to ask herself.

How much personal discomfort was he willing to put up with to come to her defense and see her one more time before she was deposed?— the queen was meant to wonder.

To what lengths would this man go, just to declare his love, and then throw himself upon the sword of a hostile regent, in order that she might swab his brow with her rose-scented handkerchief in his last moments of life?—was the idea of all this drama.

The queen was supposed to swoon at the pitiful man's devotion and fall in love. That was the plan. And after Fast Eddie completed the seduction? Who knew? Perhaps he would become king. He had entertained that notion, yes.

But what actually happened was: Watching Fast Eddie, the queen almost became impressed. Almost. Until she noticed her spotted pet pigeon Samuel clinging to his suspended pant cuff and realized all his supposed suffering was a ruse. Indeed, Fast Eddie hadn't spent innumerable uncomfortable hours hiding in the rafters and being assaulted by rats and pigeons as he waited desperately to come to her defense. No, she immediately realized, he had merely decorated himself with a disguise made of ripped clothing, fake blood, and trained animals (stolen trained animals, at that).

"Samuel! Djem-djem! Little Katerina!" she called, and her three pets flew from Fast Eddie's body over to Dahlia's outstretched arm. They were only pigeons, after all, with brains the size of currants. If she could teach them to alight on her arm and pass little hoops from beak to beak, then Fast Eddie could certainly kidnap them and make them part of his elaborate disguise. The breed was profoundly trainable.

Just then, the rat (which was really a squirrel, in disguise) fell from Fast Eddie's back, where it had been clinging. The townsfolk screamed as it flipped, end over end, down through the air, claws outstretched, jaws open. It landed on the shoulders of a beefy housewife, who spun around twice, cursed, gasped, fell to the floor, and commenced beating the rat with a hefty purse, at which point the rat turned into a redheaded woman who screamed for her life.

Aware, by this point, that his scheme had failed utterly, Fast Eddie released the rope, dropped twenty feet to the floor, right into the middle of the melee, and pummeled the housewife, himself. Assorted onlookers joined in on both sides—whether hoping to defend a loved one or just for the fun of it, who knew.

Up in his box, Zade Fandey jumped to his feet. He had an excellent view of the proceedings, as planned. "Queen Dahlia!" he pleaded. "You've got to listen to me! Don't execute that beast and monkey! You've got to bring back the magic, open the portals, and save Bumblegreen!"

It looked like someone was pulling on the hem of Zade's lab coat. Then, a gravelly voice from someplace up there rang out: "ElizabethAnn's got it covered, Zade! Just keep your mouth shut!"

"It's the eleventh hour and she hasn't done it!" said Zade, in a harsh whisper, to whomever was hiding on the floor of his viewing box. "She hasn't found the magic, hasn't saved anyone! And if the queen is deposed, what chance do we have, then?" Fandey appeared to be talking to his shoes, behind the box's waist-high wall. None of the rabble on the floor listened to any of this repartee, being far more interested in seeing real blood-and-guts action.

"Look at that portal-traveling beast!" the duchess screeched, pointing at Jackson, in the cage. "We want that beast dead! Dead, I tell you!"

The townspeople responded with a deafening roar and looked to Queen Dahlia for action. Would she give the order to execute Jackson and Earl? Would she please the crowd? The pivotal moment of her queenhood loomed, and she knew it, but Dahlia hesitated. She might have saved herself by roaring her approval of the execution, but, being a basically nice if slightly nerdy little girl, she hadn't the heart for cold-blooded murder. Her hesitation betrayed her affection for the two potentially mite-carrying beasts.

Refrains of "Traitor! The queen's a traitor!" echoed across the room.

Monkeys tore the velvet curtains to ribbons and used them to tie the queen to a drainpipe, where they forced her to witness the tedious bureaucratic reading of writs and statements and codicils against her. After all, the queen had been away overnight. She had, in fact, run away from her post. Queens don't just go on sleepovers. They don't just take exotic vacations, all alone, on whims. The clincher, in all this, was the fact that Queen Dahlia had had Jackson imprisoned for hours, yet made no formal, kingdom-wide announcement of the portal breach.

According to tradition, she should have made the beast's execution a national festival. If she really wanted to save Bumblegreen from another blight—reasoned her regents and the monkey tribunal—that's exactly what she would have done, but instead, Dahlia committed the crime of hesitation. Oh, well. Evidence of incompetence isn't that hard to come by when the queen is an uneducated, thirteen-year-old orphan.

Queen Dahlia hung her head in the face of all these accusations. They were true enough, although that hardly seemed relevant. In the dungeon, she had learned that banning imports, but not closing the portals, was the real key to ridding Bumblegreen of disease. This would, of course, require citizens to exercise self control, which was (I mean, come on) insanely ridiculous. She had to try, though. To get started, she'd have to first free Shadooda and the other magicians so they could open the portals again. Yet, tied to the drainpipe as she was, Queen Dahlia just stood there, fearing whatever the peasants planned do to her.

63

WHERE THEY'RE NOT REALLY
PEOPLE, THEY'RE MACHINES

While her scheming regents read the various writs and proclamations and dreary accusations of betrayal and what-all, Queen Dahlia became highly concerned about the potential of quite literally losing her head at the end of this (or losing whatever you lose first when dropped into a tank of angry stingrays).

The crowd—quite worked up, by now—busied itself by blaming the queen for everything from stopped-up toilets to preponderant foot fungus. In the general excitement over being united in a cause, its members chanted and threw wet foodstuffs around. Also, numerous loudmouths mentioned this business about Travel, and the portals, and wanting access to Prindal's List and some GPS equipment, and bringing back armloads of stuff, while others insisted all portals be sealed and portal jumpers executed. No one seemed to notice their ideas standing in direct opposition to one another.

Nobody watched Dahlia, anymore. By now, they objected more to the concept of her, as queen, than to her actual physical manifestation. So, she picked at her velvet bonds with her teeth, freed herself, and slunk off into the shadows of the overpopulated room, which now stank of feet and luncheon meat. She found the door and dashed outside, across the castle lawn, and into the forest, just as she had done the very day before, but this time, the queen navigated a certain path she hadn't traveled in years.

"They're not really people, they're machines. They're not really people, they're machines. They're not really people, they're machines," Queen Dahlia chanted to herself as she jogged in what was left of her fluffy royal attire, her many skirts balled up and hand-held in a useless hump of tasseled laundry at the waist.

This was the only way she could remain calm at the thought of all that rabble in her castle, demanding things—not just things, but essential things, like Prindal's List, which she had secretly stored in an unsanctioned place. Dahlia still believed the gouda to be a great hiding place, mind you, but knew nobody would agree with her maverick methods. She just hated the whole thing. She wanted her mom and dad. She wanted to go home. Unfortunately, she was already as home as she was ever going to get.

Dahlia loped on and on through the forest and finally arrived at the cheese cave. Her heart nearly stopped when she saw the broken lock, the ramshackle door gaping open, and then, the empty spot where the cheese should have been. Third from the left. The only cheese that mattered in this whole cave of non-mattering cheeses, and it had vanished.

The queen balled her fists and uttered one loud, ferocious holler that pierced the ozone, swallowed the atmosphere, and returned with gifts from imploding stars.

64

In Which ElizabethAnn
Kicks Tammy in the Shins

After their long hike from downtown Bumblegreen, ElizabethAnn and Tammy stumbled into the crowded throne room, unnoticed. They wandered through the throng until Tammy spotted Fast Eddie, her target, wrestling several housewives. At the same time, ElizabethAnn found Jackson, along with Earl, pacing behind the bars of the iron cage. Curious children taunted the animals with sticks and soggy sandwiches.

Twelve serious-looking monkeys, all in a row, squatted on the throne room's stage. The first approached a podium, glared at the crowd, then directed his malevolent gaze to the cage, where Jackson shivered and Earl made moony eyes at his crying wife, Cupcake, through the bars.

The monkey on stage rummaged through the fur on his chest, pulled it apart, and picked and picked and moved to the belly, and picked and pulled and then examined one leg, and finally, when nearly everyone had lost interest, he raised his hand high, pinching a mite: a No Oaks-brand, ordinary, live mite.

Brandishing the mite aloft, the monkey introduced himself as Commandant Deleftwich. Then, he began his rant: "See this mite? It's come here on a violation of the Universal Portal Compact! A violation by that hairy beast right there! Beast, I suppose you're bent on destroying our delicate ecosystem? Beast, I suppose you want to cause another blight, you do! So, do you people want to forgive and forget? Sure! Go ahead! Until you find mites in your own hair, own beds, own clothing! Until the blight returns. Then, you'll see!"

Commandant Deleftwich paced up and down the stage and commenced explaining the food chain and the concept of cause and effect, right down to which came first, chicken or the egg, just to make sure he appealed to everyone's sense of logic as well as whimsy. Then, he squashed the mite between his claws and smeared its guts on the podium.

Deleftwich, seemingly the chief monkey, challenged each of the other eleven members of the tribunal to come forward and produce a mite. If they could, he suggested, it would demonstrate a dangerous preponderance of the invasive insect and serious potential for a resurgence of the blight. Someone would have to be punished. Investigations would have to be made. Probably in that order.

Jackson trembled, and with him, Earl. The two looked on with wide eyes, as a second monkey loped to the podium, plopped himself down in a most ungentlemanly position, and picked over his fur, seeking mites.

"Come, girl, we have black-magic seduction to do," said Tammy (who hadn't been watching the proceedings at all) to ElizabethAnn.

Fueled by the rumbling remains of a one-cruller dinner and her single-minded dedication to saving Jackson and Earl, ElizabethAnn kicked Tammy in the shins and ran off. She wore a steely-eyed look Tammy had seen once before.

Where've I seen that look? Tammy asked herself. Eventually, she answered herself: *in my piece of broken mirror.*

As the next monkey approached the podium, the audience crouched and leaned forward, all hushed and anticipatory. ElizabethAnn sensed bloodlust curdling in the onlookers' veins, while, up in his box, Zade Fandey nervously clicked and unclicked a ballpoint pen. The sound could be heard throughout the hushed courtroom.

The monkey on stage searched himself, found various insects, and inspected each one. Finally, with a stern look at the ogling audience, he held high a prized find: a mite. He squashed it, smeared it on the podium, and banged his fist on top, to emphasize the weightiness of his find. There followed a collective gasp.

A third monkey then approached the podium.

ElizabethAnn—hiding from Tammy behind a couple of young lovers with their hands in each other's back pockets—got the distinct feeling this wouldn't end well for Jackson, not to mention Earl, and forget about Grandma, wherever she was. Shadooda, so far, hadn't helped one bit, stranded as it was down in the dungeon, and ElizabethAnn hadn't any idea how to free the magician or fix any of this, but fix it she must, so she started what can only be described as a thinking frenzy.

She thought thoughts faster than she had ever thought them before, and all that fast thinking made her thirsty. It also made her notice she had chapped lips, a parched throat, and plenty of aches and pains from climbing and swinging on vines and clinging to monkey fur and sleeping in substandard conditions over the past couple of days. Exhausted, she grasped a rung of the cage in which her poor Jackson was captured and leaned against its cool, solid iron for support.

Clink!

The sound rang through the vast room.

The third monkey inspected himself, on stage. Many members of the audience, by now, had begun wondering aloud how long before the killing began.

ElizabethAnn shook the cage's bars to see which one was loose and found the whole thing as solid as any self-respecting iron cage had a right to be. So, she leaned against the cage again and—*clink!*—heard the sound again. Turns out, that silver flask she had found in the bird's nest, still in her pocket, was clinking against the cage's bars. She took the flask out, unscrewed the lid, and, thirsty as she was, took a big gulp.

A fourth monkey had already taken the stage and triumphantly displayed a mite.

ElizabethAnn, with her skinny arms wrapped around one of the cage's iron bars, stopped thinking and started crying. Abandoning herself to total despair, the tears poured down, and soon she found herself treading water in a puddle of her own tears. She looked around, panicking, hoping for help, but the jam-packed (and now giant-sized) audience members carelessly splashed through her puddle as they jostled for a view of the trapdoor beneath the hapless dog and monkey. She heard the townsfolk eagerly discussing whether the tank would hold crocodiles or boiling oil or hungry sharks and placing bets as to which dire fate awaited the fuzzy pair.

A wave washed ElizabethAnn (shrunk now by the flask's magical elixir) right into the cage itself, right through the bars, and onto the massive but innocent paw of Jackson himself. She grasped his prodigious fur in handfuls and hauled her tiny self onto his back. Luckily, at this point, she had the good sense to reach into her other pocket and grab the duchess' fan. After a few vigorous fannings, ElizabethAnn grew back to full size. Naturally, her sudden presence on Jackson's back attracted a great deal of attention. Gulping more from the silver flask, she disappeared from sight again, but the courtroom erupted in a roar.

The duchess shouted, "Help! A shape-shifter! Alert the queen!"

"Alert the queen's regents! The queen's deposed!" shouted a peasant lady in a ragged bonnet, perhaps the only one really paying attention.

"Girl on the loose! Notify her monkey parents!" shouted others in the crowd.

The monkeys on stage kept picking their fur—every one of them finding a mite, so far. They had moved up to monkey number seven, by this time, and Earl and Jackson each vocalized the sounds of panic characteristic of his species.

The eighth, ninth, and tenth monkeys found their mites rather quickly, at which point, the crowd left off chanting for the queen and started clamoring for blood—specifically, Jackson's.

The eleventh monkey skipped merrily to the stage and pulled a mite from beneath his hat—an obvious plant. The twelfth monkey (a shy one not the least bit happy about having to stand up as the final arbiter of the beasts' fates) felt a tickle and plucked something squirmy from his back.

As the crowd roared, he looked at the mite, ready to gum it in half with his powerful, though toothless, jaws. But, indeed, he held no mite at all, but ElizabethAnn, whose tiny self had gone flying when Jackson howled himself into a sneezing fit. She was, naturally, fanning herself furiously.

In her panic, ElizabethAnn overdid it a bit. She grew to towering proportions, pushed the twelfth monkey aside, stamped one foot on the podium for order, and smashed the thing to kindling, causing the hoard to go silent and cower.

Small peasants tried to cower beneath the larger ones, while the large ones tried to cover themselves with velvet drapes and the contents of boxes labeled "Affairs of State."

"Where's the Queen?" ElizabethAnn bellowed. "I mean, who's running this show? Who's running this supposed court of law? I don't get it!"

Everyone looked at where the queen had been tied to a drainage pipe and discovered her absence. In the ensuing moment of one thousand gasps, ElizabethAnn bellowed, "Let this dog and monkey go free!"

"But sweetie, I have a pool full of angry stingrays all ready. We were going to have great fun with it," replied the duchess from beside ElizabethAnn's enormous left big toe, "and we're so hurting for entertainment these days."

"The dog and monkey are under my protection!" bellowed ElizabethAnn, although she had never before considered herself anyone's protector, "and no one here is deposing the queen without my say-so!"

"Oh, correction," replied the duchess. "I am actually deposing the queen. I have the documents right here. Now, why don't you run along and bother someone else, little girl."

ElizabethAnn picked up the duchess with thumb and forefinger. "I know a good place for you, lady: the dungeon. Unfortunately, the place is overpopulated, for now. Which reminds me, I have to find Grandma."

"First things first!" shouted Deleftwich, the spokesmonkey. "These mite-infested brutes must be put to death! Someone pull that lever!"

ElizabethAnn didn't understand the significance of the lever, but Zade Fandey did.

"Don't you touch that lever, Monkey Number Thirty-Four-Oh-Nine!"

Fandey's voice, the way it rang out over the crowd, and the way he called the monkey by his true name, made Commandant Deleftwich, Earl, and all the other monkeys freeze in place like reprimanded children.

Fandey was, after all, the original parent of each and every monkey in the place. "I, Zade Fandey, forbid it!" he added.

"Oh!" said ElizabethAnn, "Zade Fandey! I know my grandma is at that Drone place. I know she is! Can you go and tell her she can come out of hiding now? Dahlia … I mean *Queen* Dahlia knows about her, and it's okay."

"I can come out?" asked a small voice from near Zade Fandey's feet.

"Grandma?" boomed ElizabethAnn.

From below the half-wall of Zade's viewing box, a head emerged, wrapped in a hideous bonnet covered with plastic flowers so thick they obscured any view of the face on the head. A couple of narrow shoulders followed the head, and so on, until a woman holding an infant (the duchess' infant, in fact) stood next to Zade Fandey.

"Are you sure?" asked the bonnet-wrapped head.

"Sure, I'm sure!" ElizabethAnn announced. "You have to finish the job you came here for, Grandma! Bumblegreen's counting on you!"

"Counting on her?" asked the beefy housewife in the front row.

"I never heard of her," replied a nearby fruit seller.

"Who's this girl to speak for Bumblegreen?" inquired a man in a butcher's apron.

"Hideous bonnet," added an athletic-looking fellow.

"My baby!" wailed the duchess. Then, she sneezed.

The baby wailed in response, and soon, all present fell into a massive, simultaneous baby-allergy attack, including not just sneezes, but hiccups, runny noses, stuffed nasal passages, earaches, itchy eyes, and festering boils.

Only ElizabethAnn, Zade Fandey, and Grandma (the woman in the hideous bonnet) were unaffected. Queen Dahlia would also have been unaffected, but she had left the building long ago, if you recall.

Grandma removed her hideous bonnet, and her white hedgehog of hair stood at attention. "You mean, I won't be thrown in that cage, ElizabethAnn? I won't be dropped into the pool of angry stingrays? Are you certain?"

"Grandma! The only thing I'm certain of," answered ElizabethAnn, "is that Shadooda needs you desperately. You're the only one who can get the magicians out of the dungeon."

"Dungeon? But, of course, that's so logical. Zade, the magicians were in the dungeon all along!"

"How can Grandma get them out?" asked Zade Fandey. "She hasn't any magical powers. Grandma, do you have powers?"

"No, I don't have powers," replied Grandma, with a shrug.

"You'll have to ask Shadooda," answered Queen Dahlia, who, just a moment before, had squeezed between the massive doors and back into the throne room, exhausted.

You see, after discovering the missing cheese, Dahlia had galloped back, returned to the throne room, and walked through the crowd unnoticed, so engrossed were the peasants in sneezing and searching for handkerchiefs. She now mounted the stage.

"Dahlia!" exclaimed giant-size ElizabethAnn, who tried to hug the queen and nearly crushed her.

"Mrs. Grandma!" shouted Dahlia. "Thanks for coming back! Bumblegreen needs you, now more than ever, and I'm sorry about making you sign that ridiculous Universal Portal Compact. You were brave to dissent! According to Shadooda, you were right all along. Now's the time to prove it!"

Queen Dahlia grasped the iron ring on the trapdoor, pulled it open, and revealed the ladder below. Dahlia looked down, down, down, to where hundreds of tiny eyes peered up, up, up through the darkness. Hundreds of lips smacked, too. Whether they were rodent lips or magician lips, Dahlia couldn't tell.

Grandma handed the duchess' baby to Zade Fandey and descended from the box to the stage. She peered down into the trapdoor, looked at ElizabethAnn, looked down at the ladder and the eyes, looked up at Zade Fandey, looked down at the ladder and the eyes, and looked out over the sea of allergic Bumblegreenis, some of whom had already passed out from their nasal symptoms.

Others breathed through their mouths and threw cups of water on themselves. Still others stood among piles of soggy handkerchiefs as high as their own heads. Housewives ripped off petticoats to provide their husbands with additional handkerchief linen, and one man, who held his slumped wife in his arms, pounded on the throne room's heavy door, demanding escape.

"But that hatch is enchanted," said ElizabethAnn to Grandma. "Royals only."

"That's just on the way out," said Dahlia. "You can go in, no problem."

"Don't go, Grandma!" pleaded ElizabethAnn, grabbing at her grandmother's sleeve with one enormous fingernail. "You could get stuck down there! Like Zade Fandey said, you don't have any powers! How can you free the magic?"

Grandma looked at ElizabethAnn good and hard, like it might be the last time. "If Shadooda said it needed me, it must need me," she said. "I came to save this place for us, ElizabethAnn. We need a new home—not a 'home,' but a real home, and so does Shadooda, as a matter of fact."

Grandma climbed down the ladder into the gloom, looking up as she went down, locking eyes with ElizabethAnn, trying not to think about the smacking lips below.

65

In Which Grandma Gets Her Tools Back

"You might be too late," warned Shadooda, when its eyes met Grandma's—one wrinkled but spry pair confronting one wizened, useless, but wise pair.

When Grandma looked around the dungeon, she saw magicians of all shapes and sizes, though none of the shapes were upright, and none of the sizes were a ladies' six. Clad in rags, smelling like feet, they gathered around Grandma and sniffed her from head to toe. Some poked her just to make sure she was real.

Someone mumbled, "Yes, I remember her," and, "It's that one lady, the one who believed in us."

"Like I said, folks, don't get excited. She might be too late," said Shadooda, reaching out to take Grandma's hand.

Grandma grasped the gnarled hand gently and said, "Shadooda, what they've done to you … it's unspeakable."

"Oh, it's speakable, all right," the magician replied. "We got done speaking it years ago, though. No one listened. Now we sing it, and sometimes we can get someone up there to hum a few bars."

Shadooda led Grandma down the dungeon's stone passage, and the sea of magicians parted. Between their legs peeked rats the size of No Oaks house cats.

"Come this way, Grandma," Shadooda said. "We haven't any time to spare. Otherwise someone's going to have to share a cell tonight with *that*."

Shadooda pointed at a shadow on the floor, which grumbled, then moved, and Grandma judged it the widest, flattest man she had ever seen. Beside it lay a pantsuit filled with woe in the shape of a woman.

Shadooda led Grandma down past its own cell, down past Sninkletter's cobwebby enclosure, down past where water seeped in through a moldy ceiling crack, and on along to the very end of the corridor where the stairs began and the wrecked Chevelle squatted, doorless, patched with Bondo.

"We got it running once, years ago," Shadooda said. "We did it by magic, though, not mechanics. But now, we haven't enough magic left. The Chevelle's got to be fixed the old-fashioned way. Actually, new-fashioned way by magicians' reckoning, but that's splitting hairs."

"Frangipani, Shadooda! You want me to fix a car?" asked Grandma. "I risked my life coming down here to fix a car? Shadooda, can you even get me out of this place?"

"The Chevelle *is* the way out, for all of us," said Shadooda. "Grandma, don't you remember? All it takes to activate dormant magic is a breeze. Wind. But down here, the only way to produce a breeze is by getting up some speed. None of us is about to run the hundred-yard dash, are we? So, I was thinking, get the Chevelle running, you know, and it's the old wind-in-your-hair phenomenon."

"Wow, that's all you've got, Shadooda?" asked Grandma. "Wind? For an idea?"

"The wind always helps the magic—fresh air and all. What do you say?"

"Do you have any tools?" Grandma asked.

"Me? Grandma, don't you remember? You brought your own tools, years ago," said Shadooda. "Back then, when you brought the thing piece-by-piece from No Oaks, then put it back together here, just for fun. Remember?"

Grandma poked her head inside the Chevelle. The pleather seats had actually been well preserved in the dungeon's tomb-like atmosphere. She popped open the glove compartment. Yes, her tools were still there, right where she had left them.

"All right," said Grandma. "Let me get this straight. I fix this thing, somehow, and then you're going to go for a ride in it?"

"We all are! Every one of us! And you!"

"Okay, what is that, about a hundred people? We're going to get a hundred people in a Chevy Chevelle?"

"We are magicians, you know."

"I see. And what'll we do for gas?"

"Here's my idea: The Chevelle doesn't have to run. It just has to roll," said Shadooda. "We get it rolling, then push it to the end of the corridor, past that hatch where you came down."

"Then what?"

"That's where the dungeon descends down into the catacombs."

"Don't like the sound of this."

"All we have to do is give the car a push and hop on! It's not stairs on that end. It's a ramp. Plenty steep, too. Once we've got a breeze blowing, we'll have our powers restored … maybe."

"It's that 'maybe' part I'm worried about."

"A good wind will really stir the magic up—if there's even a tiny remnant of magic left in us."

"Okay. And what do we do when the Chevelle gets to the bottom and crashes into a wall?"

"Oh, we'll be gone, by then."

"Gone? You've lost me."

"If we get our magic back, we'll just vanish and reappear somewhere else."

"Well now, if you could do that, why didn't you do it years ago?"

"Some did," replied Shadooda. "Every one of them was caught, though, and thrown into a pit filled with swimming hungry sharks. The old king and queen, you know, that was their style."

"I see. Okay, so all I have to do is get these tires pumped up without the aid of an air compressor, single-handedly push the Chevelle all the way down the hall to the ramp, and make a sedan able to accommodate one hundred ancient magicians?" Grandma asked, just for clarification, mind you.

"And you! Don't forget you!"

"Mm-hmm. One hundred ancient magicians and one old lady. Do you remember I'm an old lady?"

"In my business, belief is ninety percent of the battle."

"Good point," said Grandma, who bent over the Chevelle and commenced to tinker.

One hundred magicians gathered around to watch.

"A little breathing space, please," she requested.
In awe, they retreated apace.

420

66

WHEREIN THE DUCHESS
FUELS A BLOOD-LETTING MOB

A hue and cry went up from the crowd in the throne room, which had, for so long, teetered on the edge of hysteria. At the duchess' urging—"Let's punish these portal jumpers! What do you say?"—the crowd erupted into a blood-letting mob with unsheathed fingernails, bared teeth, and jackboots of judgment.

The duchess, with a dramatic bowing out of the knees, jumped to the gleaming lever and pressed it all the way down.

ElizabethAnn, now an imposing twenty feet tall, saw the floor beneath her beloved Jackson disappearing. She lunged for the cage and, through the bars, grabbed Jackson by the tail. Jackson, in turn, lunged to save Earl, but missed.

At first, Earl clung to the bars, then lost his grip, then screamed the worst and most truly desperate of monkey screams. He fell down, down, down into the well-populated pool of angry, underfed stingrays. Jackson lunged again, and snapped Earl's tail in his teeth, but too late. One of the stingrays put a dagger-like barb right through Earl's overly sophisticated monkey heart. Blood filled the pool, and the dead monkey hung lifelessly from Jackson's moist, despondent jaws.

"Unlock that cage!" ordered ElizabethAnn. This time, the duchess complied.

Jackson let Earl's body go, and it sank to the depths of the dark and swirling pool. Those with cage-side seats attested to this fact—some with glee, others with remorse—and they passed the information back through the crowd.

With one huge finger, ElizabethAnn lifted Jackson away from danger.

Tammy had always found monkeys dirty and disgusting. The thought of a village of them raising the child that now grew in her womb horrified her. It's not that she was unsympathetic to poor Earl, it's just that she didn't understand why the gigantic girl with the messy hair was crying so many buckets of tears over a monkey—a particularly smelly one, at that. ElizabethAnn's enormous tears splashed down on the courtroom's rabble like cluster bombs.

Tammy felt, frankly, inconvenienced by all this drama, as she herself had planned to become the center of attention. She had, after all, finagled the duchess into organizing the whole deposing-of-the-queen thing and the whole gathering-of-the-enormous-crowd thing. The first was for Shadooda's sake, for whatever reason it wanted the queen deposed. Tammy felt glad to get that obligation over and done with. The second—the gathering of the crowd—was something Tammy needed for the final phase of her black magic. Shadooda had told her she would need an enormous crowd, which it called an "energy pool," to provide the psychic energy needed to complete her seduction.

Tammy had conceived this entire ultra-complex revenge scenario after many sleepless nights and scheming days spent in front of the broken piece of mirror, combing her easily-tangled horsehair extensions into wavy, susurrant tresses. And now, to complete the seduction/revenge process, she only had to capture Fast Eddie's attention, create her magic circle, do her incantations, and thereby succeed in making that bastard her frustrated slave of love. Black magic, after all, is neither a casual endeavor nor an efficient one. Tammy found it difficult to concentrate, though, as annoying butterflies kept flitting in and out of her field of vision.

Cupcake, poor thing, had seen the entire horrible event and now wept loudly and openly over her husband's cruel murder, climbing all over the cage, peering down into the stingray-infested pool, screaming her rage and sorrow.

That's the moment Tammy chose to lob her love grenades.

The idea had been for ElizabethAnn, with her small, unobtrusive, innocent, girlish stature, to sneak up to Fast Eddie, amid the chaotic crowd, and slip something into his pocket, unnoticed. But, now that ElizabethAnn had become entirely uncooperative, twenty feet tall, and the center of attention, Tammy's plan needed a quick rethinking. For the same job, Tammy figured she could use a disenfranchised monkey.

Cupcake howled, chattered, pounded her fists, and stamped her feet against the bars, but the general unfocused noise, incessant sneezing, and random bickering of the surrounding, shoulder-to-shoulder mass of humanity drowned out the widowed monkey's mournful caterwaul.

"Miss monkey! Miss monkey! Earl left this for you!" Tammy reached into one of the many hidden pockets she had had the foresight to sew into her very chic and sleek, deep purple wrap-around outfit. Waving away a profusion of butterflies, Tammy held out a tiny, gift-wrapped object.

Cupcake climbed over the cage, to where Tammy stood, and looked down upon her quizzically.

"That monkey told me if anything happened to him, I was to give this to you," lied Tammy.

Gingerly, Cupcake lifted the box from Tammy's palm, jumped to the ground, bit a few ankles to clear herself a space on the crowded floor, waved away a bunch of butterflies, and hunkered over the precious object. She turned it this way and that, stroked the orange wrapping paper and violet bow, sniffed it, shook it, licked it, then glanced at Tammy in utter helpless confusion.

"Open it," advised Tammy, as she pantomimed pulling the ends of the bow.

Cupcake pulled the ends, and the ribbon fell away, then she scratched the wrapping paper off with her claws and found a miniature music box. When she opened it, music played. Inside the box, she found a cookie—an odd-looking, odd-smelling cookie, but Cupcake ate it anyway.

Overwhelmed by the thought that Earl had left her this posthumous valentine, Cupcake collapsed in a happy heap, licked her fingers, bit the box, put it up to her ear the better to hear the tinny little concerto it magically played. She further searched the music box for any other sign of Earl, any explanation for this strange gift. Tammy gave her a few minutes, then pounced.

"Now," said Tammy, "come with me," and Cupcake did. Tammy didn't like to resort to drugging monkeys with black-magic cookies, but she had come prepared to do whatever it took. She removed another tiny package from one of her secret inner pockets, handed it to the grieving monkey, and, while flicking away an obnoxious butterfly that kept zooming into her ear, told Cupcake to run up and secretly slip it into Fast Eddie's pocket. She pointed him out in the crowd and gave the monkey a shove.

As requested, Cupcake scampered between legs, over small encampments, and around groups of teenagers sitting in social-hierarchy groups, to place the tiny gift in Fast Eddie's pocket.

Tammy retreated to a corner to watch Fast Eddie. But, after some time, he still hadn't checked his pocket, so she asked around for a pencil.

"There's some crucial information, lifesaving information, that has to be written down! My kingdom for a pencil!" Tammy yelled into the crowd.

Nobody had one, but helpful neighbors spread the request through the crowd, and soon everyone was asking someone else for a pencil. Fast Eddie heard the commotion and reached into his pocket, saying, "I might have ..."

Bull's-eye.

He found the mysterious gift, not a pencil. Some other folks did find pencils, though, and a hundred and twelve of them came sailing through the air like a volley of arrows from a hostile tribe. A few speared errant butterflies, as they flew. Tammy ducked, made a show of gathering the pencils, and retreated into a corner with a view.

"What's this?" asked Fast Eddie of no one in particular. He opened the music box he had found in his pocket, engraved *From Your Secret Admirer*.

He listened to the music, examined the object, and furrowed his brow, saying, again, to no one, "Secret admirer? Me?"

What's he thinking? Why'd he make that face? Or did he just have a crumb in his tooth? Why's he wiping his hand? Are his hands clammy? Are they clammy from fear? From passion? From knowing all my secrets? Who's he talking to? Are they talking or just standing close together? Are they whispering? Do they know it's me? He couldn't know. There's no way to know. He could be psychic. What if he's psychic? Why'd he scratch his ankle? Isn't the ankle a pressure-point for fear? Or love? Is it a sign? A signal? An omen? Tammy's mind made the leap into serious hyperspace.

With all this whizzing through her brain, Tammy knew the next step would be the hardest. She had to bide her time and wait for Fast Eddie to work himself into a frenzy of consternation, excitement, and self-adoration as he wondered whom his secret admirer could be.

"For the black magic to work," Shadooda had told her, "the energy vortex must be focused at the highest level of egotism."

In the meantime, Cupcake watched Tammy through a cloud of pink butterflies, with slave's eyes. The cookie's enchantment was a mercy, as the poor monkey widow had, for the time being, forgotten about her late lamented husband.

67

IN WHICH ELIZABETHANN CREATES THE WEATHER

ElizabethAnn found it quite awkward being twenty feet tall, but feared if she shrank herself down, the angry mob might avenge itself upon her soft and still semi-cartilaginous person. Then, when she noticed the butterflies entering the throne room through window cracks and air vents, she feared for her safety anew.

On top of everything else, all this size shifting had a serious drawback. It made her hungry. Her clothes changed size with her, but, apparently, the food in her stomach did not. At twenty feet tall, ElizabethAnn had an awfully big stomach with just the remnants of a single cruller in it, and it rumbled like anything.

ElizabethAnn stood on the stage—Jackson curled up in one palm, Dahlia sitting cross-legged in the other—while her tears splashed down on the townspeople. The three of them had to wait, relatively helplessly, for Grandma to do whatever Grandma was doing down in the dungeon. Collectively, they counted one-hundred percent on Grandma succeeding in bringing back the magic and expected profound changes any minute now.

Queen Dahlia herself wouldn't have put any money on Grandma's chances for success, but as long as ElizabethAnn waited with her, at least she wasn't alone in the hostile crowd. Meanwhile, Zade Fandey sat up there in his box, trying to shush the duchess' ever-crying infant, brush butterflies off its angry little crimson face, and hold it as far away from the sneezing, fainting, hiccupping crowd as he could.

Common sense told ElizabethAnn to stay calm, stay large, and hold her ground, so she did some deep breathing.

In through the nose.

Out through the mouth.

In through the nose.

Out through the mouth.

What with the breathing, plus her crying, plus her tummy rumbling, ElizabethAnn created, there in the throne room, a mini weather system of her very own.

Tammy couldn't give two bowls of fragrant horse piss for Prindal's List, the portals, the supposed infestation of mites, or any of it. She kept her focus on vengeance against Fast Eddie, as that old genderless spell-caster Shadooda had taught her. She walked a sacred circle, into the center of which she threw dried herbs while speaking incantations and burning incense. In grounding a space for her black-magic seduction to take place, she elbowed sniffling farming families and a sneezing knitting group out of her way. She told them to go huddle with the rest of the bellowing masses. Tammy acted important and grouchy, which convinced most of the townspeople she had something worthwhile going on. The strong winds and heavy salt-rain emanating from the newly large ElizabethAnn only enhanced Tammy's desperate focus. As she chanted and walked her circle, a sense of power coalesced in her eyes, just as Shadooda had said it would.

Then, gradually, ever so gradually—while Tammy created her space, and the butterflies filled the air, and the masses picnicked all around her, unwittingly contributing great vibrating currents of energy —Fast Eddie drew, both psychically and physically, closer. In fact, as planned, Fast Eddie wandered right into her magical circle. But just at that moment, Jackson sneezed out a puff of poor dead Earl's matted fur, which floated on the air.

Tammy looked down to check her spell-casting instructions (neatly notated on index cards) then took a moment to rearrange them into the proper order.

A tiny strand of Earl's sneezed-out fur, ever so small, landed on the sweat droplets on Fast Eddie's upper lip. He licked the sweat, ingested the strand, and a moment later (he only tasted the faintest hint of marzipan) Fast Eddie shrieked with sudden-onset Zade Fandey's disease and turned into a platypus.

Tammy heard the shriek, looked up from her index cards, and noticed Fast Eddie had disappeared and a strange animal was in her magical circle instead, which made her irate.

Fast Eddie (in his hew platypus self) found the distracted, concentrating mood of an irritated woman irresistibly sexy. Taking one look at Tammy, he fell in love again. The black magic had worked, but what with Fast Eddie being a platypus, Tammy had no idea.

As time went by, and ElizabethAnn's hope for Grandma's success diminished, and her sadness over Earl's death increased, her tears became more frequent and her sobs more profound. Her sighs and wails of despair created gusts throughout the throne room. With the onset of this new, extreme weather, the still-sneezing peasants prepared for a storm the only way they knew how. One chap pulled his sport coat up over his ears, causing his arms to flail helplessly in their sleeves. Another man clung to a railing with a python-strangling leg grip that made his knees go white. A milkmaid found a stone pillar and embraced it tight as a lover while her hair whipped back and forth with each of ElizabethAnn's gasps and sobs. Meanwhile, hundreds of butterflies got buffeted around the room like so many candy-bar wrappers catching air in a No Oaks dust storm.

Tammy looked high and low for Fast Eddie, but, eventually, miserably, concluded that he had escaped, and her witchcraft hadn't worked. Dejected, she swatted some butterflies away and tossed her index cards into a puddle of ElizabethAnn's tears. Then, she bought a soft pretzel from a clever monkey who had set up an impromptu booth, covered the pretzel with bitter mustard, sat on a pile of Affairs of State files, and sulked.

The platypus-in-love creepily watched Tammy from afar.

It's one thing to have animals run after you in a rabid or angry way, or run away from you in a shy and frightened way, but to have them sit and watch you, that's just wrong is all that is, thought Tammy.

While the strange beast flapped its beaver-like tail and wiggled its sausage-like body, Tammy stood well clear of its enormous orange bill, which clicked open and shut in excitement.

ElizabethAnn tired of crying. She got to that point, physiologically, where a crier must inhale profoundly, wretchedly, and spastically in an attempt to establish some sort of cardiovascular equilibrium. She inhaled quite a number of ticklish butterflies as she did so, making her need to sneeze. A well-raised child, ElizabethAnn knew not to blow it out over the crowd, so she bent over with the *Ah!* and released with the *Choo!* right through the trapdoor that had swallowed Grandma.

ElizabethAnn's was one of the world's most profound sneezes. The kind where she squinched her eyes shut and, for an instant, lost all consciousness and sense of time or place. When she recovered from the sneeze, ElizabethAnn noticed her shoes had sailed across the room and her hair was in a completely different arrangement. Thinking quickly, she patted her pockets—at first casually, then in a mad panic.

"Oh, no … No, it can't be … NO!" she yelled.

The flask and fan were gone.

The duchess, still enjoying her stage time, swished the train of her velvet gown to and fro with wildly twitching hips, having abandoned her hairstyle to the wind. Meanwhile, she rallied the crowd with impromptu cheers and encouraged them to ignore the fact that there was not only a typhoon in progress, but a twenty-foot-tall girl on stage, who seemed to be in league with both the queen and the wild beast currently (supposedly) infecting Bumblegreen with its mites.

Loudly, the duchess promoted the notion that the profusion of butterflies in the room was an omen of good things to come and preached to the effect that Grandma's descent through the trapdoor meant nothing. Basically, the duchess babbled on about whatever would keep eyes on her the longest. She enjoyed the attention terrifically.

Tammy made her way through the crowd and joined the group

assembled to watch the duchess pontificate on stage. Several of them were just looking up the duchess' dress. The platypus followed Tammy like a No Oaks retriever. (Although Tammy had no knowledge of retrievers as such. She would probably have found them creepy, too.)

From out of nowhere, a bird perched on Tammy's shoulder.

"Get off me!" yelled Tammy.

"Please!" it whispered in her ear. "I just want a lock of your hair. For my collection!"

The bird spread its wings wide to indicate the importance of its quest.

"What's that?" asked the duchess, from above, on the stage.

"What's what? The obnoxious platypus or the talking bird?" answered Tammy, as annoyed as she'd ever been.

"The shape on the flank of that bird," answered the duchess, taking a sudden break from pontificating.

"A bird has a flank?" asked Tammy, and she grabbed the thing like a guinea hen about to lose its head for dinner. She handed the bird up to the duchess, who took a long look at it.

A very strange, squiggly mark stood out on one side of the bird. (The bird was, of course, Bill Bramble, as you've guessed.)

"An asymmetrical design. Rather out of character for a bird, don't you think?" asked the duchess of no one and everyone.

"I've had it all my life," squawked the bird. "Now, unhand me!"

"Looks rather like a swan," said the duchess.

"Indeed, it is a swan," said the bird. I've had it ever since … before. You know, before I turned."

"So you're really a human? Enchanted? And this … you might call it a birthmark?" asked the duchess, now stroking the bird, now smiling, now looking into its eyes and searching, searching,

searching.

"My son!" she wailed. "My firstborn son!"

68

WHERE ONE-HUNDRED MAGICIANS NEARLY FILL A CHEVY CHEVELLE

"All right," said Grandma. "Let's get 'er rolling."

Just then, ElizabethAnn's sneeze—a massive, wet wind—blew briefly through the dungeon, speckling the darkness with tumbling butterflies.

"Wind! Where'd that come from?" asked Shadooda, who had assembled an assortment of blind magicians behind the stripped-down chassis of the Chevelle. It was all set to roll, for a distinctly limited time, directly on its rims.

"A breeze!" cried Grandma. "Is it enough? Was it enough to get your powers going? Can we skip the whole dangerous descent into doom? Please, say yes!"

"It certainly felt invigorating," replied Shadooda, feeling a butterfly alight on her hand and offering what might actually pass for a smile. "But it wasn't enough. The breeze has to be sustained. Maybe thirty seconds is all."

Grandma sighed. "Okay then, folks, we might as well give this a go. One, two, three … push!"

As one hundred arthritic, blind, half-crippled, half-mad magicians pushed the Chevelle, on its rims, at a snail's pace, over cobblestones, Grandma drove. She wondered how in the world they all planned to jump into the four-seater for this supposed joyride into oblivion.

The thing rolled remarkably smoothly, all things considered, but Grandma felt sure the magicians would crash it into a wall long before they got to the catacombs ramp. What with all the butterflies in the air, plus the omnipresent dense, oily darkness of the dungeon, Grandma had a terrible time seeing where she was going.

"Stop!" ordered Shadooda, who had been riding the Chevelle's hood like a seagull on a boat's prow. "What's that?"

Grandma stepped out of the car and walked over to a rectangle of white light where blue butterflies zipped around in figure eights. Here was the light from the throne room, filtering down through the trapdoor.

"It's the hatch," said Grandma, looking up.

"No," said Shadooda. "That!"

It pointed at the floor, where it sensed a magical heirloom. And there, lying beneath the hatch—in a patch made by the throne room's light—were ElizabethAnn's silver flask and antique fan.

Grandma handed them to Shadooda, who felt a butterfly alight on its nose. Shadooda popped its ears and knuckles at once, made a kissy face, and tapped a very special rhythm with its toes. It raised its eyebrows as high as it could and clucked like a leghorn rooster in order to telepathically converse with the butterflies.

Shadooda smiled and passed the flask around among the magicians, saying, "Drink up, my pretties. We've come upon a boon!"

The flask's contents did their magical work and turned one hundred crooked magicians into tiny beings who, for the first time perhaps ever, squealed and giggled with delight.

Opening the fan, the blind old magician swept it over the butterflies with grand, balletic strokes, causing them to enlarge one-hundred-fold. Finally, everyone climbed aboard the Chevelle—tiny magicians, enormous butterflies, and one very confused Grandma.

The butterflies flapped with earnest dedication, creating a pleasant and very useful breeze, all while pulling the Chevelle forward until it descended down the steep catacombs ramp. It quickly increased its speed. Grandma felt a bona fide wind in her hair.

"Wait for us!" shouted two figures, Georgie and Schrank, running behind the getaway Chevelle, reaching desperately for its bumper.

"Can't stop now!" shouted Grandma, leaving the pair in the dust.

"Catacombs ahead!" hollered Shadooda, from its post on the hood. "Begin your recitations!"

A buzz of muttered spells and incantations from the miniaturized magicians filled the air as the vehicle descended, with increasing speed, down the ramp. Grandma spent all her energy resisting the urge to stand on the brake pedal until finally, miraculously, ingeniously, the dungeon simply vanished.

69

IN WHICH JACKSON GETS A POTBELLY

Even if he had known about it, Jackson never would have been able to protect himself against Zade Fandey's disease. His nature was too pure, too instinctive, too rational. His well-meant attempt to save Earl had done him in. No matter that he meant no harm when he bit the monkey's tail. No matter that it wasn't fair. Such was the nature of the disease Zade Fandey had unwittingly created with his monkey-intelligence-enhancing technology.

Oh, before Jackson ever turned into an abominably dressed, hairy chested, complexly neurotic human, the dog knew he was infected.

There had been a tingling sensation and a ringing in the ears. He knew he would turn, but didn't know when. It was just a coincidence that it happened precisely at the moment when one hundred magicians suddenly appeared out of thin air in the throne room.

They popped into being, one by one, scattered among the sneezing townspeople. Each one squatted, hunched, put one hand gently to the ground, cocked one ear to the sky, and looked up at Zade Fandey, in his fancy viewing box. Actually, they were looking specifically at the squalling baby he held.

Preceded by his potbelly and sweating bullets through his leather pants and vest, Jackson, now human, scratched his curly head, smoothed his muttonchops, cleaned the wax from his left ear, and pounded his broad chest for courage. He stepped forward and tapped 20-foot-tall ElizabethAnn on the ankle.

"See them magicians, Princess? What you think that's all about?" he asked.

She looked down at the new Jackson and, logically, asked, "Who are you?"

"Who am I? Well, who do you think, Lemon Pie? It's me, Jackson!" said Jackson. "Say, Custard Lump, would you mind fanning yourself down to size? This is kind of awkward. I feel like I ought to get a megaphone or something."

"But Jackson's my dog. You're not Jackson!"

ElizabethAnn's voice rang out far louder than she had planned, and just as she spoke, a hush fell over the room. The hush was simply the result of the sneezing and nose-blowing and gasping for breath and calling for paramedics having stopped as suddenly as it began.

The arrival of one hundred magicians out of thin air had crowded the throne room considerably, but the gnarled, ancient beings now made their slow, laborious way through the crowd, hobbling and shuffling toward the stage.

"Yeah, Peachcake," said Jackson. "Well, I used to be fluffy and mottled and whatnot, no doubt, but this here's me: Jackson! I just … I don't know … kind of turned. Say, what are these for?" Jackson had removed his socks and sandals by now and inspected his toes. "Kind of wormy, aren't they?"

"Oh, no! Oh, my Jackson!" moaned ElizabethAnn so loudly, with her cavernous mouth, that nearby townspeople had to cover their ears.

"Quiet!" they complained.

ElizabethAnn tried to whisper to the strange man before her, "You've got Zade Fandey's disease!"

"I don't know what that means, Twinkie," said Jackson, "But I like it! Anyway, you have some kind of disease yourself, looks like. Not to put too fine a point on it, eh? Glandular problem?"

"How come you sound like Earl?" asked a very confused ElizabethAnn.

"Don't know," said Jackson's human self, "but this here's me—Jackson."

"But Jackson," said ElizabethAnn, "I've lost my magical fan and I'm stuck twenty feet tall!" Her whisper produced such a breeze it sent Affairs of State files fluttering into the air.

"You can put me down, now," said Dahlia, who still perched in ElizabethAnn's upturned palm.

"Oh, Dahlia!" said ElizabethAnn, "What are we to do?"

"Do? Do nothing, ElizabethAnn. We're saved," said Dahlia, gesturing toward the approaching sea of magicians. ElizabethAnn felt a tap on her ankle. It was Grandma.

"Hey, kiddo, I believe these are yours?" Grandma said, presenting the fan and flask to her granddaughter with a smile so broad it caught in her hair. "Nice vest," she said to Jackson, who was now doing experimental push-ups with his enormous hairy arms.

"Come on down to size, ElizabethAnn!" said Grandma.

"Wait!" said Dahlia. "Get Zade Fandey first!"

ElizabethAnn reached her enormous hand out to Zade, where he sat, high above the crowd. Goggle-eyed and disbelieving, he looked alternately at the duchess' baby and the non-sneezing populace of Bumblegreen, then back again, and back again. He might have been in some new type of shock.

"Come on down, Zade," yelled Dahlia. "It's safe, now! It's safe!"

Cradling the baby in one arm, Zade climbed aboard ElizabethAnn's enormous hand and clamped his legs around a finger, like mounting a sky horse. She brought him down and placed him beside the duchess.

"Here's your baby, Duchess," said the queen. "I think he's cured."

"My baby?" asked the duchess, breathless and disbelieving, with Bill Bramble's bird-self perched on her shoulder.

She took the child, at first hesitantly, but she didn't sneeze once. Didn't even get an itch in her eye or a stopped-up nose. She rocked the quiet, peaceful baby in disbelief. "I can't believe it," she said. "My baby. My baby!"

"Can I ..." began the duchess, and looked down bashfully.

"Can you what?" asked Dahlia.

"Can I ... can I keep him, then?" asked the duchess.

"I guess so," said Dahlia. "If the baby allergy's gone, and it seems to be."

"Can I name him?" asked the duchess, her penciled eyebrows arched impossibly high.

"The baby's yours now, Iris," said the queen. Then, to the crowd, "Guess what, everyone! All of your children are coming home!"

The crowd emitted a roar of approval, and those who still held their hats tossed them into the air. A few landed in ElizabethAnn's enormous ear.

The monkey tribunal, however, looked none too pleased.

70

WHERE JACKSON MAKES HIS FIRST BIG DECISION

Jackson experienced something new everyday. Today, it was the imprint of lawn chair webbing on the backs of his thighs. He had shuffled out of the mansion in his slippers to read the *Bumblegreen Gazette* beneath the weeping willow tree beside the duchess' swan pond.

"It's not the duchess' swan pond. It's ours, now," Grandma told him. She added, "You should shave those sideburns, I think."

"They aren't going to let us live here just indefinitely, are they?" asked Jackson. "I mean, they have to let the duchess out of the dungeon eventually. Don't they?"

"Oh, I don't know," answered Grandma, who sat beside a hillock of daisies, needlepointing a replica of her beloved International Scout. "She and her baby are all set up with a nice little nursery down there. A hot plate, a couple hurricane lamps, and Georgie and Schrank to keep them company. I wouldn't bet on the duchess coming topside any time soon. You worry too much … and trim your nose-hairs not-enough."

"Bet the duchess is going to miss her imports down there," said Jackson.

"I miss them, too," said Grandma, "and I've never even seen them! I hear those chandeliers and settees were beautiful!"

"That bonfire of imports is still smoldering, I think."

"Weird living in a big, empty mansion, but somehow," Grandma said with a smile, "I think I'll get used to it!"

"So, the duchess really isn't coming back?"

"Weren't you there when Queen Dahlia honored ElizabethAnn for bravery? Weren't you there when she rewarded us with this mansion? It's ours, man!"

"Oh, yeah!" answered Jackson. "Those facts are in that memory thing. I keep forgetting how to use it."

"You'll get used to it," said Grandma. "Just let your thoughts float around, and when you see one you want, grab it—mentally, of course. By the way, Bumblegreen barbers are still in business. Just a mild suggestion."

Jackson put down the newspaper and went for a walk. "Grab it mentally, just grab it mentally," he repeated to himself. Though he was still getting used to his two long legs and the encumbrances of clothing, Jackson enjoyed the challenge of being human, but every time he turned back into a dog, then human again, it felt like starting over. So much to learn. And now, he thought, there are barbers to deal with, too.

Jackson galloped across the thistle-strewn field behind the mansion —his and Grandma's mansion, now. When human, he didn't really miss being a dog. Sure, he had enjoyed the keen senses of smell and hearing, the ability to run for miles without tiring, and the lack of inhibitions, but the human form intrigued him. The food, for instance, was a lot better. And, there being no other dogs in Bumblegreen, he enjoyed human company, when he was human, better than the lonely existence as a terrifying fanged beast that was his fate in dog form.

When Jackson arrived at Hank's shack, he found Hank packing a suitcase.

"Beast! Oh, I mean, 'Jackson,'" said Hank. "I'm so glad you're here. I wanted to say goodbye."

Jackson helped with the packing, finding particular enjoyment in the use of his calloused workman's hands.

"Are you sure about this, Hank?" asked Jackson. "It seems awfully risky."

"For the platypus?" asked Hank, "Oh, no. They come from swamps. It'll love it there."

"No, I mean for you," said Jackson. "What if you turn into a fish somewhere along the way?"

"Tammy's going to carry my basin and a jug of water, just in case," Hank replied.

"Still!" protested Jackson.

"I know, but beast, I can't just hide out in this crappy little shack forever!" said Hank. "I'm discovering a sense of wanderlust, I guess, is what I'm saying."

"Think I'll get that?" asked Jackson.

"Don't know, Jackson," said Hank. "You got sweeping, but missed the ability to eat string cheese. You got crossword puzzles and motorcycle riding, but missed a sense of style. So, hard to say, hard to say."

Jackson scratched his rotund, hairy belly where it protruded from his dirty, too-small *T*-shirt. "Grandma says she'll build me a motorcycle out of retired pieces of cheese-making machines," he said.

"What's a motorcycle, anyway?" asked Hank.

"I don't know, but I want one," said Jackson, shrugging.

"Strange," said Hank.

"Yes! But listen, Hank?" asked Jackson. "I wanted to ask you about that bottle of potion. From Shadooda?"

"Oh, that thing," said Hank. "I'm not taking that stuff. No way. I don't want to be human permanently. It's too awful."

"I was thinking, maybe …" mumbled Jackson.

Jackson couldn't finish because just then Tammy entered the shack, shrieking, "Get this thing away from me!"

The platypus had been trailing Tammy ever since that fateful day in the throne room.

"This damn animal bugs me to death, just to death!" said Tammy, who still didn't know the platypus was really Fast Eddie, enchanted to be desperately, painfully in love with her. "I can't hear myself think with it always making those moony eyes at me!"

"I like it," said Jackson, who sat on the sofa and wrestled the platypus up into a bear hug, then held it close, like an oversized yet beloved watermelon.

"Well, say your goodbyes to it, Jackson," said Hank. "And Tammy, grab the basin. I'm ready. It's time to release this marsupial into the mangroves."

"Before you go," interjected Jackson. "About that potion …"

"No, no, nothing you say can make me take it," said Hank. "I love being a trout. I don't care about the risk."

Hank grabbed the bottle off the bookshelf and tossed it into a trash basket filled with old crossword puzzles.

"There. I feel better already," Hank said, as he and Tammy and the platypus set out upon their journey.

Jackson waited until they were out of sight, lifted the bottle out of the trash, uncorked it, and drank.

71

FEATURING A SWAMP AS THE SCENE OF A NEW UNFOLDING

As they walked, Hank and Tammy spoke of the new Bumblegreen, the way the babies had been given back to their mamas and daddies, and the worrisome sad/angry state of the now-childless monkeys. They shared inventive ideas for making a go of it in the newly inviting land. They were survivors, the two of them. Only the fact of Hank's really being a fish had prevented Hank and Tammy from realizing their love for one another. Of course, that was still the case, and yet, somehow, it didn't matter anymore.

When Hank, Tammy, and Fast Eddie (now a love-struck platypus) reached the bog, Fast Eddie gratefully entered the water. His loud sloshing concealed the beeping of Hank's wristwatch alarm.

Tammy waded in, too, to cool herself, but Hank stood ashore, afraid and agog at his human-self's absurd hydrophobia.

"Come," said Tammy, up to her waist in the swamp. Her thick black tresses spread out in the water like witchy ink. Her swollen belly bobbed like a fishing lure. "I'll teach you, Hank," she said. "It's easy."

"I don't know. I just can't swim. I don't know why, I just can't," he said.

Tammy emerged from the water, step by step, and her clothing stuck to her bulbous figure. She took Hank's hand and led him to the water's edge.

He slipped off his shoes and stepped gingerly into the swamp, feeling the spot where the water rose up and a cold ring of feeling embraced his ankle. Tammy led him deeper and deeper, until the bog water crept shoulder high.

"Move your arms like this," she said.

He did, and floated.

"Hold my hands and kick your legs," she said.

He did, and soon Tammy was holding him around the middle while he did the arms and legs at once. Hank swam: nothing like a fish swims, but swimming of a fashion. Mermaid-like, Tammy kept her arms around him. Then, it happened. Hank's watch beeped the second time.

"It's time to turn," said Tammy. "You're going to leave me now, aren't you?"

"I won't."

"Stay with me."

"I never knew you could swim. What a swimmer you are!"

"Sure," she said. "Nothing special. I had lessons. Humans do, as children."

"Do they? Really?"

"Sure. The lucky ones."

"Then, we're lucky."

"We are," Tammy replied.

"What are we going to do about this platypus?" Hank asked. "Persistent fellow, isn't he?"

"Can one ride a platypus?"

"It's not traditional, certainly."

"But possible?"

"Yes, I think, perhaps …" and that's when Hank turned blissfully, happily, perfectly into his trout self. He swam circles around Tammy, frustrated, wanting so badly to kick his pounding, muscular tail and zip away and let miles of stream bank disappear in his wake.

Tammy mounted the platypus, and it wriggled for a while before surrendering to its new role as a beast of burden.

Together, Tammy and Fast Eddie (in what was starting to look like a permanent platypus existence) darted over and under the water, enjoying its chilly embrace. They swam alongside Hank, now in his temporary trout self, who splashed and dove and smiled with secret troutish pleasure.

Tammy, on her twice-bewitched steed, surfaced for ecstatic gulps of air, then submerged once again, to swim, to float, to paddle.

"Too bad we can't stay in the swamp forever," said Tammy.

"When do you have to return to Shadooda?" burbled Hank.

"In a couple days," said Tammy. "It drives me hard with those magic lessons. But I'm learning!"

"You're the future, baby. You're the future," Hank said.

Tammy's swollen belly bobbed and floated. They laughed at it, as if at an exotic toy, and knew that soon, Bumblegreen would see new life.

72

WHERE DAHLIA PASSES
ON A RELIC OF CHILDHOOD

"Look," said ElizabethAnn to Dahlia, as they played on the castle parapet. "You can see all the way to the swampy lowlands!"

"Someone's down there!" said Dahlia, adjusting the eyepiece on her spyglass and handing it to ElizabethAnn. "I think its Tammy and Hank."

"It's just Tammy," said ElizabethAnn.

"I saw two people," said Dahlia.

"Just one and a fish, now. Things change quickly around here," answered ElizabethAnn, who watched Tammy attempting to climb aboard a beast the size and shape of a duffel bag filled with laundry.

"And look, there's the tree house!" added Dahlia, stroking her pet pigeon, Little Katerina. Sure enough, far below, they could see Shadooda and the other magicians crisscrossing the swamp on repaired rope bridges. The bog winds, the orchard's fresh apples, and the odd piece of sunshine that filtered through the leaves kept what was left of their magic alive, at least for now.

"And there's the orchard!" noticed ElizabethAnn.

"Did you know," said Dahlia, "That orchard—that's where that portal is? The one I told you about, where I fell through and landed in the belfry? It's wonderful there, as I recall. Everyone dances."

"Should we go?" asked ElizabethAnn. "Let's go see!"

Queen Dahlia put little Katerina back in the pigeon coop and checked food and water levels. "You should go," Dahlia said. "But I can't. My place is here, in Bumblegreen."

"So's mine!" said ElizabethAnn.

"Been wanting to talk to you about that," said Dahlia. "Now that the portals are open, we'll need police to make sure people don't bring imports through. I was thinking of calling them 'ambassadors,' to sound nicer, but really they're police. The job would be to travel through the portals now and then and check both sides to make sure no one's setting up souvenir shops nearby or funneling goods through underground distribution networks. That kind of thing."

"Because imports, as I understand it now, were the real cause of your blight," ElizabethAnn smartly recited. She had been studying up on the facts of life, as explained by Grandma.

"You're the obvious choice," said Dahlia.

"For a police?"

"Kind of like a gypsy police. I mean, I'll have to build an entire gypsy police force, but you'll be the first one," explained Dahlia.

"You want me to return to No Oaks?"

"Yeah. Lots of times. Come and go at will. Just keep on checking that portal, keep watch over it."

"Where would I live?"

Dahlia shrugged. "A little bit here, a little bit there, I guess. Plus I want you to check the other portals, too, like the one in the orchard. Shoot through a couple portals a week, check both sides. Get little apartments in some of the other worlds, so you can come and go. Gotta keep checking. Can't let any trade develop between worlds."

"But … but … but … I'm ten!"

"I became queen at nine," said the queen. "You're capable. That's what matters."

"Would I get to live with Grandma, in the mansion?"

"When you're here."

ElizabethAnn paused and let all this sink in. Even though Queen Dahlia was her friend, ElizabethAnn could tell this was no request, but an order.

"So I wouldn't really have a home," she said.

"You'd have a lot of homes. Think of it that way."

ElizabethAnn twiddled her fingers, cracked her knuckles, and popped her ears. Finally, she smiled and said, "Actually, that could be kind of fun."

"Good. It's settled. That reminds me, I have a gift for you," said Dahlia.

Dahlia reached deep into her voluminous skirts and pulled out a chocolate tin, old and worn. Long ago, she had written something on it with awkward strokes of crayon: *bits of string too small to save*.

ElizabethAnn accepted the relic with a full understanding of its meaning. This simple toy was for her, now. In spite of her adventures and her new, important job, ElizabethAnn was still a kid, and a kid could partake in such playthings. She opened the tin and removed a loop of string.

"They're not really too small, you know," ElizabethAnn said, stringing the loop between thumb and pinky. "They're the perfect size."

"Too small for me to save," said Dahlia. "You save them. I'm a queen. I can't be saving childish things."

ElizabethAnn pulled and pinched and wove the string until she made a shape. "Cup and saucer!" she said.

"Or a crown," said Dahlia.

"Yes," said ElizabethAnn, looking out over Bumblegreen's restored, disease-free, but still delicate landscape teeming with sad and angry monkeys. "It can be whatever we make it."

Just as soon as ElizabethAnn left the castle to be fitted for her new ambassador costume, a potbellied man in a leather vest, too-tight pants, and muttonchop sideburns galloped up the stone steps to the castle parapet. There, he panted inelegantly at the queen and leaned on the pigeon coop to catch his breath.

Queen Dahlia yelled, "Guards, an intruder!" but then perceived something familiar, good, endearing, snuggly, and innocent about the man. Something generous and loyal, yet spontaneous and fun.

Guards ran upstairs and, wheezing all the while, attempted to subdue the man.

"Wait a minute," said Dahlia, with a commanding wave of her arm. "Unhand him, please."

She asked the man, "Don't I know you?"

"You once called me 'The Beast,' Your Majesty? It's me. It's Jackson."

Brow furrowed, Dahlia took the man by the shoulders and

examined his bashful face. She stroked his unruly mess of curls and looked deeply into his brown eyes.

"Yes," she said, "Those eyes. They're the same. It's you, Beast. It really is you!"

"Queen, I love you," said Jackson. "Please forgive me."

"Forgive you for what?" she asked.

"I took a potion," he admitted. "It was presumptuous, but I drank a magical potion that'll make me human, forever. I did it for you. I'll be a beast no more, all so I can hold you in my arms."

"Oh, Beast!" cried the queen, who then initiated Jackson into the joys of hugging, and then, much to his surprise and delight, kissing.

It had been love when they met—he, a captive animal; she, a lonely monarch—and their love had survived.

ElizabethAnn returned to the parapet just then, outfitted in her Traveling gear, and watched this strange reunion. Sad at the loss of her loyal pet, she was even sadder that Jackson hadn't let her have one last pet of his shaggy head before ending his dog-life forever. Even so, she could tell Jackson's human self was driven by something beyond her understanding.

Though disgusted by the kissing, ElizabethAnn knew this meant the end of one thing and the start of another. Moreover, it meant she had finally found, for Grandma and Jackson, if not for herself, a home.

IN WHICH ELIZABETHANN JUSTIFIES HER FIVE SYLLABLES

ElizabethAnn frowned and pressed a button on the Favra watch-of-the-future, which hung loosely on her tiny wrist—more like a manacle than a piece of jewelry. Birds sang in the treetops far above, and a magic wind tousled her hair. As usual, the insects circling ElizabethAnn's head found something about which to bicker.

"You looking for that portal back to No Oaks?" asked the first tiny insect voice. "It's to your left, at the base of that tree, under the leaves!"

"No, it isn't!" retorted a second voice. "Now, all the portals are labeled with red, *Do Not Import* signs."

"What would you know about red? We're colorblind!" admonished the first voice.

"And we can't read, either. Talk about putting on airs!" contributed a third tiny insect voice.

"I was told so by a reliable source," said the second voice. "I never claimed to be a scholar, but I've a memory like a steel trap!"

"Excuse me, Mister Steel Trap," said voice number one. "Can you name all the counties of Bumblegreen and their capitals?"

"I never said ..."

"Would you all please shut up?" ElizabethAnn mumbled. She was trying to concentrate, after all. The watch's GPS feature indicated she should be near her destination. She did recognize the nearby cliff face and the tree she had climbed, so long ago, but still, the portal eluded her.

"Over here!" cried a distant insect voice. "Up the mountain!"

ElizabethAnn remembered how she had tumbled down a hillside when she first popped out on this side of the portal, so she hiked uphill, and there it was, beneath an overhanging rock.

It's a wonder Earl found this thing at all, thought ElizabethAnn, who missed the smelly old monkey, with his food-oriented pet names and love of adventure. The cute dress and patent leather shoes she had worn on that long-ago day were gone, replaced by a miniature, beanpole-girl version of the rugged gear once worn by portal-traveling gypsies. She had insisted, however, that the royal stylist embroider her pockets with flowers and add some sparkly embellishments.

"After all," she told him. "I'm five syllables ..."

"I know," the stylist had replied, rolling his eyes and inserting another rhinestone into his bedazzler, "'worth of girl.' Grandma already told me."

The heavy responsibility of being Bumblegreen's only portal policewoman had certainly changed ElizabethAnn's status in this land, but it was the dense, oddly shaped knapsack on her back that changed her outlook. All she needed to survive in any world clung to her back, now. This was a Zade Fandey invention, of course, with a little help from Shadooda, the magician.

The contraption contained, in techno-magically condensed form, changes of clothes, medicines, a tent, a fire starter, a helmet, a snow parka, a sun hat, and innumerable denominations of money, but also a respirator, an ice pick, and an assortment of weapons. The "Fandeypack," as Shadooda dubbed it, was going to be, essentially, ElizabethAnn's new home. Sure, it would have been nice to live a life of leisure with Grandma and Jackson in their fabulous mansion, but being entrusted with this important job made ElizabethAnn feel like she was finally living up to her five syllables.

"Here goes nothing," she said aloud, then dove, headfirst, into the slot under that overhanging rock. As she fell through dark, gravity-less nothingness, ElizabethAnn felt her body parts disjointing from one another, then the sensation of having them juggled by a circus professional, then a series of jolts where they got snapped back together, one by one. Meanwhile, she heard that familiar, eerie sound particular to portal jumping: *kedank shooshreek.*

A moment later, a bit lightheaded but none the worse for wear, she found herself in No Oaks, at the base of the One Remaining Tree, where, long ago, she had been warned to Never Ever Go. Her old home smelled the same—burning plastic, hot tar, insecticide—but knowing neither Jackson nor Grandma were here to greet her made it seem even less like a real home than ever.

First, ElizabethAnn did her job: snooping around the area and looking for footprints, parcels, drag marks, or other evidence that portal jumpers had been lugging imports around the vicinity. She saw no signs of life, though, only the swiftly flowing Treacherous Prohibited Stream, piles of dead leaves, and plenty of untrammeled mud.

The job itself, thought ElizabethAnn, *is a cinch*. She could have popped right back into Bumblegreen, if she felt like it, but portal travel, with all that *kedank shooshreeking*, takes a toll on a body, and anyway, she had an errand to run.

Somebody had fixed the fence Grandma rammed through, so long ago, with her original orange International Scout, so ElizabethAnn just climbed the One Remaining Tree, skootched out on a branch, hung from it by her beanpole arms, and dropped to the ground on the other side of the fence. The ease with which she did it would have been impossible for the girl she used to be, but so what.

She crossed the plastic, grass-like expanse of the No Oaks Golf and Country Club and ducked into the alley between tall, brick buildings that her dog Jackson had once carried her through in a wild frenzy. At the end of the alley, she emerged in front of the dumpster Grandma had smashed with her Scout and felt comforted to notice it was still smashed. That seemed to be the only evidence left of the fateful day, only a few weeks before, that ElizabethAnn, Grandma, and Jackson had made their spontaneous exodus from No Oaks.

She walked to the end of the trash-strewn alley, then thoughtfully retraced the trajectory of Jackson's wild frenzy—crossing a street, jogging down an embankment, climbing up an escarpment, and finally confronting a busy four-lane thoroughfare. Loud traffic zipped past in both directions.

ElizabethAnn pushed a button on the Fandeypack, pulled out a bonnet, and affixed it to her head. That was to make sure her hair didn't get caught when a propeller emerged, spun at a furious speed, and lifted her up and across the intersection. Of course, people stared and pointed, but she didn't care. She was, officially, a visitor from another world and figured she might as well act like it.

The busy boulevard she next encountered was overhung with a cloverleaf of highways and exits, so she pushed a button to retract the propeller, pushed another to extend four instant-inflating wheels, and simply joined the traffic, as a human car. On the other side, with the press of a button, ElizabethAnn became a normal little girl again, albeit with a dense, strangely shaped backpack and a weird bonnet she kept on for the shade it provided from No Oaks' relentless sunshine.

When she finally arrived at her neighborhood's familiar roundabout, ElizabethAnn identified her old house by counting: first, second, third, fourth from the intersection, for the houses all looked the same. But no, something was different. Her house had a sign in front, with her own picture on it, saying, "Missing, ElizabethAnn, ten years old, beloved daughter."

There was no sign about Grandma.

She walked up to the house, where her father laconically swept plastic bags and candy wrappers off his lawn and onto someone else's. ElizabethAnn stood there, unavoidable intelligent, just the way Tammy had taught her. Mr. Von Earp looked at ElizabethAnn, glanced away, and looked again.

"You're the spitting image of my daughter," he said, providing her with a thorough up-and-down evaluation and adding, "but she's not so … creative looking." He was being nice.

Through the kitchen window, Mrs. Von Earp eyeballed ElizabethAnn, pursed her lips, and shook her head.

ElizabethAnn reached into her pants pocket, pulled out an acorn, and offered it to Mr. Von Earp. He shrank away from the thing.

"Where'd you get that?" he asked.

"From ElizabethAnn," she said. "She isn't missing. She just moved away."

"How does a ten-year-old move away?" Mr. Von Earp asked, logically.

"With Grandma," she said. "They're in a 'home' of sorts, together. She said to tell you to stick this in the ground."

"I don't want to," said Mr. Von Earp. He knew what that thing was.

"Okay," his daughter said, and meant it. Some folks just prefer No Oaks. She added, "Keep it, though."

She placed the acorn in his palm and folded his fingers over it.

Satisfied, ElizabethAnn—bonnet, knapsack, bedazzled cargo pants, and all—walked back the way she had come.

Mr. Von Earp pulled the *Missing* sign out of the ground, leaving a garish hole in the plasti-lawn, where the stake had been. He clucked his tongue at the hole, said, "Ugh, dirt!" then brought the sign inside and told his wife what had just transpired.

"ElizabethAnn sent us an acorn?" asked Mrs. Von Earp. "She must be under my mother's influence!"

"Wish I hadn't put this sign up," said Mr. Von Earp. "Now, there's a big hole in the lawn."

"Well, she's left us, then. It's official," said Mrs. Von Earp, adding, "I don't want this thing!"

With all her might, she hurled the acorn through an open window.

It landed on the plasti-lawn.

Mr. Von Earp stuffed the *Missing* sign in the garbage can.

The acorn bounced a couple of times and rolled.

Mr. Von Earp returned to the lawn, to finish the sweeping.

The acorn picked up speed.

Mr. Von Earp filled a watering can and approached a flowerbed.

The acorn plopped, soundlessly, into that brand-new hole, where the *Missing* sign had been.

Mrs. Von Earp, at the kitchen window, heard a faint, faraway sound that startled her. It went *kedank …*

She yelled to Mr. Von Earp, "What's that …"

… Shooshreek

"SOUND?" she finished, startling her husband so much he jumped and dropped his watering can.

Water splashed out of the can, all over the plasti-lawn.

Mr. Von Earp cursed his misfortune.

A rivulet trickled past the flowerbed, across the lawn, and right into that hole in the ground, where it dribbled down in a clear, promising stream.

The sight prompted Mr. Von Earp to mumble, "Ugh, mud!" and fast-walk in the other direction.

Beneath the little spot of mud, that acorn settled in, real comfortable-like.

It, too, had found a home.

THE END

Ruby Peru is a sloppy workaholic and independent operator with weird sleep habits and limited knowledge of pop culture. She drives a beat-up pickup truck, and some opine she's a little bit of a badass. Studying under Kurt Vonnegut in the eighties and David Foster Wallace in the nineties made her want to never be a writer and instead be a person who surfs, climbs, and looks cool on a motorcycle. She isn't and doesn't. Ruby has spent decades as a ghostwriter of memoirs and other nonfiction for clients. You hold in your hands the first book published in her own name: *Bits of String Too Small to Save*. Ruby makes her online home at www.rubyperu.com.

Join Ruby Peru's fan club today, and receive a fascinating album of Philip Harris' preliminary artwork for *Bits of String Too Small to Save*!

Here's the link:**https://rubyperu.com/fan-club/**